TO KILL
A GHOST

J. Warren Weaver

Copyright © 2022 by J. Warren Weaver

Independently published.

Library of Congress Cataloging-in-Publication Data available upon request.

ISBN 979-8-9856251-0-3
eISBN 979-8-9856251-1-0

Printed in the USA

Acknowledgements

THIS ENDEAVOR WOULDN'T be possible without the unwavering support of my friends and family. To my wife Ceci, my muse, my every version reader, my sounding board and my everything, thanks for putting up with my self-doubt, my wandering mind, my need for validation, and your help in crafting this story. To my parents, Chris and Christa, who have pushed me, believed in me and supported me through years of half-finished ideas and stories. Without your love and patience, none of this would be possible.

To my friends and early readers; Mario Quimiro, Marty Messer, Mike Darron, Megan Silvertooth, Amber Pitts, Jason Mattingly, Ty and Josie Bailey, thank you for your time, your interest and your insights. Reading an incomplete, working version manuscript isn't always the easiest task, especially when the author is waiting to interrogate you upon completion.

To my editor, Laura Joyce, thank you for gently pushing me to continuously improve this story, to flesh out even the smallest aspects and make this novel as complete as it could possibly be. Your guidance has been invaluable.

If you're going through hell, keep going.

- Sir Winston Churchill

Prologue

VICTOR BROWN AWOKE at his usual time and began going about his day just as he had every day since Marga had died. He arose from his full-size bed, which he promptly made with military precision, used the bathroom, and brushed his teeth. He made breakfast; two eggs, ham and whole-wheat toast because Marga had told him it was healthier than white, and he'd live longer. That meant little to him now, but he liked to live right by her memory. After breakfast, Victor retrieved *The Wall Street Journal* from his front stoop and retreated to his favorite chair. He sipped hot tea, because coffee gave him heartburn, and spent the next hour combing the gritty pages, digesting the articles and storing talking points for his morning rounds.

When he was finished, he folded the paper just so and put it in the recycling bin. He took a quick shower, never one to waste water, shaved and combed the wisps of white hair that still clung stubbornly to his scalp. He donned his trademark three-piece suit, tying a double Windsor knot in his tie and picked out a complementing felt fedora. Today, the suit was light gray, the tie was baby blue, and the fedora was black with a baby blue band. It was the last ensemble Marga had picked out, and she had always had a keen eye for a bolder sense of style. Victor checked himself meticulously in the mirror, his faded blue eyes straining in the morning light. He needed glasses but refused to wear them: those old eyes could still see what was right in front of them.

Satisfied, Victor left his single-story home with the unfinished basement and the failing yard because gardening had always been Marga's thing. He walked down the front steps, down the concrete path and out the waist-high picket fence, latching the gate carefully behind him. He turned left at the street and made his way towards the park. He had the gait of a man that'd always taken care of himself. His steps were sure and his shoulders back. Only the sag of his cheeks and the wrinkled skin around his eyes spoke to his advanced age.

He entered the park and joined a group of fellow seniors around the chess tables. They chatted about the weather, their grandchildren and made jokes only people who'd lived through the 1940s would understand. When angry, dark clouds rolled in they said their goodbyes and went their separate ways. Victor made his way to the store, bought ingredients for dinner, and waited out the storm with another hot cup of tea. He made idle conversation with the teenager behind the counter before the rain slowed and he made his way home.

He walked through the open front gate. Hadn't he latched that? His feet slowed as he picked his way between smudges of dark mud dotting the concrete path. Who'd made those? He slowly made his way to the front steps, casting a wary glance around him before climbing up them. He fumbled in his pocket for the house keys, his eyes going wide as the blurry reflection of a masked man appeared in the glass panel of the door.

A loud bang ripped through the quiet neighborhood, followed by the sound of breaking glass. A few neighbors rushed to their windows, but the majority were unaware anything out of the ordinary had occurred.

Mrs. Kozłowski rang the police, complaining about what sounded like a gunshot, and she'd know because she'd grown up in Soviet era Poland and witnessed enough bloodshed to last a lifetime. The operator on duty assured her they'd send a unit and Mrs. Kozłowski assured them she'd be waiting.

True to her word, Mrs. Kozłowski was waiting as the patrol car rolled up. She practically jumped off the curb to flag the cruiser down and the two officers inside sighed loudly. They'd been hoping to just drive through the quiet neighborhood and confirm all was well, but they should've known better.

And so, the officers exited the patrol car and greeted Mrs. Kozłowski. She assured them that she'd heard a gunshot, no way she was mistaken. Sounded like it came from the Browns' place. She'd heard breaking glass too, she sure did. The officers assured her they'd check it out and that she should go inside where it was warm. They'd come talk to her before they left.

With hands relaxed over the butts of their guns, unlocked just in case and ready for action, the two officers made their way through the broken front gate, swinging in the wind on one hinge, up the muddy walk, new smudges running the opposite of the old, and to the front steps, a river of blood running down them, still steaming in the cool air.

And so, Victor's corpse was discovered with a fatal gunshot wound to the back of his head.

Chapter 1

ERIK BROWN, VICTOR'S youngest grandchild, was at the gym when he got the news. The gym was a place he went to center himself; Victor had taught him that. *A healthy body keeps a healthy mind*, he'd always say when Erik was feeling down. Now in his second year of medical school, the gym was where he went to wash the stress from his body. Others drank, but Erik had never developed a fondness for alcohol. Victor had always warned him, *Alcohol does nothing more than numb your senses. You want to be sharp, always.*

Erik showered off after finishing his six-mile run. He shaved, as Victor had taught him to. Every day to the skin. He combed his short hair; the same cut Victor had always gotten before losing most of the hair on the top of his head. Erik scanned his appearance in the mirror until he knew Victor would be satisfied. Victor was never slow to voice his complaints.

Erik dressed in a pair of grey slacks and a light blue button-up. He tucked in his shirt then put on his gleaming black dress shoes. He'd always dressed nicely and had gotten over the teasing when he was still a kid. Victor had always stressed looking your best. Erik had never seen him in anything other than his suits, collar buttoned, and tie knotted.

Erik retrieved his belongings from the dented orange locker, shoving his wallet and keys in his front left pocket, harder to steal a wallet in the front pocket. He picked up his phone and it vibrated in his hand, letting him know he had some missed notifications. Erik unlocked it and the home screen informed him he had twelve missed calls and twenty-three text messages.

"The hell?"

Erik sifted through the texts and his stomach dropped out of his body. His legs, already weak from their work out, gave way under him and he slumped down to the wooden bench just behind him.

All the air exited his body, his core tightening with anguish. A gurgle escaped his throat and tears welled in his eyes. His phone clattered to the hard locker room floor. Erik grew dizzy and realized he was holding his breath. A rush of air filled his lungs as he gasped, then whooshed back out of him in a pathetic wail. He fought to regain control of his breathing while more tears sprang to his eyes.

The men around him gave him weird looks as another deep breath turned into a restrained sob. One raised an eyebrow as Erik doubled over and let out another smothered sob. Erik finally saw the looks and sprang to his feet, fleeing their judgement.

He burst through the gym's front doors and rushed to his car, a beat-up blue Honda. He sat down in the worn bucket seat and yowled his misery. Victor was dead. Tears streamed down his cheeks, unchecked.

A knock at his window stunned those tears as Erik went rigid in his seat. A sympathetic face looked in on him, holding up his phone. Erik rolled down his manual window, struggling with the weakness that plagued his whole body.

"Hey, forgot your pho—"

"Thanks," was all Erik could manage as he tugged it out of the man's hand.

Erik tossed it onto his passenger seat and then started the process of rolling his window back up. The man put his hand on the window, making the process more difficult and Erik shot him a questioning glare.

"You alright?"

Erik was taken aback for a moment. He struggled to respond, fighting over which words to use with this stranger. Finally landing on somewhere around the truth.

"Not really. I... I lost my bestefar... my grandfather, today."

Sympathy flooded the stranger's face, and he removed his hand from the window.

"Tell me about him."

"What?"

That was the last thing Erik had expected him to say.

"Let's grab a coffee and you can tell me about him."

Erik hesitated; his grief momentarily held at bay. "No, that's OK, thank you. I should go to my family. They need me right now."

"No problem," the stranger replied, handing a business card to Erik. "If you change your mind."

"Thank you," Erik responded. The man walked away as Erik looked over the card: 'Jeffrey Grant, Grief Counselor'.

"What are the odds?" Erik wondered aloud before retrieving his phone from the passenger seat. He unlocked it, took a deep breath and dialed his father.

"Hey, Dad. How are you doing?"

Chapter 2

ERIK'S OLDER BROTHER and sister had beaten him to their father's house. He wasn't surprised. He'd stopped by his apartment to grab his phone charger and pack an overnight bag. He intended to spend the next few days helping Selene with the funeral arrangements and going through Victor's house. Anything to keep his mind occupied. It still hadn't fully sunk in, Victor's death. He knew enough about grief to know he was in denial, or shock, or whatever. He didn't really care. He just wanted to be with family.

He entered a quiet house, leaving his shoes at the front door. It smelled like pizza, and he realized how hungry he was. He always ate a nice protein-rich meal of chicken and rice after the gym, but in his haste to get over there he'd skipped it. He dropped his bag by the stairs and walked into the kitchen. A single pizza box sat open on top of the stove. Only a few slices left. Old habits made Erik hesitate before grabbing one.

"Sorry, Bestefar."

He devoured the slice in a few bites and grabbed another.

"Erik Brown, eating pizza. Well, now I've seen everything!"

Erik smiled at Selene's reflection in the glass of the microwave door. She was standing with her hands on her hips in mock outrage.

"Shut up, I'm hungry."

Erik wolfed down the last of his slice and turned to Selene, wrapping her in a big hug. She was much shorter than him and had to stand on her tip toes just to rest her chin on his hunched shoulder.

"How are you doing, Kid?"

Erik could hear a waver of restrained grief in her voice. Oh, Selene, Erik thought. Always had to put on a strong face for her little brothers.

"Shitty," Erik finally responded, fighting back the tears that filled his eyes once more. "I can't believe he's gone."

Selene patted his back and hugged him tighter. "I know."

Lars, Erik's older brother, chose that moment to join them in the kitchen, skirting by them both for the pizza box.

"Who ate all the pizza?" Lars' voice always held a note of animosity and Erik could tell it was going to be directed at him soon enough.

"Erik. He just got in. You'll survive, Lars. There's fruit in the fridge."

Lars flashed with anger and narrowed his eyes at Erik. "I didn't bring fruit, Selene. I brought pizza."

"Good to see you too, Lars. Tell me, how are you doing?"

Erik was rigid with anger, but Selene still clung to him and started backing him away from his older brother, out of the kitchen.

They'd always had a difficult relationship. Erik was the baby in the family, seven years younger than Lars, ten years younger than Selene. And besides that, Lars blamed Erik for their mother's death. Erik entered the world and, ever so shortly after, their mother left. She'd had enough time to hug her newborn baby, kiss him and name him. When the nurse checked on her the next morning, she was dead.

In truth, it was a medical snafu that was to blame for her untimely demise but try explaining that to a grief stricken seven-year-old. So, the boys had grown up without much love between them, but today, on the day of Victor's death? Erik wasn't having Lars' sour attitude.

"Swell, Erik. I've been here since five dealing with our father. Where have you been?"

"Not all of us are as available as you are, Lars."

Lars' eyes shot daggers at Erik.

"Is this a contest to see who's more miserable? Really? If so, I think I'm winning because I have to take care of a room full of children!" Selene fumed.

"He started it," Erik replied indignantly.

"And you took the bait. Jesus, Erik. Every time. And you, Lars, give it a rest! I'll order another pizza if it's that much of a big deal."

Selene cast a withering glare at Lars, turning its intensity on Erik as he began to mouth a snide comment. He marveled at how much she'd perfected it over the years. She was less sister in those moments and more mother. Michael, their father, had always been an emotionally fragile man. He'd retreated into a ball of depression after their mother's death and proved unable to rise to the task of raising three children alone. For eight years she'd been forced to raise her little brothers. When college came around Michael finally stepped up to the plate, promising to be better, to be a father again. So, she left, believing Michael would rise to the occasion. He didn't. To his credit, he tried, but dealing with an eight-year-old and a fifteen-year-old was beyond him. That's when Victor and Marga stepped in, and that's how they came to raise Erik.

It started with afternoons, twice a week and then became afternoons five days a week. Lars was mobile so he was of no concern, even though he was screwing up in school and getting into trouble. When Lars left home at eighteen and joined the Marines, Erik was eleven and alone. Michael had lost his job for poor performance, hard to teach a college class when you never showed up, so they moved in with Victor and Marga. They lived with them until Erik was seventeen, and Michael finally got his life back in order. He started teaching again, writing books, and was able to buy a small home, the one they were in now. Erik moved with him but only for a few months before he left for college.

Erik could've gotten into any number of schools, but he chose to stay close to Victor and Marga. Lars resented him for it. That and his success.

"Not the point, Selene. I was saving those slices for Dad." Lars was still mad, but Selene's outburst had cowed him enough to let it go.

"Where *is* Dad?" Erik said into the brief silence.

"Bed."

"Of course," Erik sighed. "I'll go say hi. Let him know I'm here."

"Erik here to save the day. Good for you, Champ!"

"Lars! Knock it off!" Selene was mad now. Her usually placid features were taut with anger. The scar above her left eye was pulsing red. Lars and Erik called it 'The Beacon'. When it came out to play it was best to just scurry away.

Lars threw up his hands in defeat and walked out of the kitchen. Selene turned her dark gaze on Erik, and he realized he wasn't out of the woods quite yet.

"He started it," Erik stammered, wilting under that hot glare.

"Twenty-four years, Erik. And you feed into his bullshit every damn time. You both need to grow the fuck up."

Selene never swore. She just saved it for when she was really trying to make a point.

She stormed out of the kitchen leaving Erik to consider her words, and he almost did, but then he started thinking about what Victor would've told him and he lost it. Tears streamed down his cheeks as he fought the gut-wrenching sobs that begged to be set free. He buried his head in his hands and decided to just let it all out.

He nearly jumped out of his skin when a hand landed gently on his shoulder. Erik spun around to meet his father's puffy eyes, his heart racing. Victor would be so disappointed. Erik had let his guard down, lost control of his surroundings. *"Never let someone catch you by surprise,"* Victor had warned him. *"It's a sign of weakness."*

Michael pulled Erik into a tight hug and began to cry. Erik fought the urge to join and lost. What a sight, Erik thought. Two grown men bawling like children. But Erik didn't push Michael off of him, instead he allowed himself to find comfort in his father's arms, such a foreign feeling.

Chapter 3

THE NEXT MORNING, Erik finally found out Victor had been murdered. He'd assumed it was a stroke or a heart attack. Victor was old, old people die suddenly. Marga had beaten him to the grave two years earlier. Cancer. She'd battled for several years before finally succumbing. Watching her die, all the tubes going in and out of her body, the rhythmic beep of the heart monitor keeping time for his grief, until it suddenly went silent one morning. It was a big reason Erik decided to go into the medical field. Erik had been glad to be spared that sight with Victor, but the image of his blood-soaked front steps–the barely recognizable face Selene described in tormented breaths as she attempted to describe what she'd found when she'd identified the body–dashed those thoughts from his mind.

"Shot?" Erik stammered.

Selene snapped back to reality and met Erik's eyes again. "In the back of the head. It was… it was so hard to even identify him…"

Erik slumped back in his seat. Who would want to kill Victor? He was loved by all that met him. When Erik voiced that thought Selene shrugged.

"They think it's a botched robbery. Maybe Victor came home and surprised them. That reminds me, they want us to take a look at his house and see if anything obvious is missing… Do you think you can handle it?" Selene looked tired; the to-do list she had compiled laid out in front of her in her perfect penmanship.

"Sure, Selene."

"And what about me?" Lars butted into the conversation with his usual grace.

"Why don't you get on the phone with the funeral home," Selene responded in the growing silence. "I'll call Pastor Davis."

And so, they went their separate ways. It was unclear what Michael was going to do but that was fine. Erik guessed they'd find him in bed when they got back from their responsibilities.

Chapter 4

ERIK WAS FORCED to wait outside of Victor's home for a police escort. It was an active crime scene they'd explained to him. The property was taped off at the front gate, so Erik just sat on the curb, staring at the broken hinge as the gate swung idly against the yellow tape. The officer that they'd sent was fifteen minutes late.

He offered Erik a pair of latex gloves as he led him past the tape, pausing to make sure Erik knew he wasn't allowed out of his sight.

"Sure," was all Erik responded, his mind elsewhere.

They walked down the concrete path up to the stairs. In front of the door was a pool of dried blood and a chalk outline. Victor's final resting place. Erik gasped, nearly collapsing. The officer was the only thing that kept him upright.

"You're alright," the officer told him as he got an arm under his shoulder. "Hard to see, I know."

After that, the officer was all business again. Erik marveled at his ability to turn his compassion on and off so quickly.

Once inside, Erik did his best to center himself. He looked around the small living room, immaculately clean and organized as always.

"Did your grandfather own a TV?" The officer asked.

"No. TVs are for lazy people with no imagination."

"That a fact?" The officer raised an eyebrow and Erik realized the officer thought Erik was putting him down.

"That's what my grandfather thought. Me? I like my downtime."

"Uh huh, so no TV."

Erik nodded an affirmative and turned to look at Victor's bookshelf. He scanned the books, not really looking, and moved on to the shelf of pictures. Everything was as he remembered, except the torn patch of hardwood floor just inside of the doorway.

"That's new," Erik said, pointing to the offending mark.

"Bullet hole... from the..."

Erik raised his hand and motioned for the officer to stop. "Say no more," he said, before turning back to the vacant house, the memories, the hollow feeling creeping up his spine as he strode through the past looking for something missing, something other than Victor's warm presence.

They made their way to Victor's bedroom, passing the picture-filled walls, Erik's family smiling at him in perfect innocence. He fought the urge to take them down, to remove their mocking grins, the silent vigil of his grief. Victor's room was much like the rest of the house, immaculate. The floor swept, the clutter an organized time capsule of Victor's daily routine, everything carefully put into its place. Erik riffled through his drawers, trying not to displace the perfectly folded, undisturbed, clothing. He moved on to the closet and found more of the same. Victor's suits dominated one side, wrapped in plastic meant to keep out moths and dirt. Hat boxes filled the shelf above, each holding several felt fedoras and other wide brim hats. Marga's side held little in contrast, but what was there brought tears to Erik's eyes. He ran his fingers down her preserved wedding dress, ancient and beautiful.

"Anything?" The officer interrupted.

"No."

Erik led the officer into the unfinished basement. More an unfinished landing. Partial dirt walls made up half the room, the crawl space under the house a foreboding darkness which the naked, overhead light bulb failed to fill.

"These basements give me the creeps," the officer said, stopping a few steps above the dirty concrete landing.

Erik made his way to the safe propped against one of the two concrete walls. He jiggled it, making sure it was still anchored to the wall. It was. He kneeled in front of it and tried the door. Locked. He spun the combination and unlocked it, swinging the door slowly open, afraid what he might find, but everything was as it should be. Marga's jewelry box, Victor's gun collection as well as Erik's rifle, pistol and other personal effects, all undisturbed.

"All there?"

"Yeah."

Erik moved on to the next corner, wondering what he'd find under a black tarp. He pulled it off and just stared.

"What is it?" The officer said from the stairs, squinting into the meager light but refusing to descend those final few steps.

"A grave marker," Erik responded in disbelief.

"A what?"

Erik couldn't help himself, a begrudging chuckle escaping his lips. "A gravestone, head stone, whatever you call it."

Erik shook his head, a smile dominating his lips for the first time since he'd gotten the news.

"The hell?" The officer said, also in disbelief. "What's that doing down here?"

"My bestefar must have made it after my bestemor died."

"Bestefar?"

"Grandfather. It's Norwegian. My grandfather is Norwegian... was Norwegian." Erik ran his finger along the smooth stone. "He made my bestemor's gravestone when she was diagnosed with cancer."

"Well, that's morbid."

"He tried to make her coffin," Erik laughed, the memory of Marga telling him about it with her trademark deadpan playing in his mind: *we all deal with grief in our own way.*

Victor must've crafted his own gravestone to deal with his grief after losing her. He was never a man to sit idle. He was a firm believer that time was limited, and that everyone was obligated to fill it with more than television and sleep. *It's on you to live rather than just exist,* he'd always schooled Erik. *Your father, he just exists.* It was a poignant example, Erik never forgot it.

Erik covered the gravestone again, making a mental note to let Lars know about it ASAP and they resumed their tour through the house for a couple more hours, even walking the outside perimeter before Erik could be sure nothing worth stealing was missing.

"It doesn't make any sense," Erik lamented. "Nothing's been touched. No locks or windows show signs of tampering—"

"And how do you know that?"

The officer's response caught Erik off guard, and he had to think about it for a second. "My bestefar taught me what to look for."

"What?" The officer gave him an incredulous stare. Erik shrugged in response.

"He was a kid in Nazi Norway. Made him paranoid I guess."

"Wait, your grandpa was a Nazi?"

Anger surged through Erik and he had to bite his tongue to keep from lashing out. "No. He was a *kid* in Nazi occupied Norway during World War II. He hated the Nazis."

The officer threw up his hands and turned his attention to the mantle above the fireplace. "That your grandpa?" He asked, pointing to an old black and white photo.

Erik crossed the room and picked it up. It was a picture of three teenagers, smoking cigarettes. They sat on a stone wall; rifles propped next to each of them. The middle one was Victor, the other two were friends of Victor that Erik had never met. Victor never really talked about the war Erik realized as he put the picture back.

"Yeah. Just after liberation I think."

"Cool," the officer responded in a neutral voice.

"Hey, do you guys have any leads on the killer?"

"I wouldn't know," the officer responded.

"Who would?"

"Detective working the case. You done here?"

"Sure. Can you tell me who that is? The guy working the case?"

The officer shrugged. "It's a she. Detective Kincaid. Surprised she hasn't contacted you already. Anyway, it's an open investigation so don't expect her to clue you in on much."

Erik nodded his understanding and then motioned towards the door. They left the house, and the officer replaced the crime scene tape.

"So, you wanna be a cop or something?"

The question caught Erik off guard. "What do you mean?"

"The way you walked the house, noticed the locks weren't tampered with… Same thing detectives do."

"Oh, no, I'm in med school. I just learned how to cover my tracks as a kid. My bestefar, now he would've made a great detective. It was nearly impossible to pull one over on him. He once caught me sneaking out by leaving a hair in the door jamb of the back door. Who does that!?"

Erik let himself laugh at the memory. Victor had been furious. Erik had been grounded for a week.

"Grandparents," the officer said, laughing along with Erik.

They parted ways at the street, the officer thanking Erik for coming down.

Chapter 5

ERIK WAS HALF-WAY back to his dad's when his phone rang. He took one look at the caller ID and swore. He pulled the car over and answered.

"Erik? Where are you?" Samantha's voice was worried.

"Sorry, Samantha. I should've told someone. My grandfather passed away yesterday." Erik barely managed to get the words out.

"Jesus! Seriously?"

"Yeah. I just… I just came from his place. I'm not…" Erik had to fight to keep the emotion from his voice. "I'm gonna miss a few days of class. I'll shoot out an email and let everyone know."

"Yeah, OK. I'll tell Dr. Clark. He was wondering where the hell you were. Not like you to miss class. Are you still gonna make the dinner next week?"

"Dinner? Totally forgot. Yeah, I'll be there. How much do I owe you? Meant to pay you yesterday, but…"

"Don't even worry about it, just bring me a check when you can."

"I'll just Paypal you. I'd rather do it while it's on my mind."

"Sure, but can we do bank to bank? You're with Lake Harvest Credit Union, Right? I only remember cuz you're like, the only other person that's even heard of it!" She broke into an awkward peal of laughter, her mood such an opposite to his own.

"Oh, no, that was my… that was my grandfather, but sure, no problem."

"Oh my God. I'm so sorry! Insert foot into mouth."

"Not your fault. Wanna text me your info?"

"If you have a pen, I can just tell you, I have it in front of me right now."

"Yeah, sure. Shoot."

Samantha read out her routing and account number and Erik typed it into his phone.

"And Erik? No rush, OK?"

"OK, I'll shoot you over the money ASAP. Thanks, Samantha."

Erik hung up and tossed his phone onto the passenger seat. He rubbed the grit from his tired eyes and slumped against the steering wheel.

So much to do, he realized. He needed to contact all his teachers and let them know what had happened. He'd forgotten all his responsibilities. "Get it together, Erik."

Erik straightened back up and checked his rear-view mirror. A black sedan caught his eye and he stared at it for a moment. The driver seemed to be watching him. But that's crazy. Erik shook the thought loose and pulled away from the curb.

Chapter 6

HIS FATHER'S PLACE was empty when he returned. Selene had probably forced Michael out of bed. Forced him to join her on whatever errand was her responsibility. Erik couldn't remember. His mind was clouded. It took the rumble of his stomach to tell him to eat. He entered the kitchen and riffled through the fridge, condiments and little else. He checked the freezer and found a stack of assorted microwavable meals. Of course. His father had never been much of a cook.

Erik heated up a chicken and rice bowl and wolfed it down. He tossed the carton into the trash and sat down in the living room, retrieving his laptop from his overnight bag. He logged into his email app and composed a message to his teachers and study groups. He was numb as he typed out the words saying Victor had been murdered. He struggled with sending it before changing the words to just say Victor was dead. No sense in over sharing he figured. Maybe he was moving to the next stage of grief. He'd come to terms with the fact that he would never lay eyes on the old man again, the damage from the bullet made that impossible.

Erik shot off the email and decided he needed to go for a run, clear his head. He retrieved his workout clothes from his bag and changed. He looked at his reflection in the mirror and was dismayed by the growth of stubble coating his cheeks and chin.

"After the run," he decided.

Erik left from the side door of the garage, opting to leave the front door locked. He hit the side of the road and took off. If he was running for speed, he could comfortably do a mile in under six minutes; for distance, he paced himself at eight minutes. Today, he wasn't sure what he was going for, so he set himself on pace for something in between.

It'd been about six years since he last ran this route, and back then, he was a cross country runner for his high school. He'd never taken first place in the competitions, but he was consistently in the front of the pack. "*Always a competitor*," Victor would say.

The residential neighborhood he ran through was quiet. Not a surprise since it was 11:30 a.m. on a Tuesday. Erik allowed his mind to wander, the steady rhythm of his breathing the only sound he registered. He rounded a sharp corner and was surprised by a parked car. He dodged to the left of it, barely managing to spin around it, putting himself into the middle of the road. He stumbled, off balance, and nearly fell. He put his hands down to catch himself and just managed to keep his feet under him. He scrambled upright, finally finding his balance and couldn't stifle the laugh that poured out of him.

He looked around for any witnesses, casually turning his head to see behind him. There, just down the block was a black sedan. Couldn't be the same one from earlier, right? The sedan seemed to hesitate for a moment, deciding whether to speed up or park, eventually deciding to speed up. The sedan sped past Erik, the driver ignoring him. Erik watched the car go, eventually convincing himself it was all in his head. No way a car was following him. That only happened in movies.

Erik returned home and was doing some stretches in the living room when the doorbell rang. He was pretty sure he was the only person home so he toweled off as best he could and answered the door. A striking black woman in a loose-fitting suit waited on the other side.

"Michael Brown?"

"No, I'm his son, Erik."

"Good, saves me the trip. Hi, Erik. I'm Detective Kincaid. Is your dad home as well?"

"Sorry, he's out with my brother or sister I think."

"No problem. Mind if I come in? I have some questions for you about your grandfather."

Erik stepped aside and motioned for her to come in. They took a seat at Michael's small kitchen table and Det. Kincaid pulled out a pen and a note pad.

"Ok, before we get started, I just want to say these are routine questions, so don't be offended by anything I might ask. I don't know you or your grandfather, so this is just to help me fill in any details that might help me to see a bigger picture. Ok?"

Erik nodded, the sense of numbness climbing back into his extremities, erasing the calm his run had given him only moments before.

"Ok, where were you on day of the event?"

"At the university until around four and then the gym."

"You're a student?"

"Med student… second year."

"I'm sure your family is very proud of you. How close were you to the deceased?"

"He raised me… for the most part, while my dad got his life back together."

"So, you were close?"

"Yes."

"When was the last time you spoke to him?"

Erik paused, unsure of how long it'd really been, trying to remember what their last conversation was about. Tears welled in his eyes as his mind wandered.

"Few days? Couple weeks?" Kincaid said, interrupting his thoughts.

"Couple days. We were supposed to have dinner this weekend."

"Was he at all off to you?"

"Off?"

"Acting funny? Did he say or do anything out of the ordinary?"

"No."

"Can you think of anyone that might wish him harm? Hold a grudge?"

"He was loved by everyone that met him. He had a way with people. He'd cut to the core of you, give you comfort without you even realizing it was happening. He just knew how to talk to people... I've spent the last twenty-four hours trying to wrap my head around it, and none of it makes sense. None of it." Tears streamed down Erik's cheeks as Kincaid nodded along, scribbling notes in her note pad. "Do you have any leads?"

"I'm sorry, Mr. Brown. I'm not at liberty to say, but as soon as I have something concrete, I'll be sure to let you know."

All in all, Det. Kincaid spent about twenty minutes talking to Erik. The whole process just helped to make Erik feel more and more numb to reality. It was a relief when Michael and Selene walked in, they took his place and Erik retreated to the couch where he fell into a fitful sleep.

Chapter 7

"STUPID KID RAN into a parked car and spotted me. I had to drive on," Feliks tried to explain to his dour companion.

"Why were you so close?" he growled in response.

"I was not close! I was down the street but stopping and letting him get his feet under him might have tipped him off!"

"Shut up! I tire of your excuses, Feliks. You are lucky that I do not reward your incompetence."

Feliks shrank into himself, too afraid to meet the big man's eyes. "What do we do?"

"He is with policewoman now, so he is not going anywhere. I will check in with Gerwazy. You will go get us dinner." And with that, the big man exited the car.

Feliks breathed a sigh of relief and put the vehicle in drive. When he'd been assigned this detail, he'd seen it as a promotion, but now, after spending some time with his companion, he wasn't so sure.

Chapter 8

VICTOR'S FUNERAL WAS four days later. Selene had spared no expense on the beautiful flowers piled up around the closed coffin, a blown-up photo of a young Victor and Marga dominated the space between them. Erik stood in front of Victor's coffin admiring the flowers. The coffin was a shiny gray, understated but still nice. It's exactly what Victor would have wanted. He'd never been crazy about flash or pizzazz. He had always preferred to blend in, not stand out. Lars had done a good job, Erik hated to admit.

Erik imagined Victor lying peacefully beneath the lid, bedecked in a fancy suit, a fedora clutched between his lifeless hands, a photo of Marga next to his head to keep him company in eternity. Erik followed his teachings, dressed in a navy-blue suit, his hair combed as precisely as possible, his cheeks smooth once more. His tie was a dark grey with little blue swirls. His shirt was cream. It was one of Victor's suits. One he'd passed down to Erik when he got his first interview for medical school. Erik felt like a million bucks in it. He and Victor were of a similar size, or they had been when Victor was younger. As he'd aged his muscles had softened and his shoulders had slumped. The suits from his later years would be too small for Erik, but that was fine, Victor had already lined Erik's closet with hand me downs. Now Erik could raid Victor's hat collection, a treasure trove he'd fantasized about as a kid.

Erik smiled at the thought. He'd always loved Victor's fedoras and flat caps. It was a style he very much wished would make a comeback. Victor would want Erik to have them, maybe it was even in his will.

"How you doing, Kiddo?" Erik had watched Selene's approach in the gleam of the coffin.

"Ok, I guess. Good job with the flowers." Selene nodded her thanks and put her hand on his shoulder.

"If you need to talk, just let me know. I know you and Bestefar were close."

Erik grabbed her hand in his own and turned to face her. "Thanks." She gave him a sad smile and walked away.

The mourners arrived shortly thereafter. The number of them surprised Erik. He'd never realized how popular Victor was. The little funeral hall filled up quickly, until there was standing room only. Pastor Davis took his place at the podium and began the service. It was very Lutheran. Erik's mind wandered, not hearing the good Pastor as he relived his favorite moments with Victor. He had to pick one as the center piece of his eulogy. Lutherans didn't typically allow them in the funeral service, but Erik refused to send Victor to the afterlife without one last thank you for everything he'd done, and Pastor Davis had granted Erik the chance.

Selene's kick to his ankle brought him back to the present and he realized everyone else was kneeling for one of the prayers. Erik quickly went to his knees and mouthed a silent apology to Selene. He fought his mind's effort to wander further, and eventually Pastor Davis called on him for the eulogy. Erik took his place at the podium and looked out over the crowd of unfamiliar faces. He took a deep, calming breath, cleared his mind and let his shoulders relax, just as Victor had taught him.

"I knew Victor was loved, but I had no idea he'd touched so many lives. Guess we should've sprung for a bigger funeral hall." The crowd laughed softly. "I'd like to thank Pastor Davis for allowing me the opportunity to say something here today. I'm guessing most of you called him Victor. I called him Bestefar. I've been told it's Norwegian for grandfather, but when you directly translate it, you get best father, and he was... he was a best father. He took us in when my mother died, and when my father went back to work, he became a best father to me. I've been profoundly lucky to have two father figures in my life."

Lars harrumphed from the front row and Selene kicked him in the ankle hard enough to elicit a yelp. Erik ignored it, pressing on with his eulogy.

"As Pastor Davis spoke, I found myself lost in thought... lost in reflection. It wasn't that I was ignoring the good Pastor, I was just trying to pick the best story to tell you about Victor, his selflessness. I realized, there are far too many, so I'll just tell you the first one that popped into my mind as I walked up here.

"Victor liked to play a game with me. He called it the guessing game." Erik smiled at the memory that tumbled from his lips. "We would sit on the park bench and watch people. We would watch people and guess their life stories. Victor had a knack for identifying special characteristics for each person; the way they did their hair, the clothes they wore. Dirty fingernails implied manual labor, pressed slacks an office job. The way they walked could tell you their fitness plan or speak to old injuries. Victor was a wizard with identifying things. He knew how to get straight to the heart of people. He could take one look at me and know if I'd had a rough day.

How? I'd ask. The way your shoulders are slumped, the way you keep playing with your hair. He just knew people, and he knew how to talk to them. I'm guessing that's why so many of you are here today." The crowd murmured their agreement and Erik smiled.

"Victor was a great man. He came of age in Nazi occupied Norway and fought them until the Allies liberated him. He volunteered because he knew what they were and what they were capable of. He never spoke about it to me, or anyone really, but the medals he locked away in a drawer in his office told me enough."

Erik stopped speaking and looked around the room, taking in the faces in front of him. He fought the sadness growing in his stomach and knew he had to finish the eulogy before it overtook him.

"I can't wait to hear the stories you all must have. I can't wait to get to know a man I thought I knew already, even more. I miss you, Bestefar, but I'll never forget what you taught me." Erik's voice cracked on the last word. He tried to hide his tears by turning to the coffin and placing a hand on it. He stood there for probably too long as Pastor Davis approached him and patted him on the shoulder.

"You did his memory proud, Erik. That was beautiful."

"Thanks, Pastor."

Pastor Davis led Erik back to his seat and retook the podium. The rest of the service was a blur.

Chapter 9

THE WAKE WAS held in an old diner that Victor had frequented. Erik knew it well. He'd spent many mornings reading the newspaper with Victor there. It was the first place he'd ever had coffee. Victor thought he was too young, but Erik was desperate to emulate the old man. Victor finally gave in and, years later, he told Erik he'd had them water down the decaf for him.

Victor had a way of handling things. So deft and capable. How many times had he allowed Erik to believe he'd won?

Erik found himself the center of attention over the course of the night. It seemed people took his request for stories quite seriously. He found the only alone time he had to himself was when he was in the bathroom, and, even then, men would start telling him about Victor from the adjacent urinal.

Erik learned a lot about Victor. He learned that Victor had led a chess club in the park, that he liked to sing karaoke on Tuesday nights. He learned that Victor had a whole life after Erik went to college. He was a bird watcher. He played basketball in the senior league. He was never idle, especially after Marga died. One mourner swore he visited her grave every day to lay her favorite flowers at the gravestone he'd carved for her.

Erik was thankful for the stories. He did his best to commit them to memory. He was in the process of just that, when the man from the gym parking lot approached him. Jeffrey Grant, grief counselor.

"Erik, beautiful eulogy, Victor would've been proud."

"You following me?" Erik said with a smile he didn't feel.

Jeffrey paused for a moment before lighting up with recognition. "I thought you looked familiar. I hardly recognize you out of your gym clothes."

"Took me a moment too. So, how'd you know Victor?"

"I worked with him for a time," Jeffrey said.

"Worked with him?" Erik said with a frown.

"Well… In a professional sense, but I can't get into that…"

"Really? He hated psychiatrists, didn't trust them."

"And apparently for good reason! Me and my big mouth. He took Marga's death hard, I helped him through it." Erik gave Jeffrey another frown. "Shouldn't have said that … Listen, if you ever need to talk, you have my card, right?"

"I think so, thanks. Good to see you again."

"Here, have another one. I have stacks of 'em," Jeffrey laughed, handing Erik the card. They shook hands and Jeffrey moved on to give his condolences to Selene.

By the end of the wake, the majority of people were pretty drunk. Lars was obliterated, slurring his words, stumbling around the room. Selene was flushed and giggly, and Michael was morose and quiet. Erik was sober, as always. The mourners' stories slowly became harder and harder to decipher and Erik became more comfortable brushing people off. Eventually, he was able to slip into a dark corner and just people watch. He practiced the game Victor had taught him so many years ago, sizing everyone up, guessing who they were and what they did. He created back stories for everyone worthy of note and smiled at his little inside jokes. "For you, Victor."

His eyes found an immaculately well-dressed man in an Italian silk suit, perfectly tailored. His hair was thick and white, his blue eyes sharp. The two men just stared at each other for a moment, sizing one another up. Erik assumed he was drunk, the way he openly met Erik's eyes, his features void of any emotion. Eventually, he rose from his seat and moved towards Erik with a vitality not typical of a man his age, his stride confident in each step, his back straight. Not drunk, Erik realized as the elder man seemed to glide towards him, his dark leather shoes flashing in the meager light of the diner. The dark suit hugged his frame, showing off the athletic physique he must have labored a lifetime and more to achieve.

Erik watched, entranced as the stranger continued his path towards him. How Erik hadn't noticed him earlier he didn't know, for the man was unlike anyone else there. Everything about him screamed wealth and power. Erik finally rose to his own feet when it became obvious the man meant to talk to him.

"Erik Brown, what a pleasure to finally speak with you." His tone was refined, with a slight accent. Erik tried to place it but couldn't.

"I'm sorry, sir, have we met?"

"Why, of course not, but I've heard so much about you. Call me Gerry, all of my friends do." Gerry offered a hand, his mouth turned into a slick smile that caused a wave of anxiety to wash over Erik. Erik accepted it, an uncomfortable energy flowing into him. "I know... Victor... From his time in Europe. I was a very close friend of his wife's."

"Bestemor Marga?"

"Yes... Marga. Not what we called her back then, but so much changes with age. I was heartbroken to hear of her death, and so recently. I wish we could've reconnected sooner, but fate has a way of playing by its own rules." Gerry's smile deepened, a sinister element filling it.

Erik withdrew his hand from the man's grasp and immediately felt better for it.

"I've been told you knew the old man best?" It was less a question and more of a statement of fact; one Erik silently acknowledged with a nod.

"Good. Our reunion was short-lived and I'd love to know more about the man in his later years."

"Oh, OK." Erik didn't know what to say, what to do, only that he wanted to be done with the conversation as quickly as possible.

"Victor... did he ever talk about his time in Poland?"

Erik shook his head no. "They didn't ever really talk about their time in Europe."

"Ah, well, then I can see why you might be confused. That is where we met, so long ago. Oh, what I'd give to relive those days with him, but alas, fate plays by its own rules."

"I'm so sorry, Gerry, I think I need to help my sister with my brother. I'd love to continue this conversation sometime, in a better setting though." Erik didn't wait for a response. Gerry watched Erik make his way over to Lars and Selene before he motioned to a brute of a man in the corner of the room, his face decorated with a grotesque pink scar running along his cheek. The man came to Gerry like an obedient servant, his eyes wary of anyone who was watching.

"He doesn't leave your sight."

"Of course, Gerwazy," the man assured him before returning to his vantage point in the corner of the diner.

Chapter 10

AS THE LAST stragglers staggered out of the diner, Erik gathered his family. He was forced to walk Lars to the car as he could barely stand. Michael shuffled in their wake as Selene led the way.

Erik struggled with Lars' mostly limp body while everyone else got in the car. Erik finally got Lars' legs in and slammed the door in frustration. He was deep in thought, wondering why people got so drunk, when he noticed a black sedan parked down the block and across the street. He took a step towards it and had to shield his eyes when the headlights flipped on. He took an involuntary step backwards when the car pulled away from the curb and drove by him, techno music suddenly blaring. The interior of the vehicle was shrouded in darkness as his eyes tried to readjust to the moonless night.

"You're losing it, Brown." Erik shook off his paranoia and got in the driver seat. "Everyone buckled up?"

A series of grunts seemed to affirm as much, so Erik started the car and drove them all home. He dropped Lars off first, begging Selene to help him get Lars up his apartment steps. They left Michael sleeping in the back seat and struggled against Lars' dead weight. Erik had to pin him against the wall next to the front door so Selene could unlock it. She giggled as she dropped the keys, Erik groaning against Lars' weight.

"Selene, please," Erik growled, not nearly as amused as she was.

"Chill, little bro," Selene said as she bent over to pick them up. Her balance shifted and she ended up head butting the door and going down on her knees. Selene burst into laughter and Erik tried to hide his smile.

Selene was still laughing when she finally managed to get the door open. She stumbled through the threshold and gasped.

"What?" Erik asked following her in with Lars in a fire man's carry.

Lars' apartment was a mess. His bookshelves were empty, their contents all over the floor. Broken picture frames littered the floor, glass cascading out from where they'd been spiked to the ground.

"Jesus, Lars," Erik murmured, carrying Lars to his couch and tossing him onto it. "Anger issues much?"

"You think he did this?" Selene asked.

"Of course. Probably when he found out Bestefar was dead. He's always had an anger problem."

"Fair enough!" Selene laughed, grabbing a blanket from the floor, giving it a good shake to remove any debris. "My angry little man," she cooed as she tossed it over Lars' prone form.

Erik took another quick scan of the room and shook his head; it was absolutely destroyed. It was as if Lars cared nothing for his own possessions. Demons from the war? He wondered silently. Selene skipped out the door in front of him and he closed it behind them, locking the handle, figuring it was enough of a deterrent.

Michael was easier to deposit. Erik just shook him awake and told him he was home. Michael thanked him for driving, thanked him for the eulogy and for being so great throughout the whole tragedy. He hugged Erik tight and cried drunkenly on his shoulder. Erik let him until Selene reached over and honked the horn, ruining the moment. Michael apologized for being overly emotional and staggered up the front walk, fumbled with his keys at the front door, then disappeared inside. Erik watched him go, then got back in the car.

"Well, that was rude."

Selene started to giggle and slapped Erik on the leg. "Would've been here all night and I'm tired. Take me home, chauffer!"

Erik couldn't deny her logic, so he let the subject drop. Selene lived in the next town over, on the way home for Erik. She dozed for the first half hour and Erik enjoyed the silence. His mind was awash with the stories he'd heard that night. He ran the whole evening over again in his mind, digesting every moment. Selene stirred back to the land of the living right around the time Erik got back to his conversation with Jeffrey.

"Did you know Bestefar saw a therapist after Bestemor died?" Selene didn't say anything, so Erik assumed she'd dozed off again.

"Really?"

"The guy was there tonight; he didn't say anything to you?"

"Describe him."

Erik hesitated. He tried to place Jeffrey in his mind. All he could remember was what Jeffrey was wearing. "Dude in grey slacks and a white button up..."

"Did you just describe half the funeral and expect me to know who you're talking about?" Erik smiled despite himself.

"Pretty much. I think he was wearing glasses, kinda plain looking, short light hair maybe. I don't know. I met a lot of people tonight."

"Oh yeah, that guy? Yeah, he was real, yeah..."

"What'd he say to you?"

"I was kidding, Erik. I have no idea who you're talking about. But if Bestefar was going to him that's good. I was worried about him after Bestemor died. They were together for like, a bazillion years!"

Erik laughed; he couldn't help it. "Sixty-five years. Yeah, I just... It's weird to find out so much I didn't know about him. I thought... I just thought I knew everything about him."

Selene leaned over the center dash and laid her head on his shoulder. "He had a long, long, long, long life before you came around, kid. I wish I got to know him half as well as you did. That story you told about his game? I would've liked that."

"The guessing game? That wasn't even the best part. After I'd come up with my guess, he'd make me go confirm it."

Selene shot up in her seat and gave Erik a playful smile. "Confirm it? How?"

"We'd come up with characters to play and go talk to the people."

"You're joking..."

"Nope. Bestefar would make me come up with a backstory and everything. He'd even quiz me before setting me loose. It was like I got to be someone new every day."

"You know that sounds crazy, right? Like, who does that! How old were you?"

Erik laughed at the disbelief in her voice. "We did it for years. The last time was like six months ago. Bestefar always wanted to make sure I wasn't slacking on my skills."

"Your skills? What!?"

"I mean, the character stuff, I'll admit, was kinda weird, but the guessing game is super helpful in my field." Selene grunted doubtfully. "For real!" Erik protested. "I see plenty of patients that don't want to tell me everything. Do you know how handy it is to be able to just tell if they're lying to me by their body language?"

"Their body language?"

"Yeah, roll their eyes one way as opposed to the other, nervous tics, the works."

Selene shook her head in resumed disbelief. "Remind me never to play poker with you." They shared a laugh and let the silence envelop them.

They drove for a while before Selene spoke up again. "You know what the last thing Bestemor told me about him before she died? After she caught him making her headstone? He said he just wanted to keep his all with her when she died, so she wouldn't be lonely."

"Well, everyone deals with death differently, I guess," Erik said, fighting the tears welling in his eyes.

"Some better than others... Maybe we should send Dad to that therapist. Hell, maybe all of us should go. I know it helped me when Mom died."

Erik didn't say anything. Their mother was always a sore subject for him. Erik had never known her. As far as he was concerned, Selene was the closest thing to a mother he'd had before Marga and Victor took over his upbringing.

"You'd have liked her, Erik, and she would be so proud of you."

"Guess we'll never know for sure." The words sounded wrong, even to Erik, but he was drained. He didn't have anything left for mourning a woman he'd never met. She was a character in a fantasy novel to him. All he had were stories told with a warm reflection that went cold as soon as it reached him. He had pictures where the rest of his family had memories. They simply weren't the same thing and no matter how hard he'd tried to explain it, he was always met with icy disapproval.

A soft sniffle made Erik look over at Selene and he realized she was crying. "You OK?"

Selene nodded her head. "I just miss her sometimes."

"Sorry... I... I'm sorry, Selene." She flicked a hand at him and turned to the window.

"I wish you'd known her, that's all."

Erik sighed, turning his attention back to the road ahead, his mind a cluttered storm of memories. Behind them, a sudden pool of light illuminated a black sedan behind them.

"Hey, Selene…"

"Huh?" she responded; her exhaustion obvious in her voice.

"You ever noticed how many black sedans are on the road?"

Selene was slow to answer. "Uh, no?"

Erik's eyes returned to his rearview mirror, hunting for the black sedan. He was about to give up when another pool of light illuminated it in the distance. Erik changed lanes, going from the far-left lane to the far right, and waited. His breath caught as the lights he'd attributed to the sedan followed.

"No way," he murmured in disbelief.

"What?" Selene asked halfheartedly.

"Nothing," Erik said as he started to speed up.

His blood went cold as the sedan appeared to speed up with him. Erik rapidly slowed down, jerking Selene fully awake in her seat.

"What the hell, Erik!?"

He ignored her protest as the sedan rapidly slowed down to stay a distance behind him.

Without warning, Erik rapidly changed lanes again, no signal, and slammed on the gas, flying around a couple cars, putting them between him and the sedan. One of the other cars honked at him but he just kept his foot on the gas and left them in his dust.

"Erik! Jesus Christ! What the hell's wrong with you! Pull over this instant!"

Erik complied, swinging rapidly into an off ramp and only slowing down once he'd started to descend it.

"Erik Brown! Are you drunk? Jesus!" Selene was wide awake now, the Beacon visible in the meager streetlight.

"Sorry," Erik responded, his eyes on his rearview mirror, waiting for the sedan to appear behind him.

"Green, Erik," Selene said, bringing Erik's attention back to the light in front of him.

"Right, sorry."

"What the hell's gotten into you all of a sudden?"

"Nothing, just... I don't know. I miss Bestefar."

"Oh, Erik... Me too."

Chapter 11

FELIKS WATCHED IN disbelief as Erik's car careened into the other lane, zipping past traffic, horns blaring in his wake. He tried to follow suit, but the opening disappeared, trapping them behind the cars Erik had cut off.

"Idiot!" Loren bellowed from the seat next to him, his face red with anger.

"He is a drunk, driving like an asshole! How can I follow that?"

"Do not make excuses, Chudy!"

"Feliks, my name is Feliks."

"Your name is what I say it is!"

Feliks squealed around the other cars, but Erik's blue Honda was nowhere to be seen.

"Skurwysyn!" Loren yelled at the empty road, smacking the dash with a balled fist, the thick pink scar on his cheek twisting his features into a demonic scowl.

Feliks cringed into himself. "What do we tell Gerwazy?"

"Gerwazy will not know," Loren growled.

Chapter 12

A FEW WEEKS later, Erik received a text from Michael, asking him to join the family for the reading of Victor's will. He had tried to return to his usual routine, fighting the crush of sorrow by throwing himself into his studies, a simple feat for a second-year medical student. Step one of his medical boards were just around the corner, so every free moment was spent studying. He made the library his home, only taking breaks to eat, sleep and work out. The routine was good for him. It allowed him to push the paranoia to the back of his mind and stop thinking about the black sedan, about Gerry. He was finally starting to put Victor's murder behind him, a short reprieve, it turned out.

Expecting that Victor had left him his hat collection, or the rest of his suits, Erik got dressed in a nice suit, the first one Victor had given him, combed his dark hair, and drove to the lawyer's office.

Lars and Selene were already there. Lars wore jeans and a holey T-shirt and sneered at Erik as soon as he walked through the door.

"Little over-dressed, aren't we?"

"Thanks, Lars," was all Erik had the heart to respond. He found the walls of depression closing in on him as Victor's death regained a vicious hold on his mind once more.

Selene draped a sympathetic arm around his shoulder and laid her head on him. "Ignore him. He's just bitter because he knows Bestefar didn't leave him anything." Selene playfully stuck her tongue out at Lars and, just like that, pushed the toxic air right out of the office.

Michael was late. The lawyer was about to begin reading the will when he finally rushed in. His eyes were puffy, and his nose was raw. He's been crying, Erik thought. But of course, he'd been crying. That was Michael. A gentle, fragile soul. An orphan. Tears began to well in Erik's eyes, but he quickly wiped them away before anyone had time to notice.

"Sorry kids, my therapy session went long."

That surprised Erik. He'd been unaware Michael was seeing a therapist, but Michael spared no time for questions as he took his seat and motioned for the lawyer to begin.

"Victor Brown had a modest estate. He wanted his finances to be split equally between you all, so four ways—"

"How much?" Lars interrupted, suddenly sitting straight on the edge of his seat.

The lawyer looked over his glasses at Lars, obviously not happy to be interrupted. "Depends on what he owes. Probate should take several months. He had $120,000 spread out among multiple assets."

"Probate?" Lars said, plowing on with his single-minded greed.

"Yes. We need to liquidate his stocks, pay what he owes as far as bills, take inventory on his possessions, etc. The process is quite involved and takes time, now please, this goes a lot faster if you save your questions for after the reading of the will."

"Sure," Lars nodded, slumping back into his chair. It didn't take a mind reader to guess Lars was having money problems. Erik made a mental note to talk to him about it after the reading, not that he expected Lars to open up to him about it.

"Moving on. Erik?"

Erik sat up in his seat, pushing the thoughts of Lars out of his head. "Present." The lawyer cracked a smile, clearly not expecting Erik's response.

"Very good, Erik, glad to hear it. Victor left you his house."

"What?" Lars and Erik said at the same time. Lars cast an angry glare at Erik. Erik shrugged in response. He was as surprised as anyone.

"That's bullshit! We should sell it and split it!" Lars raged. He looked to Michael, trying to appeal to him, but Michael was zoning out. It was hard to tell if he'd even heard the lawyer.

"Mr. Brown... err, Lars. It was your grandfather's will that Erik have his house. This is indisputable. Now, please, allow me to continue. To Selene, Victor left Marga's figurines and jewelry."

Lars made a strangled noise in the back of his throat and Erik expected another outburst. The lawyer was quick to move on. "To Lars, Victor left his gun collection."

"Oh, hell yeah!" Lars exclaimed, smacking Michael on the knee. "That's got to be worth Twenty-K, easily!" Michael jumped and looked around the room batting his eyes as if he'd just awoken.

"Yes, Lars, he says in his will that there should be some collector's items among them. Michael? Your father left you his 1966 Chevelle."

"Oh, I was unaware he still had that. Very good," Michael said, as jealousy surged through Erik for a moment. He almost channeled his inner Lars and said something. Victor had taught him to drive in that car. His mind flashed back to squealing around an empty parking lot, Victor laughing in the seat next to him.

"Now, pull up on the hand brake and crank the steering wheel." Erik followed Victor's directions and sent the Chevelle into a controlled slide. "Now, hit the gas!" Erik did and the vehicle pulled out of the slide with a screech, barreling forward.

Erik felt like a stunt driver, imagining he was Jimmy Doyle in *The French Connection*. Victor had set up orange construction cones all around the parking lot. He'd even made cardboard cut outs of pedestrians for Erik to swerve around. They pretended Erik was being chased and had to get away. Victor sat in the passenger seat, smiling ear to ear, as he relayed how close the pursuit was.

"Left at the next street! Going to have to put her into a slide!" Erik did just that, careening into a row of orange cones. "Oh no! You blew a tire! They're on us now!"

Victor pretended to shoot out the back window as Erik laughed beside him. "Oh no! I'm hit! Going to have to run for it my boy. Leave me, I'm through." Victor slumped over in the passenger seat and Erik let the car slow down to a stop.

"Bestefar! Say it ain't so!" Victor broke from his faked death slump and ruffled Erik's hair.

"You did pretty good there, Erik. Just need to remember to time the brake and the gas."

"Where'd you learn to do all this?" Erik asked. Victor took on a distant look, the smile falling from his lips. "Bestefar?"

Victor snapped back to reality and gave Erik a sad smile. "Where I learned most of life's hardest lessons, and I hope you never have to learn them as I did."

Erik knew that was code for the war. Victor never talked about the war, and as Erik got older, he understood why. He did a report on the Nazi occupation of Norway when he was in high school. He tried to interview Victor, but he just laughed, saying that the history books had a better recollection of that time than he did.

Erik discovered that the Norwegians were starved, abused, murdered for being 'patriotic'. That they were raped and bombed. Erik gave his report with a heavy heart, knowing Victor had come through all of that, somehow.

"Erik?" Selene's voice snapped him back to reality. "We're going to get lunch. You have time?"

"Oh, yeah, sure." Erik took a moment to right himself, looking around the small office. The lawyer was packing up the files, shaking Michael's hand. "Guess I zoned out. Did I miss anything?"

Selene laughed and shook her head. "Nah, just a bunch of legalese."

"Erik?" Erik turned his attention to the lawyer who was holding out a ring of keys for him. "I expect you to facilitate the doling out of Victor's will. You're going to have to file the paperwork, etc., but the house is yours."

Erik took the keys, turning them over in his hands. His only thought, of the bloodied front steps to the home he now owned.

Chapter 13

ERIK PUT OFF going to the house as long as he could, a fact that drove Lars to near madness. Erik received daily calls and texts that grew in desperation as they went from asking, to demanding Erik let Lars in so he could collect the guns and start getting them appraised. Lars accused Erik of holding them hostage just out of spite. He accused Erik of some endgame, of which he could provide no specifics. It hit a point of begging that threw Erik off. Lars had never pleaded for anything from Erik. Had he been doing it intentionally, Erik would have reveled in the moment, but he was trapped in a schedule of study and class, with a healthy dose of pity from professor and peer alike. Secretly, Erik wondered if Lars was just going to break in and try to take them. Good luck. Erik was the only one living that knew the combo to the gun safe, so Lars needed him.

After a miserable few days of knowledge overload, Erik met Lars and Selene at the house. It had been like pulling teeth to get Selene to come out. She'd said she was in no rush, but Erik wanted it done with. Eventually, she agreed. Lars met Erik with his standard animosity, although, if Erik really concentrated, he thought he felt an edge of uneasiness coming from him. It made Erik wonder what Lars had gotten himself into. Probably had something to do with Lars' pizza place. Why Lars went into the pizza business, Erik would never understand.

The three were forced to step over the darkened blood stain on the front porch. Erik hesitated before unlocking the front door, his eyes fixated on the broken glass. The hole punched through it looked like a small-caliber handgun, Erik thought. He was about to stick a finger into it when Lars interrupted his thoughts.

"Can we go in, please? I'm freezing my nuts off."

"Why you decided to wear shorts and a t-shirt, is your own fault, Lars." Selene said it with a smile, intending it to be lighthearted, but Lars snapped at her anyway.

"Can you stop playing mommy for five minutes, Selene? Seriously, give it up, we're all adults here."

A storm raged in Selene's eyes, the Beacon lighting up over her left eye, but before she could unleash it, Erik unlocked the door and swung it open.

"Can we keep this cordial, please? This is going to be hard enough without everyone fighting." Lars and Selene both looked at Erik in surprise and nodded OK. He motioned them in and followed, closing the door behind them, his eyes still stuck on the hole in the glass.

Lars quickly went into the basement where the gun safe was, and Erik followed Selene into the bedroom.

"Jewelry's in the safe, Selene."

"I know. I just wanted to see their bedroom one more time, as they left it." She turned to Erik and gave him a big smile. "Before you turn it into whatever weird recluse den you thrive in."

"Erik! What's the goddamn combination?" Lars yelled from the basement. Erik smiled at Selene and rolled his eyes.

"Do I have to do everything?" They both chuckled, not really putting their hearts into it.

They walked down the stairs to find Lars leaning against the safe, his head resting on the cool steel frame.

"What's going on, Lars?" Lars looked up and glared at Erik.

"None of your fucking business. Just open the safe so I can get on with my day."

Erik paused, crossing his arms over his chest. He almost started tapping his foot but restrained himself. Lars flushed in response and looked like he was about to go on a tirade but held it in check.

"Listen, I just need to get the ball rolling on this, OK?"

"Do you owe someone money? Are you in trouble?"

"None of your business. Just open the damn safe."

"What if I don't know the combination?"

The blood drained from Lars' face and Erik felt bad. Of course, he knew the combination. He and Victor had gone shooting almost weekly until Erik had started med school. Two of the guns in that safe were his; a beautiful Colt 1911 Victor had given him when he got into med school, and an old M1A1 Carbine Erik had fallen in love with when he was younger. He'd always picked it to go shooting, so Victor eventually just gave it to him. It was the first gun Erik had been tasked with maintaining. Until then, Victor had cleaned all the guns. After that, Erik started helping. He'd bonded with Victor over their care. Victor was methodical, his attention to detail unrelenting. Every weapon got scrubbed down to the last inch.

"Then we need to hire a safe cracker." Lars turned away from Erik running both hands through his hair. "Shit. Shit!"

"Lars, what the hell's going on? And don't you dare lie to me, you know I can tell."

"Fine, OK? Fine!" Lars took a moment to gather himself before turning back to Erik and Selene. "I owe some bad people money."

"Lar—" Selene started.

"Shut up!" Lars paced around the small basement, trying to decide how much to tell them. "Remember when I made the rounds asking for a loan for my pizza place?"

He'd gone to Michael for money, but Michael was helping Erik with medical school. He'd gone to Selene for money, but Selene had just bought her house. Erik knew all of this because last, he'd gone to Victor. Victor had turned him down flat, no excuse, just no. Lars blamed Erik, of course.

"I thought you got a bank loan?"

"Like a bank is going to trust a vet with no capital. No, I had to go to a loan shark. I've been making my payments but—"

"What do you mean? I thought you said you were already making a profit. You've been waving it in everyone's face for months." So like Lars. Everything was posturing to him.

"It's so close." Lars looked on the verge of tears.

"Explains why your apartment was wrecked last time we were there," Erik said to himself.

"Jesus, Lars," Selene murmured.

"Screw you, Selene. Maybe if someone would've helped me out, I would be in a better place, but you all chose yourselves so here we are. I'm just trying to make something of myself," Lars said, his voice rising with each word as he flushed red with anger.

"Maybe if you hadn't lost everyone's money with your stupid T-shirt company we would've!" Selene shot back.

"How was that my fault? Explain to me, Selene, how you can blame me for that?"

Erik ignored the two of them and walked over to the safe. He spun the lock until a series of clicks sounded and he swung the heavy door open.

"The 1911 and the Carbine are mine," Erik said, refusing to get pulled into the argument.

"The hell they are. Bestefar left me the gun collection!" Lars' angry face contorted with spite and all the pity Erik held for the man evaporated. He slammed the door shut again and spun the lock.

"The 1911 was a gift from Bestefar and the carbine's been mine since I was twelve. The rest are yours or I don't open this safe again. Got it?" Erik looked Lars dead in the eyes, his own anger making him shake just slightly.

Lars had his fists balled at his sides; his jaw clenched. Erik wondered if he was going to throw a punch, but he stood his ground anyway. Lars might have military training, but Erik had been kickboxing since he was a kid, plus, he was in much better shape than Lars and taller by half a foot.

"You're such an asshole, Lars. I can't stand you right now," Selene growled as she stomped back up the wooden steps, snapping Lars out of his rage fueled stupor. He unclenched his hands and relaxed his shoulders.

"Fine. Just open it back up." Erik nodded and opened it back up.

"You know, Lars? You've been an asshole to me my entire life. I don't know why I thought Bestefar dying would change that. Bestemor dying sure as hell didn't do anything."

Lars ignored Erik, instead, shuffling through the deep safe. Erik threw up his hands in disgust and walked out of the basement. Selene was waiting in the kitchen, the tea kettle warming on the stove.

"Meh, he's not all bad, Erik. Somewhere in that rodent brain of his, he loves us."

"Yeah, right. You sure cooled off quick." That was all Erik said as he tried to walk past her, heading for his childhood bedroom, but Selene grabbed him gently by the elbow, forcing him to turn back to her.

"Come here," she whispered, herself on the verge of tears. Erik crumbled into her embrace.

Tears streamed silently down his cheeks, splashing on her shoulder, spreading out in damp pools on the cotton of her sweater. Erik tried to fight them but couldn't, and before too long he realized he felt Selene's tears on his shoulder.

They'd have likely stayed in that sad hug for a while longer, but the shrill whistle of the tea kettle brought them to a sudden parting. Selene giggled, wiping the wetness from her eyes with the cuff of her sweater while Erik turned towards the cabinets to hide his own. He grabbed a couple mugs and set them on the counter. Selene poured the hot water in each and splashed tea bags in afterwards.

"Sit with me, little brother." Selene grabbed both mugs and set them on the kitchen table before taking a seat.

It was with a heavy heart that Erik complied. He wasn't feeling much like talking, but when Selene made a request, it was foolish to refuse, especially when it was about opening up. She'd stalk and hound you until you finally relented and unloaded the full breadth of your worries to her. It was a strength, getting people to open up.

"How are you doing?" Her question hung in the air between them as Erik tried to craft the answer he knew she was looking for, but the raise of her left eyebrow, a subtle reminder of the Beacon, stayed Erik's lying tongue.

"Terrible."

"Duh," was her quick response.

"I feel... so distracted. I read and study and quiz and... nothing stays in my head. I find myself re-reading every paragraph a dozen times before anything sticks. All I can think about is Bestefar, him being gone."

"I know the feeling. It's not like when Bestemor died. I was ready for that. I got to say goodbye."

"Exactly! I just can't stop asking myself, who would want Bestefar dead? Why? It makes no sense. It dominates my every waking moment, the questions. I can't turn them off. I can't focus on anything else, and the police—"

"You've talked to them? Since Dad's?"

"No," Erik admitted stupidly. "I keep waiting to hear something, but no, nothing so far."

"Well, I'm sure they'll be in touch as soon as they have something."

"Yeah," Erik said, his doubt ringing in his ears.

Silence settled over the room once more and the siblings sipped their tea, reflecting on the world around them.

"I'm jealous, you know?" Selene looked around the clean kitchen. "You got to grow up in this, a family home, with a whole family."

"What're you talking about? You got how many years of Mom and Dad? Back before Dad was… what he is now."

"Yeah, it was pretty good for the first few years, probably." Selene broke into laughter. "I don't really remember a time before Lars. But I'd trade those few years with Mom, the heartbreak of her dying, Dad going to pieces, for just half the time you had with Bestefar and Bestemor."

"Grass is always greener," Erik said, ending the conversation. He got up from the table and shuffled into his childhood bedroom, closing the door in his wake. Fresh tears sprang to his eyes as he crashed onto his bed and allowed the fabric of the pillowcase to absorb his misery.

"Well played, Selene," she said with a sad sigh.

Chapter 14

ERIK STAYED IN his bedroom until Selene popped in to say she was leaving. He got up and hugged her goodbye. She warned him that Lars had split about twenty minutes earlier. "Might want to make sure he kept his word. Otherwise, I doubt you'll ever see your guns again, not that that's a bad thing…"

Erik sighed, walked her to the front door, hugged her again and headed to the basement. The safe was still open and Erik held his breath as he peered in. To his surprise, his colt and his carbine were still in there, and that was about it. Lars had cleared out all of the ammo, the cleaning supplies, even the stack of rags Victor had kept.

"Figures."

Erik spent the rest of the day puttering around the house, taking note of what was there. He'd have to let Michael go through everything and take what he wanted to keep. Selene had already washed her hands of it, only taking what Victor had specifically left her. Lars was likely to disappear until the money was distributed, whenever that was going to be. After he was finished with that Erik turned his attention to the blood stain at the front door. With tear filled eyes Erik scrubbed at it until it was a wet, rust colored smear.

The weight of Victor's death finally fell on him, crushing him beneath it. Who would want to murder him? The police still thought it was a botched robbery, but Erik doubted it. Why would they kill him and run away? Why not just leave and try again? Obviously, Victor hadn't caught them or anything. They shot him in the back of the head not the front. He'd died trying to unlock his door. None of it made sense.

Erik got to his feet, bloody rag still in hand and studied the bullet hole in the glass window of the front door. He stuck his finger through it, mindful of the jagged spears that threatened to slice him up. Small caliber handgun. The trigger was pulled point blank. Erik didn't need an autopsy to tell him that. A bigger round would've destroyed the window, not just punch a hole in it. He put his eye close to it and peered through it, lining up his gaze with the hole in the floor inside. Low trajectory meant Victor had been hunched over. Maybe he'd dropped his keys, maybe he needed to get as close to the lock as possible for his failing eyes to see the keyhole.

Erik pushed open the door and stepped through. He used the overhead light in the entrance to get a good look at the doorknob. No tell-tale scratches or marks to imply it was picked. If Victor had surprised the robbers there would've been something, and what kind of burglar worth their salt would break in through the front door? The yard was lush but anyone walking by the front walk had a straight on view of the front door.

Erik closed the door behind him and made his way to the hole in the hardwood floor. He squatted down and ran his fingers over it. The wood was splintered, the hole uneven. He stuck the same finger he'd put through the hole in the glass into the one in the floor. It was much bigger. Erik got down on all fours and put his eye as close as possible to it. He could just make out scratched grooves in the bottom of the hole. Someone had removed the bullet with a knife. The police maybe? Probably not. They would've used forceps or tweezers or something along those lines. Erik rolled onto his butt and hugged his knees, finally realizing he still held the bloody rag.

He stifled a body shaking sob, almost managing to do the same to the next ones. Almost.

Chapter 15

THE NEXT DAY, Erik found himself at the police station. He wasn't sure what he was doing but he knew he had to satiate the part of his mind that wouldn't rest. He had to try and puzzle out what had happened. If he waited for the police, he might never understand. So, he walked up to the desk sergeant and nodded hello.

"I'd like to speak to Detective Kincaid? About an ongoing investigation."

The sergeant looked up and took in Erik's appearance. Erik had meticulously groomed himself, dressing in one of Victor's suits. He wasn't their typical customer, he imagined. "Name?"

"Erik Brown." The sergeant nodded and picked up the phone on his desk.

"Yeah, Kincaid? Yeah, got a lawyer out here, wants to talk to you about a case you're on. Yeah, Erik Brown." The sergeant raised an eyebrow and looked Erik up and down again. "Student? Huh. Ok, I'll let him know."

The sergeant put down the phone and pulled out a piece of paper, scribbling on it. He plopped it down on the desk in front of Erik. "Sign in and I'll have an officer take you to the homicide department."

Erik did as he was told and then took a seat in the lobby at the direction of the sergeant. Outside, the black sedan parked, Feliks, clad in a black leather jacket, his hair freshly shaved to the scalp, exited the vehicle. He entered the station and walked right past Erik.

"Here to parole my brother," Feliks told the sergeant. After a few minutes the sergeant let him know his brother wasn't there. "Must've been another station, thank you for your time."

The man took a seat just down from Erik and pulled out his phone. He pretended to dial a number, pretended to let it ring and then pretended to have a conversation. He pretended to wait for someone on the other line to figure out where his brother was, and Erik was so absorbed in unraveling the mysteries that plagued his mind, he missed all of it.

"Detective Kincaid will see you now." Erik looked up and nodded. He followed the officer out of the lobby and Feliks pretended to end his conversation and exited the building.

Erik followed his escort past rows of desks, all with busy officers and detectives. Phones rang continuously as sullen perps sat handcuffed to uncomfortable steel benches. It was sensory overload for Erik. He started to question what he was doing, and then he was standing in front of a desk with a name plate that read 'Det. J. Kincaid'.

"Take a seat, the detective will be right with you."

So, Erik sat. Moments later, Det. Kincaid sat down on the other side of the desk. She extended a hand and said, "Good to see you again, Erik." Erik shook her hand. "The desk sergeant said you had some questions?"

Erik nodded. "I... I just... It makes no sense, your theory."

"Oh?" Kincaid responded. "I was unaware we'd made a theory public."

Erik shifted in his seat; this wasn't going how he'd hoped. He took a deep breath and centered his mind as Victor had taught him. "Think before you speak," Victor had always warned. "Sometimes a moments breath is the difference between a wall and a door."

"Sorry, Detective Kincaid—"

"Call me Jo."

"Sure, Jo. Allow me to start over. The officer that walked me through the house, he told me the going theory was that my Bestefar... grandfather's death was the result of a botched robbery."

Kincaid stared at him from the other side of the desk, her face betraying nothing. Erik fought the urge to shift in his seat, forcing a sense of calm to blanket his body and reveal as little as she did. "Why an officer would offer that sort of information to you, I'm not sure, but, as I said, we have no public theories at this time."

"Do you have any suspects?"

Kincaid shook her head. "I can't divulge information on an ongoing case, Erik. Just rest assured we're working on all possible angles. If you have any information you think might help us in our investigation, by all means, give me a call." Kincaid grabbed a business card off her desk and slid it over to Erik.

"Oh, that reminds me, do you guys reimburse for the damage made by your forensics crew, or is that on me?"

"I'm sorry?" Kincaid leaned in, off balance from Erik's sudden change of topic.

"Yeah, they messed up the floor real good removing the bullet from the floor."

"Sorry, Erik, but we didn't retrieve a bullet from the crime scene." The look that washed over her face told Erik she hadn't intended to tell him that.

"Oh, OK. My bad." Just as he'd thought, the 'robbers' removed it.

"I appreciate you coming down here, Erik, but I—"

"See, that just doesn't make sense." Kincaid gave Erik a quizzical look. "There not being a bullet recovered. I mean, I know it was a small caliber and there's the possibility that the bullet went to pieces, but then there's a bullet hole in the floor, plain as day."

"Who told you it was a small caliber handgun?" Kincaid said, an edge to her voice.

"Not trying to get anyone in trouble…"

"Same officer that told you about our *ongoing theory*?" Her response told Erik everything he needed to know, the way she suddenly straightened in her seat. Her tone was passive, but her body language told him he'd hit the nail on the head.

"Honestly? I can't remember. I've just been in my head the last few days, running through everything over and over again."

"You two were close?"

"He raised me," Erik said, letting his eyes drop to the business card in front of him.

"Well, Erik, I'm sorry for your loss. Do you know if he had any criminal connections? Loan shark? Bookie, maybe?"

"Not Bestefar. He was as clean as they come, but honestly, I'm finding out he didn't always share everything with me, once I moved out."

"Like?"

"Little stuff. He led a seniors chess league in the park, was in a senior's basketball league down at the rec center. Stuff like that. Nothing that explains why someone would assassinate him, point blank in the back of the head." Erik noted the surprise in the way Kincaid was sizing him up suddenly and decided to lay all his cards on the table. "They were so quick to get out of there they broke the front gate off the hinges but were calm enough to pick up Bestefar's keys, unlock the front door, go into the house, find the bullet and take it? And then they lock up behind themselves?"

"And who told you any of this?" Kincaid's voice was stern, unamused, telling Erik he was close to the truth.

"No marks on the locks, so they didn't try to pick them, and why would they try to break in at the front door? Where anyone who walked by could see them? It's a small neighborhood with nosey neighbors and my grandfather was well known and liked," Erik continued, ignoring her question. "Nothing missing, nothing even out of place. Did you know Bestefar didn't even own a TV? He didn't own hardly anything worth stealing, so why his house? Why in broad daylight? What could have possibly brought his murderers there other than one thing?"

Erik went silent and just watched Kincaid as she tried to sort through everything, her body language confirming much of what he said, the way her head bobbed from side to side, the rapid eye movement as she tried to avoid eye contact as she formulated a politically correct response. And when she finally did respond, Erik already knew what she'd say.

"This is an ongoing investigation so I can neither confirm nor deny anything about your... theory. Listen, I know it's a lot to compute, Erik. I really appreciate you coming and talking with me. It's been a pleasure, but I really need to get back to work." Kincaid stood up, offering her hand. Erik followed suit.

"Bestefar wasn't involved with the mafia, by the way." Kincaid's eyes widened in surprise just long enough for Erik to confirm the theory that'd been building in the back of his mind since she'd asked about Victor having any criminal connections. Victor's death was a mob hit, or at least Kincaid suspected as much. It made sense when Erik really started to toy with the idea. The broad daylight assassination right out in the open. But why? Mistaken identity? Wrong place at the wrong time? What else had Victor hidden from Erik? What else did Erik not know?

"Good to know," Kincaid responded with a forced chuckle. They shook and said their goodbyes.

Erik walked out of the station in a fog. He passed the black sedan where Feliks and Loren sat, completely unaware, as they tried to look inconspicuous. Had he been paying attention, Erik would've noticed Feliks and wondered why he was still there. Had he been paying attention; he would've recognized the car. He'd noticed it several times over the last few weeks. Victor would have been disappointed; he'd taught Erik better.

64

Chapter 16

"WHY DOES HE meet with Kincaid?" Loren asked as they resumed tailing Erik.

"Who knows. The kid spent a night in the house, spent all evening scrubbing Victor's blood from the steps."

Loren shook his head. "This 'kid' is not what we see. There is something under the skin. We need to scratch off the surface and reveal it."

"Why we do not just loot the house. Why do we wait? Why do we follow this kid? Like the rest of his family, he does nothing, knows nothing!"

"Because that is what Gerwazy told us to do," Loren growled.

"What about Lars?" Feliks said, trying to skirt the edge of Loren's ill temper.

Loren shook his head again. "Came to Konstantyn with a trove of guns, desperate to pay off his debt. Must have paid it three times over." Loren broke into gruff laughter, his scar twisting his grin into a macabre sneer.

"Konstantyn back to his normal self?"

Loren looked at Feliks with a wary eye. "Konstantyn is always his normal self. I do not know what you are talking about."

"Come on, Loren. Something happened back there and then—" Feliks was completely unprepared for the swinging back hand Loren delivered to his chin.

"What are you talking about, saying these things? Are you stupid?" Loren's face was a mask of rage as he prepared another swing. Feliks cowered away from him, blood running down his split lip.

"This kid holds the keys to the kingdom, so we follow. Who knew Victor best? This kid. You would be smart to forget any thoughts about Konstantyn, Chudy. Just do your fucking job."

Feliks looked from Loren's angry face to the gold gilded pistol hanging out of his open jacket and shuddered.

Chapter 17

ERIK DIDN'T GO back to Victor's house... his house. He went to his apartment instead, the next city over. He attempted to go back to his routine of study, gym, class, study and sleep, but his mind refused to play along, stuck on the revelations he'd had at the police station. His desire to unravel the mystery swirling around Victor consumed him. He ignored the looks of pity, flubbed his way through conversation of his loss, condolences, etc. The realization that Victor was assassinated haunted him. It haunted him until he decided to go back to the scene of the crime. He blamed it on meeting a glazier he'd hired to fix the front door window, but the truth was he couldn't shake the feeling he'd missed something.

The glazier was quick to do his job. He saw the rust-colored stain in front of the broken panel of glass with the bullet shaped hole in it and gave Erik a sad smile, refraining from making a comment or asking a question. Once he was gone, Erik went to work riffling through Victor's possessions.

It felt dirty, going through Victor's underwear and sock drawer. He pulled them out and laid them in a cardboard box, only pausing when he found the plastic bag full of firing pins. Victor always removed them before storing the guns. "For safety," he'd always claimed. Erik smiled to himself, wondering whether he should tell Lars he had them or not, and deciding on not before moving on to the next drawer where he found stacks of neatly folded undershirts. He repeated the process for the whole dresser until all of the drawers were empty and three cardboard boxes were full of clothes, destined for charity or whoever would take them off his hands.

Erik moved on to under the bed where he found a few shoe boxes with knick-knacks and photos. He sifted through them realizing how old they were after damaging the corner of one. He held the photo up into the light and realized he was looking at a picture of Victor when he was young. He stood in front of a pretty young woman and a handsome soldier in dress uniform, the name 'Larssen' on the lapel below several ribbons and medals. They must've been his parents. Erik turned over the photo and discovered the date, 1939. Victor was twelve.

"Larssen." Erik leaned back against the bed frame. How had Larssen become Braut? Braut was Erik's un-Americanized last name. Victor had immigrated to America, Viktor Braut. He'd changed his name to Victor Brown to better fit in, Braut sounded too German. Marga had refused to change her name, so they became Victor and Marga Brown. Everyone thought they were Russian, Marga being short for Margarita. It was no wonder she went by Marga in America, Erik thought fondly.

Maybe the man in the photo wasn't Victor's father. Or maybe Victor's mother remarried years later. It could've even been her maiden name for all Erik knew. Scandinavian last names were notoriously difficult to trace, so any number of things could be possible. Before 1923, last names changed with each generation so Larssen just meant the man in the photo was the son of Lars, but Victor being born in 1927 would've meant he should've shared the same last name as his father. Erik had so many questions, but Victor had never spoken about his childhood, only that he'd grown up under Nazi rule.

Erik put the photo to the side and kept sorting through the stack. He found a picture of Victor and Marga smiling at the camera next to a Christmas tree decorated with nuts, apples, glass baubles and what appeared to be handmade ornaments. Erik recognized none of them, but Victor and Marga looked so young, younger than the photos that dotted the walls of the house. He found a photo of Marga, pregnant, with Victor standing over her. The photo was damaged, the corner ripped off, obscuring most of the face of the man on the other side of Marga. It looked accidental, like the photo was just that old. Erik had essentially just done the same thing to the photo he'd just poured over. The date on the back was 1951. But Michael was born in 1959, Aunt Ingrid in 1957. The one could be a seven though, if he squinted. The more Erik flipped through the photos, the more confused he became. It felt as if Victor and Marga had led a secret life before his dad was born. He'd have to remember to ask Michael about the photos.

Erik abandoned the boxes from under the bed, putting them to one side, making sure they were separate from the donation boxes. He moved on to the small walk-in closet. He pulled the beaded steel chain and clicked the naked bulb on. He stood motionless for a bit; the chain clutched, forgotten in his hand. His eyes roved over the neatly hung suits, up to the old hat boxes. He realized with a start that all of Marga's things had already been removed, except for her wedding dress, something he'd already discovered but had forgotten in his grief. He wondered if that was part of the grieving process as he went to work pulling the suits down and laying them out on the bed. The newer ones he'd have to donate. Victor's shoulders had slumped in his old age. The flat stomach he'd worked to maintain in his youth had gone soft. As Erik sorted through the stack of custom-tailored suits he began to wonder if any of them might fit him. Victor had become so much smaller in his old age.

It wasn't until he got to the back of the closet that he discovered a suit wrapped in brown paper. It looked old, untouched for years, a slight layer of dust coating it. Erik held it up in the orange glow of the closet light. To his surprise he discovered writing in black Sharpie. 'To Erik, with love, Bestefar.' Erik walked it out of the closet in a daze. He removed the brown paper carefully, trying to preserve it as if he were going to use it again. Once it was removed it revealed a classic cut brown three-piece suit. Erik just stared at it. He tried to remember if he'd ever seen Victor wear it. How long had Victor waited to gift it to Erik?

Erik removed the suit he was already wearing, slowly putting on the new one. The fabric was nice, soft. The waist was a bit tight, probably tailored to measurements taken before Erik left behind the skin and bones distance runner's physique he'd worn throughout high school. The vest was also snug but manageable. Erik donned the jacket with apprehension, fearing what he already knew. The jacket was tight along the shoulders to the point of discomfort. It'd all have to be let out, as if he had time to go to a tailor and Victor's penchant of removing any tags made it impossible to remember who his tailor was in the first place.

Erik walked to the mirror hanging on the closet door and laughed. He looked ridiculous, like an overstuffed sausage casing, the sleeves of his button up protruding comically from the jacket cuffs, the vest buttons straining against his stomach and the slacks clinging to his muscular legs like skinny jeans. Erik shook his head and started to navigate his way out of the jacket. As he carefully slid one arm out, something stiff scraped against his forearm.

"Ouch!" he exclaimed more out of surprise than pain. He delicately finished removing the jacket and checked his forearm. A faint pink scratch ran along it, tiny droplets of blood pooling and drying. "Must be something caught in the sleeve," he said out loud.

He started turning the sleeve inside out to find the culprit and hit something stiff just above the elbow. He felt along it with his fingers, perplexed, until he found a little needle imbedded in the seam. What a strange place to find a tailor's pin. He tugged on the little barb and to his surprise the seam gave way in a long slit. "Damn!"

Erik looked at the ruined seam and silently cursed his luck. Not like he would've been able to wear it anytime soon, but to ruin it on day one with his carelessness? "Dammit," he muttered as he fingered the tear, and then he felt something within it.

With a curious frown he let his fingers probe deeper into the seam until they landed on something small and cylindrical. His fingers couldn't quite navigate the small space, so he took the jacket into the master bathroom, rummaged around in the drawers until he found tweezers, and then carefully probed the hole again until he was able to find the mystery object again. With some real effort, he was able to pull the object free.

It was a small plastic tube the size of a ballpoint pen tube.

Chapter 18

ERIK FORGOT ABOUT the suit jacket, about how ridiculous he must've looked in the tight vest and tighter slacks. His full attention, the entirety of his mind, was focused on the tiny plastic tube he held in his hand. At first, all he could do was just look at it, turning it over slowly in his hand, his mind trying desperately to discern something about it, to identify it. He'd been to the tailor several times and could say with some certainty that it was unlike anything he'd ever seen them use. Upon further inspection, he discovered that the ends had been melted together, but why? Erik's stomach dropped as he realized the small tube had something trapped within it.

"Holy…" Erik murmured as a surge of energy shot into his limbs, leaving a tingling feeling in his toes and fingers.

Erik rushed to the kitchen and retrieved a sharp knife. His goal was to slice the top off and free its contents, but it proved more difficult than he'd hoped. The small tube was tightly packed, and he feared damaging the contents. Erik wished he had access to a scalpel, but this wasn't one of his labs. The knife felt clunky in his hand, too big for the delicate task but, after what felt an eternity, Erik managed to slice off the tiniest piece of the plastic. He rushed back to the bathroom to retrieve the discarded tweezers and gently freed a small rolled up piece of paper from its plastic tomb. Erik just stared at it for a moment, disbelief stopping his fingers from functioning. What was this thing? Did Victor know about it? Did Victor put it there, hoping Erik would find it? It was so difficult for Erik to believe it had all been intentional, but then, how could he claim it wasn't? The suit had been specifically marked for him, tailored to measurements Victor must have known wouldn't fit him. The way the sharp piece in the lining caught him and then sliced open, with such ease, as if by design when he explored it…

Erik slowly unrolled the small slip of parchment and revealed a series of nine numbers in incredibly tiny print. Why would Victor hide a series of apparently random numbers in the lining of a jacket? Erik left the slip on the kitchen counter and returned to the suit jacket. He spent the next half hour poking, prodding and pinching the jacket. He started with the lining, turning the coat inside out, and moved on to the interior. He found nothing, so, he removed the vest and performed the same procedure finding about the same. Then, he removed the slacks, turning them inside out and continuing until that too revealed nothing.

Erik sat down heavily on the edge of the bed; mystified, certain he was missing something. He ran the numbers through his head over and over again. What did they mean? They had to be important, for why else would Victor go through the trouble of hiding them like he had? And why would he want Erik to be the one to have them? It made no sense. Perhaps more clues were hidden around the house? Erik got up from the bed and went back to the closet. The hanging rails were empty as he'd already sorted the suits, but the shelf above them was lined with hat boxes and old shoe boxes. Erik decided to start there, sorting through the shoe boxes first. He grabbed a stack three high from the shelf and carried them back to the bed. He put them down and started shuffling through them.

To the eye, they held little more than knick-knacks. He discovered an old lighter, stainless steel, the etched writing on the side so worn and faded Erik could only make out the 'L' at the front and the 'N' at the end. Underneath was what appeared to be some kind of insignia, or coat of arms. There were marbles, little tin pins, a pocketknife, dull with age, the grip worn with use. He found no notes, no clues, no nothing. He moved on to the next stack and found little more, repeating the process until all of the shoe boxes were void of content and a pile of junk filled the middle of the bed. Besides a few items, the majority were trash. Erik would of course catalog them and check if they had any worth before discarding them. Victor had always taught him the value of another man's treasure. It was entirely possible that some of the pins were a part of some rare set, but that was as far from his mind as could be in that moment.

Disheartened, Erik put on a pair of sweatpants, jamming his phone into the pocket. He looked around the bedroom and sighed. The only things left were the hat boxes and Erik already knew what resided in them. He'd explored their contents too many times to count. Victor had always laughed when Erik suddenly appeared with a fedora hanging low over his eyes. He'd get a rag to pad along the inside of the hat band so Erik could wear the oversized thing without it falling over his eyes or wobbling chaotically around his head. Erik doubted he'd get rid of any of them. He'd put them to good use he promised himself, before heading to the basement.

The basement proved to be just as empty of clues as the bedroom had. He searched through countless old cardboard boxes, mainly finding his old clothes and toys packed safely away. Erik teared up as he took in how carefully his old possessions had been taken care of. Victor clearly was hoping to meet his great-grandchildren. Why else would he keep the old things?

Erik left the basement and found a comfortable place on the old sofa in the living room. Mentally exhausted, he put his feet up and started to doze off, but his phone had other ideas as it sprang to life in his pocket. He shot up on the couch, his exhaustion temporarily forgotten as surprise pumped adrenalin into his veins. He laughed at himself as he removed the vibrating phone from his pocket, but by the time he freed it the call had gone to voice mail.

"Samantha." Erik said as he stared stupidly at the caller ID, trying to figure out why she would be calling him. He ran over a list of possibilities before the voice mail notification buzzed. Erik quickly accessed it and hit play.

"Hey Erik, it's Sam. Duh, I know, obviously... Anyway, I just wanted to call about the dinner. Did you have a chance to pay me back yet? I might've missed your transfer so just let me know one way or the other! This is Samantha... Talk to you later. Bye!"

He'd totally forgotten. Erik sighed as he found the note in his phone with her bank info. He logged into his own bank website and copy and pasted the router number into the correct space and paused, just staring at the numbers, an odd feeling of familiarity invading his thoughts until realization lit him up like a light bulb.

Erik rushed into the kitchen and picked up the tiny piece of parchment paper, comparing the numbers to the ones staring back at him from his phone. They were identical.

"Holy shit..."

Chapter 19

ERIK JUST STARED at the numbers until he finally decided to give Victor's lawyer a call, but an answering machine informed Erik that he'd missed office hours, so he called Michael instead.

Michael's voice was subdued when he answered. Erik wondered if the man had gotten out of bed that day but left the question unasked.

"Hey Dad, how you holding up?"

"Oh, doing my best. How about you, Erik? You OK? I know you two were close."

"Yeah, just going through his stuff, wondering how well I really knew him, which is why I called... I was hoping you might be able to fill in some blanks? I keep finding pictures of him and Bestemor that make no sense."

"Oh? How so?"

"Well, there's one with Bestemor when she was pregnant but the date on the back is from 1951, and then there's a picture of Victor with some soldier with the last name Larssen—"

"Oh, Erik, I don't think I'm going to be much help. Your grandparents never talked about their life before I was born. Even after I was born, I always felt like they kept things from me."

"What do you mean?" Erik asked, surprised by Michael's statement.

"Well, we moved a lot when I was a kid, always suddenly and without explanation. And when I asked questions, they never gave me a straight answer. Was like that my whole life, until your mother died…" Erik could hear Michael restrain a sob. "I never really felt close to your grandparents. I think I was always a disappointment. It wasn't until…"

"Sorry, Dad. Didn't mean to dredge up bad memories. I just never realized… I guess I just thought you were closer to them."

"I know they loved me, Erik, and that's always been enough for me. You know how much I love you, right? I wish I'd been stronger—"

"I know and I love you too, Dad. Get some sleep, we'll talk later."

His conversation with Michael had been illuminating. He made more sense to Erik somehow, but the mystery around Victor had only deepened. Erik found little sleep that night, finally drifting off in the wee hours of the morning, but he couldn't escape his body's programming as sleep deserted him with the rising of the sun.

He spent a tortured couple of hours waiting for the lawyer's office to open, mostly sifting through the clutter he'd created in his mad search for more clues. He wasn't sure what he was going to say but figured that didn't matter in the end. He dialed the office and was immediately put on the line with the lawyer.

"Hi, Jim? It's Erik Brown, Victor Brown's grandson. How are you?"

"I'm well, Erik. How can I help you? My secretary said you had some questions for me about your grandfather's finances?"

"Yes. I was just wondering if he still had an account at Lake Harvest Credit Union?" The other end was silent except for the click clack of keyboard keys.

"Nope, doesn't look like it, Erik. Why do you ask?"

"Oh, I just seemed to remember him having one there."

"Well, if he did, it must've been under another name."

"Thanks for checking."

"No problem. We should be done putting everything together here in the next few weeks. I know your brother is in a hurry to get his portion of the inheritance. Do you have any questions?"

"What? Sorry, not really," Erik responded, distracted by the new information. He hung up the phone and picked up the parchment paper, scrutinizing the routing number like it'd eventually crack under the pressure and tell him why Victor had wanted him to have it.

Erik spent most of the morning puzzling out how he could move forward with the routing number. Clearly, there was something at the bank that Victor wanted him to have. His focus should have been on his classes, on studying, on anything other than the nine-digit number, but he was like a dog with a bone. He was determined to get to the end of it. He had half a mind to go down to Lake Harvest Credit Union and simply ask about Victor, but that seemed stupid. They'd never willingly give out their customers' information. Maybe if he brought Victor's death certificate and his passport? That could work.

Erik finally landed on going down there with Victor's IDs, his proof of death and his own ID to prove his relation. So, later that morning Erik drove down to the credit union. He had no idea if his plan would work, but he had to try. He was a detective, unraveling a great mystery. The murder of Victor still weighed heavily in his thoughts as the police continued to turn up nothing. The case was more a cold case than an active investigation, and Erik knew it. Det. Kincaid didn't have to tell him she'd moved on, it was what he expected, the first forty-eight hours and all. It'd been a few days since he'd visited her and still nothing. Victor's neighbors had seen nothing, or if they had, they kept their mouths shut. Erik had half a mind to go and ask his own questions, a grandson just looking for a little closure.

Erik walked into a stark lobby. He looked around for a manager but saw nobody. Instead, he walked up to a teller, one of three working. She was an older woman with bright red hair. She peered through the glass at him from behind thick glasses in a tortoise shell frame. Her smile was sincere and put Erik at ease.

"Hi sweetie, how can I help you?"

Erik hesitated, getting his story together before uttering a word, just as Victor had taught him. *"Be clear, be concise and don't talk just to fill the silence."*

"Hi Ma'am. I recently found out my deceased grandfather had an account here, or at least he used to. I just wanted to make sure the proper steps were taken with it after his death." Erik offered her the death certificate with the passport on top of it. She let him slide it under the glass and picked it up, scrutinizing it briefly before pushing it back to him.

"Let me grab my manager. He's better suited for this type of thing." She rushed away leaving Erik to wait. He didn't have to wait long as a bald man in a cheap suit came walking through the lobby towards him. The man had an outstretched hand and a smile.

"Hi, young man, I'm Arnie Joseph, branch manager. My teller informed me of your situation, and I'd love to help. Why don't you follow me back to my office and we can get to the bottom of it."

"Sure." Erik shook Arnie's hand and followed him out of the lobby.

Arnie took him to a drab office with a single window overlooking the parking lot. Arnie's desk was cluttered with pictures of teenagers. His chair squeaked loudly as he plopped his bulk into it, pulling his keyboard towards him. Arnie motioned towards the seat across the desk from him and Erik obliged, sitting delicately on the edge.

"Sorry to hear about your loss. Mary said you had a death certificate and a passport?" Erik nodded, placing them on the table and sliding them over to Arnie. "Thanks, and can I get your ID?"

Erik complied, pulling out his ID and sliding it over. "I also brought along photos of the two of us if you need more proof of our relationship."

"Oh, that won't be necessary," Arnie picked up Erik's ID and looked it over. "Won't be necessary, Erik." Arnie started typing into his computer, double checking Victor's name. He frowned, typed in Victor's info again. "Not seeing an active account here. It would appear your grandfather closed his account with us... Ten years ago."

Erik tried to hide his disappointment. He slowly reached across the desk to gather his things. "Oh, OK. Well, that makes sense since this account didn't show up in his assets."

"Sorry, Erik. Is there anything you'd like to do with your account today?"

"My account?" Erik was dumbstruck. Since when did he have an account at the credit union? Had Victor opened it for him and forgotten to tell him? "Yes, that'd be great. Can you give me an overview of it, please?" He said, doing his best to hide his shock and succeeding.

"Absolutely." Arnie started typing then clicked enter on his keyboard. A printer to his left roared to life and the two men waited for the pages to emerge. Arnie grabbed them, double checked them and pushed them across the desk to Erik.

Erik quickly scanned through them, surprised by a balance of $10,000. He was even more surprised to find that the account had been active for fifteen years. Victor had created the account for Erik when he was a child. But why, and why keep it from him? There had been plenty of time for him to tell Erik about it. Account activity showed that money came and went from the account regularly. Was Victor hiding money, hiding it under Erik's name? But Victor had wanted Erik to find it, at least, after his death anyway.

"I see here I have a safety deposit box; can I take a look at that?"

"Sure! All you need is your ID and a key."

"Oh, I lost my key. Any way I can take a look without it?"

Arnie frowned in response, shaking his head no. "Sorry, Erik. The box needs two keys to unlock. Did you lose both of your copies? If so, I suppose you could have the locks changed. Costs about one-hundred bucks and you'd need to set up an appointment. If you just lost the one, we can replace it for twenty-five bucks. Anyway, I can't get you in there today."

"Yep, seem to have misplaced both keys. To be honest, I can't recall what the dang keys even look like." Erik gave Arnie his most disarming smile and Arnie laughed, playing right along.

"Well, let's see," Arnie said as he pulled out a bristling key ring. He fiddled through a few keys before landing on some squat bronze keys. He isolated one of them and held it up for Erik. "Gonna look just like this little guy."

"Perfect! I'll be on the lookout for one just like that. In the meantime, let's cover all our bases here and get an appointment in the books for a locksmith."

"That I can do, Mr. Brown." Arnie started typing on his computer again. "How does Tuesday of next week sound?"

"This coming Tuesday?"

"Oh, no. Sorry. I meant Tuesday of the following week. I never know the correct terminology for that." Arnie broke into a gruff laugh and Erik did his best to hide his disappointment.

"And that's the earliest you can get a locksmith in here?"

"Sure is. All kinds of red tape to go through first."

"Of course." Erik resolved to tear the house apart in search of those stupid keys.

Chapter 20

"WHAT IF MARGA remarried," Feliks mused out loud. Loren turned to him and scowled.

"Then Lars lied to us."

"Yeah, well he also said they emigrated from Norway. This kid, he knows nothing." Loren's scowl deepened and Feliks finally noticed it. "Just saying is all."

"Petulant child, always complaining, I tire of it. This bank is not a development? Ever stop to think the book might be there? Bałwan."

"But Victor does not even have an account there."

"Or that lawyer lied to us. Maybe we should pay him another visit." Loren's smile was vicious as he relished the idea. Feliks shivered next to him. He knew that look and he never wanted to be on the other side of those sick machinations.

Erik exited the bank and made his way towards his car.

"Finally," Feliks said.

"Indeed," Loren grunted before opening the passenger door.

"Where the hell are you going? Kid is on the move."

"Then follow him, Bałwan," Loren said as he got out of the car.

Feliks hesitated, "What about you?"

Loren leaned into the car, using the door frame to loom over Feliks, his gold gilded gun on full display, and smiled his macabre grin. "Need to talk to a banker. Go, he is leaving, do not lose him, Chudy, or there will be consequences."

Loren slammed the door and trotted off across the parking lot. Feliks didn't hesitate to comply. He was glad to be away from Loren. The man scared him. He'd found himself on his bad side more and more. He needed to learn to hold his tongue, he needed to get off that shit detail and back to what he was good at, back to where he was safe from Loren's glares, his dark machinations. Feliks shuddered as his imagination ran wild.

Chapter 21

LOREN ENTERED THE bank and looked around the empty lobby. Only one teller was on duty as closing time loomed large. Loren made his way to the little plastic cubicle and smiled down at the red-haired woman. She smiled uneasily back at him.

"My nephew, he was just in here and forgot his wallet, such a foolish young man. Perhaps it was you that helped him, Erik Brown?"

Mary just stared at the big man, mouth agape.

"Erik Brown?" Arnie Joseph said behind Loren.

Loren turned to regard him. "That's him."

"Mary, have you seen his wallet?" Arnie asked with a grin.

"Na-no," Mary managed.

"Must have dropped it in my office! Follow me, sir."

Loren turned to regard Mary, reveling in the state he'd put her in. "Thank you."

Mary shivered despite herself.

Arnie led Loren back to his office and immediately dropped to his hands and knees to look under the chair Erik had sat in.

"Not seeing anything here…"

"Stand up," Loren growled. Arnie's good mood evaporated as he took in Loren and the big gun hanging out of his jacket. "Sit down," Loren commanded and when Arnie looked to protest Loren unbuckled the clasp on his holster. Arnie trembled, frozen. "Now!"

Arnie jumped to his feet and scurried into the closest chair.

"What did Erik Brown want?"

"I… I can't tell you th—"

"I assure you, you can," Loren growled, the gun sliding out of the shoulder holster with a metallic scrape. Loren slammed the gun down on Arnie's desk making him jump.

Loren stood near the front entrance of the bank, a cigarette dangling out of his mouth, his phone pressed firmly against his ear.

"No, Victor had no account here, but I am told the kid does. The bank manager seemed to think the kid was mostly interested in a safety deposit box."

"Does he know what is in it?" Gerwazy asked.

"Doubtful. The kid has no key, so he ordered a locksmith to open the box."

"Can we get in there first?"

"No. Bank man only has one key. The box needs two."

"Good work, Loren. I assume you were delicate?"

"Of course, boss. The bank man is shaken but unharmed. If he says a word, I will put a bullet in his gut. I made sure he understands." Loren's scar tugged at the corner of his dark smile as he imagined shooting Arnie.

"Good, and Feliks is still following the kid?"

"If he is not, I will put a bullet in *his* gut," Loren said, bursting into a gruff laughter.

"Good," Gerwazy said before the line went dead.

Loren shoved the phone in his pocket and took a long drag on his cigarette. "What a beautiful evening," he said as a black SUV entered the empty parking lot, coming to a stop in front of him. He tossed the butt of his cigarette into the gutter and climbed in.

Chapter 22

ERIK TURNED THE house upside down again. And, again, he found nothing. He should have been studying. He should've been at the gym. He should've been doing anything other than pursuing the clues Victor had left him, but he was locked in. With the same determination that had gotten him into medical school, he was determined to figure out why Victor had led him to the safety deposit box. He tapped on walls, searched for false bottoms in drawers. He opened the safe and dismantled his two guns in search of another clue. He even braved the yawning maw of darkness that was the crawl space under the house. It all proved fruitless. That is, until Erik found himself in Victor's closet for the fourth or fifth time.

Erik stared up at the hat boxes perched on the upper shelf. He racked his brain trying to remember if he'd checked them yet, realizing no, he hadn't. He'd planned on keeping them, so he hadn't taken them down to go through them. The more he reflected on them the more he was convinced the missing key was in one of them. Victor knew how obsessed Erik had been with them. Victor would set his hat down for no more than a second before Erik would steal it and go running through the house pretending to be a P. I.

Victor had always indulged him, pretending to by a surly person of interest. Erik would interrogate him, and Victor would make him read his exaggerated body language as to whether he was lying or telling the truth.

It was probably why Erik was so good at reading people. Victor had a knack for those kinds of games. They seemed innocent to a kid but when reflected upon as an adult, they all had a life lesson built in.

Erik fought off a wave of tears as his mind danced through the fond memories. He wiped them away and pulled down one of the boxes. He took it to the bed and started unpacking the felt fedoras. He carefully searched the inside lining of the hat band, felt around the brim to be sure nothing was sewn into it, and finding nothing, moved to the next one.

It was the second box he searched that held the key. Erik had already searched the top two hats when he pulled out a honey brown, wide brimmed fedora. Erik looked at it and tried to remember it, but if Victor had worn it, it was never around Erik. He turned it over and peeled back the sweatband, moving slowly around it until his fingers felt something hard and cold. Erik's heart surged, his pulse quickening. It took a little effort to pull the key free, it was wedged in there so well. He held it up to the ceiling light and smiled. It was a match for the key Arnie had shown him.

"Yes!" Erik barked, jumping off of the bed to do a quick dance around the bedroom. "Yes!" He whooped again.

Chapter 23

SUNDAY WAS TORTURE for Erik. With the bank closed, the key was only capable of jump starting his imagination. What could be hidden in the safety deposit box? Why did Victor want Erik to have it? It was the same questions over and over, and Erik never got closer to a realistic answer. Erik went to the gym near Victor's house at one point, but he didn't put much into it. The day seemed a waste, and his nerves frayed under the stress of not knowing. Not knowing why Victor was assassinated or by who. Not knowing why Victor had left him the clues.

Erik was up bright and early the next morning. A plan firm in his mind. The bank was on the way to his lecture, so he'd stop in quickly, see what Victor had wanted him to have, and decide whether he wanted to still go to the lecture. He had plenty of time to figure it all out.

He arrived shortly after the bank opened and hurried inside. He spoke to Mary and she told him to grab a seat while she fetched Arnie. He must have been busy because Erik was forced to wait for around forty minutes. He tried to distract himself on his phone but found it hard to focus. He was so close and running out of time. All the answers he needed were just a few steps away. Where the hell was Arnie, and why was he taking so long?

Finally, Arnie materialized. He walked up to Erik and offered his hand, his former friendliness nowhere to be seen. "Good morning, Mr. Brown. Were you able to find your key?"

"Sure did! Been so long since I accessed the safety deposit box, I barely remember what's in it." Arnie forced a laugh along with Erik and led him back into the vault. Erik noticed but chalked it up to a bad day, or maybe Arnie still needed his morning coffee.

Arnie inserted his key into the lock on his side and Erik followed suit with the one on his side. They both turned the keys and a gratifying click sounded. Arnie pulled out the large box and set it on the table in the middle of the small vault then took a step back, crossing his arms behind his back. Erik gave him a friendly smile before stepping up to the box. He ran his finger along the metal lid and looked back up at Arnie.

"I'm sorry, Arnie, can I have some privacy please?" A grimace flickered across Arnie's round features before he unclasped his hands and nodded at Erik.

"Of course. Just let Mary know when you're through and she'll come grab me and we can lock it back up."

"Thanks, Arnie. Really appreciate it."

"Just doing my job," Arnie laughed, the good humor never moving past the edge of his lips.

Arnie vacated the vault leaving Erik alone. Erik watched him go and waited for the click of the door closing before turning back to the safety deposit box. Arnie's behavior, so different, tugged at Erik's thoughts. He was missing something, but his prize was right in front of him. He grabbed the lid of the box, his heartbeat pounding in his ears. The lid squealed as Erik lifted it. He pushed it up and let it fall backwards on its hinges. All of Erik's anticipation whooshed out of him like a deflating tire. The box was empty except for a folded scrap of paper.

"Gotta be kidding me, Bestefar." Erik grabbed the scrap and opened it, revealing a name: Per Larssen, and a phone number. Erik looked at it, disappointment seeping into his every fiber. He fought the urge to crumple it up and toss it away.

"Everything, OK?" Arnie's sudden reappearance made Erik jump. He spun towards Arnie and caught him craning his neck to see inside the safety deposit box. Erik instinctively put himself between the box and the man and scowled at him.

"Yeah, I'm fine, Arnie. Can I please have some privacy in here? If I need anything, I'll be sure to let you know."

Arnie nodded stupidly, blind to Erik's brewing anger. "Sure, sorry, Thought I heard you call for me."

"Then you need to get your ears checked, Arnie. I can recommend a good otolaryngologist."

"A what?"

"It doesn't matter. I don't need help and frankly, I find this intrusion to be very rude." Arnie looked miserable. It wasn't embarrassment, it was something else. Erik finally allowed his mind to chase the thread it'd picked up on earlier, and he realized Arnie had been off since the start. Sweat beaded his brow, his cheeks were flushed. The man couldn't stand still, dancing nervously from foot to foot, his hands kneading something between them… the safety deposit key.

"Is everything OK with you, Arnie? You seem… distressed."

Arnie let out a loud laugh void of humor and gave Erik a fake smile. "Couldn't be better." He did an about face and rushed out of the room. What was going on? Erik wondered; the slip of paper almost forgotten in his hand.

Erik held the paper for a time, the name Larssen mocking him. He was done with the box, ready to retrieve Arnie and wallow in defeat but as he reached for the bronze handle of the windowless door, he faltered.

Larssen… The picture he'd discovered under Victor's bed flashed into his mind. The picture of Victor and his mother with the soldier, Larssen prominent on the breast of his uniform. Was he Per Larssen? He'd have to be in his nineties, hundreds even. What if Victor had family? What if there was a whole Larssen clan Victor wanted Erik to find? Would they know why Victor was murdered? Erik's mind exploded with possibilities that continued to multiply as his excitement surged.

The sharp beep of his phone brought his feet back to the ground as it signaled ten minutes to the start of lecture. "Shit," was all he managed as he scrambled to fetch Arnie. Erik swung the door open and discovered Arnie lurking just down the hall, pacing back and forth as if he were waiting for Erik. They were able to lock up the box in short order.

"Anything of interest in there?" Arnie asked, his casual tone far too forced to be honest.

Erik bristled against the question, his distrust of the man growing by the breath. "Nah, just some old paperwork I've been looking for."

Erik thanked him and rushed out of the building into the parking lot. He barely managed to keep himself from running to his car. He started it from across the parking lot and barely took the time to fasten his seatbelt before hitting the gas. He sped by Feliks and Loren who just gaped at him as he drove past. Erik's eyes flicked over them but hardly noticed them. It wasn't until he was halfway to the lecture that the shocked horror on their faces registered.

It wasn't until he was pulling into the school parking lot that his brain recognized the black sedan. Erik parked and did his best to shake the thoughts from mind, but he couldn't escape the sense of paranoia that was building in his bones. Arnie had been so off... and the sedan, was it the same one as before? He grabbed his book bag and rushed into the lecture hall.

Chapter 24

THE BLACK SEDAN crept into the parking lot and took up its vigil from the back corner, below the thinning branches of a large tree.

"You are getting lazy, Chudy." Loren was in a mood. Feliks knew it well. It was better if he didn't respond. "Maybe it is time we switched cars. Get out."

"What?" Feliks could only stare at Loren.

"Get out. I am going to switch cars. You stay here, wait for the kid. Call me if he changes from his schedule. I think I will pay bank man another visit on my way."

"Sure," was all Feliks could manage before Loren started to push him out of the door. "I am going! Jesus, man!"

As soon as Feliks slammed the car door, Loren sped off. Feliks waited until Loren had turned the corner before flipping him off. "Diabeł, psycho."

Feliks looked around the busy campus parking lot and slumped. He pulled out a pack of smokes and lit one up, sighing loudly. "Shit job with an asshole psycho. Chudy, do this. Chudy, do that. My name is Feliks!" He made his way over to a bench in front of the building and sat down.

Chapter 25

THE LECTURE SEEMED to stretch on forever. It was all Erik could do to pay attention. He had to fight to keep his mind from wandering over the possibilities of who Per Larssen was. He was constantly forced to implement Victor's strategy on staying focused. He'd take deep breaths, clear his mind and turn his full attention to the lecturer at the front of the room. By the time the lecture finally finished, Erik had little to show for it. The notepad on his laptop, which typically would have had pages of study material, was mostly empty. Erik did his best not to dwell on his poor performance for the day.

"Hey, Erik!"

"Hey, Samantha." Erik had seen her picking her way over to him but was surprised that he was the focus of her attention. He'd thought for sure she was coming over to talk to Diana. Out of the corner of his eye, he saw Diana wink at Samantha. To his surprise, Samantha blushed. The hell is that about, he thought to himself, missing every signal that was so clearly in front of him.

"Hey, Erik, so, Diane, Jason, Prisha, Devon and I are all going out for drinks tonight, and we thought maybe you'd want to join us, blow off some steam?" Erik missed the naked plea in her voice and went about packing up his things.

"Oh, thanks for the invite. I'm not much of a drinker though."

"Oh yeah, forgot." Samantha looked to the floor, her smile slipping. "Well, if you just want to hang out, we can do that too."

"Thanks for the offer but I'm kinda swamped right now."

"Oh, right. Your grandpa." Erik's attention piqued and he fixed Samantha with a wondering frown.

"What do you mean?" His voice held more menace than he'd intended, and Samantha shrunk away from him.

"Just that, he died and stuff… I'm so sorry!"

Erik immediately softened. He regained his senses, took control over his racing mind and put to work Victor's teachings. Was she being honest? Sincere? Probably, but Erik couldn't shake the since of paranoia Arnie had instilled in him earlier. "Trust no one," Victor would always say.

"I'm sorry, Samantha. I know you're just trying to help. I didn't mean to jump down your throat."

"It's cool. If you need anything, just know I'm here for you." Samantha hesitated, fixed Erik with a sad smile and retreated.

Erik continued to feel terrible playing the conversation on repeat, wondering if there was anything to his distrust of her. Why the new attention? Was it because of Victor's death? Was she just trying to be a friend? Erik had precious few of those. First thing was first though, he had to call the number Victor left him. He had to call Per Larssen.

Erik retreated to his car, walking right past Feliks. Feliks watched from behind a pair of dark sunglasses, his hood up against the gusting wind. Erik looked at the scrap of paper, took a deep breath and dialed it. The line rang and rang. Erik waited for the voice mail to click on, but it didn't, instead it continued to ring. Erik was about to hang up when the line clicked, and the ringing stopped.

"Hello?" Silence. Erik decided to try again. "Hello?"

"Who is this," came a grizzled voice full of menace.

Erik hesitated, was this the right number? He fought the urge to double check and plowed on with his mission. "I'm looking for Per Larssen?"

The silence on the other end stretched on and on, before, "Who is this?" The voice had softened, and Erik heard genuine curiosity.

"Mr. Larssen? You probably don't know me; my name is Erik Brown. Victor Brown was my grandfather—"

"How'd you get this number?"

"My grandfather left it for me. I think you guys might be related."

"Wrong number, don't call here again." The line clicked off and Erik's phone beeped the end of the call.

Erik held the phone out in front of him and marveled at what had just transpired. He checked his call history and made sure the numbers matched. They did. "What the hell was that?" Erik wondered out loud.

He leaned back against his seat and closed his eyes against the anger that slowly built inside of him. Why had Victor left him that number? Why the scavenger hunt to find a dead end? Erik fought with the reasons and the only thing he could land on was Victor was playing one last joke on him. He should be happy with the surprise of $10,000. He should be happy with the house. Maybe this was just Victor telling him to just be happy and to move on, but Victor didn't know he was going to be murdered. Victor couldn't have known how much this would all weigh on Erik. So many questions and no answers.

Frustrated tears sprang to Erik's eyes and he didn't fight them. He was exhausted and maybe it was time to let things go. That was when Erik saw Jeffrey Grant's business card, right where he'd left it the night he found out about Victor's death, and then an idea sprang into Erik's mind.

He dialed the number. It rang twice. "Jeffrey Grant's office. Is this a crisis?" answered a woman's voice.

"Hi, uh, no crisis. I was just hoping I could make an appointment with Dr. Grant?"

"Your name?"

"Erik Brown."

"Let me check if he has any openings." Erik waited in silence for a moment before her voice roared back through his phone. "Can you come in today?"

"Today?" Erik was shocked. He'd figured it would take a week or two to get him in.

"Yes. You're in luck, we just had a cancellation. How does 4:30 sound?"

That gave him forty-five minutes after class ended. "Sure, 4:30 works."

"Excellent, see you then."

If anyone could shed some light on Victor, it was Jeffrey. That is, if he really did treat Victor, which Erik still had a hard time believing, but he was figuring out that there was a lot to be learned about his mentor, his friend. Erik passed by Feliks, deep in thought as he approached the table Samantha and some of his classmates were at.

"Hey, Samantha," he said, trying to let it go, his paranoia, his fear. "Can I still join you guys for that drink tonight?"

Samantha's smile was ear to ear. Genuine, Erik reflected. "Yay! So glad to hear that! We're meeting up at nine at the Trusty Goat but you can stop by my place beforehand if you want to pregame a bit."

"Pregame?" The terminology was lost on Erik which seemed to delight Samantha.

"You really don't party much do you..."

Chapter 26

JEFFREY'S OFFICE TURNED out to be not too far away from campus which gave Erik the much-needed opportunity to stop by a coffee shop on his way and get a pick-me-up. The shop was almost empty, not surprising as the clock on the wall rolled over the four. Erik yawned as he stepped up to the counter and tried to blink away the fatigue from his eyes.

"Americano, please," Erik said to the barista. He paid and found a nice corner with a wall to his back to wait for his caffeine. The shop had two exits and he could see both clearly from his seat. Victor had taught him that, to be aware of your surroundings, to always have a wall at your back. "Never know what can happen," he'd say, letting Erik's imagination run wild.

The ding of the door right next to him caused him to jump. He'd been zoning out he realized after a quick scan of the room told him a young woman had entered via the door next to him, and that his coffee was ready at the pickup counter. The woman gave him a quick smile as she glided past him to put in her drink order.

Erik followed her for a moment and was transfixed by the smell of vanilla that wafted in her wake. He nearly passed the pick-up counter, so entranced by the smell, but managed to stop himself before it became awkward. He retrieved his coffee and took a long pull on it before spinning on his heel and heading back to his corner.

4:05 p.m.

Another ten minutes to kill. Did he want to do it in the shop or in his car outside Jeffrey's office? He was pondering the question when the scent of vanilla invaded his nostrils once again. He looked up to see the young woman sitting at the table next to him, pulling out a notepad and a bag of pencils.

Student, was Erik's first thought as he took in her overstuffed backpack. The paint flecking her hands, her hair, said she was an art student. Erik watched as she sharpened a pencil and just managed to avert his gaze as she started to look around the small shop.

Erik took another sip of coffee before allowing his eyes to find her again. She was busily sketching in the notepad, her eyes flitting to a sad looking man in a rumpled suit just across the walkway. The man looked dejected, the coffee forgotten in his hands, his eyes far away. Erik could relate, that feeling of loss, lack of purpose. It's how he'd felt since that day in the gym, the day his life got flipped upside down.

"Rough day at the office," the woman said, just loud enough for Erik to hear. His eyes snapped towards her and saw her looking at him.

"Sorry?" Erik responded, unsure if he heard her right.

"Suit over there," she said, motioning towards the man with a tilt of her head, "rough day at the office." Her smile broadened as Erik lit up in realization.

She'd seen him staring at the man and come to the same conclusion he had. Erik looked at the man and smiled. "Rough *month* at the office would be my guess."

The woman laughed. "And what about you?"

Erik's smile slipped and he saw a flit of anxiety pass over her eyes. He took a moment to form his response, deepening the silence between them. "Insomnia," he said just moments before things became awkward.

The woman gave a relieved laugh and shook her coffee at him. "I know what you mean."

"Erik."

"Kelsey," she responded, holding her hand out to him.

"Pleasure to meet you," Erik said, taking her hand.

"And you!"

A silence descended as Kelsey got back to sketching the man. Erik's eyes flickered from her emerging sketch and her oblivious subject.

"Wanna see?" She said eventually.

"That obvious?" Erik chuckled.

"At least you're staring at my hands. Most guys stare at my boobs."

Erik's cheeks burned bright red. "I am so sorry!"

"As long as you don't suddenly become most guys, I think we're ok. Come here." She motioned for Erik to take the seat next to her and he complied, bringing his half empty coffee with him.

She turned the sketch towards Erik, and he looked down at it. "Wow!" The sketch was messy, but Erik knew most sketches were in the beginning. Erik was amazed by how much of the man's soul she'd captured. Erik had always respected art, he just had no talent in it, but he knew enough to realize that Kelsey was talented.

"Thanks?"

"Seriously. Wow! The way you captured the sadness in his face, his hands around the cup... Wow."

Kelsey lit up next to him, clearly surprised by the precision of his accolades. "You a fellow artist?"

"What makes you say that?"

"Certainly, not the suit!" she quipped merrily. "Maybe just wishful thinking."

"What am I then? Guess." Erik was suddenly very interested in what this beautiful woman thought of him.

"Guess?" Erik nodded expectantly. "Ok. Suit says banker, but you don't look like someone with a desk job."

"That a compliment?"

Kelsey burst into laughter before continuing. "Yeah, that's a compliment. Anywho, as much as I want you to be an artist, I doubt it. Young professional, career unknown."

"What if I said I was a musician?"

Kelsey just raised an eyebrow and shook her head. "Jazz?"

It was Erik's turn to laugh. "How'd you know?" he said, sarcasm rich in his voice. "No, I'm a student, just like you."

"So, I'm a student then?" Kelsey's voice was deadly serious, and Erik's heart caught in his throat. Kelsey must have noticed because she broke into a smile and put a comforting hand on Erik's arm. "Kidding! Of course, I'm a student. Have you seen my backpack!?"

A wave of relief washed over Erik, only to be ruined by the sudden ringing of the alarm on his phone. His eyes shot to his watch and he realized he had to get to his appointment.

"Wow, sure you're not a banker cuz that is some kind of watch!"

Erik quickly hid the watch in the cuff of his sleeve and fixed Kelsey with a smile. "Not a banker, the watch was a gift from my grandfather for..." a lump caught in his throat and he couldn't finish the thought. "I have to go," was all he was able to get out.

Erik was halfway out of his seat when Kelsey stopped him. "Hey, you want my number or something?"

Erik was taken aback, thoughts of Victor disappearing as if they were mist on a sunny day. "Sure," he said stupidly.

"Well, don't let me force you into it..."

"Sorry, just a lot happening at once. Let me try again. That'd be fantastic!" Erik put every ounce of enthusiasm he had into it and was rewarded with a smile.

"Ok," Kelsey jotted her number at the bottom of the sketch of the sad suit and pushed it towards Erik. "Use it wisely."

"I will, and thanks. I needed this."

"A girl's phone number?" Kelsey said.

"No, a real conversation. It's just… It's been a while since I had a real conversation… And ignore me, please, before I make this weird."

"Yeah, I'm gonna need my number back here soon," Kelsey laughed.

"Well, this is awkward…"

Kelsey's laughter intensified and Erik felt himself let go, and for the first time in weeks, his laughter was genuine.

Chapter 27

ERIK WATCHED THE clock on his dash click over to 4:30 p.m. and sighed. He looked out his front window at the small, beat-up building that housed Jeffrey Grant's office. The sidewalk was coated in a dusting of garbage and dirt, the building itself stained and crumbling. Erik checked the address he'd written down for a fourth time and shrugged. He wasn't sure what he'd been expecting.

He made his way through a pair of heavy glass doors and entered a sterile white hallway. To his right was a directory with faded white letter tiles forming different business names. Erik scanned through them and found Dr. Grant's. The letters looked new in comparison to the yellowing tiles around it, but Erik didn't pay it much mind.

He made his way to the back of the hallway and found a sign for Dr. Grant. He pushed open a cheap wooden door and stepped into a small waiting room. A middle-aged woman sat at a desk near the only other door in the room. She looked up and gave Erik a big, matronly smile.

"Erik Brown?"

"Yeah, sorry I'm—"

"Not a problem!" she said, interrupting him. "Dr. Grant is ready for you."

She motioned towards the door behind her with long, pink, fake nails. Erik paused; confusion etched on his face. The woman's smile faltered.

"Do I need to fill out any paperwork?" Erik said after a brief, awkward silence.

The woman blushed, a lilting laugh flooding from her open mouth. "Of course! Sorry, I'm new. Still getting into the swing of things. Go ahead and give me a valid ID and your insurance card and I'll get everything together while you're in with Dr. Grant."

Erik fished out his ID and insurance card from his battered leather wallet and handed them to her. She snatched them out of his hands and gave him another big smile.

"Go on in!" She chirped merrily.

Erik nodded his thanks as he walked past her and opened the door. Jeffrey Grant sat behind a cheap wooden desk, busily typing on a laptop. He looked up and smiled. He got to his feet and walked out from behind the desk.

"Erik! So glad you finally called." Jeffrey put out his hand and shook Erik's enthusiastically. "Go ahead and have a seat!"

He motioned for Erik to sit in one of the two leather chairs. Erik complied and the scent of brand-new leather wafted up at him. "You just move in here?"

"You can tell?" Jeffrey looked around at the sparse decorations, the mostly empty bookshelf and laughed. "Pretty obvious, I guess. I wanted to be closer to my at-risk clientele. If I didn't already tell you, I'm a domestic abuse advocate as well. I've found I'm more effective being closer to the... seedier part of the city where a lot of the abuse takes place. There's a shelter nearby. I'm a regular there."

Erik loosened up a bit. "That's tough work."

"It's pretty rewarding though. Sometimes I'm the last line of defense for people. Makes you feel pretty special. Enough about me though, tell me about your grandfather." Jeffrey's question was met with silence as Erik tried to gather his thoughts.

"He was a great man." That's all Erik could come up with. He'd been put on the spot. The question had thrown him off. The whole day had thrown him off. First the dead end with Per Larssen, then the moment of normalcy with Kelsey, now talking to a therapist. Erik began to second guess his decision to come there as the silence lingered, then he remembered the real reason he was there.

"He helped raise me, him and my grandmother. My mom died when I was born and my dad was... weak, emotionally."

"That must make his passing even harder."

"Yeah. He was my mentor, maybe even my best friend. I don't think I'd be where I am today without him. I mean, my sister helped a lot before she went to college, but—"

"Tell me more about your grandfather... would you say you knew him best of your family?" Jeffrey interrupted, steering the conversation.

Erik paused, the echoes of a different voice saying the same thing tugging at his mind. "Sure, I mean, he was long retired by the time he took me in, so we spent a lot of time together. He taught me to shoot, taught me to drive. Tutored me in math—"

"Tell me about the man, not what he did for you," Jeffrey interrupted again.

Erik was very put off by the interruptions, but ignored the uneasy feeling building in the back of his mind. "Sure... like what?"

"Who was he? What did he do? Give me his history!" Jeffrey said.

"Ok. Well, he was born in Norway and lived through World War Two. I'm not really sure what happened after the war, but he met my grandmother at some point, and they got married, immigrated to the US and had my dad. Bestefar worked as—"

"Bestefar?" Erik cringed at the interruption; it was really starting to bother him.

"Norwegian for grandfather."

"Oh, sorry. Carry on."

Erik was forced to gather his thoughts again. "Is this part of the therapy?"

"What?"

Erik saw his opportunity to flip the script and pounced. "You knew him, didn't you? I mean, I bet you know more about him than I do. He was a quiet man and he never talked about his past."

"I'm not sure I follow," Jeffrey said defensively.

"He was your patient, wasn't he?"

Jeffrey's face brightened in realization. "Oh! Right. Sorry. I'd forgotten I let that slip at the funeral. Unprofessional of me to say, I know, but I hadn't seen him in some time before his death," Jeffrey laughed awkwardly.

"Well, it couldn't have been that long, Bestemor died two years ago."

"Wow, two years? That's it? Feels like an eternity." Jeffrey laughed merrily, shaking his head in reflection. "Well, Erik, we didn't talk much about your grandfather. His sessions were spent talking about your grandmother. I find forcing the patient to talk about their loved one is a good first step towards healing."

"Oh. Makes sense, I guess. But, still, I bet you know more about his past than I do?" Erik let the question linger, hoping Jeffrey would take the bait.

"It's possible, but I want to hear it from your perspective. It helps to get our thoughts in order, to remember who our loved one was to us."

"Ok… Well, Bestefar questioned everything. That was one of the early lessons he taught me. Never trust anyone you don't know and, even those you do, with a grain of salt. But don't get me wrong, he had a lot of friends. You were at his funeral."

"Why do you think he believed that?"

"I think a lot of it had to do with World War Two. Nazi occupation, all that crap."

"And did he ever tell you how Marga and he met?"

"Just that it was after the war. I think they met after my bestemor fled Poland. They never talked about the 'old days' as they called them. A lot of pain and misery, they said."

"Bestemor?"

"Norwegian for grandmother…"

"But she was Polish?"

"Yeah, but I thought we were focusing on Victor?"

"Just getting the lay of the land. These cultural things, they really interest me. Apologies." Jeffrey shrugged and gave Erik a plastic smile. "Did Victor ever work in Poland?"

"It's possible…" Erik said, leaving an opening for Jeffrey to finish his thought.

"I feel like he said that was where he met Marga."

"Like I said, they didn't talk much about their lives before America. Just a bunch of sad memories or something." Erik stopped and the voice tugging at his mind finally found a face. "Gerry," Erik said out loud.

"Sorry, what was that?"

"Sorry. Your questions… they reminded me of this old dude at Victor's funeral. His name was Gerry. Guy gave me the creeps."

"And why was that?"

"The way he talked about my grandparents… His words should've felt warm but the way he said them… it was like there was this undercurrent of anger. I don't know. It's hard to pinpoint. The dude was just creepy. Said he met Victor in Poland. And then I kept seeing this black sedan in my rear-view mirror, like I was being followed or something. I don't know, guess Bestefar being murdered has made me paranoid."

Jeffrey just nodded along in understanding. "Everyone takes death differently. Victor was taken from you so suddenly so there's no surprise from a psychiatric standpoint that paranoia might be a stage of grief you'd experience. The thing to remember is that a black sedan is a common car on the road, and that meeting strangers is always a coin flip of first impressions. It's entirely possible that this Gerry fellow is just a harmless well-wisher."

"Yeah, you didn't meet him. Just thinking about him gives me the heebie-jeebies."

"But you can't pinpoint why?"

Erik had to think about it for a second, really trying to understand the feeling the man gave him. "No... just, I'm pretty good at reading people, and he came off as... evil. Does that make sense?"

"Doesn't have to make sense to me, as long as it makes sense to you. Again, grief is a terrible thing. It can make an otherwise normal person do crazy things. Let me ask, how have you been feeling since the incident?"

"Sad. Angry. Confused."

"All normal responses to a sudden loss. Let's explore those emotions and how they relate to Victor."

Erik found himself being drawn into the conversation, answering honestly, putting himself out there. It was the opposite of what he'd expected. In the end, Erik couldn't help but feel like Jeffrey had more to offer on Victor. Erik had managed to confirm Victor had spent some time in Poland but that was it. So, he put another appointment on the calendar, vowing to be better prepared.

Chapter 28

ERIK WENT STRAIGHT to the gym afterwards, did his workout, showered and headed over to Samantha's apartment. He spent the drive in his own head, running over his therapy session, analyzing it. The way Jeffrey asked questions, it felt like an interrogation. The way he tried to steer the conversation. The more he thought about it, the more it rubbed Erik the wrong way. He'd be ready for it next time.

He found parking about a block away from Samantha's and got out. He walked down the sidewalk, still lost in thought, when a white van squealed to a stop next to him. Erik looked over in surprise and saw two masked men leap out the sliding side door. They charged Erik and he had about enough time to fall back into a defensive stance. The first man reached for him, attempting to grab him by the arm while the second one did the same. Erik slipped the first man's grasp while the other one got a hold on his arm. Erik acted fast, surging forward with a right straight, catching the man holding his arm square in the jaw. The man slumped and hit the concrete with a thud. The other man abandoned his attempts to grab Erik and threw his own punch.

Erik slipped under it and came back with a left uppercut. The man's teeth clicked together loudly but he stayed on his feet, dancing back from Erik to reassess him. The other man stirred on the ground next to Erik prompting him to send out a quick kick that caught the man on the side of the head. The standing man growled angrily and flew forward with a series of swings. Erik danced back away from them, blocking the ones he couldn't altogether avoid. He tried to throw his own counters, but his opponent was quick and flowed with the experience of numerous fights. Erik had never been in a real fight, but he'd trained for years at the behest of Victor.

Erik was so focused on the man in front of him that when he noticed another masked assailant to his left, it was too late. Erik heard a bang and dropped to the ground with 50,000 volts rushing through his body.

"Get him in the fucking van!" A woman's voice commanded. Erik felt the big man he'd been facing pick him up and toss him into the van.

Erik landed with a thud and then a black hood was put over his head while his hands were tied behind his back.

Chapter 29

LOREN HAD ABOUT enough time to pull his gilded pistol from the folds of his jacket before Erik disappeared into the depths of the van.

"Was that us?" Feliks asked, worry stamped all over his face.

"No. That was someone else. Follow them," Loren said as if this were an expected turn of events. "Follow the fucking van!"

That was the last thing Feliks wanted to do, but after a moment's hesitation he popped the black SUV into drive and started to tail the van. Loren pulled out his phone and dialed. "Tell Gerwazy our kid just got caught in a snatch and grab." Loren let the other person respond. "I was hoping you would know. Well, we are tailing them now... Yes, yes, just watch."

Loren hung up the phone and turned to Feliks. "We have a new player in the game."

"Who?" Feliks was on the verge of panic, barely keeping it together.

"You think I know? Głupek!" Feliks cringed away from Loren's anger and tried to focus on keeping the van in his eyesight.

Chapter 30

"JESUS CHRIST! WHAT the hell happened back there?" Came the woman's voice as the van sped down the street. "It was supposed to be an easy bag and grab!"

"He got in a lucky punch," a man mumbled. He'd be the one Erik dropped, he thought. The voice had the sound of a bruised jaw and a fat lip.

"Dropped you like a bitch!" Laughed another male voice. That'd be the one that distracted Erik while the woman snuck up on him with the taser. Erik silently cursed himself for being too focused on the man in front of him. Always be aware of your surroundings, no matter the circumstances.

"Lucky punch!" The injured man retorted hotly. "And, if you'd secured his other arm, it wouldn't have happened."

The other man let out a deep laugh and Erik could hear him slap the other man on the shoulder.

"You're both lucky nobody saw us. That was sloppy."

Erik stayed quiet on the hard metal floor of the van and continued to listen to his abductors. The man he'd dropped groaned and his jaw clicked as he tried to work it out. Erik smiled from within the darkness of the bag covering his head, a small victory in an otherwise terrifying situation. He had to keep calm. He had to keep his head on straight.

He worked his wrists against their zip tie restraints and found little wiggle room. His feet found a similar situation. He turned his attention from escape to scouting. He knew there were three. One large man, another his size and a woman. The woman seemed to be in charge and was likely the driver as well. He strained his ears, listening to the breathing of his captors. He could only distinguish three separate breathing patterns. His mind flashing back in time, trying to remember Victor's lessons.

"When you have no eyes, trust the other senses. Let them take over," Victor said, helping Erik out of the Chevelle. Erik was blindfolded and had been for the last twenty minutes. "What do you hear?"

Erik held his breath, straining his ears. "Birds."

"That's it?" Victor's voice rang with disappointment causing Erik to double his efforts.

"The interstate. Running water."

"What does that tell you?"

"The city's close."

"Good. What else can you tell me?"

"We took the interstate here, due west."

"What told you that?"

Erik thought about it for a moment. "The sun was on my face for the majority of the drive."

"Very good!"

"We're at… The wildlife reserve," Erik said as the distant quack of ducks sounded.

Erik jumped as Victor smacked him on the back. "Very good, Erik! Very good!"

The van lurched from side to side as it turned, Erik had lost track of how many times they'd gone left or right but knew the exact moment they turned onto a gravel road. The van's floor vibrated against his cheek, the crunch of rocks filling his ears. They must be close to their destination. Erik wasn't surprised when they lurched to a stop and the squeal of the door sliding open filled the van.

"Any complications?" It was the voice from the phone, Erik was sure of it.

"Dropped Donny but that's about it," the female voice responded.

"Mac missed his arm," Donny protested.

"Shut up!" The voice from the phone interrupted. "Did anyone see you?" The captors must have shaken their heads no because the voice continued shortly after. "Good. Get him inside and strapped up."

Erik was lifted bodily from the vans floor; he was sure it was the big man. Erik made his body limp, and the big man struggled to carry him. "Knock it off, muthafucka! Make this easy or I *will* knock you out."

"What's the problem?" Came the woman's voice.

"He's acting like a dead fish!" The big man's voice was angry, and Erik wondered if he really was going to hit him. Might as well get in the first strike.

Erik went rigid in the man's grasp and drove his feet into the vans floor, using it to spring backwards. As he straightened his body, he swung his head backwards and connected with the big man's nose. Erik heard a satisfying crunch and felt the spray of warm blood on his neck.

The big man grunted loudly and stumbled backwards, tripping and falling. Erik could hear the man's skull bounce against the rocks and quickly rolled off of him straight into a kick to the stomach. The air whooshed out of Erik's lungs and he crumpled to the gravel, stunned.

"Was it worth it?" The female voice sounded as another kick connected with Erik's ribs. He grunted and tried to curl into a protective ball but was seized by each arm and hauled upright. "Take a shot, Mac. Freebie."

"Little bastard broke my nose."

Erik readied himself for the strike. He could only guess where it'd land, but it never came.

"Stop fucking around and get him inside!" Shrieked the voice from the phone.

"He broke my nose!" Mac tried to explain but the man from the phone interrupted him in his shrill, angry voice.

"Then you let him! You're twice his god damn size, and if that isn't enough, he's bound and blinded."

Erik could hear the crunch of his retreating steps. "Sorry, Mac," the woman said.

Erik was dragged across the gravel road, his feet digging two trenches in the stones in his wake. They arrived at a building, Erik guessed a warehouse based on the acoustics of their steps as they dragged him to a chair and threw him into it. They quickly zip tied his wrists to the arms of the chair and his ankles to the legs.

One of them ripped off the black bag and revealed a pitch-black room. Erik's eyes strained against the darkness, exactly as they'd wanted as they flipped on a white-hot spotlight. Erik squinted away from it and he heard Mac laugh in response. Erik slowly opened his eyes against the light and tried to see around it. A few human shapes were just visible but as far as their features, Erik couldn't tell anything about them.

"What's your name?" It was the voice from the phone. Erik hesitated. Did he tell them the truth? Was this a huge misunderstanding? Were these Victor's murderers? But then, why would Victor have left Erik their name and number?

"Dane Sversen." Erik wasn't sure why he'd lied. Maybe it was Victor's voice in the back of his head telling him to never give up anything without first getting something. "This is some huge mistake... I... what is happening?"

"Dane Sversen, huh? I don't believe you. You said your name was Erik Brown last time we spoke." That confirmed it. It *was* the man from the phone call. "Were you lying then? Or are you lying now?"

"Per Larssen?" The man laughed and moved around behind the light.

"How do you know that name?" He asked.

Erik fought with the story he wanted to tell, slipping into the game he'd always played with Victor. He couldn't see his captors so he couldn't build a profile, but nothing was stopping him from building his own.

"A friend."

The man laughed. "A friend? A friend gave you that name and that number? Do you think I'm stupid?"

"No, I don't know anything about you, Per. A friend gave me a slip of paper with your name and your number. I thought it was in connection with a murder."

"Someone gave you my name and my number in connection with a murder... Stop fucking with me, Erik. I'm starting to get upset." His words were cold, he annunciated each syllable and slowly rose from his seat to loom over the table, just the dark shadow of a medium sized man. Suddenly, a gun dropped onto the table in front of Erik. "Time for some honesty, Erik."

"I swear! I got a number and a name. I called it. That's it!"

"Who gave you that number?"

"Victor Brown! My grandfather! He was murdered." The truth flew out of Erik in a panic and shame filled him. They probably already knew everything. They'd probably killed Victor. What had Erik gotten himself into? What had *Victor* gotten him into?

"Victor Brown. Am I supposed to know that name?" Erik could distinguish the man's naked honesty in the question.

"I don't know. He... he left me your name and number in a safety deposit box, I swear!"

"Victor Brown?"

"Yes! I don't know why he left me it. I'm just a—"

"Med student. I know." It was like a slap in the face how casually the man threw that out. "We know everything about you, Erik. Except how you got that name and that number."

"I found it. I swear!"

"I believe you, Erik. What I don't understand is how your grandfather got it or why he gave it to you." The man sat back down and removed the gun from the table. "Ok, get him out of here."

"What?" Was all Erik had the time to say before a needle was jabbed into his neck. Erik tried to fight it but whatever was in it was in his blood stream before he could react. His chin sagged into his chest and fight as he may, he couldn't keep his eyes open.

Chapter 31

ERIK AWOKE IN his car, alone, his head ringing, his ribs sore to the touch. He looked around with scratchy eyes, bloodshot and puffy. His memory of the night was a void, a dark chasm swallowing his thoughts as he tried to probe its depths. He tried to rub the moisture back into his eyes and blinked against the meager light coming from the streetlamp above him. He looked to his watch, a sleek black faced piece with an eighteen-karat gold case and a black leather band. A vintage Zenith. It was a graduation gift from Victor and Marga before she passed. Victor had worn it since the late 1950s. Erik had never seen him without the watch, so he was moved beyond words when Victor parted with it after nearly sixty years of continuous use. It was most likely a collector's item at that point, but Erik was never tempted to see what it was worth. The thought never even crossed his mind until Lars started to speculate about it.

2:00 a.m.

He struggled to get a hand into his tight pocket, awkward in the confined space of the car. His hurt ribs protested as he finally retrieved his phone.

Five missed texts and two calls complete with voicemails.

Erik felt terrible, his skin crawled, his mouth was dry. He felt like he'd been jumped, but he'd already subconsciously established all of his possessions were still with him, his fancy watch among them. How was it even possible to be in that much pain and not recall how it happened?

He scrolled through his missed texts. They were from Samantha and they went from sober to drunk. They asked him if he was still coming and ended with telling him he was a jerk for standing her up. Erik looked at them in disbelief. He looked out his car at the cross streets and was even more confused. He was at Samantha's apartment. He listened to the voicemails and they were both from Samantha. She slurred her words as she told him how much of a dick he was. He thought about texting her back but didn't know what to say.

He did the only thing he could think of and drove home, to Victor's house. He parked on the street by the front gate, still swinging idly on its one hinge. Getting out of the car took some effort as his ribs screamed in protest. He walked down the front walk prodding them with his fingers, discovering a large area of tenderness. His neck was painfully stiff too, and further investigation found a painful lump.

He stepped onto the porch and stopped. The muffled thud of feet on the hardwood floor just barely reaching his ear. Was someone in his house? Slowly, he stepped down from the front step and crept along the side of the house. A flashlight crossed the window and Erik stopped, pressing himself against the side of the house.

Erik's heart raced. Someone *was* in his house. He pulled out his phone and dialed 911. He stayed where he was, too afraid to move.

"911, state your emergency."

"Someone's in my house," Erik whispered.

"I'm sorry? Can you please speak up?"

Erik didn't dare. "My house is being robbed." Erik quickly rattled off his address.

"OK, we have a unit in the area. Get somewhere safe and don't intervene. Please stay on the line with me."

"OK." Erik lowered himself into a crouch, leaning against the house, too afraid to move.

The flashlight beam reappeared across the window and Erik pressed himself flat against the side of the house.

"Hey! We have to go," came a loud whisper from the other side of the window.

"What?" Another responded.

"We have been made; someone called the cops."

"Shit."

Erik listened with wide eyes. How did they know? He heard the back door open and heard the robbers coming. He prayed they didn't come his way. He scrambled to get behind the AC unit as footsteps sounded along the dirt path behind him.

"Sir, is everything alright?" Erik didn't respond, instead he set the phone down and waited.

The footsteps grew louder and then a man dressed in all black rushed by. Erik's heart stopped, but the man kept going, oblivious. Erik almost breathed a sigh of relief but before he could another man dressed in black surged by.

The man yelped in surprise, stopping in his tracks. Erik reacted with all of the defense training he'd been taught. He leapt up from his squat and drove his whole weight into the robber. They crashed into the hedge running the length of the walkway.

"Help! Help!" the man yelled, trying to tie up Erik's hands and keep him from striking.

Erik finally got a hand free and smashed a fist into the robber's face. The man yowled in pain as they tussled in the bush. The crunch of approaching feet told Erik the accomplice was back, and he pushed himself off the other man falling into a defensive stance just as the accomplice rounded the corner.

The flash of metal told Erik that he had a gun, and he wasted no time in leaping back behind the AC unit. A shot rang out, the whistle of the bullet going right past Erik as he crashed to the ground.

"Move!" bellowed the man with the gun.

The sound of the two men fleeing caused a wave of relief to sweep through Erik. The sudden sound of police sirens filled the quiet neighborhood. Erik remained as still as possible. The roar of a car sounded, and the squeal of tires announced its departure. Moments later, bright red and blue lights reflected off the windows of the neighbor's house.

Erik slowly got to his feet, pain shot through his hand, drawing his attention to his split knuckles. He stumbled around to the other side of the AC unit and recovered his phone.

"Sir? Can you hear me? Sir? Are you OK?" The dispatcher's voice was cool and controlled but the ring of worry was clear.

"Hello?" Erik finally managed, his voice wavering like the lines on a heart monitor.

"Sir? Are you OK? We heard shots?"

"Yes, I'm fine... The robbers... they found me. I fought one and the other one shot... shot at me. Jesus Christ." Erik's legs went rubbery and he almost fell. He took a deep breath and willed his heart to normalcy. He leaned against the house for support as two police officers rushed onto the property. "I'm over here!" Erik yelled. "The robbers are gone!"

The officers rushed around the side of the house; guns drawn. Erik threw his hands into the air reflexively.

"Which way did they go?" Demanded one of the officers.

"Out the front. I heard a car leave, I'm not sure which direction."

"Did you see the car?"

Erik shook his head no and the officers holstered their guns. "Why don't you come out to our cruiser, sir." Erik nodded his agreement and accepted the steadying arm of one of the officers. They lead him down the walk and out to the street where their cruiser flashed its red and blue lights.

Chapter 32

IT TOOK MORE than an hour for Erik to give his statement, making sure to leave out the part when someone tipped the robbers off. He was still having a hard time believing that's what had happened. He walked around the house, from room to room and couldn't find anything out of place. Had the dispatcher not heard the confrontation and the gun shot, Erik would've sworn it was a dream. The police were equally confused. No sign of forced entry, nothing missing.

Detective Kincaid showed up at some point and sought Erik out, sitting him down at Victor's kitchen table while the other officers cleared out.

"Forensics pulled a slug out of your back fence, but I doubt it'll lead to much. These guys were pros, and they were looking for something specific. Any idea what it was?"

The question caught Erik off guard. Did Kincaid really think he was involved somehow? Holding something back? But then, he kind of was.

"I woke up in my car earlier this morning, around 2:00 a.m."

Kincaid raised a confused eyebrow.

"I don't know how… I was going to go out with some classmates and then I woke up in my car… with bruised ribs and a lump in my neck." Erik turned his neck towards Kincaid and found the lump with a finger. "Can you see anything?"

Kincaid pulled out her flashlight and spotlighted the area Erik was pointing to. She leaned forward and squinted. "Yeah, looks like a needle puncture mark and some blood on your collar."

Erik went white as a sheet and leaned back in his seat. "I think I was drugged and left in my car."

Kincaid clicked off the flashlight and stared at Erik, the wheels turning behind her dark eyes. "Let me get the facts straight. You were drugged and left in your car and subsequently robbed?"

"You think they're related?" Erik said with heavy sarcasm.

"I doubt it's a coincidence." Kincaid sighed. "Listen, Erik, I think it'd be a good idea if you didn't stay here for a few days. I'll be sure to put a car on the street outside, but I'm worried whoever's involved here might escalate things, and if you're not completely bullshitting me, drugging you to rob a house is already a pretty escalated point to jump off from. Now, is there anything you want to tell me about your grandfather? Anything you might have discovered since last we spoke?"

Erik thought on it for a few moments before turning back to Kincaid. "Only that I don't think I knew him very well... at all."

"Have you noticed a black sedan hanging out around the property?" That perked Erik's ears up.

"What do you mean?"

"One of your neighbors told us there's been a black sedan lurking around the property of late. Two guys hanging out in it at all hours of the night. She thinks they were staking the place out."

Erik's mind flowed backwards over the last few weeks and pinpointed each time he'd noticed a black sedan. Each time he'd tried to rationalize it as a coincidence. How many black sedans were in this city? He started to hyper ventilate as a panic attack approached.

"Whoa, kid! Calm down, breathe. Breathe." Erik fought the fear that threatened, beating it back with deep breaths.

"I've been seeing one in my rearview for a little while now. But it can't be the same one, right? Cuz that's crazy, right?"

"This whole mess is crazy, kid. Be on the lookout, if you notice someone following you, call me. Write down the plate, memorize it, do whatever you can. and you get it to me, OK?"

"OK."

"You have some place to go, other than here? Your dad, sister?"

"Yeah."

"Go there. I'm not trying to scare you, but this whole thing screams organized crime. If it were the one event? I'd say it was random, but the murder, the drugging, the robbery, too much is stacking up. Whoever is behind this, they have their shit together, they're after something very specific, and they want it bad enough to kill for it. That tells me they're powerful, that they have plenty of resources. This isn't the work of a couple of goons. I just can't figure out an angle on how your grandfather was involved. None of it makes sense..." Kincaid trailed off, clearly thinking out loud before she returned her focus to Erik. "Listen, Erik. There are a couple of crime families that operate in this area, and neither of them are good. Silver lining is if they wanted you dead, we wouldn't be talking. If anything feels off, call me. If someone approaches you, call me."

"Wait," Erik said before Kincaid could stand up. "They knew I called the cops."

"What?" Kincaid responded; shock heavy in her voice.

"Must've been a minute after the operator told me units were on their way. One of the guys was by the window I was hiding under... I heard the other guy tell him they had to leave, that the cops had been called."

"Did you tell anyone else that?" Kincaid said with a sudden seriousness that deepened the pit already in Erik's stomach.

"No, of course not. I'm only telling you because I think I can trust you... Right?"

Kincaid shook her head, her face edged with worry. "Yeah, of course you can," she said, getting up from the table and throwing her jacket on. "But no one else."

"Sure," was Erik's weak response.

Chapter 33

ERIK WAS STILL shaking by the time he got to his small, one-bedroom apartment. A moldy odor assaulted his nose as soon as he pushed open the thin, plywood door. It reeked. Erik dropped his bag by the door and rushed into the small living room/kitchen, on a mission to discover the foul smell. He discovered dirty dishes in the sink and quickly cleaned them, then took out the trash. He returned and sprayed Febreze all over the room, wiped down the counter, did anything but think about his night, the last week.

From there, he went to his room and gathered his laundry, stripped his bed and made his way to the building's basement where he started a load. He returned to the apartment and threw on a pot of coffee, started cooking breakfast, the sun just then peeking over the eastern horizon. He yawned against the sleep that longed to engulf him. He burned his tongue on hot coffee and tended to his laundry, switching it over. Anything to keep his mind from wandering, to keep it from Samantha and pick at her involvement in the night before.

Erik's thoughts kept coming back to her, wondering if she set him up, wondering if her texts, her voicemails were genuine. Anyone could pretend to be upset, even he could pretend to be drunk, Erik figured, even though he'd never personally experienced it.

He fought the urge to call her, to confront her. Instead, he turned his thoughts to his apartment. He tried to remember the last time he'd been in it. It'd been a while. The more he thought about it, the more he realized how much his schedule had been messed up. He should've been studying or at the gym. He should've been well rested and ready for a day of lectures. He sat back on his couch and closed his eyes. How far behind was he?

No matter how hard he tried to focus, his mind found its way back to his night. A shiver ran through him and he fought the urge to yell out. *Separate your fear from your reason*, Victor's voice told him. *Fear is the killer of thought*.

Erik took deep, restorative breathes, centered himself and looked beyond his emotions. What were they looking for? And suddenly, Erik remembered Per Larssen and the phone call flooded back to him.

Was this the doing of Per Larssen? Did he drug Erik, rob Victor's house? The picture he'd found under Victor's bed sprang to mind. Who was Per Larssen?

Things had been off ever since he'd discovered that name, the phone number. First Arnie at the bank. Erik could clearly recognize something was wrong with the man, his interest in what Erik found in the safety deposit box. The way his face had fallen, fear edging the corner of his eyes when Erik brushed him off, and then, back to Samantha… Her sudden interest in him after a year of shared classes. Could she have lured him to her apartment? But why drug him when she could've just kept him distracted at a bar while her pals searched his house for whatever it was they were looking for? And what *were* they looking for? The biggest question of them all.

Erik should've gone to bed, he should've just let it lie and let his mind wind down, but he didn't. Instead, he took to the internet. Unsurprisingly, he didn't find much. He tried to look up Larssen's phone number, but it wasn't listed. He searched for Per Larssen on social media, but again, nothing. Finally, Erik decided to call the number again, one last time before he turned it over to Kincaid, hoping she'd know what to do with it.

He dialed the number and just stared at it on the screen of his phone. Was this a stupid plan? What was he going to say? He tried to get it together before he hit send. What did he know about Larssen and his people? They were organized, ruthless and had deep resources. Worst case scenarios ran through his head and continually landed on murder. But if they wanted him dead, they wouldn't have just drugged him. If they wanted him dead, he would be, like Victor.

Erik took a deep breath and hit send. No turning back. Separate fear from reason. No fear. No fear. No fear.

"What do you think you're doing?" The voice was immediately familiar, and Erik knew he was talking to Per Larssen.

"Did you drug me?" Laughter sounded from the other end and Erik's heart raced. "And rob my house?"

The laughter stopped. "Why would I rob your house?"

"But you're not denying you drugged me?"

"Erik Brown. Med student. Son of Michael and Fiona Brown, the latter deceased. Two siblings: Lars and Selene. Grandson of Victor and Marga Brown, both deceased."

"Did you murder Victor?"

Silence. Erik thought maybe Per had hung up.

"No." The silence resumed.

"I'm not afraid of you," Erik bluffed. "You know everything about me. Congratulations, you know how to use the internet."

"You should be." The words sent shivers down Erik's spine. "You should be very afraid of me."

Erik paused, making sure he kept his voice firm. "Do you know who murdered Victor?"

"Drop it. Move on with your life."

"He's my grandfather…"

"Do you even know who he was? Truly?"

"I don't care. He was my grandfather. I owe him everything, so either you can help me, or you can talk to the police."

"Don't threaten me, you little shit. You keep going in this direction and I *can't* help you."

"What, by drugging me and robbing me?"

"Let it go. You have bigger things to worry about, like checking on your laundry." And with that, the line went dead.

Chapter 34

"HE BEAT YOU because you were scared. You froze and he used the opportunity," Victor told him when he'd come home from school with a fat lip. "He pushed you and you shut down. You let the fear win."

Erik had been ten at the time. Victor never saw a kid though. He saw the clay that would one day be the man. He'd enrolled Erik in kickboxing within the week and Erik was never on the losing side of a fight again, until now.

Erik forced himself out of the memory, sifting his way through the fear, finding its edge and pulling it back from blanketing his mind. He forced himself to slowly get up from the couch. Forced the tremors that threatened from his limbs. Was his apartment bugged? How would he even check?

Erik forced himself to be calm, then proceeded to tear apart his apartment, dismantling lamps, unscrewing the back of his TV. Checking anywhere he could think that might hide something. The morning sun beamed into the room by the time he was done. He'd been awake for twenty-four hours, he finally realized. He looked around the destroyed room, his body trembling.

"Get it together," he said to himself.

He quickly composed an email to his teachers telling them about the robbery and saying he wasn't going to make it to lecture. Next, he picked apart his decision to call Larssen again. That was stupid, foolish. What had he gained from it? He knew Larssen had been in his apartment. He knew Larssen knew everything about him, was actively monitoring him. Erik had learned nothing that would help him, except, the robbery might not have been Larssen, but who then? The mob? Erik rubbed the lump on the side of his neck absent mindedly. Larssen hadn't denied drugging him, but if not to keep him out of the house, then why? Maybe he was asking the wrong questions.

Erik found himself calling Samantha, unsure of what he was going to say but knowing he needed to say something.

"What," she answered, her dislike obvious.

"Samantha, about last night—"

"Yeah, thanks, Erik. Read you loud and clear."

"Do you know Per Larssen?"

"What? What kind of question is that?"

"Do you know Per Larssen, yes or no."

"You know what Erik, screw you."

"Are you part of this? Did you drug me? Did you lure me to your apartment to drug me and rob my grandfather's house?" It all just poured out of him, his voice hysterical even in his own ear.

"Jesus Christ, Erik. You need fucking help!" And then she was gone, and nothing was any clearer.

Erik thought about it as he stuffed his backpack with fresh clothes and his most important possessions. She hadn't denied anything, just deflected his questions. Had someone recruited her to spy on him? Was it really at all plausible? He was no closer to an answer by the time he hit the road in search of somewhere Larssen didn't know about.

He hopped onto the highway and let his mind wander back to his conversation with Kincaid the other night. The question of the black sedan loomed over him. Had he noticed a black sedan following him, or were there just simply more black sedans on the road lately? He checked his rear-view mirror and saw no black sedans.

He looked at his left side mirror and then his right. Again, no black sedans.

"Paranoid," he muttered to himself as he pulled off the interstate. A black SUV followed from a few cars back. Erik paid it no extra attention as he made a right into street traffic.

He kept driving for a bit before he spotted the black SUV a few cars behind him. This time, his interest was piqued. Was it the same one as the interstate? Erik's mind was drawn back to his driving lessons with Victor, squealing around corners, pretending to shake a tail. How much did he truly remember?

Erik took a quick look in his rear view, absorbing the details of the SUV; the look of the grill, the curve of its head lights. Anything he could see, he tried to commit to memory. When the light turned green, he jumped off the line, accelerating rapidly to try and see if they followed. To his absolute surprise, the black SUV jumped into the other lane and did its best to pass the two cars between them and catch up.

"Holy shit," Erik breathed to himself in disbelief.

He quickly changed lanes and turned at the closest street. He punched the gas and sped down the street, his eyes flicking from the road to his rearview mirror. The black SUV squealed around the corner and Erik fought the feeling of dread taking hold of him

Chapter 35

"NO FEAR, NO fear. Just reason," he whispered to himself as he made another turn and punched it again. He wasn't sure where he was going, but it didn't matter. He just wanted to lose his tail.

He squealed into an alley a short way down the block and accelerated. He sped recklessly down it and came out back on the main road, leaving a little tire rubber on the curb. Without realizing it, he'd put himself on track for the police station, for Det. Kincaid. He found himself watching his rearview mirror as much as the road but the black SUV didn't reappear.

He was so focused on watching for it he missed the light turning red and nearly rear ended the car in front of him. At the last second, he slammed on the brakes and screeched to a halt. His heart was racing, sweat was dripping from his brow. He must have looked a mess to the driver of the car in front of him as they locked eyes via the rearview mirror.

"Sorry!" Erik mouthed, giving them a meek smile. The driver just shook their head and turned their attention back to the light.

Erik looked away just in time to see the black SUV drive through the intersection in front of them. Erik ducked under his steering wheel as if it was him they were looking for instead of his car. The driver of the black SUV sped past without even a glance Erik's way. He looked angry, his mouth curved into a snarl as he smacked the steering wheel and yelled something. Erik could only gawk. He recognized the man but wasn't sure from where. Erik was so focused on the retreating SUV that he failed to notice Feliks straddling a bike on the corner next to him, out of breath and talking emphatically into his phone.

Erik left him behind as traffic started to move, none the wiser as Feliks struggled to keep pace in his wake. Erik breathed a sigh of relief as the police station came into view. He was reasonably convinced he was being followed and equally convinced he'd lost them. He parked his car and jogged towards safety, completely unaware of the black SUV parked just down the road. Completely unaware as Feliks sped past him on his bike and stopped at the driver's side window for a moment before pedaling off into an alley.

Erik was led back into the homicide department where he found Kincaid at her desk, trapped behind a mountain of manilla folders. She looked as tired as Erik felt.

"Erik, I was just about to call you. Forensics managed to match that slug they pulled out of the fence to a couple of unsolved murders in a heavily Eastern European part of town. My guess is it's either the Poles or the Russians. There are a couple different families of note vying for control in that neighborhood."

"Larssen didn't sound Russian or Polish," Erik reflected out loud. Kincaid raised an eyebrow in confusion. "Yeah, I should probably fill you in on a few... developments. Anywhere private we can go?"

Chapter 36

"SPILL IT, KID," Kincaid demanded after leading Erik to a private room, probably meant for lawyers to speak with their clients, Erik guessed.

"Right. So…" Erik struggled for a moment, trying to decide where to start and how much to say. He finally landed on the truth, the whole truth. He tossed the dice and hoped they came up seven.

"My grandfather hid a message for me, in a suit he left me—"

"In a suit?"

"Yes, I know, it sounds crazy but that's what happened." Erik paused. "I found it in the lining of a suit… The message… it was a routing number for a bank. I went there looking for an account for my grandfather but discovered he'd opened one for me—"

"You pulling my chain, kid?" Erik shook his head no and Kincaid leaned forward, eyes locked with Erik's. "Your grandfather left you a routing number in the lining of a suit so he could lure you to a bank where he had secretly opened an account under your name?"

"Yes, but that's not the important part—"

"Not the important part," Kincaid laughed in disbelief.

"No," Erik responded, an edge creeping into his voice. "There was a lock box… Err, safety deposit box. The only thing in it was this scrap of paper with a name and phone number on it." Erik produced the scrap and slapped it down on the table.

Kincaid slowly pulled it towards herself before picking it up. She looked it over for a moment, turning it in her hand before putting it back down. "What am I supposed to do with this?"

"I called that number yesterday, before I was drugged and left in my car. Before my house was robbed. I told them where I'd gotten the number... Who I'd gotten it from... I called it again last night and they didn't deny drugging me. They knew everything about me, they'd been in my apartment!" Erik could hear the desperation in his voice and fought to stifle it.

"Slow down, kid!" Erik went silent, his hands clenched in his lap. "This Larssen, did he threaten you?"

"He drugged me, probably robbed my house! I think he murdered my grandfather; I think it was him and I think he paid off one of my classmates to lure me to her apartment last night. Samantha Kint, we were supposed to grab drinks..."

Kincaid picked up the scrap of paper again and studied it with renewed interest. "Samantha Kint and Per Larssen lured you to her apartment..." Erik could tell Kincaid was having a hard time believing him. "And why didn't you mention this last night?"

"I wasn't myself; I was overwhelmed." And then Erik remembered the tail on the way there. "And, I'm being followed."

"You what?" Kincaid asked in disbelief.

"A black SUV followed me from my place. I lost them, but I know they were following me. Remember when you asked about the sedan? Pretty sure they switched cars."

"Jesus, kid. This is a lot to take in. Are you sure you're not just being paranoid?"

"You're the one that asked me about being followed!" Erik said as he surged forward in his chair and pointed an accusing finger at Kincaid. She threw up her hands in acquiescence. "Someone murdered my grandfather and I think I'm next." Erik's words rang in his own ears, a secret thought finally spoken out loud.

Kincaid, for her part, remained as calm as could be, digesting Erik's words before speaking. "I'll look into this," she said, holding up the scrap of paper. "Per Larssen. I'll look into him and see if he's connected with the Russian mob because I think that's who's behind this, and honestly, I hope it is."

"Why?" Erik asked, fear rising in is throat.

"Because as bad as they are, at least I know something about them."

"What do you mean?" Erik said, the fear starting to seep into his mind. "What if it's the Poles?"

"Do you have any reason to suspect them over the Russians?"

And then Gerry was staring back at Erik, his arrogant smirk, the power resonating from his eyes, through his words. *"Our reunion was short lived…."* Gerry had said. Erik hadn't really thought about the statement in the context of Victor's murder, not until Kincaid sat across from him, worry lining her cheeks, her jaw clenched.

"At Victor's funeral… a man told me he knew my grandparents from Poland. He gave me the creeps. He said his name was Gerry, that his reunion with Victor was short lived."

"Jesus," Kincaid exhaled.

"What?" was Erik's frantic response.

"We've heard chatter about a guy, high up in the Polish mob, they call him G, that's it. He's an enigma. We know he's ruthless but he's more careful than anything. No known pictures, no known names even. If it's the same guy, you might be one of the few people living that can identify him."

"What the hell's that supposed to mean?!"

"Be very careful who you share that information with. Don't mention him on the phone, text, or email. You never know who might be listening."

"Detective, you're scaring me," Erik said, trying to will away her words, her worry.

"Good! You need to be very careful, Erik. These guys don't mess around. If you think you're being followed again, you call 911. You tell them who you are, and you tell them what's going on and you don't stop for nothing until you see someone in blue, OK?"

"What if they're in on it? The police?"

Kincaid's expression froze in thought, a grimace pulling at the corner of her lip. "Gonna have to trust the odds, Erik. I know someone here is dirty, I've suspected it for a long time, the way evidence just turns up missing, or informants disappear… but I can't begin to believe it's that wide…" Kincaid let the unsaid thought die. Erik knew what she was going to say and left it at that, nodding along instead, trying to keep his calm.

"Do you have anywhere to go? A friend? Someone no one would expect?"

Erik thought hard for a moment. "Maybe."

"OK, don't tell me. Don't tell anyone, OK?" Erik nodded yes. "Be careful and don't do anything reckless. I'll look into Ms. Kint and see what I can dig up about Larssen. I'll be in touch."

Erik left the police station shrouded in disbelief. It was all happening. He hadn't imagined it. He was in a fog as he got back into his car, so much so, that he just sat there for a bit, working through his frantic thoughts.

Finally, he picked up his phone and dialed Selene.

"Erik? Hey, what's up?" Selene's voice was so comforting, so unaware. Erik had to find his own voice before he could respond.

"Hey, Selene. Just wanted to give you a heads up, I'm going to be out of town for a bit, didn't want you to get scared or whatever."

"Don't you have school?" Selene's voice was filled with confusion and Erik's heart broke. He wanted nothing more than to tell her what was happening, to cry on her shoulder, for her to tell him he's OK, but he couldn't. She might already be in danger.

"Yeah, school trip. Totally spaced it." The words came effortlessly to him as he slipped into the old game he'd played with Victor back on those sunny days in the park. "Some conference I signed up for back before... Bestefar. I already paid for everything so..."

"Don't wanna waste the money. Ok. Does Dad know?"

"Think you can tell him? Lars too? I have a lot on my plate right now. Sorry!"

"Yeah, sure. No problem. Doubt Lars will care but, anyway, have fun, lil' brother."

"Thanks, Selene. I love you."

"I love you too!" Selene laughed on the other end. "You sure everything is alright?"

"Yeah, it's just... There's so much going on right now. I feel like I'm drowning underneath it all."

"Oh, Erik. I know what you mean. Wanna talk about any of it? Mama Bear's here." Erik could practically hear the smile accompanying those words on the other end of the line.

"Thanks, Selene, but I think I just need to work through it on my own."

"Ok, little brother, but just remember, I'm here for you. No matter what."

"Thanks, Selene. We'll talk later."

"Ok! Have fun! Bye!"

Erik hung up the phone and rubbed his temples with one hand while he figured out his next move. Inspiration struck, and he picked up his phone.

"Dr. Grant's office. Is this a crisis?"

"Hi, yes, actually, I think it is a crisis. This is Erik Brown. Can I talk to Dr. Grant?"

Chapter 37

ERIK WATCHED HIS rearview the entire way to Jeffrey's office, his body rigid in the seat, his hands like vice grips on the steering wheel. He breathed a sigh of relief when he arrived without seeing the black SUV or any other car of note for that matter. He parked down the street from Jeffrey's office, an attempt to hide his presence from prying eyes. He willed his limbs to loosen, pushing the stress and anxiety from his mind just as Victor had taught him. Once centered, he walked the short distance, mindless of the trash crunching under his feet, his eyes roving the streets for any familiar faces.

He entered the office building's stark white lobby and quickly made his way down the sterile white hallway to Jeffrey's small suite. He pushed open the door to find Jeffrey's secretary watering the small ferns that dotted the suite's lobby.

"He's in his office, head on in," she said with a plastic smile.

"Thanks," Erik responded giving her a plastic smile of his own.

Erik pushed open the door to find Jeffrey sitting at his desk, looking out the window towards the parking lot. He spun around and smiled at Erik.

"Erik! What's going on? Is everything OK?"

Erik shook his head and plopped into one of the open leather chairs. Jeffrey got up from his desk and came around to take a seat in the other one, concern dotting his face.

"Truth is," Erik started. "I… No, it's not."

"Ok… Tell me what's going on then. Maybe I can help?"

Erik fought with how much to tell him. How much did he trust the man? The question hung above him, smothering the room. "My grandfather was murdered. I think someone wanted something from him—"

"Do you know what?" Jeffrey interrupted.

Erik shook his head no. "But I think I know who killed him."

The blood left Jeffrey's face. "Did you go to the police?"

"Yes, but all I have is a name and a number that my grandfather left for me." Erik paused and Jeffrey leaned in, his interest obvious.

"What do you mean, left for you?"

"He left me a series of clues… I know, sounds ridiculous. I called the number and as a result… I was being followed, and I'm pretty sure that's been the case since Victor's death."

"You were being followed?"

"I lost them, so there's that, but yeah…"

Jeffrey leaned back in his chair, overwhelmed. "Jesus, Erik."

"That's actually why I'm here. I'm so sorry to involve you, but I need somewhere to lie low while the police investigate this guy. He… my apartment's not safe, obviously. I don't want to involve my family; they're probably being watched too. You're the last person anyone would expect to be helping me, and I know you're an abuse advocate, so if you have, like, a safe house to stick me—"

"Sure," Jeffrey interrupted, placing a comforting hand on Erik's knee. "I have a guest bedroom for exactly this reason, typically different circumstances but you'll be safe there, I promise."

"I… Thank you."

"Not a problem, Erik. Can you tell me who's doing this to you? In fact, tell me everything. Maybe I can help."

"I really don't think that's a good idea, Dr. Grant."

"Erik, I insist and call me Jeffrey, or Jeff, or Jefe. Consider it repayment for staying with me." Jeffrey leaned forward, a glimmer in his eyes. Erik's plight had struck a chord. Erik wondered if he could use it to learn more about Victor.

Erik relayed his story, glossing over most of the details, just giving Jeffrey enough of the truth to whet his appetite. He relayed his conversation with Kincaid, that she thought it was organized crime looking for something specific.

"And Detective Kincaid... she thinks they're Russian?"

"Russian or Polish. The bullet they recovered matches a couple of unsolved murders in a heavily Eastern European neighborhood."

"Wasn't your grandmother Polish?"

"Yes, and if she really did meet Victor in Poland like you said, that could be a big connection"

"Indeed. Victor easily could've made enemies in Poland during his time there. But, Larssen doesn't sound Polish or Russian."

"It's not. It's Scandinavian. At first, I thought it was some long-lost friend of my grandfather's, but now, I don't know."

"Interesting. Well, if that's everything, I don't have another appointment for another hour, why don't I run you to my place?"

"That'd be great. I'm parked around the block."

"Nah, leave your car. If what you say is true, they're probably looking for it. Better if we just take mine."

"Good idea."

And so, Erik found himself lying on the floor in Jeffrey's back seat. It felt a bit unnecessary, but Erik played along. Jeffrey didn't live far away so the ride was brief.

"We're here."

"Did you see any suspicious cars?"

"Nope. I think we're good."

Erik sat up and pulled himself onto the back seat. "You think I'm crazy don't you."

Jeffrey smiled at Erik in the rearview mirror. "Nah. I'm not sure what you are but whatever it is, you believe it's happening. I'm inclined to trust you… and you're not the first last minute guest I've entertained trying to leave a bad situation. Do you think Victor left you any other clues?"

"I tore that house apart looking. I didn't find anything else, but then again, the first clue was hidden in the lining of a suit so who knows."

Jeffrey chuckled from the front seat. "Sounds like a James Bond movie." Jeffrey didn't wait for Erik's response and got out of the car. Erik sat in the back seat for a moment realizing Jeffrey was right. A knock on the window brought him back from his stupor. Jeffrey smiled at him and nodded towards the small townhouse he called home.

Erik grabbed his bag and got out of the car. "What makes you think Victor made enemies in Poland?"

"What?" Erik had caught him off-guard. Good.

"You said he easily could've made enemies while he was there…"

"Oh, just that, the nature of his work and him being a foreigner."

"Nature of his work? Funny, I don't even know what his work *was* before coming to America."

"I think he said he worked in manufacturing, but we mostly talked about Marga," Jeffrey said with a shrug.

Jeffrey said no more as he led Erik into his townhouse. It was stark, just like his office. Erik marveled at the bare walls, the threadbare furniture. The dining table was a simple folding plastic one with folding plastic chairs. If Erik hadn't known better, he'd have thought Jeffrey was squatting. Jeffrey noticed Erik's perplexed look and chuckled.

"Just moved in, remember? I wanted to be closer to my new office. A lot of changes for me in the past few weeks. Nothing like what you're going through though."

Erik laughed softly. "I'm not here to judge. You're doing me a huge solid."

"You're upstairs, follow me." Jeffrey led Erik upstairs and pushed open the first door at the top. The room was empty. "Gonna have to buy an air mattress, I let my last guest keep my last one. They were really going through it. Poor kid." Jeffrey trailed off in thought for a moment before turning back to Erik with a sad smile. "I'll do it on my way back from work tonight. Sound good?"

"Sure," Erik nodded, tossing his bag into the corner. "What's your WIFI?"

Erik could swear he saw Jeffrey's face pale for a moment before a smile appeared. "Haven't gotten the internet hooked up yet. Embarrassing."

"All good. I'll just go to a coffee shop or something."

"There's one down the street," Jeffrey offered.

"Cool. Thanks again, Dr. Grant."

"Come on, Erik! Jeffrey, Jeff, Jefe. No need to be so formal. You're my guest here, not my patient," Jeffrey laughed, slapping Erik on the shoulder. "Well, I better get going. Oh, and hey, please let me know where you end up, I don't want to worry."

"Sure."

Chapter 38

JEFFREY WAS BARELY out the door before Erik grabbed his laptop and slipped out of the house. He'd donned a dark hoodie and a knit beanie to disguise himself. He knew it was half-assed, but it was the best he could do with what he had.

The coffee shop turned out to be the one from the night before, just a different barista and much busier. Erik ordered a double Americano, the lack of sleep over the last few nights weighing him down. He set himself up in the same corner, turning the chair so only the wall was behind him and he had a vantage point of both exits. Victor had taught Erik to keep his back to a wall at a young age, and when mass shootings started to become more and more frequent Victor would always reiterate it. Sage advice, Erik thought as he logged into the shop WIFI.

Erik didn't have to wait long for his coffee and burned his tongue again. The browser was slow to connect so while he waited, he pulled out the slip of paper Victor had left him at the bank. He looked at the name and phone number, boring holes through the paper with his tired gaze. Why had Victor left it? Why had he wanted Erik to have it and not the police? The clue felt so incomplete that it nearly made Erik scream in frustration. Not for the first time, he wished he'd grabbed that photo of young Victor with what Erik assumed was his mother and some man named Larssen. Not for the first time did Erik wish Victor had been more open about his past.

Erik sighed and turned his attention back to his laptop. His fingers hesitated over the keyboard, unsure of what to do. Erik sighed again and started typing. He'd already Googled Per Larssen, so instead he searched for Viktor Braut. Maybe he could find a family tree for his grandfather. His first search proved unfruitful, so he amended the search to 'census Norway'. Erik perked up when a website popped up. He opened it but was dismayed to find the records only going to 1910. If he'd ever learned his great grandfather's name, maybe he could've searched for it.

Dead end. Next, Erik typed in 'Norway citizen database'. Again, little to go on until he found a link to the National Archives of Norway. He looked around the site for a bit before discovering a whole section on tracing your ancestry. Erik spent the next few hours trying to find Victor. He knew Victor was born in Oslo, he knew the date, Victor's Norwegian name, everything he needed to know but nothing came up. It was like banging his head on the wall over and over again as he double checked the information.

Erik took a long pull on his cold coffee, nearly spitting it back out in disgust. He forced himself to swallow and went back up to the barista. He ordered another double Americano and the barista gave Erik a raised eyebrow.

"Didn't sleep this week," Erik joked in response.

The door dinged as another customer entered the shop, Erik watched them walk up to stand in line next to him in the reflection of the pastry display case. The face was vaguely familiar, but too distorted by the glass for Erik to recognize it. He saw the person look at him but ignored it as the person quickly looked away. The barista returned with Erik's order and he thanked her before returning to his perch in the corner.

He took a sip of his piping hot coffee, glancing over the plastic lid at the man that had been standing behind him. Erik coughed out hot liquid as he tried to place the man. It sprayed out over his laptop. Erik, in a flurry, set down his coffee and quickly grabbed a handful of napkins from the holder in the center of the table and furiously started wiping off his laptop. In his haste he sent his cup of coffee teetering until it slammed on its side and belched out a jet of black coffee over the table.

Erik raised his laptop in one hand as the black sludge surged towards it. He managed to right the downed cup with his other hand. Erik looked up and found himself to be the center of attention. He smiled stupidly, laughing to himself in embarrassment. The barista leaned over the counter with a rag and gave Erik an amused smile. The man in line looked horrified as Erik locked eyes with him.

As Erik made his way over to grab the rag the man turned and left. "Hey!" The barista called after him. "Don't you want your coffee?" The man didn't turn around.

"Some people," the barista joked as she handed Erik the rag. "Paid for his coffee and everything. Must be his first cup today."

"Probably," Erik said, a sense of unease creeping up his spine.

Erik made his way back to the coffee lake that was his table on shaky legs and started to wipe it up, trying to force the strange man from his mind. He removed the brown, soggy napkins and tossed them in a nearby trash. He turned back to the table to discover the slip of paper Victor had left him submerged in coffee.

"Shit," Erik mumbled to himself, his mind racing as he retrieved it from the table. He tried to dry it with the rag, being extra careful not to tear it in his trembling hands. He wiped at the front and was relieved when the ink didn't smear. It was thick paper, luckily, so he was pretty sure it'd be OK. Not that it really mattered as Per Larssen had proved to be less than helpful. Erik turned the slip over to wipe the back side and gasped, his mind grinding to a stunned standstill.

There, revealed by the hot liquid, was a secret message. Erik sat down heavily and gawked at it. Of course! How had he been so stupid? Memories of Victor flooded his sleep deprived mind and for a moment he was back in the days when Victor and he would exchange secret messages with invisible ink. Just add heat and the message appears. Why hadn't he thought of that? The gravity of the discovery snapped him back to the present and he brought the slip close to his face, trying to read the tiny message written in impossibly small letters.

The front door dinged again, and Erik snapped his attention away from the tiny message. Erik's blood went cold as he stared up at the man that had been driving the black SUV. Terror hammered at Erik's mind and it took all his effort to tear his eyes away before the man noticed his stare. Erik forced his eyes back to the coffee-soaked table and tried to act as normal as possible. It couldn't be, he thought. He wiped at the table, pretending to ignore the man, but watched him in the reflection of the metal napkin holder. The man gave the room a quick scan, located Erik, and walked up to the barista.

"My friend, he forgot our coffee. Skinny guy, dumb as a doorknob," the man explained in a thick accent.

Polish, Erik realized. Marga didn't really have an accent, she'd spent years training it away but when she'd gotten mad, it sounded just like that man. Erik's heart was a kick drum in his ears as he realized Larssen had found him. But how? He needed to stay calm. *Don't tip them off they're blown*, Victor's voice whispered soothingly in the back of his mind. It was true. They were just watching him or waiting for him to leave so they could kill him, grab him, do whatever they wanted to him.

"Breathe," Erik muttered out loud. The woman sitting at the table next to him gave him a concerned look.

"You OK? You need any help over there?" Erik looked up, locking eyes with her, his confusion obvious. "It's cool, I spill coffee every other day. Here," she said, getting up from the table and putting out an expectant hand.

"Kelsey... right?" Her smile slipped in surprise and she gave Erik a once over.

"Erik! Holy shit! I didn't even recognize you!"

"Yeah," Erik laughed, his attention split between Kelsey and the man with the scar. "Decided to go casual today."

"I see that! Quite the change if I'm being honest. Here, gimme that," she said with a smile, motioning to the rag in Erik's hand.

Erik looked down at the table and realized he'd been wiping at the same spot over and over again. He looked up and forced a smile, handing her the rag. She took it and started wiping at the table, using the rag to soak up the coffee and then ringing it out in the trashcan next to them.

"I find it's easiest to soak some up and wring it. Like I said, I do this all the time." She gave Erik a big, reassuring smile and went back to soaking up the coffee on the table. "Is your laptop OK?"

"What?" Erik replied, still paying more attention to Loren in the corner of his vision than the beautiful woman taking pity on him.

"Your laptop? Did you spill coffee on it?"

Loren grabbed his two cups of coffee and walked out without giving Erik another glance. *Just making sure I'm still here.* Erik allowed his eyes to stop straining towards the door and finally allowed himself to engage with Kelsey. "Right, sorry. Need caffeine," he joked, allowing his body to flood with a confidence he didn't feel as he picked up his laptop. He made a show of investigating it before closing it. "All good!"

"Glad to hear it. Insomnia?"

"You remembered!" Erik laughed, trying to force the anxiety out of his voice.

Kelsey fixed him with a broad smile, a glimmer in her eye. "Memory like a steel trap," she said, knocking gently on the side of her head. Erik tried to smile at the comment but found himself turning it over in his mind. She remembered their conversation, but not his face? Was his change in appearance that radical? Who was this woman that had magically appeared in front of him a second time?

"Your turn." Kelsey said, trying to hand Erik the rag. "Geezus! Your hand!"

Erik looked down at his bruised knuckles and quickly pulled his hand back.

"Kickboxing," he tried to explain, his mind floundering. He tried to recall how he'd messed his knuckles up. The robber? But that was one punch...

"Nice! I do Krav, but we wear padded gloves when we spar," Kelsey said with a laugh, her bewitching smile firmly back in place. "You live in the area? Sorry, just, I'm here about every day and before yesterday, I'd never seen you here."

"Oh, ha. Yeah, I'm new to the neighborhood. Just staying with a friend for a bit." Erik wanted nothing less than that conversation. He wanted to take off out the side door and sprint into the city. He wanted to be as far away from those strange men as he could get. He wanted to do anything other than gaze into Kelsey's brown eyes as she tried to feel him out. And with that thought, Erik realized that was exactly what Kelsey had been doing. Could it just be coincidence running into her again? Was she there every day? His paranoia was like a vice squeezing his mind, forcing him to see nothing but evil in everything around him.

"Erik?" Kelsey was looking at him with a raised eyebrow.

What had he missed? "Sorry, mind was elsewhere." Erik forced a laugh. Forced himself to be calm and collected, to give Kelsey a chance. Victor's lessons flowed back into his mind and he forced himself to take a couple deep breaths, to collect himself. Erik looked at Kelsey with a calm mind.

"I was just wondering when you planned on giving me a call. Typically, when I give a guy my number, we go on a date the next night…" She laughed as she leaned in closer, hand planted on the coffee-soaked table, rag still in hand.

"Ha! About that… I swear I was gonna call," Erik lied. "Just been swamped with school, what with midterms coming up."

"So, what you're trying to tell me is that you really are a student and not some high-powered banker?" Erik gave her a big grin and motioned to his computer.

"I was in the middle of studying when I created lake espresso."

Kelsey let out a melodic laugh. "Student of what? And you better not say art because we already crossed that one off yesterday."

"Nope, you're the art student. I'm the art aficionado," Erik lied again. "Together I'm sure we can create quite the conversation," Erik laughed, slipping into character.

"What was that?" Kelsey laughed. "Was that a pick-up line? Cuz if so, yuck!"

"Geez, usually works so well too!" Erik laughed, picking up the coffee-soaked rag and admiring the clean tabletop. "Hold on a sec, just gonna return this."

Erik didn't wait for a response, cutting to the front of the line at the counter. He offered the dirty rag to the barista but held on to it for a moment longer as she tried to take it.

"That woman, she here often?"

The barista was clearly taken by surprise, her eyes jumping from Erik to Kelsey. "Kelsey? Yeah, like clockwork." The confusion left her eyes and a smile blossomed in its wake. "She's a spitfire, don't get yourself burned."

Erik thanked her and apologized to the woman he'd cut in line. Kelsey raised an amused eyebrow at Erik as he made his way back to her.

"Hey, funny thought," he said, "you wanna get out of here?"

"Really?" Kelsey said.

"Sure, why not? Other than you just met me and know practically nothing about me."

"There is that," Kelsey said with a laugh. "But I suppose you do already have my phone number, or did you forget? Cuz I'm still waiting for that call…"

"Just a second," Erik said, pulling his phone out of his pocket.

"What are you doing!?" Kelsey laughed.

"Just a second, I'm making an important call."

Led Zeppelin's 'Immigrant Song' started playing from Kelsey's backpack and she burst into laughter. "Seriously!?"

Erik shushed her, "Important call, here. Nice ringtone by the way."

"Yes! Fine! I'll go out with you! Geez!"

Erik hung up his phone and slipped it back into his pocket. "Good, cuz I think I've embarrassed myself enough for one morning and would love to take a walk with a fellow art lover," Erik said with his most winning smile.

"Let me grab my things."

Kelsey was quick, shoving her laptop into her backpack and gathering up her notebook and pencils to accompany it. She slammed the last dregs of coffee from her paper cup and tossed it into the trashcan.

"Ready?" She asked as Erik finished wiping off his laptop.

"Let's go!" Erik said, his eyes going to the front entrance. He scanned the parking lot through the wall-to-wall windows but couldn't see a black SUV. That didn't mean they hadn't switched cars though. At least now Erik had seen both men's faces, and he'd never forget that pink scar snaking down the second man's face.

"Second thoughts?" Kelsey said, interrupting his thoughts. Erik snapped back into character and fixed her with a big smile.

"Not at all! Follow me," Erik said with a wink, leading her out the side exit. If Kelsey thought it was strange, she gave no indication. Erik walked slowly to the corner and peered around it, making the movement as fluid as possible.

"Whoops!" Erik said, crouching down to tie a shoe that was already tied. "Stupid laces never stay tied."

Kelsey laughed in response. "That's why I wear flats." She stuck out a foot for Erik to admire. White slip-ons with pink polka dots and little flecks of paint, probably a result of her studies. *Probably*, Victor laughed in the back of Erik's mind.

"Very nice," Erik said after a cursory glance. He looked around the shoe, glad for the dark lenses of his sunglasses, and spotted Loren glaring out from the driver side of a blue coup towards the back of the lot. He was watching the entrance while Feliks rubbed his jaw miserably.

Erik stood up and used Kelsey to shield himself from his stalkers. "There's a park this way, right?"

"Oh! Wanna walk it?" Kelsey's eyes were bright, her smile eager. Erik hardly noticed, so trapped within his own mind, his own worries.

"Read my mind!" He smiled, looking over her shoulder as they walked into the city and away from the immediate danger.

Chapter 39

ERIK HAD TO FORCE himself to relax as they walked through the large park. It was a marvel of multi-tasking as he was somehow able to stay engaged with Kelsey while remaining fully aware of his surroundings. He was enjoying their conversation, even if he was doing nothing more than spouting white lies with little bits of truth sprinkled in for comfort, a trick Victor had taught him while playing their games so many years ago. It'd been so long since Erik had played the character game with Victor and thinking about it made his passing hurt anew. What had Victor gotten him into? He desperately wanted to look at the impossibly small message on the scrap of paper but forced the thought out of his mind. First, he needed to get as far away from his watchers as possible. Once he was safely back at Jeffrey's, he could go about figuring it out.

"Favorite artist?" Kelsey asked, playing the 'get to know you game' necessary for every real first date. It was a first date, Erik realized.

"Jacek Malczewski," Erik said with little hesitation. He'd been Marga's favorite artist. *Stick with what you know*, Victor concurred with him.

Kelsey stopped walking and did a comical sizing up of Erik. "Seriously?"

Erik smiled, not sure if he cared whether she was impressed or disappointed. "Seriously. He was the father of Polish symbolism!" Marga's words out of Erik's mouth.

Kelsey laughed and started walking again. "I would've pegged you for a Banksy lover."

"What? Why?" Erik said, legitimately engaged in her response. Turned out he did care what she thought.

"Hoodie, beanie, dress pants and what looks to be a collared shirt underneath? You look like a hipster," Kelsey said with a laugh.

"Ouch," Erik responded. "I do like his stuff though."

"Duh, he's a genius."

"Who's your favorite?"

"Depends on the day," Kelsey shrugged. "Today? Edward Hopper."

Erik couldn't believe his luck. Nighthawks by Edward Hopper currently hung on the wall in Victor's living room. Erik had bought Victor the poster years ago and Victor had framed it. He'd always told Erik it reminded him of when he and Marga had met. He never explained why.

"Big fan of Nighthawks," Erik said, playing it cool.

"You and everyone else. I was more thinking about Woman in the Sun," Kelsey laughed. "Favorite band?"

As Kelsey and Erik made their way through the park, Erik realized he didn't want it to end. He'd originally planned on faking an excuse to leave her behind once he was a safe distance from his followers, he could always call her if things ever went back to normal, but he was finding it more and more difficult to disengage. Kelsey peppered him with questions and for a moment, all his worries slipped to the back of his mind. His eyes never stopped scanning his surroundings, searching for the faces of his followers, but he allowed himself to enjoy the conversation, the only one he could remember that wasn't with family or didn't center on his recent loss in a real long time.

They walked a circle around the park a few times before Kelsey stopped, an anxious look spread across her soft features.

"Hey, Erik. Question."

"Shoot," Erik said with a ready smile.

"I know we just met... yesterday, and maybe I'm crazy but I feel like we've known each other for so much longer than that and this is definitely one of the better first dates I've ever been on. Would you like to see some of my work? At my studio?"

Erik fought the urge to decline and carry on with his personal hell, but something wouldn't let him. "Sure! I'd love to," Erik said, his voice ringing with the truth he felt. He really did want to see her work, and what could it hurt? "And I agree. Hands down, one of my better first dates."

Kelsey smiled, her cheeks flushing ever so slightly with relief. "Follow me!"

They walked out of the park and into the gray city, so uninviting after their journey amongst the grass and trees. Kelsey kept up her barrage of questions and Erik kept trying to differentiate the character he was trying to play from his true self and failing. The only real difference, Erik realized, was the new Erik didn't have the same hang ups, his grandfather hadn't just died and more importantly, no one was hunting him. Erik desperately wanted that Erik to be the real Erik, but he was a means to an end, an end he'd already achieved but couldn't seem to disengage from, no matter how reckless it was becoming. What was the end goal? Where was he going with it? Where was he taking this beautiful woman? *Heartbreak*, Victor said, breaking whatever myth Erik had been trying to engineer.

"The Sydney?" Erik said, forcing himself out of his reverie as they passed a rundown apartment complex with the name, The Sydney, running along the side of the building in bright gold lettering.

"Don't ask," Kelsey laughed.

"Someone's got a sense of humor," Erik said, making Kelsey laugh harder. Music to his ears.

Shortly after The Sydney, they reached the entrance of an old brick building, and Kelsey informed him her studio was on the second floor. She bit her lip as she said it and Erik gave into his weakness and followed her past the elevator with the 'out of service' sign, up the winding stairs with the stained floor tiles and to her front door, a small floral image painted around the peephole. She unlocked it and led him into an open studio, a single door in the far corner, probably the bathroom, Erik thought, casing the room as Victor had taught him. True to her word, easels and art supplies dotted the room. Half-finished paintings sat discarded in the corner, next to a futon shoved up against one of the walls. A mini fridge, and small, two-person table with mismatching chairs, the only other furniture.

"What do you think?" Kelsey was suddenly serious as she regarded the room with open arms.

"Wow," Erik stammered, the reality of what he was doing finally setting in. "This is amazing." Kelsey glowed in front of him.

"No, it's not. Also, I want to paint you," Kelsey said with an abruptness Erik had come to expect from and enjoy about her.

"Oh?" Erik forced a smile as he ran through his options once more. Could he just leave? Did he want to? He didn't know where this was going but all his worries were slipping away, and it felt good. He was away from his pursuers. He'd found another clue in Victor's mystery that burned a hole in his pocket, begging to be read, but it'd still be there later. Mostly, did he really want to get Kelsey involved in the hell that had become his every waking moment?

"Also, please don't be weirded out and I promise I'm not some thirsty perv, but I want to paint you… nude," Kelsey added with a raised eyebrow and a smirk.

Erik turned bright red and was suddenly aware of the little he truly knew about the woman in front of him. His mouth worked up and down like a fish out of water as he tried to center himself. Kelsey crossed the short distance between them standing just inside his personal bubble.

"Embarrassed?" She said shyly, gazing into his eyes. Erik forced a confidant grin and was about to speak when Kelsey moved in closer, looking up at him, her eyes asking permission for an unspoken question. She hesitated but Erik didn't back away and something unsaid passed between them before she pressed her lips to his.

Erik kissed her back, funneling the torrent of repressed stress into passion. He wrapped his arms around Kelsey's waist and pulled her close. When they finally broke the embrace, Kelsey gasped, pushing herself back from Erik.

"Check," was all she said before coming back for more.

Erik's phone vibrated in his pocket, but he didn't care, and if Kelsey did, she said nothing as she slowly led him towards the futon tucked against the wall. When she reached it, she broke away from Erik's lips and unzipped his hoodie. She looked up into his eyes and her cheeks reddened. With trembling hands, she started to undo his belt, pulling it loose from his jeans in a flourish worthy of a magician. She tossed it to the side and unbuttoned his pants. Erik couldn't stop himself from helping her, and then with anxious fingers, unbuttoned his own shirt, practically ripping it off.

Kelsey stopped, taking a step back, her eyes traveling the length of Erik from his feet to the tip of his head. He quickly removed his hoodie and button up while she appraised him like a prize horse. Suddenly feeling awkward as an impish grin crested her lips.

"Slow down, tiger," Kelsey laughed, taking another step back. Erik looked at her in confusion, any form of response lost within the pounding of his heart. "Sorry, got caught up for a moment. I just really wanted to… kiss you…"

"Ok," was Erik's eventual response. He had never been less sure of himself as in that moment.

"Can I paint you?" Kelsey asked, her nose scrunching up as she gave him a nervous grin.

"Nude?" Erik responded, his cheeks a burning testament to how uncomfortable the prospect made him.

"Please?" Kelsey responded. "I know it's a weird request, it's just, when you're inspired… you're inspired… and I'm in this art show in a few days and the more work I have—"

"Yeah, I don't know about that," Erik said honestly.

"No problem!" Kelsey was quick to respond, her disappointment obvious. "I just have Woman in the Sun stuck in my head and thought it'd be a cool parallel to paint you in the same way, just in my style."

"Remind me what Woman in the Sun looks like again?"

Kelsey's eyes lit up and she rushed over to a stack of books, pawing through them until she found the one she was looking for. She riffled through the pages until she found the painting and eagerly held it up for Erik to see.

"Beautiful, right?" She wasn't wrong.

"And you just want me to stand in profile like the woman? Looking out your window, in the sun?"

"Yes," Kelsey nodded, a hopeful smile engulfing her brown eyes, beaming into Erik, willing him to play along.

"Yeah, I… I don't know how I feel about hanging out all by myself in my birthday suit," Erik said honestly. Erik's heart broke as the hope fled her gaze and was replaced with disappointment.

"No worries! It's a really weird ask, I know." Kelsey paused, her eyes going distant before they refocused on him. "What if I got naked too? Then you wouldn't be all alone in your birthday suit…"

Erik's pulse quickened and he couldn't help the glimmer that came to his eye. Kelsey didn't miss it either. Her smile deepened as she set the book down and crossed the small distance between them. Erik wrapped her in an embrace as quickly as he could and started kissing her again. She ran her fingers between his belly and the elastic of his briefs and started pulling them down with his pants. Erik broke the kiss to tear his under shirt off, flinging it onto the futon.

Erik trembled with excitement as the cool air of the studio washed over his bare skin. Kelsey ignored it, pushing him backwards onto the futon. Erik landed with a smile, still trembling. He'd never wanted a woman so much before. Kelsey removed his shoes and socks, then pulled off his pants. She grabbed Erik by his wrists and pulled him back to his feet, putting one hand on his hip, causing another tremble to wrack his body. She gently turned him to face the open window, the sun streaming through with its golden rays. Erik felt the warmth licking his skin and smiled.

Kelsey stepped back and looked Erik over, closing one eye and framing him between a square she made with her pointer fingers and thumbs. Erik should have felt uncomfortable, but he didn't. The whole thing had his hormones raging. Kelsey looked Erik over from his feet up to his face, locking eyes with him.

"Those sparring sessions are no joke, goodness!" She said as she picked up an easel and a canvas.

"What?" Erik said, honestly confused until he looked down at the motely display of bruises along his side. "Oh, that."

"Don't get me wrong, I have my own bruises from sparring, but nothing like that," she said as she set up her workstation. Erik watched her, suddenly very aware of how exposed he was.

"You comfortable?" Kelsey said with a devilish grin.

"Uh, yo... I... aren't you forgetting something?"

Kelsey's cheeks flushed and Erik realized she was just as nervous as he was. "About that…"

Erik looked from Kelsey to his pile of clothes and back again, the chill of the studio finally warranting his attention. "Too late to back out?" he said, covering himself as best he could as he started to move towards his pile of clothes.

"Wait!" Kelsey said. She took a deep breath and kicked off her slip-ons, unbuttoned her sweater with shaky fingers. "Deals a deal."

Kelsey stripped to her underwear before walking back to Erik and prodding him back into the right pose.

"Stay," she commanded. Erik complied. Kelsey smiled triumphantly. "Good boy."

She turned and walked back towards her easel, turning on some calm music on her way past a paint splattered boom box. She turned and looked Erik over once more, and a wave of discomfort washed over him again.

"How, explicit is this going to be?"

Kelsey laughed. "I can leave some things out."

Erik flushed and turned back towards the window, suddenly very self-conscious.

"Hey, Erik…" Erik looked back towards her and watched in awe as Kelsey removed her bra and underwear. "Deals a deal. Now, look straight ahead."

Erik stared at her with a desire he'd never known. All his worries seemed so far away it was as if they were from a different life all together. Erik relaxed into his stance; eyes focused on the woman he'd just met as she blushed back at him, covering herself against his hungry eyes.

"Hey! Eyes forward!" she demanded with a laugh.

Chapter 40

KELSEY PAINTED FOR a few hours, specks of paint dotting her exposed skin. It took a while for Erik to relax against her critical stare as she poured over the details of his body. He could scarcely remember having more fun though. There was something freeing in standing there. Nothing to hide and no worries of judgement. When Kelsey was finished, she informed him by crossing the room and kissing him. Erik forgot what he was running from. Erik Brown was a different person, with his own worries and his own life. The Erik in Kelsey's studio knew nothing of it and was better for it.

As Erik sought to explore her body, she stopped him with a gentle finger to his lips. "Not yet."

Erik was confused, his body locked into position, his arms wrapped around her, her skin so warm against his. "What?" was all he could say as she tore herself from his embrace.

"I… can we just not rush it? I think I like you and…"

Erik didn't make her say it. "You want to take things slow."

She nodded emphatically, a hopeful smile cresting her lips. "Yeah, sure," was all Erik could say to the beautiful naked woman in front of him. "Probably gonna need to get dressed then, cuz this is torture." Kelsey laughed; her smile filled with a relief Erik didn't share.

"I know it's weird, and we've already impressed each other with our naked bodies—"

"So, you were impressed?" Erik asked with a grin.

"Oh, just get dressed, asshole," Kelsey laughed as she retrieved her own clothes.

Erik just grinned at her as he pulled on his pants and was quickly reminded of reality as his phone buzzed in his pocket.

Jeffrey had texted nine times and called as many times more. Erik silently cursed at himself for not having warned Jeffrey his tail had caught up, but as he scrolled through the texts something replaced that worry. Jeffrey had every right to be upset, but something didn't feel right. His tone was almost frantic from the start, and then Jeffrey was trying to call again.

"Jesus," Erik whispered as the call vibrated in his hand. He looked over at Kelsey and smiled apologetically. "Sorry, gotta take this."

"Your girlfriend?" Kelsey said with a laugh.

"Yep, how'd you guess?" Erik responded; a stupid grin plastered on his lips.

"Sure," Kelsey said, rolling her eyes dramatically. "All the good ones are taken, right?"

"I promise, it's just the friend I'm staying with. We were supposed to hang out and I blew him off, for obvious reasons. He's not taking it well."

"Uh huh," was all Kelsey said as she picked herself up off the futon and returned to her painting.

"I'll be right back, promise." Erik didn't wait for a response as he stepped into the small bathroom. "Hello?"

"Erik! Are you OK? Jesus, you gave me quite the scare! You can't tell me all the shit you told me today and then ghost my texts and calls! That's not how I run my safe house." Jeffrey was angry. Erik could hear it bubbling underneath his otherwise pleasant tone.

"Jeffrey, I'm so sorry. You're absolutely right… It's just… my tail caught up with me at the coffee shop."

"What? Are you sure?" Jeffrey's tone was incredulous, and Erik couldn't understand why.

"Yeah. I saw 'em and had to slip out. It was crazy because I'd just discovered another clue and—"

"I thought you said you didn't get a good look at the guy following you…" Jeffrey said interrupting Erik.

"That's what I thought but when I saw him today… it was him. I'm positive."

"Sorry, didn't mean to talk over you there. Did you say you found another clue?" Erik smiled at the immediate change in tone.

"Yeah. My grandfather left me a message on that slip of paper using invisible ink."

"Invisible ink? Crazy. What'd it say?"

"I haven't had a chance to read it yet," Erik responded sheepishly.

"Well, what the hell have you been doing all afternoon?" A hint of anger flared up in Jeffrey's voice catching Erik off guard.

"Avoiding my tail," Erik said, his own anger starting to stir.

"Sorry, Erik. Why don't you just tell me where you are, and I can pick you up. We can decipher the clue together."

But suddenly, Erik didn't really feel like letting Jeffrey know where he was. Why was it so important? Knowing Erik was safe should've been the end of it.

"All good, Jeffrey. I'm in the middle of something right now but I'll be back in a bit."

"Erik, come on man. Just let me pick you up. It's getting late and this isn't the greatest part of town."

"I appreciate it, but I'll be fine."

"Sure, well at least let me know where you are, that way if we lose contact again, I can give the police an area to look." Jeffrey sounded desperate and Erik hesitated to respond. Jeffrey had a good point, but why was it so important he knew where Erik was? He'd have to wait forty-eight hours to declare him missing anyway.

"Don't worry about it, man. I'll be fine. I'll be back later," Erik responded coolly, careful not to betray the doubt lingering in his gut.

"Erik. Give me a fucking break here. You can't expect to unload that bullshit on me and then not let me know where you are. You brought me into this shit, I deserve to be in the fucking loop." Erik's jaw tried to drop at Jeffrey's bald anger, but he forced himself to remain calm. The best tool to fight anger is calm. Victor had drilled that into him.

"Jeffrey, chill dude. I'm fine, and you're right, I shouldn't have brought you into this. I'm sorry, but I'm not going to tell you where I am. I can't, I don't know the address. I'll be back soon, I promise."

"Fine. I guess that's what I get for putting up a practical stranger in my house."

"Listen, I have all my stuff, you want me gone and I'm gone," Erik growled, done with the whole conversation.

"No! Sorry. I'm just worked up. You gave me a hell of a scare. That's all. Just come back and we'll figure it out," Jeffrey said with a forced laugh.

"Yeah, sure. See you later." Erik hung up the phone in disbelief. Something was off. He ran the faucet and splashed cool water on his face and tried to gather his thoughts. Was some information on Victor worth dealing with Jeffrey's attitude? Information he'd have to coerce out of the man in the first place.

Erik exited the bathroom to find Kelsey still at her easel. She regarded him with a raised eyebrow. "Have a good chat?"

"Nope, not really. My friend is acting like a real dick." Erik plopped back down on the futon and watched Kelsey continue to paint.

"I never do this by the way," Kelsey said without looking at him.

"What?"

"Bring people back to my studio."

"Good to know…"

Erik watched her paint for a bit before his curiosity finally won out and he walked across the room to stand next to her. She turned the easel to face him and left him gawking. The painting was beautiful. It wasn't finished, not even close, but what was took his breath away. He felt odd staring at a painting of himself, made no less weird by his being naked.

"Thanks for the extra muscles," Erik said with a grin. Kelsey blushed and spun the painting away from him.

"I just paint what I see, everyone's body is different." Erik broke out in laughter. "You're gonna call, right?"

"Of course, how could I not? I can barely keep my hands off of you!" Erik was smiling so hard his cheeks hurt. He really liked this woman. In all the hell he was living through, a bright spot.

"Don't get too many ideas, fella. These hands are registered weapons," she said, stepping back into a defensive stance, her hands balled into fists. "But, if you play your cards right," Kelsey said, trying not to smile, "Maybe I will let you touch me again."

"I think I'd enjoy that," Erik said, going in for another kiss.

Chapter 41

ERIK WAS WALKING on clouds when he left her building. He'd completely forgotten that he'd hidden the real Erik from her piercing gaze. She didn't even know his last name. She didn't know the trouble that dogged his steps, the danger. She thought he was some confident, smooth-talking man. She knew a caricature he'd created to escape his very real and present problems. It wasn't until he had returned to the park that the realization hit him.

"Shit," he muttered to himself in dismay, plopping down onto a park bench. "Shit," he reiterated sadly, and just like that, he was plunged back into the depths of hell.

Erik leaned back on the bench and sighed. He closed his eyes in misery and stayed there until his phone started to vibrate. He sighed again and fished it out.

Detective Kincaid.

"Hello?"

"Erik, hey. I have a development on the phone number. I put it through my sources and they're pretty sure it's a black site number."

"Sorry, a what?"

"They think it's a government number. The company it's listed to is a defunct plumbing business. When they looked a little closer, turned out to be a shell company owned by a John Smith. I'm not sure what your grandfather was involved in, but I need you to be careful. I'll let you know more when I do."

"And Samantha?"

"Ms. Kint? Seemed genuinely shocked when I turned up asking questions. So, either she's a good actor or she just has a crush on you."

"Oh. OK, thanks." The line went dead and Erik sat there, stunned. He put his phone back in his pocket and felt the scrap of paper. He bolted upright and fished it out. He squinted against the dying light, trying to make out the small message.

He struggled for a few minutes, unable to make out any concrete words, before a thought dawned on him. He pulled out his phone and took a picture of the message. He then opened it in his photo editor and zoomed in on the writing. It worked just like a magnifying glass, just a little blurry. Erik smiled at his own genius.

The message read: Hello, Erik, my barnebarn. Understand I'm sorry. Just or not, I've lied to you. How I've lied to you all. Your bestemor was the only one who knew the truth as she lived it with me in life and in death. Ultimately, if you're reading this, my death has been tragic. Let me pray it was an honest tragedy, but I suspect foul play is what has brought you here and placed my all with Marga once more. Understand, I am not Viktor Braut. It pains me still, but Viktor Braut died in the snows of Norway in 1945. Just one of the many victims of the Gestapo. Erik, my name is Per Larssen. Best known as a name that lives in infamy in the criminal worlds of Poland and Russia. Understand that it is a name attributed to a man thought dead by the American government. Dutifully, I tell you this now, and this way, because to know that name is to live in constant danger. Bad men with long memories would be very interested in that name. Understand, I believe you can trust the people on the other end of that phone number, but I caution you none-the-less. Trust no one. What I ask is, remember my teachings. Understand, Erik, I love you and I'm sorry. Here on and forever, remember my teachings and be smart, be safe, be fearless.

Bestefar

Erik held his phone in numb fingers. His heart beat the dirge of a funeral as he lost all feeling. He stared at the message trying to comprehend it. He read it over and over again, refusing to absorb the words. It gave credence to what Kincaid had said about the crime families. It strengthened her argument that the number was a government number. The message confirmed everything that had seemed too fantastical to be believed. Fear gnawed at the edges of Erik's thoughts, but he forbade them entry to his mind. He slowly began to accept what the message had told him and let the dots connect. Be cautious, he thought, realization dawning on him as to how exposed he was in that park.

With new attention to detail, he surveyed his surroundings. The park was deserted, the lights flicking on in the darkening evening to illuminate small patches of sidewalk. He was directly beneath one such light. He quickly got up from the bench and walked into the dark, sitting down heavily on the cold grass. Again, he looked around the park, trying to peer into the shadows. He stayed there for a bit, making sure he didn't see any movement. His phone vibrated.

Jeffrey.

Will you be back soon? It asked

Suspicion swirled within Erik. Jeffrey's concern had entered an uncomfortable realm. Erik had told him he'd be back, why was it so important Jeffrey knew exactly when? And then it hit him. Erik scrolled back to the first text Jeffrey had sent asking where he was. It had been forty-five minutes after he'd slipped out of the coffee shop. Coincidence? He'd told Jeffrey where he was going, Jeffrey had no reason to question his whereabouts, unless... unless Erik's tail was connected to Jeffrey.

Erik went cold with dread. Was Jeffrey in danger? And then another thought invaded his mind. What if

Jeffrey wasn't who he said he was? All the coincidences started to coalesce in Erik's mind. The gym, the funeral, Victor, the coffee shop. Either could be true, he realized, but there was only one way to find out.

He texted Jeffrey he was on his way back.

Chapter 42

IT WAS FULLY dark by the time Erik made his way into Jeffrey's subdivision of cozy townhouses with tiny yards. Erik moved from shadow to shadow, using trees and bushes for cover when he could. He passed a blue coupe, holding his breath as he skirted by. That'd been the car they'd been driving at the coffee shop. It was empty. He continued towards Jeffrey's house. The lights were on, but he couldn't be sure if anyone was inside. He made his way towards it, slipping over the decorative picket fence and flattening himself to the grass.

He crawled into the bushes by the front window, mindless of the stains his transit had left on his slacks. He picked his way through the bushes with as little noise as possible, finding a gap between them and the side of the house. He rose to his knees and tried to peer through a small gap in the blinds. He could just make out movement inside.

Erik yelped in surprise as the gold gilded barrel of a gun jutted through the blinds just above him, revealing a pair of staring eyes, a menacing scar running along one of them. Erik crouched into himself and held his breath. The eyes stared straight ahead, looking to the street. Erik stayed as still as possible until the fingers retreated, and the blinds settled back into place.

"This is your fault, Chudy!" bellowed a heavily accented voice. Polish, was Erik's fleeting thought.

"Patience, Loren. He said he's on his way back," Jeffrey responded.

"That was twenty minutes ago! Text him again, god dammit."

"I've texted him twenty times already, you want me to tip him off that something's up?" Jeffrey's voice rang with confidence and Erik's stomach dropped.

Jeffrey was dirty, and suddenly everything clicked into place. Erik had lost his tail until he'd linked up with Jeffrey. Jeffrey's insistence on knowing where Erik was, his panic when Erik gave his tail the slip. His empty house, sparse office, the probing questions... How he'd been waiting when Erik found out about Victor, how he'd weaseled his way into Erik's family. It was a setup, and he'd missed it.

"Fine, then we just sit here like assholes and wait. I am sick of this shit. I am sick of watching, waiting. It is about time we sit this kid down and get the information we need. You said he had new clue?"

"Yes, that's what he said."

"You are worthless. I do not know why we put up with you." The menace in the man's voice made the hair stand up on Erik's arms.

Erik needed to isolate Jeffrey and get some answers. He slid his phone out of his hoodie pocket and shot Jeffrey a text.

"He just texted me!"

"What does it say?"

"He's lost. He sent me the crossroads. He wants me to pick him up," Jeffrey said happily.

"Good, me and Chudy will get him. You stay here."

"What? Why?"

"This kid is tricky, what if he is lying? You stay here in case he comes back."

"Fine," Jeffrey responded, defeat in his voice. "Well, leave me a gun at least."

The front door slammed open and Erik scrunched back into a ball, just barely avoiding detection as two men raced out of the house. Jeffrey stood in the doorway, watching them depart with crossed arms. "They get to have all the damn fun," he muttered as he turned around, closing the door behind him.

Erik was frozen in his hiding spot, his mind laser focused on Jeffrey, and the more he thought about everything, the more his fear boiled into anger. It rose in him, filling his chest, seeping into his head. He fought the urge to rush into the house and throttle Jeffrey. He needed to be smart. He had no idea how dangerous Jeffrey was.

Erik waited for the blue coupe to take off towards his false coordinates and then a few minutes more before he slipped out from behind the bushes. He skirted between the closely stacked town houses and went around to the back of Jeffrey's. He pulled a lock picking kit out from his backpack. A gift from Victor when he was still just a kid obsessed with reruns of 'Get Smart'. Victor had taught him how to pick locks and made him promise not to abuse it. Victor had always said it was a good skill to have. You'll never be locked out of your house.

It took Erik more time than he felt comfortable with to slip the two locks, sweat beading his brow in the cool night air. He was rusty, but he finally got it. He opened the door as slowly as he could, making sure the hinges didn't groan a warning. He was inside with the door shut silently behind him in mere seconds. He took off his backpack and placed it against the wall, out of the way. He removed his shoes and placed them next to it. He took a deep, calming breath, and made his way into the long hallway, disappointed with himself for leaving his Colt 1911 back at Victor's house.

He crept down the hall, so close to the wall that the fabric of his hoodie brushed it ever so slightly. He crept slow and deliberate, hoping upon hope that Jeffrey wouldn't round the corner before he was close enough to strike. His luck held and he found himself positioned between the living room and the stairs. His ears strained for any sound of Jeffrey. Finally, the creak of floorboards sounded from upstairs, followed by the pounding thump of feet coming down the hardwood steps.

Erik had enough warning to leap backwards and press himself flat against the opposite wall. Jeffrey rounded the stairs within an arm's length of Erik, but continued into the living room, completely oblivious to Erik's presence. Erik crossed back over to the other wall and peered around it. Jeffrey shuffled around the room for a moment before taking a seat at the plastic folding table. He pulled a shiny silver pistol from behind his back and tossed it loudly on to the table. He sighed his disappointment at being stuck in the townhouse while his compatriots had all the fun, and pulled out his phone, just holding it, willing it to buzz news of Erik's capture.

Erik watched from just around the corner, sizing up the odds. Was he quick enough to cross the room and surprise Jeffrey before the gun found his hand? Should he creep towards the man just as he'd crept down the hall, silent and efficient until he could strike? Patience, Victor had always taught him. In all things in life, the patient man takes the prize because all the greatest things come to those that wait. That had been one of the many lessons Victor had taught him on their hunting trips and time after time they had been rewarded with trophy kills.

Jeffrey yawned loudly and started to scratch his leg. "Bullshit," he muttered, getting up and heading into the kitchen, leaving the gun forgotten on the table.

Erik slid around the corner, moving just slow enough to keep his feet from thumping the hard floor, just slow enough to keep the swish of his clothing silent. He crept towards the table, his eyes never leaving Jeffrey's back. Jeffrey was too busy scrounging around in the empty fridge to notice. "Least they could do is leave me some God damn food!" He exclaimed before turning around.

"Hey, Jeffrey. How's it going?" Erik said, gun in hand, leaning lightly against the cheap table.

Chapter 43

JEFFREY'S EYES TRIED to secede from his skull, his body going rigid as if death had already found him hours before. A convolution of disbelief and shock bubbled out of his mouth, combining into muttered gibberish until his brain took control of his vocal cords once more.

"Erik! I'm so glad you're back!" He said, attempting to force the waiver of fear trembling within his words to the wayside, punctuating the lie with a slimy smile that dripped with fake gaiety. "I was so worried about you!"

Erik smiled back, but when Jeffrey started to move towards him, Erik pointed the gun at him and shook his head. "Go ahead and stay over there, Jeffrey."

"Whoa! Hey, watch where you point that thing!" Jeffrey said, throwing his hands up and forcing an awkward laugh. Erik remained straight faced, doing his best to keep any emotion from his features. "I'm guessing you're wondering what I'm doing with a gun."

"Who are your friends? Jeffrey?"

"Who?" Jeffrey deflected, his body language telegraphing his discomfort.

Erik stood up straight and racked the pistol with a loud click, the movement made ever so smooth with years of training under Victor's critical eye.

"Who are your friends, Jeffrey? In fact, why don't you tell me everything, you lying snake," Erik growled, every ounce of anger he'd gathered over the past few weeks flowing into his words.

The smile slipped from Jeffrey's face, replaced by a cold, menacing glare. "Might not want to take that tone with me, Erik." He took a step closer, his hand reaching out towards Erik.

"One more step and you'll have a hole in your leg," Erik warned, forcing equal menace into his own words.

Jeffrey stopped and cocked his head to the side in disbelief. "You ever shoot a gun, Erik?"

Erik couldn't help himself; he broke into a broad grin. "Never shot a TT-33 before, but then again, it's just a low caliber, Russian Colt 1911 knock off. Now, that's a gun. Colt 1911. Smooth as silk on the recoil but still packs a punch. I'm guessing this model's been specked for a .38 special round? Nothing compared to a .45 though."

Jeffrey just stared at Erik, clearly surprised by Erik's response. "Now, why don't you just take a seat, right where you are and we can have a chat," Erik commanded. Jeffrey continued to just stare.

Erik's grin slipped into a scowl and he grabbed a folding chair in his empty hand and flung it at Jeffrey. Jeffrey yelped in surprise and just managed to block the chair with his outstretched arm. It clattered to the kitchen floor, echoing off the cheap cabinets.

"Sit down," Erik growled, the pistol trembling in his grip. He wanted so badly to pull the trigger, not to kill Jeffrey, he wasn't sure he could go through with that, but just to wound him and show him he was serious. Jeffrey watched Erik and must have seen the murder in his eyes because he scurried to pick up the chair and took a seat in it. He lifted up his hands in a show of surrender.

"Now what?" he asked as calmly as he could, fear still causing his words to waiver.

"Now you tell me who the hell you are. You can start by telling me what the hell you want with me."

Jeffrey burst into unsettling laughter and Erik snapped, surging across the room before Jeffrey could blink, pistol whipping him across the face. Jeffrey grunted in pain, falling off the chair and clattering to the floor. Erik danced away from him, leveling the pistol at him again.

"You think this is funny? This is my life you're messing with! Now tell me why, you cockroach."

Jeffrey slowly turned to look back at Erik, blood leaking down his face from a cut above his eye.

"Talk!" Erik screamed making as if he was going to pistol whip Jeffrey a second time.

Jeffrey responded by cringing into himself and putting his hands between Erik and his face. "OK, OK!" He roared; all the arrogance gone from his voice. "Just, chill!"

Erik glared at the man, his hate for him swirling nakedly behind his eyes. Was this the man that had pulled the trigger on Victor? If not, did he know who did?

"I work for Gerwazy Zatorski," Jeffrey finally said, wilting under Erik's fiery gaze.

Erik let the silence hang in the air between them, the gun still pointed at Jeffrey.

"Give me your phone," he finally said, breaking the silence.

"What?"

"Give me your phone." Erik motioned towards the thin, rectangular bulge in Jeffrey's front pocket. "Take it out, unlock it and toss it to me."

Jeffrey just stared at Erik with a confused look. "Now!" Erik screamed, surging forward, the pistol raised above him in the threat of another pistol whipping.

"Jesus," Jeffrey exclaimed as he scrambled to take the phone out. Erik stepped back, giving Jeffrey some breathing room. Jeffrey's eyes darted from the phone to Erik and back until his shaky fingers were able to unlock the phone. He held it up to show Erik the home screen and then tossed it near enough to Erik that his reflex was to reach out for it, but Erik fought that reflex and let the phone go sailing past him to land with a clatter on the hardwood floor.

Erik just stared at Jeffrey, ignoring the phone all together. He waited for Jeffrey's tensed muscles to relax, for him to lean back against the cold, stainless steel refrigerator. His plan had been obvious as soon as he tossed the phone. Erik knew he was supposed to lunge for it, take his eyes, and more importantly, the gun off of Jeffrey and then Jeffrey would charge him. Erik didn't feel like finding out which of them was the stronger man. He knew nothing of Jeffrey. For all he knew, Jeffrey had special ops training, though he highly doubted it.

Erik slowly stepped backwards until the phone was between him and Jeffrey. He crouched down, never breaking eye contact, and retrieved the phone blindly. Once he had it, he held it up. The screen had gone dark. A fresh bout of anger raged through Erik's blood and he clenched his teeth against it. *Be calm*, Victor cooed from the back of his mind, a deep breath purging the ill will that festered within him.

"Well, that was stupid," Erik remarked calmly as he tossed the phone back at Jeffrey. The move took Jeffrey by surprise as the phone thumped off his chest. He was barely able to catch it. "Unlock it and if you try that again, I'll put a hole in your knee."

Jeffrey met him with a glare, clearly not believing Erik's threat. Erik, for his part, prayed Jeffrey didn't make him back it up. Jeffrey unlocked the phone and tossed it back to Erik.

"Why? Why did Gerwazy have my bestefar killed? Why is he having me followed? What does he want?" Jeffrey's abrupt laughter was chilling. Erik pushed down the fear that tried to invade his mind. Deep breaths, deep breaths.

"You don't remember, do you?" Jeffrey's laughter doubled as he shook his head back and forth, his eyes trying to bore into Erik's soul. "Gerwazy... You don't remember meeting him, do you?"

"Gerry," Erik mumbled in realization.

"Gerry, Gerwazy, one and the same. You're a dead man and you don't even know it!" Jeffrey laughed

"You're just as in the dark as I am. Jut a peon," Erik responded with a forced smile he hoped looked genuine.

Jeffrey's laughter ceased as abruptly as it began. He glared at Erik, menace in his dark eyes. "Victor took something from him, a long time ago. But I think you know that. I think this game you're playing..."

"Game?" Erik interjected.

"Yes! You're playing stupid. What did the new clue tell you? I wonder..."

Erik's fingers worked casually on the phone in his hand, his familiarity with the model making it simple for him to navigate it as he'd done so many times before. Jeffrey was oblivious as Erik went into his safety settings, oblivious until Erik held up the phone and double checked his work.

"The hell are you doing?" Jeffrey finally asked.

Erik ignored him, finishing his work with the phone and then slipping it into his pocket. "Changing your password. Do you have duct tape?"

Jeffrey looked at him in disbelief. "What?" Was all he could think to respond, but Erik didn't mind as he raced forward and smacked Jeffrey on the side of the head with the butt of the pistol. Erik used just enough force to knock Jeffrey into a crumpled heap on the kitchen floor.

Erik was on him in a flash, the barrel of the gun jammed into Jeffrey's back as he grabbed Jeffrey's wrist, twisting it behind his back and pinning him to the ground. Jeffrey failed to resist, and Erik realized he was out cold. He must've hit him harder than he thought.

Erik quickly jammed the pistol between his belt and the small of his back and grabbed the other wrist, pinning them both behind Jeffrey's back. He held them firm with one hand as he scanned the empty kitchen for something he could use to secure them. His heart dropped when nothing presented itself. Finally, he settled with pulling a shoelace free from one of Jeffrey's shoes. He secured Jeffrey's wrists in makeshift handcuffs deciding they'd have to do while he searched the house for something better.

Erik took off one of Jeffrey's socks and shoved it into Jeffrey's slack mouth. He rushed upstairs to Jeffrey's room and found the door locked. He jiggled the doorknob in disbelief. Why would the room be locked? Erik pushed against the door, testing its strength. It rattled in the door frame making Erik think the lock was more symbolic than preventative. He took a step back and launched a front push kick against the door just next to the handle. His foot passed right through the cheap wood and Erik barely managed to keep his balance.

He hopped on one foot as he tried to pull his foot back through the hole. At the same time, Jeffrey's phone vibrated in his pocket. Erik managed to pulled it out of his pocket, doing his best to balance on one foot while he unlocked it. It was a text from someone named Chudy. Polish for skinny, Erik realized. Obviously, a nickname.

"Kids not here," was all it said. Erik smiled as he texted back.

"Just got a call from the kid, got scared and hopped a bus back to his apartment."

Erik knew it'd be a decently long drive for them to get from where Jeffrey had sent them to his apartment.

"Going to kill this skurwielu," was the rapid response.

Erik's blood ran cold as he read the text. He wasn't sure what a skurwielu was, but that part didn't matter. Were they really going to kill him, just like they'd killed Victor?

Erik forced himself to put the phone away and focus on his trapped leg instead. His ruse wouldn't keep them busy forever, he needed to get as far away from Jeffrey's as he could before they figured it out. Erik jimmied his leg free, taking large chunks of the door with it, and reached back through the hole he'd made and unlocked the doorknob.

Erik pushed open the door and flipped on the lights revealing a room full of stacked, plastic boxes. "What the hell?" Erik muttered as he approached one and popped the lid off. He peered inside and let out an involuntary gasp.

The box was filled with tightly wrapped bricks of what Erik could only guess were drugs. Heroin? "Holy…" Erik exclaimed as he moved on to the next box and revealed more of the same. Erik had little knowledge of drugs, but it sure looked like heroin to him, or at least, what Hollywood portrayed it to look like.

This is a stash house, Erik realized, the alarm bells ringing. Erik moved on to one of the bigger plastic boxes, more rectangular than square. He popped off the top and revealed a gleaming row of rifles, neatly packaged away. Boxes of ammo lined the front of the box.

"Jesus," Erik muttered. He turned his attention away from the guns and opened the sliding closet door next to them. Inside, he found shelves lined with all kinds of goodies; ammo for the pistol he carried in the small of his back, loaded clips for it, a series of knives, big to small zip ties, duct tape, rope, a roll of plastic sheeting, rolls of money, hack saws and other menacing things Erik could only imagine the purpose for. Erik took one look at it all and knew exactly the fate they had planned for him. They *were* going to kill him and then simply make him disappear.

Erik should have been terrified, but he wasn't. Instead, he felt calm. The fear gnawed at his edges, but he refused it entry. He was in control. They didn't know where he was, what he knew. He held the cards. He had a name, a face. Finally.

"I can beat this," Erik stated out loud. The confidence in his words ringing in his ears. "I can do this," he reiterated more softly.

Erik gathered up the supplies from the closet, shoving the loaded clips and rolls of money into his hoodie pockets, slipping a medium sized pocketknife into his pant pocket and a much smaller one into his sock, wedging it in his shoe. It wasn't very comfortable, but the feel of it gave him solace. He gathered up the zip ties and duct tape and went back downstairs.

Jeffrey groaned softly on the floor, coming to, but not fully aware yet. Erik rushed up to him with abandon and sat down hard on his lower back. Jeffrey coughed out the air in his lungs with a gratifying whoosh. Erik grabbed both of his legs and wrapped the roll of duct tape around them. Once, twice, thrice, and a fourth time for good measure.

"Get off of me!" Jeffrey eventually wheezed; the words barely intelligible from behind the sock in his mouth. Erik smiled as Jeffrey tried to work the shoelace handcuffs. Erik had put slip knots on them so that when Jeffrey pulled, they tightened.

Jeffrey's flesh bulged around the tight bonds as he tightened them more and more. His hands turned bright red before Erik felt sorry for him and fashioned him a zip tie set of cuffs and applied them. He took out the knife he'd stuffed into his pocket and cut the shoelace free, allowing circulation back to Jeffrey's swollen hands.

"I should have left those," he whispered in Jeffrey's ear.

"Bastard," was Jeffrey's barely intelligible response.

Erik laughed merrily as he rose from his seat on Jeffrey's back. He rolled Jeffrey over and grimaced at the dark and bloody evidence of his final pistol whipping. A massive purple bump jutted out from the side of Jeffrey's face; a slow stream of blood leaked from its bulbous peak. The wound had swelled to the point that Jeffrey's right eye was but a slit.

"We're going to kill you, boy," Jeffrey said, finally working his sock out of his mouth. "You're already dead. Just like your scumbag grandpa." Jeffrey smiled a ghastly smile, made all the more haunting by the blood slicking each cheek.

Erik surged forward and that smile slipped as Erik shoved the sock back into his mouth and wrapped duct tape around Jeffrey's mouth, wrapping the roll around the back of his head and around the mouth a second time. Erik stood up and regarded Jeffrey with a frown.

"That's gonna be a bitch to get off. Good luck." Erik turned and walked out of the kitchen, Jeffrey's duct tape muffled screams nothing more than ambient noise in the wake of the victor.

Erik walked down the hallway towards the back door, retrieved his shoes, and transferred the pistol magazines and money from his hoodie to his backpack. He slipped the backpack around his shoulders and pushed the back door open, a gust of chilled air rushing past him into the townhouse. He walked into the night, calmer than he had a right to be. He didn't know where he was going, just that his enemies had even less of an idea than he did. He took comfort in that, letting the realization wrap around him like a bulletproof blanket.

As Erik left the neighborhood, being sure to stick to the shadows, he pulled out Jeffrey's phone and dialed 911.

"911, what is your emergency?"

"Yes, I think my neighbor is in trouble. I heard screaming and what sounded like a fight. Possibly a gun shot. Please send someone as soon as you can!" Erik rattled off Jeffrey's address and hung up the phone, popped off the back and pulled out the sim card. He tossed it into the bed of a pick-up truck as he walked by and then shoved the phone into his backpack. He pulled out his own phone and quickly checked his notifications.

One new text. Kelsey. "Hey, whatcha doin?"

Erik's smile held the tendrils of pain within it as he responded. "Thinking about you. I'll try to call later."

And then he popped off the back and removed his own sim card, shoving it into a small pocket in his backpack along with his phone. *No reason to take risks*, Victor agreed.

A few minutes later, the ring of police sirens broke the nights quiet calm. Erik smiled to himself as he continued down the shadow-enshrouded sidewalk.

Chapter 44

THE MORNING SUN found Erik still on the street. He'd decided it was safer for him to be homeless rather than bring someone else into his chaos. Sifting around that stash house had really opened his eyes to the gravity of his situation, confirmed his worst fears. Those guys were serious. Real players in the underworld. True criminals like you see on TV or in the movies. Drugs, guns, stash houses. They'd murdered Victor. Why wouldn't they murder him? Especially now? How much money had they lost in that stash house? Of course, Jeffrey would tell them who was to blame.

Erik couldn't decide if he'd improved his lot or made his situation even worse. So, he walked, just following where his feet led, unsure of where they were taking him but sure that he needed to stay on the move. He passed an electronics store and stopped. He gazed through the front window at a display of single use cell phones. Burners. He thought about the two phones in his bag, no SIM cards inside, cut off from the world, from anyone who might be trying to track his location. They couldn't do that with a burner, he realized. Erik popped inside and bought two phones, both single use phones with a finite number of minutes and data on them.

"Perfect," he said to himself as he continued his aimless journey down the cold city streets.

His next stop was a coffee shop. He paid for his breakfast and a giant coffee with the cash from the stash house and found a table in the back corner, near the side exit, just as he had the day before at a different coffee shop. Another life, he thought to himself. So much had changed in just twenty-four hours. He'd gone from paranoid to sure, from what might be to what was. It was a scary and sudden metamorphosis.

He placed his back to the wall and pulled out his personal phone. He scrolled through it and transferred the important contacts to his burner. Satisfied with his progress, Erik pulled up Kincaid's contact info, pushing call. The phone rang a few times before it was abruptly picked up.

"Kincaid."

"Detective. It's Erik... Brown. There's been some developments."

"You OK, kid?" Erik detected genuine concern in her voice and relaxed just a hair.

"Yeah, I'm safe. Listen, Jeffrey Grant tried to abduct me. Him and the two goons that have been following me."

"What? Who?" Kincaid's voice rang with alarm and Erik relaxed another hair.

"Guy I was going to for grief counseling. Jeffrey Grant. Claimed to be my grandpa's counselor after my grandma died, so I trusted him. I think my dad was seeing him too. Anyway, I went to him thinking no one would think to look for me at his place. I barely even knew him for God's sake. It turns out he was a plant from the jump—"

"A plant?" Kincaid interrupted. "Whoa, time out, take me to the beginning."

"Sure," Erik said with a sigh, not really wanting to relive his trauma. "Grant approached me the day Victor was murdered. He was waiting for me to get the news or something. Shadowing me at the gym. I forgot my phone in the locker room and he brought it out to me. He said he was a therapist. I blew him off until everything started to heat up and I thought I was losing my mind.

Remember how I told you about a guy named Gerry at Victor's funeral? Turns out he works for him. His real name is Gerwazy Zatorski. They killed Victor, Jeffrey admitted to it, said I was next unless I helped them find something. That's all I could get out of him before I had to disappear. The other two guys are still looking for me. I called their stash house into the police, so I'm guessing they're real pissed at me right now."

The silence stretched out for a few seconds before Kincaid cleared her throat on the other end. "What was the address?" Erik rattled it off and waited for her to respond. "You sure that's right?"

"Yeah, why?"

"I have no report on a case at that address, that's why."

"What? That's impossible, I called it in. I heard the sirens. I left Jeffrey tied up in the kitchen!" Panic filled Erik, trickling through his extremities as it boiled over in his mind. His breath came in short wheezes as his chest restricted. Erik became aware of curious eyes turned in his direction and realized he'd yelled that last bit. His cheeks flushed, the distraction proving just enough for him to regain control and push the overwhelming feeling of terror out of his mind. No fear. No fear.

"Nothing, kid."

And then Erik connected some dots, some big ones. "When I called in the robbery a few nights back, my grandpa's place... Victor's place... As soon as I did, the guys inside knew. Someone called them, I heard it. What if they have cops in other precincts?"

"Erik, I don't usually say this, but I think you might want to avoid the police for the time being. Something stinks. And the name, Gerwazy Zatorski? I'm not finding a damn thing in the database. Are you sure that's the right name?"

"Positive. Sounds like a Bond villain. Hard to forget. Didn't you say there was a G in the Polish mob, couldn't that be him?"

"Not much of a stretch... I'll keep digging then. Maybe the organized crime division will have more on him. Can I reach you at this number?"

"It's a burner phone," Erik responded, still lost in disbelief.

"Good. Give me until this afternoon then check in. And let me know if things change."

Erik nodded, realized Kincaid couldn't see him and said, "Yeah." The line went dead on the other end, and Erik leaned back in his seat, exhaling his disbelief in one big, slow breath.

Gerwazy, Gerry, G. Alias'? Was his real name so protected that no one knew it? Probably why Jeffrey had let it out so easily. Erik was no closer to the truth than he'd been the night before. Anger surged into his blood stream and he fought the childish urge to punch something, anything. It was a welcome replacement for the hopelessness that had been building in him.

"Screw it," Erik muttered to himself as he retrieved the scrap of paper Victor had left and typed the phone number into his new phone.

Erik hit send and held it to his ear, the tendrils of a plan whipping in the breeze, in the hurricane within his head. The phone rang, and rang, and rang. Erik started to worry that the man behind the voice was gone, that he'd missed any opportunity of using the clue to its full advantage. He silently cursed himself and was about to hang up when a loud click sounded, and the ringing stopped.

"Hello?" Erik stammered into the silence.

"Erik Brown. New number? Haven't seen you in a bit..." The voice was arrogant, raising Erik's hackles.

"Who are you?" Erik responded, finding a corner of courage to grasp on to.

"Per Larssen, I thought." Erik could picture the smile those words emanated from and wanted to punch it. For a moment, he marveled at how much emotion could come from such a simple sentence.

"I know who Per Larssen is. He's dead, so who are you? Or will your handlers even let you tell me?"

Laughter bubbled through the phone and Erik shifted in his seat, pushing down his discomfort. The man had practically admitted they weren't watching him as of now. Nothing to fear, he thought.

"Let me tell you what I do know, spook." Silence greeted him so he just plowed forward. "Per Larssen was a resistance fighter in Norway during World War Two. He was recruited by the US government thereafter. He did some work behind the iron curtain and had his cover blown. He stole something off of some guy named Gerwazy Zatorski, pissed him off real good and had to disappear. He faked his death, or just didn't let the US government know he was still alive and lived out the rest of his life in hiding. That is, until Zatorski caught up with him and murdered him on his own front step. Per Larssen was my grandfather, Victor Brown. The real Victor Brown, Viktor Braut, died during the war, but no one really paid attention to that. Now, Zatorski is after me because he thinks I know something I don't."

More silence greeted Erik, but the line didn't go dead. Erik prayed his bullshit was at least close to the truth. It was a shot in the dark, just expanding on the little he knew. He waited for a response that didn't come, and finally succumbed to the urge to fill the silence. "I figured the US government might be interested in that little story. Maybe I was wrong." Erik was about to hang up when the voice finally sounded.

"We should meet." That was all he said as the silence returned, lingering like the smell of a dead animal entombed in the wall.

"OK," Erik said.

"6:00 p.m., Washington park. I'll find you. Come alone and be smart. You've awoken a sleeping dragon, Erik Brown."

The line cut off and Erik was left holding the phone to his ear trying to decide if that last part was a threat or a statement of fact.

Erik let the question fade from mind and checked his watch.

9:45 a.m.

That gave him plenty of time to stake out the meeting location, and if the mystery man was going to find him, Erik could dictate where he was to be found. Erik realized he held more cards than he thought as he poured over the possibilities.

Chapter 45

ERIK WAS AT the park by 12:30 p.m., disguised in his hoodie, sunglasses, and a couple days growth of stubble on his cheeks. His Viking ancestry served him well as the scratchy whiskers grew in thick. At first, Erik simply walked the perimeter of the park, scouting out the best place to sit and wait for the mystery man to make contact. He decided it should be somewhere public but also secluded. Somewhere where the mystery man could be spotted coming, or anyone else for that matter.

Erik found a park bench outside the restrooms and considered it. The bench faced out on to the grass lawn, the brick walls of the restroom not far behind it. It would be hard for someone to sneak up on him, especially if Erik were to add some gravel to the concrete behind the bench. The only problem was it was too out in the open. A milieu of pedestrians made for a constant obstacle as they passed within earshot of the bench. Also, he'd be a sitting duck for a long-range rifle, dead before anyone heard the shot, the shooter gone before anyone realized he was down. No, the bench wouldn't work. He had to find something better.

Erik continued his search, entering the park proper. He walked the concrete path that wound its way through the playground and the soccer fields, into and out of the patches of trees that dotted the lawn. Finally, Erik came to a somewhat secluded, graffiti and trash filled tunnel. Dried leaves crunched under his feet as he wandered into the short tunnel, the crunch echoing down the length of it. He stopped in the middle and looked from one end to the other. A bend in the landscaping on both sides made it difficult to set up a long-range shooting location. Not impossible but the shooter would have to be in the berm, out in the open. Erik would see him coming.

Light traffic trickled by him as he leaned against the stone wall. The scraping metallic roar of skateboards echoed around him as kids on skateboards raced by, paying him little to no attention. The panting stomp of runners, their breath ringing out in the tempo of their feet, headphones just loud enough in their ears for the murmur of music to reach Erik as they passed. For the most part, all were oblivious to him. His only concern for prying ears were those of the mothers pushing their strollers silently through the tunnel, but the coo of babies or the mother's soft praise would be enough to alert him to their presence.

The spot would do, Erik decided as he pushed his back against the cool stone to propel himself forward into a standing position. One of the bricks wiggled against his weight prompting him to turn around and push on it. It gave a little, the mortar around it crumbling a bit at the pressure. An idea blossomed in Erik's mind and he ran his fingers along the brick masonry of the wall as he walked towards one of the entrances, walking until he found a loose brick that nearly fell out of the wall. He looked around himself first, making sure no one was watching, and pried the brick out with little effort. Erik stuck his hand in and measured the holes depth. He put the brick in his bag and walked out of the tunnel.

A few minutes later, Erik found himself at a mom-and-pop hardware store across the street from the park's gated entrance. The shop looked like it had been there a long time. The signs old and tattered, the shoulder high shelving dinged and scratched to hell by years of use and abuse. The single room of the shop had the smell of an old book, at the same time oily and woody, with a hint of something metallic. Circular mirrors dotted the corners of the room so the cashier could watch customers browse without standing behind them. Erik took in the shop with a single glance. He landed on the bored cashier who took his eyes off of his magazine for just enough time to acknowledge Erik before returning to the fine print on the page. Erik pulled out the brick and approached the man.

"Hey, weird question. Can you cut this brick for me? I'm on a job down the way and my saw broke on me. Last piece too. What luck, right?" Erik laughed.

The cashier smiled up at Erik and shrugged. "One of those days, huh?"

"Don't you know it!"

"Follow me, let's see what we can do."

The cashier lead Erik towards the back of the store, stopping at a wall of used tools. "Usually, you'd have to rent the angle grinder, but seeing as you only have one brick left to cut, we can cut you some slack."

"Really appreciate that," Erik said handing the brick to the man with a thankful smile.

The man pulled down the angle grinder, plugged it into the wall. "How much you want to take off?" The man said, pulling down a small framing square.

Erik measured the amount with his hand, using his knuckles to gauge the depth he'd measured back in the tunnel. "That ought to be good," he said letting the cashier mark the spot with a pencil.

"Interesting way to measure," the man laughed. "Must not be too tight a fit we're going for here."

Erik shrugged. "What can I say, I'm ready to go home."

The man laughed as he used the square to draw a line down the brick's length. "Plug your ears," he cautioned. The grinder roared to life and he lowered it to the line, cutting through it without any apparent effort, the debris bag attached to it sucking in most of the dust the grinder created.

The cashier handed the brick back with a flourish. "Easy peasy."

"You're a life saver. Thank you!"

"No problem," the man said with a proud smile. "Just do me a favor and make us your preferred hardware store from now on."

"You got it!" Erik promised.

Within no time, Erik was back at the tunnel. He looked both ways before pulling Jeffrey's gun from his backpack. He stuffed it into the hole he'd revealed and shoved the brick back into place. It jutted out a fraction of an inch to Erik's delight. Just enough for him to see it, but not enough for anyone to think twice.

Erik smiled as his plan slowly started to take shape. He left the tunnel and proceeded to walk around the park, familiarizing himself with an escape plan, multiple escape plans. If he had to run, he wanted options. After an hour or so, he had them. He made sure that they all ran back to the same location, a bus stop where he pulled his burner phone and a small wad of cash out of his backpack before shoving it into a locker.

He took the key and walked away, head on a swivel. No one seemed to notice him, and no one looked familiar to him. He walked about a block away before turning down an empty alley, slowing his pace as he eyed the space. Finally, Erik saw what he was looking for. He walked up to an empty dumpster. He did a circle around it, checked his surroundings and stashed the locker key in the hollow where the trash collector's arms went to lift the dumpster and empty it.

If the mystery man patted him down, he'd only find the money and a phone, and if Erik had to run, his bag was safe, so long as he could get back to it. Erik checked his watch.

3:13 p.m.

What was he going to do for the next two and a half hours?

Chapter 46

ERIK FOUND HIMSELF in a tiny, hole in the wall diner. The dining area had the floral smell of scented soap, and the way the floor glistened, Erik figured they'd just mopped. It was a seat yourself affair, so Erik took one of the booths in the back, sitting on the side that faced the door. He guessed the other exit was through the kitchen door just on the other side of the seat across from him. If he was in a pinch, he would rush it and disappear into the clamor of bubbling pots and hissing fryers and use the alley to disappear.

Erik was thinking about his escape when a middle-aged waitress sauntered up to him, a plastic smile stamped across her face. The smile said hello, but her body language screamed, "Get me out of here!"

"Hey sugar, anything to drink?" Her voice sounded as if it had been turned to gravel through years of cigarette use and Erik figured she was likely younger than she appeared.

He ordered a water, a sandwich and a heaping plate of fries. It arrived in no time, taking just as much time as the fries needed to cook. Erik wolfed the sandwich down and started to do the same with the fries until the grease hit his stomach and it rejected the intrusion into his otherwise clean diet. Erik pushed the majority of the fries away, wishing he'd stuck with a salad. He checked his watch and thought about Victor.

"Nice watch," the waitress said as she dropped the check off at the table.

"Thanks," Erik responded, fishing a twenty out of his pocket. "Keep the change."

"Thanks, sweetie. Have a good one." The waitress retreated towards the kitchen and Erik returned his gaze to his watch, forcing Victor from his thoughts.

Almost five. Time to head back to the park. Time to get his head on straight.

Erik found a bench at the edge of the park, one with a view of most of the grassy lawn, playgrounds, even the tunnel where he'd stashed his gun. He started watching the people spread out below him. The park was much busier than when he'd been there earlier, but most people were getting off work, so he wasn't surprised. The tunnel saw few people passing through it, to his relief. Five thirty hit and Erik made his way towards it. All his precautions would be for naught if the mystery man caught up with him away from his spot.

Erik hid the relief that flooded his body when he leaned up against the wall of the tunnel, the pistol hidden just an arm's length from him. He ran over how he'd retrieve it in his mind, playing out scenario after scenario just like Victor had taught him.

"Always be thinking. Prepare for anything. Imagine what you'd do if an armed assailant burst through the door. Where's your exit? What if you're cornered?" Victor believed that preparation started in the mind. Visualize what you'd do if something happened and you're that much more likely to be ready to do it.

Erik leaned his shoulder against the wall and let his hand settle as naturally as he could manage on the loose brick. He imagined the meeting going wrong and pulling the brick out in one fluid motion, throwing it at his assailant, distracting him just long enough to retrieve the gun. It sounded silly in his head, but he convinced himself that someone not looking for it wouldn't have time to react. Erik's heart raced as he played the image over and over in his head, familiarizing himself with the actions and the various fall outs. He'd already plotted his escape in multiple directions. He was ready.

The crunch of leaves brought Erik back to himself, his eyes darting to an older woman with a cane that had entered the tunnel, walking towards him. He smiled at her, willing away his sudden burst of nerves, and she smiled back as she shuffled by.

"Pay attention," Erik mouthed to himself, chastising himself for gathering wool. He checked his watch.

5:52 p.m.

The mystery man could appear at any moment.

Erik shook the fantasy from his mind, letting it drip into his subconscious where he hoped his brain would continue to refine it and regurgitate it at a moment's notice. He put his head on a swivel and really started to watch the approach of everyone who entered the tunnel. When the mystery man arrived, Erik knew it without a doubt.

The man wore a lose jacket, too heavy for the mild weather. Erik guessed it hid the shape of a gun. He wore a baseball hat pulled low and oversized sunglasses. The collar of his coat was turned up and he shrugged his shoulders to allow the lower part of his face to disappear into it.

Erik watched his approach from the corner of his eye, making sure no one as similarly obvious was approaching from the other side. The only thing he saw was a teenager doing flip tricks on his skateboard, but he'd been there since before Erik arrived. Erik forced himself to stay relaxed as the man closed the distance between them. He turned his full attention to the man when there were just a few feet between them. The man smiled, coming to a stop.

"That obvious, huh?" It was the voice from the phone, a chill surging down Erik's back.

"Dressed to hide your identity, not for the weather. You armed?"

The man's smirk deepened. "Are you?"

"No," Erik responded, opening his unzipped hoodie, lifting his shirt and doing a graceful twirl for the man.

The man's grin deepened, and Erik feared he'd be looking down the barrel of a gun at any moment. Time slowed down as his adrenaline spiked, and he nearly went for the brick, but the gun never materialized.

"Let's walk and talk," the man suggested.

"Nope, I'm good right here." That got a laugh from the mystery man.

"Why, so you can be near your gun?" The man's words froze Erik and his eyes darted to his hiding spot. "Aw, so that's where it is. Smart move, Erik. I figured you had it hidden somewhere nearby."

Erik fought the despair creeping up his back, forcing himself to be more confident than he really was. "Smart move. Played me good. Mind if I retrieve it? Level the playing field?"

"Go right ahead, Erik. If we wanted you dead, you would've been the moment you stepped into this park."

Erik didn't turn his back to the man as he reached for the brick, removing it and letting it drop to the concrete. He pulled the pistol free and shoved it behind his belt, letting his hoodie fall over it.

"You're a lot smarter than we gave you credit for. My colleagues had their doubts, but I knew. Why would a scared college kid show up to a meeting five and a half hours early? They said nerves, I said he's casing the place. When you chose the tunnel I thought, that's where I would've gone. What else do you have up your sleeve? I'm curious…"

"Why'd you want to meet? Cuz I don't care what you think about me. I'm here for one reason. Information. If you don't have any, I'll be on my way." Erik's pulse drummed in his ears, but he kept his face calm, forced any signs of his anxiety to lie dormant. He'd always been a good poker player; Victor had been sure to teach him how to bluff.

"Ballsy, Erik. You really think you're in control? Snap of my fingers and I'm not alone."

"You're not alone right now," Erik smiled. "Unless you expect me to believe the skateboarder isn't with you." Erik turned to the skateboarder and waved. "A little rusty, aren't you? Been a while since you last skated, huh?"

The skater's eyes darted to the mystery man. Awaiting orders, Erik thought. Erik turned back to the mystery man and allowed his smile to deepen as he waved the skateboarder off. "I'm fine, Max. He's not a threat." Max nodded and quickly skated away, probably to rejoin his colleagues in the oversized van Erik had noted in his walk around the park.

"Not like they can't hear you right now anyway."

The man smiled again. "See? Much smarter than we gave you credit for."

"Who are you?" Erik responded.

"Not necessary," the man shrugged.

"Is to me," Erik retorted.

"Fine," the man lamented. "Call me John. John Smith." His smile was ear to ear and Erik fought the urge to punch him, realizing it wouldn't end in his favor. Who knew how many people still lurked around them, waiting to intervene? *Where there's one, there's many*, Victor warned.

"Fine. Why are we here? What'd you want to say to me? You called this meeting after all."

"I did. See, I figured it was time to connect some dots. At first, we didn't know what we had. You see, Victor Brown wasn't someone we knew about, so it rattled some people when some dumb kid called saying he left him Per Larssen's number. Per Larssen. See, that's a name with some weight. No one outside the company knows that name, or so we thought.

"Per Larssen. Recruited out of the Norwegian resistance fighters at the end of the war. Turned out he was really good with explosives and had ice in his veins. Rumor had it he was interrogated by the Gestapo on multiple occasions but was able to get out of the shit every time. Smooth talker, reliable. Single-minded in his hatred of the Nazis. Turned out his dad was a commando that'd escaped to England during the invasion. Ended up making things difficult for the Nazis at the end of the war with William Colby. You know who that is?"

Erik shook his head no.

"Of course not. Well, you should. He ran the CIA at one point. Anyway, Sver Larssen didn't make it, but Colby didn't forget what he'd done and when he found out Per was a fighter, orphaned by the Nazis, well, he decided to take him in, in a sense." John Smith paused, his lips turning up in a smirk. "Ain't it something? Me telling you about your grandpa?" He broke into a laughter Erik didn't appreciate.

"He couldn't tell us, asshole. He was too busy protecting us." Erik's rush of anger channeled into his words and nipped that laughter in the bud.

"OK, OK. Take it easy. Didn't mean any offense. Where was I?"

"My grandfather was taken in by William Colby..." Erik was growing more irritated, word after word. The mystery man was taking too much delight in stringing out the story. Erik wanted answers and this guy was skirting them.

"Right. I can't give you the details, but Larssen ended up in Poland. His work there was something else. They write lectures based off that shit, real spy shit. Need to know stuff, so when you called, we all wondered, how'd you get the number and how'd you know about Larssen? Our first conversation didn't illuminate much." Smith caught the confused look on Erik's face and laughed. "Oh yeah. You don't really remember that do you?"

It didn't take much effort for Erik to realize Smith was admitting to drugging him only nights before. "So, it was you," he growled, his fists clenched at his sides.

"Nothing personal, Erik. Company business. Someone makes contact on an old company line, spouting a dead spy's name? Gotta check it out." Smith's grin thickened and Erik allowed a fantasy of him breaking Smith's teeth to play in the background while he reasserted his calm.

"Who's Gerwazy Zatorski?" The smile slipped from Smith's lips as the reality of things caught up with him.

"I was getting there," he murmured, all his previous humor evaporated. "He was a party boss in Poland. Real sicko, took the lessons the Gestapo taught him to heart. Young for a party man, but when you stand up to the Nazis and live to tell about it, sky's the limit. Larssen was greasing him at the time. Word is he fell in love with Gerwazy's girl. Shit got hectic and Larssen's cover got blown. That's the last we heard of Per Larssen. His star is on the memorial wall in Langley and so ends his legend, until now. Did some digging after we spoke. Your grandma was Marga?"

"So?"

"Funny thing. Was a Marga associated with Gerwazy. Margarete Lupinski. Pretty close to your grandma's name, right? Margarete, Margarita… Yeah, that's what we thought. Got us to thinking," Smith paused and locked eyes with Erik, drawing out the moment, toying with Erik. "We think your old man's old man stole her away. Stole Gerwazy's woman right out from under him and disappeared with her. Poof. Until Gerwazy caught up to him, few years too late it'd seem, and put a round in his head. Case closed, kid. You already know more than you should, go home and let life go back to normal."

"Would if I could," Erik said from behind clenched teeth, "but Gerwazy wants something else. I don't know why they killed my grandfather before getting it, but they think I have it now. They're gonna kill me unless they get it. One of em told me that before I knocked him out. Tried to give him to the police but turns out the cops are dirty. Let the guy walk and you better bet he told Gerwazy I was the one that fingered his stash house." Erik paused, letting his words sink in. "Turns out you don't know any more than I do about that, huh? Same with the police. Gerwazy doesn't even pop up in their database. So, now my question is what do you know about him? Because I'm a dead man if I can't get in front of this."

Smith let out a slow whistle and shook his head. "Tough break, Erik. Wish I could help, but as far as we're concerned, Gerwazy Zatorski disappeared shortly after the iron curtain fell. If he's still operating, it's under a different name. Crazy, the guy must be in his nineties by now. What I can do is tell you about the Polish mob, but I doubt it's gonna make you feel too good.

"They've been operating in this area for a handful of years. Used to be all Russian territory and those Russians, woo-wee! They're a mean bunch of bastards but turns out the Poles are meaner. All of a sudden, they started finding dead Russians all over the place, third eyes in their foreheads, pretty obvious shit really. Started hearing chatter about some psycho that was cutting them up, leaning on their guys, stealing their dope. Isn't named Gerwazy though. Goes by the name Konstantyn. But here's the thing, he ain't the boss. No one knows who the boss is. Wouldn't be a stretch of the imagination to think that might be Gerwazy. Fits with his past MO anyway." Smith paused before going on, deciding how much to tell Erik, how much he thought Erik could handle.

"These boys don't mess around. Once they came to town, people just started disappearing. And with the disappearances came the drugs. Heroin. If I were you, I'd just as soon disappear myself as go toe to toe with them. Well, it's been fun. Go ahead and lose that number, you won't be reaching anyone there anymore. Good luck, I'll try to keep tabs."

"Why don't the police know all this?" Erik asked, just able to hide the waiver in his voice.

"Cuz, they own the police, Erik. They own judges, politicians. Any investigation that's permitted doesn't get too far, if you catch my drift. Forget Gerwazy's name, it'll just get you killed."

"And why don't you do anything about it?"

"And how would I do that? I'm not even here," Smith laughed. "But hey, if you're dead set on suicide, there's a shop on 7th and North. Seems to always be a black sedan parked out front. Might be worth checking out… if you're suicidal of course."

With that, Smith just walked away. Erik fought to keep his jaw in place, but it dropped anyway. He couldn't believe all that had just happened. His adrenaline still coursed through his veins, but the effect dissipated quickly, and he was left with a feeling of numbness. Another dead end, Erik lamented as he turned and walked out of the tunnel. He ran over the story Smith had given him and shook his head in disbelief. Victor *was* a spy. When he thought about it, it made complete sense. All the life lessons he'd given Erik, all the games they'd play. Victor was bored, reliving his better years with his grandson. It was so obvious when Erik thought about it. But if Victor trained Erik to be a spy, couldn't he use that? And, with a flash of realization, it dawned on him that he already had.

The days preparation washed over him, and he saw it for what it was. Even Smith had been impressed, a working spook. Tendrils of hope wormed their way into his gut, a feeling he'd not realized how much he needed. Those gangsters didn't know what they were up against. Erik had already bested them a few times. As long as he could stay out in front, he could beat them.

The feeling was gone as quickly as it had arrived. What was he thinking? These were killers! Criminals! Luck had gotten him this far, not skill. But maybe skill could get him the rest of the way. What choice did he have?

Erik took his time in retrieving his backpack, making sure that he wasn't followed. His paranoia had taken over his world and everything he did was done looking over his shoulder. He'd feared that Smith knew more than he was letting on, that he'd taken the key hidden in the dumpster, but it was undisturbed, and a thorough search of his backpack found everything where he'd left it. Erik sighed in relief and took a seat on a city bench. He pulled the hood tight around his face and took off his sunglasses, thinking about his options as the sun dipped over the city, her buildings like fingers reaching for the sky, trying to grasp a piece of the cosmos.

"What am I missing, Bestefar?" he muttered into the rapidly cooling night.

The gun felt cold, heavy in the small of his back, but the feel of it gave him comfort. He'd never killed a man, never even aimed a gun at someone, just Jeffrey, but Victor had been sure to take him hunting, forced him to dress his own kill, get his hands dirty. Probably a big reason why blood and gore didn't faze him. It made him an ideal medical student. In anatomy lab, when the class was told to remove the top of a cadaver's skull, Erik did it without hesitation while other students hyperventilated and hesitated. He was done before some students had even started. It didn't go a long way in netting him any friends, but his teachers had been impressed.

Erik lost track of the time, sitting there in his own head, running through everything Smith had said, every question Gerry asked. He should've gotten more from Jeffrey before he ran, but did Jeffrey know anything? Erik doubted it. He'd only used Gerwazy's name like a shield against Erik's probing. Erik needed to find what Gerwazy was after and try to broker a deal to get out from under it all, reclaim his life, but if Victor's note held anymore clues, Erik was struggling to unravel them.

Erik shivered against the dropping temperature and rubbed his hands along his forearms. He tried to think of where he could go. He couldn't go to his family. That would be putting them in danger, plus they were probably already being watched as well. That left only one real option to escape the dawning cold, Kelsey's studio.

He pulled out his burner and tried to call her. When had it gotten so late? Erik's heart sank as the line just rang, an automated voicemail clicking on to confirm the number he'd reached and to leave a message. Erik wasn't sure what to say.

"Hey, Kelsey, it's Erik… I know it's late, but remember that friend I was staying with? Yeah, didn't work out…" Erik fought with the urge to spill the truth to her, but pulled back with a sigh. "I was wondering if it'd be cool if I crashed at your studio? Hopefully you don't live too far away… I don't know… just don't want to spend the night on the streets again. Call me back when you get this." Erik cringed against the desperation ringing so heavily in his ears.

He left the bench and began his solemn walk across the city, Jeffrey's words echoing in his head, but was he walking towards a bad part of town, or did Jeffrey just say that so Erik would accept his offer of a ride? Did it matter? The icy feel of cold, hard steel pressing up against his back with every step gave him confidence that he could handle just about any situation. His slept in, nearly homeless, appearance was doing him some favors as well. His pants were ruined, stained and fraying. His hoodie was covered in mud. He could only imagine how dirty his face was, how bad he smelled. He needed a bed and a shower, assuming Kelsey would let him stay.

Chapter 47

THE SUN HAD fully set, the icy claws of cold, fall wind raking at his cheeks, exploiting the thin fabric of his slacks as if they were a lace negligee by the time Erik found himself in the neighborhood where Kelsey's studio was. The hidden lines of one neighborhood into the next couldn't have been starker. On one side of the road, a little everyday discarded trash gathered in the gutter, whereas when Erik set foot on the opposite sidewalk the ripe scent of unwashed bodies cascaded down the opening of a nearby alleyway. He'd been so enthralled with his own worries, scanning faces and keeping up with Kelsey's questions that he hadn't noticed the barred windows, the cracked stoops leading out from rundown buildings, the overflowing trash cans.

Erik shuffled by the prone bodies of homeless men and women hidden under layers of blankets and clothes, their worldly possessions gathered in a shopping cart just within arm's reach. Soft snores were like a sad symphony resonating from the benches and gutters, stoops and walkways. Erik hoped Kelsey was never at her studio after the sun went down. As Jeffrey had warned him, the neighborhood was rough. Thoughts of Jeffrey warred with memories of his afternoon with Kelsey, creating a jumble of emotions that vied for Erik's attention.

He shook it off and turned his attention outward. As Erik pressed deeper into the neighborhood, the more his surroundings began to change. From the homeless to the restless, as groups of people began to pop up, jamming the front steps of apartment buildings, smoking cigarettes crowded around benches. The sounds were at odds with the dilapidated buildings. The people laughed and joked, sang, played music. It was like some strange night club unrestrained by brick and mortar. If anyone paid him any mind, they didn't voice it as he glided silently by, his hood pulled over his eyes, his hands jammed into his hoodie pockets.

Erik continued his solemn trek through the city he'd never known, his eyes scanning the buildings, hoping to find the landmarks he was seeking, something that told him he was close. He stopped on the corner of a four way stop and gazed up at one of the buildings, the sign running along its side immediately familiar to him. The Sydney, in its glittering gold lettering. It was a sign that promised so much more than the building offered, Erik had no doubt. He could hear Kelsey's musical laughter as he walked by, a smile turning the corners of his mouth.

"You lost?" Growled a deep voice, bringing Erik out of his reverie.

Erik snapped back into himself and found a group of men standing just off to the side of the dirty concrete sidewalk. Erik's eyes scanned the grim faces, not sure who'd asked the question.

"What you looking at, bitch?" One of them called out to Erik.

Erik lifted his hands up in response and shuffled backwards a step, keeping his tongue still while he did his best impression of a junkie. He made his eyes stare forward, willing them to gloss over as if he wasn't sure if the men were real or not. He worked his jaw, chewing on his tongue as if it were too big for his mouth, hoping it would explain his silence to the group. He stumbled over his own feet, managing to keep his balance, just barely. He'd seen enough drug addicts while working in the hospital. He was fairly certain he could mimic them.

"Leave him alone! Probably doesn't even see us right now!"

"Junkies, man. I fuckin hate em," another man said. "Stain on our neighborhood."

The person Erik could only guess was his aggressor just watched Erik back away, his expression never changing. Erik was convinced he was going to do something but as the distance increased between them the man turned back to his friends.

"Man, fuck that guy, coming into our neighborhood all fucked up," he growled to his friends and turned his head up at Erik in disdain.

"So, mess him up then! Send him packing."

Erik's apprehension soared as the man turned back to regard him. "Nah, he ain't worth my time, plus, you ever knocked down a crack head? They just jump right back up!"

"Man! That ain't even your joke!"

"Shut up, *Calvin*." The group roared in laughter and Erik beat a hasty retreat. Last thing he needed was a fight, although it might shake the rust off of his training.

"You're a joke thief! That's all I'm saying!"

Erik slipped into the dark and left the men behind him. It didn't take long after the confrontation for him to locate Kelsey's studio building. He tried the front door, but it proved to be locked. He tried buzzing the studio, hoping it was the right number as much as he hoped she might be there. There was no response and Erik's heart sank. He checked his phone, but if Kelsey had gotten his message, she hadn't responded. He needed to get out of the cold. He needed a cup of water, a shower and a toilet. He didn't care in which order but as far as he could discern, Kelsey was home, wherever that was.

Erik sighed, his stress weighing him down like a concrete vest. He looked around, made sure no one was watching and pulled his lock pick set from his backpack. He crouched down on one knee and went to work on the old lock. He had it sprung in no time to his own surprise. He pushed the door open and made sure it clicked shut behind him. The warm air of the building enveloped him like a down blanket and a tiny piece of his stress slid off his shoulders like melting ice.

He removed his hood and beanie and checked his hair in the reflection of the row of metallic mailboxes dotting one wall of the dimly lit lobby. He made himself look as normal as possible, straightening his clothes as best he could, frowning at his stained and ruined slacks before mounting the winding stairs. Kelsey's studio was on the second floor, at least he hoped. When he'd left the other day, he hadn't expected he'd be back so soon, or without Kelsey's permission. The thought made him feel like a dog, but he quickly pushed it aside. He was doing what he had to do. She'd understand, if he ever got to tell her.

He reached what he was pretty sure was her studio and smiled after spotting the little floral design painted around the peep hole. Definitely her studio, he thought as he wrapped his knuckles on the door in a soft knock. He was greeted by silence and his guilt subsided. She'd never know he was there.

Erik had a quick look around and saw no one. He crouched to one knee and started picking the lock. Nerves made his fingers stumble through the distantly familiar process and it took way longer for the gratifying click to sound. Erik went to work on the deadbolt and found it equally elusive. His adrenaline spiked as the time ticked by, his position becoming ever more precarious. He'd foolishly approached his current position without a well thought out escape plan. If he was caught, well, he could always just run for it. He could be down the stairs and out the front door before the dispatcher even picked up the 911 call. What if they had a gun? The thought made him shake off all other thoughts and focus on the lock.

Finally, it gave. Erik stood up like a rocket, shouldered his backpack while giving the hallway a quick scan and pushed the door open. He entered the dark studio and turned to close the door with a quiet grace that belied his crime. As soon as the door clicked shut, he reached to lock the dead bolt but before his hand found the metal knob, a blunt object found the side of his head.

Erik grunted in response, marveling at how quickly the feeling in his legs had disappeared. He crumpled like a paper bag, collapsing in on himself. His head smacked against the front door with a thud and the blunt object found his shoulder, nearly deflecting off of it and back into his head. The object whooshed by and Erik did his best to roll away from his attacker. All he managed to do was hit the floor and lay there, his brain sending orders to a body that wasn't listening. The object came down on Erik's leg and another grunt squeaked out of his clenched teeth, and then the light blinked on.

Erik's eyes dilated and he blinked against the sudden illumination. He tried to move but his body was still misfiring. He tried to look up at his assailant, but his vision was blurry.

"Erik?" Kelsey's voice emanated from a blob standing over him and his cheeks relaxed into a numb smile. "The hell are you doing!"

Erik heard the terror leaving her voice as anger overtook it. He wasn't sure if it was the blows he'd taken or the fact that he'd scared her, but his head hurt.

"I didn't think anyone was here," he mumbled stupidly, as if that made it all OK. "I buzzed up, knocked…"

"And I ignored that shit cuz I never open my door this late! Jesus, Erik. I almost killed you!" Erik's eyes started to adjust, and his vision cleared. Kelsey stood over him with a baseball bat, red cheeked and angry. "Did you seriously just… break into my studio!"

"I'm so sorry," Erik replied weakly. "Made me pay for it though if that's any consolation." He forced an embarrassed smile that Kelsey dismissed with an angry snort.

"It is now." She brought the bat back up and Erik flinched, throwing his hands up to protect his face. Kelsey laughed, the humor never reaching her eyes. "Now I feel better. Oh, and Erik? Get the fuck out of my studio."

Kelsey stalked away from Erik and hit the futon with a shriek. The bat bounced off the cushion and smashed into the wall, making a decent sized hole. Kelsey whirled back towards Erik, bat still in hand, and shrieked again. "See what you just made me do?"

"I can fix that," Erik mumbled as he forced himself into a sitting position, his head still swimming. He reached a hand behind his ear and found a large bump, a trickle of blood leaking out of it and dripping down on to his hoodie.

"Whacked me good," was all he could think to say as he looked at the hot blood coating his fingers in disbelief. Kelsey noticed and went white as a cloud.

"Jesus! Are you alright?"

"Sure. Probably have a nice concussion, bruising on my shoulder and leg, but sure. Other than getting the shit kicked out of me, I'm peachy." Erik tried to stand up but ended up falling forward instead and crashing back to the ground. Kelsey shrieked in surprise and was at Erik's side instantly.

"Let me help you to the bed," she offered, worry coating her words. Erik let her, and with some effort, they arrived at the futon. As soon as Erik was sitting on it, his senses went haywire once more as a hand connected with his face. "Why did you break into my apartment you shithead?!"

Erik's eyes shot open, water overwhelming his tear ducts and trickling out the corner of one eye. He opened his jaw against the burning sting on his cheek and brought a hand up to rub it. He looked up at Kelsey and saw the storm cloud had returned. She reared back to deliver another slap, but Erik raised his arm defensively to intercept it.

"Chill, Kelsey! Chill! Did you get my voicemail? Cuz that will go a long way in explaining things."

"Seriously?" She struck a no-nonsense pose, arms crossed, foot just a twitch away from tapping the floor.

"Yeah, I called. That asshole I was staying with... shit didn't work out. I needed some where to stay. When you didn't respond, well, I didn't think you'd still be here this late."

Kelsey's jaw dropped against the outrage that filled her eyes. "You didn't think I'd be at my apartment!? Why would I be anywhere else!? And I don't have any missed calls from you, and definitely no voicemails."

"Shit, new number. Didn't even think about it. No wonder you never called back." Erik laughed at his own stupidity. "Probably thought it was a telemarketer... Just check your voicemails. I swear I'm not lying."

"Regardless, why the hell did you think it was OK to break into the place I live!?"

Erik finally looked around the apartment and marveled at how stupid he'd truly been. Of course, she was living there, the mini fridge, the futon pulled out and made into a bed, dishes in the sink. Idiot, was all Erik could think.

"I'm an idiot," he said out loud.

"You think?" Kelsey said.

"I thought this was just your... art studio. I never even thought about you living here."

"Oh, because art students are typically so wealthy and can afford multiple rents."

"Yep, as I said, I'm an idiot."

"Well, I won't debate that, but that doesn't explain why you thought it'd be OK to break in! I don't even have anything worth stealing!"

Erik fought with how much of the truth he should give her. He owed her a little, at the very least. Making up his mind, he leaned forward, resting his elbows on his knees, and sighed. "Remember that guy that was blowing me up yesterday?" Kelsey nodded; her glare unrelenting. "Turned out to be a real scumbag."

"Takes one to know one," Kelsey interjected.

"Yeah, I deserve that." Erik sighed again and tried to look up at Kelsey. The light behind her hurt his eyes and he was forced to look back at the floor instead. Definitely a concussion, great. "He was supposed to be helping me out with a problem. He lied to me. Turned out to be a really bad dude," Erik said.

"Ok, how about you get to the point." Kelsey's expression hadn't changed.

"Yeah, that's a much bigger story than you think."

"Try me."

"Ok. Truth is, he's involved with the Polish mob, but I didn't know that until last night. This is going to sound unbelievable but, I was going to the guy for grief counseling and when my place became unsafe for me to stay at, I went to him, but he turned out to be working with the guys that killed my grandfather. So, when I found out, I stole a bunch of money from him and dipped. I spent last night in an alley; I didn't know what to do. I didn't want to do it again, that's for sure, so I thought I'd come find you here and see if you could help me. When you weren't here, I figured what's the harm? I'd be outta your hair before you even knew I was here."

"Wow, you're a piece of work, you know that?" Kelsey's tone made it obvious she didn't believe him. He was doing a terrible job of explaining himself and he knew it. He had to get it together or he was going to finish the night in a jail cell. Or a ditch, he thought, when he remembered there were dirty cops involved now.

"I was stupid to come here, to get you involved in this, just... please don't call the police. They have connections in the police department."

"You're not gonna give it up, are you?" Kelsey laughed to herself in disbelief. "Wow, Kelsey. Sure know how to pick em."

"I'm not lying, believe me or not, doesn't really matter. Why would you? I barely believe it myself and I'm living it." Erik deflated, unsure of what he could do to make her believe him. He channeled the stress of the last few nights and poured it into his words, finally deciding to give her his full reality.

"Kelsey. My grandfather was murdered a few weeks ago and I'm pretty sure the Polish mob was behind it. They're looking for something he took from them a long, long time ago. They think I know where it is, so they've been following me. I was able to get away from them last night, but that was after I found out Jeffrey, the guy I was staying with, was one of them. I don't expect you to believe me. I know how crazy it sounds, but look." Erik got up from the futon on wobbly legs and opened his backpack, dumping the contents out.

"Holy shit," was all Kelsey could say as she stared at the wads of money bouncing across her bed. "You're serious."

"Yes," he responded. "Listen, Kelsey. I'm not a bad guy. I'm just in a bad situation. I just need a place to crash for one night and then you never have to see me again. I promise."

Kelsey uncrossed her arms, the confrontation of her thoughts passing across her beautiful face. Her eyes were distant, staring into the corner of the room but when they finally moved and settled on Erik, he felt his breath catch. Why did he have to meet her now? Life was unfair, he concluded, the longing in his heart deepening his sorrow. Kelsey must have felt it for she crossed the small distance between them and placed a comforting hand on his shoulder.

"I want to believe you, but if you're lying to me, I'll fucking kill you, and you better believe me when I say I know how." Her words were firm, resolute. Erik had no doubt she meant them. Life truly wasn't fair, was it?

"Thank you," was all Erik managed to say into the ensuing silence, the gravity of where his life had arrived raining down on him like the first rain drops of a hurricane. His resolve splintered under the weight and fat tears rolled down his cheeks to drip off his chin and splash on to the hardwood floor. Erik buried his face in his hands and fought the emotions that roiled him.

His thoughts were a parade of the last few days, of Victor's death, the discovery of his life, the lies, the pain. He'd been a medical student, completely focused on boards as little as a week ago. Now, he was balling his eyes out in front of a beautiful woman and she didn't even know who he really was. He'd broken into her apartment! His life was a shamble, and the tears came quicker at the thought.

"Whoa, hey…" Kelsey was caught by surprise, the doubt in her mind slowly washing away with each tear that pooled on her floor. "Hey, Erik. Hey." She stepped in closer to him and grabbed his chin between both hands, lifting his face out of his hands. She forced his head up and locked eyes with him, assessing the grief she found there and deeming it real.

"They killed my grandfather," Erik let lose in a flood of grief, not sure why he needed to say it again. The sense of relief itching at the back of his skull as he finally faced the truth made him realize how much he needed to talk about it all, and so he resolved to tell her everything, in as vivid detail as she wanted, but when he attempted to unload his misery on her, Kelsey just pulled his face into her stomach and started running a hand through his hair. She winced when her hand landed on the bump behind his ear. She lifted it up and stared at the blood on her fingers.

"Jesus, Erik." That's all she said as she continued to comfort him.

Erik cried until he was empty, a small lake at his feet, Kelsey's midriff showing where her shirt had caught some of those tears. Her fingers were coated in blood trying to dry and harden.

"Let's get you into the shower." Erik nodded his consent and Kelsey helped him into the bathroom where she deposited him on the toilet seat and turned on the water in the shower. She turned back to him and started to help him out of his clothes, unzipping the hoodie and pulling his arms out of the sleeves. The icy brush of the pistol against Erik's back brought him to his senses and before Kelsey could take a hold of his shirt, he stopped her.

"Can you get me a glass of water, please? I'm so thirsty…" He'd burdened her with so much already, the gun was too much, Erik decided.

"Sure," she responded with a sad smile.

As soon as she was out of the bathroom, Erik removed it, scanning the small space for a place to stash it, finally landing on the cabinet beneath the sink. He dropped to his knees and threw it open. He was greeted by a stack of toilet paper and random cleaning supplies. He stuck his arm in as far as it would go and wedged the gun into the corner behind the cleaning supplies.

"What are you doing?" Erik spun around and looked up at Kelsey.

"I…" He had to think fast. "I was looking for some paper towel… To dab the blood with."

Kelsey smiled, taking Erik's hand and pulling him to his feet. "Don't worry about that." She pulled his shirt over his head, tossing it into the corner and tugged his belt free. "I'll take care of you."

Kelsey removed all of Erik's clothes, wincing when she revealed the bright red spots where the bat had impacted. She guided him into the shower taking a bottle of soap and a luffa and started scrubbing him down. Erik trembled against her touch. She was not gentle, and Erik couldn't blame her. He had no right to put her through any of what he just had. He had no right and they both knew it.

Erik had never felt as clean as he did when Kelsey tossed him a towel before she left, a trail of drips following her into the next room. Erik toweled off as quick as he could and joined her in the studio. She stood near the futon, her wet pajamas on the floor beside her as she wiped herself dry with a fresh towel. Erik stood in the doorway appreciating her for a time before she turned a wary eye his way.

"I'm not sure what to think about you right now, Erik." She turned away from him and grabbed a dry shirt, pulling it over her head. "So many alarms are blaring in my head, but..." She didn't follow up with whatever thought was plaguing her, so Erik started to close the distance between them.

She held up a hand and stopped him in his tracks.

"I've been hurt before, and I'm really not in the mood for a repeat."

"I promise you," Erik started, slowly working out the words he wanted to say to her. "I never want to hurt you. I'm not that kind of guy. You just met me at a really strange point in my life."

"Yeah, I'm having a hard time believing anything you say right now."

"I'm having a hard time believing it's really happening to me." Erik dropped his eyes to his feet. "A week ago, I was just mourning the death of my grandfather... Today... I never should've come here; I just didn't know where to go. I'm gonna go. This isn't fair to you."

"Stay. I would've kicked you out if I wanted to. This is a rough neighborhood; you probably have a concussion and I've already proven I can kick your ass... Multiple times now. So just do yourself a favor and stay."

Erik nodded, relief flooding over him. "Kelsey, I owe you the truth and you deserve to get answers to any questions you might have." And so, Erik unloaded his story, sparing no detail as Kelsey listened with disbelief firmly in her eyes, but as Erik unraveled his tale, that disbelief softened until it was replaced with shock, shock that Erik could possibly be telling her the truth, shock that she was starting to believe him.

By the time they'd finished, the sun was starting to brighten the sky outside, and Kelsey invited Erik to curl up in her embrace, and with the weight of the world temporarily off his shoulders, Erik slept.

Chapter 48

"I KNOW IT'S instant coffee, but geez," Kelsey said, interrupting Erik's thoughts with a scowl. He had a lot of making up to do, the way he'd broken into her apartment. He'd certainly paid for it already, his pounding headache and achy back testament to that.

"A woman gives you coffee, you don't complain, especially if she's threatened to kill you once or twice before."

Kelsey fought to keep the smile from cracking her lips and burst into laughter instead. "Shut up, asshole. So, assuming I believe everything you said last night... how do I help you?"

Erik couldn't hide his surprise. When he'd unloaded his tale of woe, the last thing he could've expected was for her to offer to help. Would he do the same if their roles were reversed? He'd like to think he would, but would he? His first instinct was to refuse her offer, but with the weight off his shoulders, and how good he felt after putting it all out there, he realized he really needed allies.

"Ok, well, honestly, I don't have much to go on, except I know it's the Polish mob, and I have some idea of where their base of operations is out of. John Smith did say something to me ... said there's a shop at 7th and North that always has a black sedan in front of it."

"So, what?" Kelsey responded with a quizzical look. "You want me to go check it out... and do what? Tell you if I see a black sedan? Aren't there like, a few thousand of those in the city?"

Erik couldn't help but laugh which only seemed to deepen her frown. "If you're just trying to get rid of me, don't beat around the bush, Erik. I'm really offering my help. Take it or leave it."

What was the point of sending Kelsey to the shop? Was he just trying to give her some meaningless task? Erik sat up as inspiration struck. "I am being serious. I think Smith was trying to imply that I might find the guys chasing me at that shop, and they've never seen you before, but I have seen them. I can describe them to you and if they're there, then I could follow them to Gerwazy. I could turn the tables on them."

"Ok... so... who am I looking for, since, you know, I've never seen them either?"

And so, Erik rattled off a description of Loren and Feliks and Kelsey surprised him by pulling out her pencils and a sketch book. She started to draw them as if she were a police sketch artist and they spent most of the morning getting it just right. When she held up the sketches Erik could only stare.

"Those are them. Holy shit. Wow."

Kelsey beamed under his praise, his lack of words. "So, go to the shop and see if I can see one of these two guys?"

Erik just nodded his head, unable to speak still. How had he gotten so lucky? Why did this talented young woman trust him so much? Did she not understand the danger she was putting herself in?

"You don't need to do this, by the way. It's dangerous and I shouldn't have gotten you inv—"

"Erik, just shut up. I'm not some frail flower. I thought I proved that to you last night. I didn't grow up in some fancy neighborhood, with loving parents and an overprotective grandpa. I had to learn to take care of myself a long time ago and I turned out just fine, so take my help or take a hike, because I won't have you looking at me like that."

Erik wiped the worry from his face and smiled. "Ok, just wanted to make sure. Don't do anything crazy, OK? I just need to know if they're there, if there's something to what Smith said."

"Perfect. I'll head over to the shop after class, oh, and my gallery meeting of course." Kelsey paused, lost in thought for a moment. "You'll be here when I get back, right?"

"Of course. Not like I have anywhere else to go," Erik laughed.

"Good," Kelsey said with a relieved smile. She picked up her bag and walked towards the door. "I'll let you know what I find at this shop."

And then she was gone, and Erik was left with nothing but his problems to keep him company. Erik's joy quickly disappeared, and reality set back in, and he realized how ridiculous it was to think he could have a normal life with her. How was it all going to end? Odds were not in favor of anything good and Erik realized just how screwed up it all was, bringing her into his hell, burdening her with the truth. The chain of thoughts brought mirth-filled laughter to his lips and he was forced to just lean back and accept the things he couldn't change.

Victor had taught him that. "Problems are worth thinking about only when you can affect them." Victor had been so wise. Erik wondered what Victor would've done in his situation, and then it dawned on him, memories of the word games they would play, writing coded messages and passing them back and forth, leaving them in drops, as Victor called them. More spy games, Erik realized.

He retrieved his phone and brought up the picture he'd taken of the message on the Larssen clue. He zoomed into it and started to really look at the words.

Victor was too smart. His clues were impossible for anyone who didn't know him like Erik did. Even for Erik, the clues were at the edge of his abilities. The wording of the message had bothered him since he'd first laid eyes on it. Victor had been in the states for decades, yet his message had the ring of an immigrant still mastering the language.

"Caesar's cipher!" Erik realized. The words at the beginning of each sentence were so deliberate it had to be a clue and Victor had always loved Caesar's cipher. Erik frantically searched Kelsey's small studio for a pen and paper, finally finding them next to a pile of art textbooks stacked next to the futon. He quickly went about jotting down the first letter of each sentence, much as he had in his youth.

Hujhyuluijebudbutwuh.

It was gibberish, of course. Only the proper shift in the alphabet would decode the message, if there was one. There had to be one though. Erik leaned back in the chair, racking his brain. Victor was always very clever; the shift could be any number really, but Erik wanted to believe it would be something obvious only to him. It had to be, otherwise, why leave the message in the first place?

Victor had come to America in 1952 and was twenty-five at the time. Twenty-five didn't work with the cipher, so it couldn't be that, plus, too many people knew that. He had two children; Aunt Ingrid had died when she was four. Again, too many people knew that. What was something Victor had confided in Erik? Something that only they knew. They'd made many secrets while Erik was growing up under his care, but few had anything to do with numbers, especially numbers between one and twenty-five.

Erik was coming to terms with the idea that he'd have to just plug in each number and check the shift against the first letters of each sentence he'd jotted down when an idea sprang into his mind. Victor always said your life changed at sixteen, whether there's a war on or you get a driver's license. Erik always wondered what Victor had meant. The driver's license was for Erik, but what had happened in Nazi occupied Norway that'd so changed Victor's life? Erik had far more context now. Perhaps that's when the real Viktor Braut died in the snows of Norway.

Erik started decoding the letters with a sixteen-letter shift, his breath coming in nervous gasps, the fear that the whole thing was futile in the first-place dancing in the back of his mind. About halfway through decoding the letters something started to emerge. Erik's adrenaline spiked and his confidence grew. 'Retrieve' appeared in the letters in front of him and his worry slid from his shoulders. Then, 'stolen' followed it. Retrieve stolen, Erik's mind exploded with possibilities. This was it; this was what the gangsters wanted from him. The final word emerged, and Erik just stared.

'Ledger'.

That was it.

'Retrieve stolen ledger'.

Erik read it over and over again. There had to be more. He was missing something, he had to be. He pushed himself back from the table in disgust. He'd come this far, and for what? He was no closer to the ledger than he'd been before he even knew it existed. This was worse, he thought as he considered the weight of the knowledge. He knew it existed, he knew what Zatorski wanted but even under the worst torture possible, he'd still be unable to deliver it. He was a dead man. The thought sent a shiver down his spine. He was a dead man, and no one could do anything about it. Not even Det. Joanna Kincaid. For her, Zatorski didn't even exist! To the government, Zatorski was a ghost. How could Erik take down that which didn't exist?

Erik got up from his seat and walked away from the offending cipher. "Shit!" He growled as he shoved his phone back into his backpack next to Jeffrey's phone and the burners he'd bought the other day. And then it dawned on him. He had Jeffrey's phone! He'd totally forgotten about it. At first, he'd only taken it to make sure Jeffrey couldn't call anyone if he broke out of his restraints before the police arrived. Little good that had done, but now he realized he could use the numbers in Jeffrey's contact list! If he could find some names, maybe Kincaid could chase them down. Maybe he could unearth Zatorski, bring the fight to him!

Erik pulled out the burner phone and dialed Kincaid's number. The phone rang twice before Kincaid's voice boomed, "Hello? Erik?"

"Det. Kincaid."

"Jesus Christ, Erik! I told you to call yesterday afternoon! Where have you been? Are you safe?"

"Shit, sorry. I… There's been some developments, nothing major, but the full picture is starting to become clearer."

"You're goddamn right there's been some developments! Care to explain to me why there's a dead man in your apartment?"

Erik's stomach dropped out and all he could do was stutter, any response dying still born in his throat. "What?" He finally managed.

"You saying you had no idea?" Silence stretched out between them until Kincaid broke it. "Shit. I want to believe you, I do. I'd say we should meet, that you should let me bring you in, but something isn't right on my end. Way too much interest in what I'm doing, in you all of a sudden. It's got me looking over my shoulder and jumping at shadows. If it wasn't you, it's the people coming after you."

"I… I… holy…" Erik was in shock, fear clouding his thoughts until Victor's voice reminded him to banish it. It took some effort, but Erik finally managed it. "It wasn't me; I promise you that... Who was it? Do you know his name?"

"Peter Wacowski. Ring any bells?" It didn't.

"Can you describe him to me?" Erik was grasping at straws, a nightmare already forming in the back of his mind.

"Tall, skinny, sandy blond hair. Looks like someone beat him up before putting a hole in his head. Thing is, kid, they found a gun registered to Victor in a dumpster around the back of your apartment. Pretty sure that's the murder weapon."

Erik just absorbed the information, trying not to react. But Lars had Victor's guns, or had he sold them? If Erik was being followed, why not Lars too? If so, they'd know who Lars sold them too, they could easily buy one of them for exactly this purpose.

"My brother... Victor left his guns to him in his will. He said he was going to sell them. What if they're following him too? They could have bought one. Also, you just described Jeffrey Grant. Of course, that's not his real name." Erik fought the desperation clawing at him. "I pistol whipped him twice, just above the eye. There should've been a couple abrasions there."

"I think this is your guy."

"They killed him. They killed him for giving me Gerwazy Zatorski's name, and then they pinned it on me! Shit!" Erik screamed into the empty apartment. "Detective Kincaid, can you check in on my brother? Check if he's OK? I swear to you, I didn't do this. I have an alibi."

"Save it, don't tell me. This conversation didn't happen, OK?"

"Wait," Erik said, sensing Kincaid was about to hang up. "Can you run some names and phone numbers?"

"What? You serious? After what I just said?"

"I stole Jeffrey's phone. I have his contacts. I thought, maybe you could run them, and we could see what shakes out?"

"You telling me you have the dead man in your apartment's phone?" Erik's heart sank.

"Yeah, and I'm beat up right now. Shit, this doesn't look good at all."

"You're beat up? How the hell did that happen?"

"Part of my alibi…"

"Jesus Christ, kid."

"I'm innocent. I swear. Haven't been back to my apartment since I came and saw you and you told me to lay low. That's what I've been doing. I'm sick of running. I just want to know what I'm up against. Maybe I can surprise them, bring the fight to them, clear my name." Erik felt stupid as his plan started to sift through his fingers. "Sorry, Detective Kincaid. You've done enough for me. I'm sorry I got you involved." Erik was about to hang up, but Kincaid stopped him.

"I believe you, and it's my job, kid. Everything feels so off… Just give me the names and numbers." Erik could hear the resignation in her voice, but he forced himself not to care.

"I'll send you an email with all of them. One of em is named Chudy, Polish for skinny, doubt it's his real name, but he's one of the guys that was following me. He… he said he was going to kill me, in a text to Jeffrey. Just send back what you find. We gotta stop these guys, we… my life depends on it."

"OK, kid. Stay safe, and I can't believe I'm saying this, but avoid the police, and get a good disguise cuz your face is gonna be everywhere before too long."

"Thanks," Erik said, fighting to keep the worried waiver of emotion from his voice.

Be smart, be safe, be fearless. The other end went dead. Erik grabbed his laptop and plugged Jeffrey's… Peter's phone in, transferring all of his contacts. He found an unsecure WIFI signal, bakery across the street from Kelsey's place, and sent them to Kincaid. He lamented not getting Kelsey's WIFI password but then again, he'd been busy. A sad smile found his lips as he ran over the last few days in her company and then his heart sank. What was going to happen once his face was everywhere, wanted in connection with a murder? His alibi had a hole, he realized. Between the spook, John Smith, and Kelsey's apartment, he had an hour or two where he was unaccounted for. Not like anyone would be able to track down Smith or believe his story anyway. Erik grabbed his things and left the studio in a hurry. He wasn't sure what he was going to do, he just knew he needed to do something.

Chapter 49

ERIK FOUND HIMSELF walking down the street, hood up, sunglasses on. His hand found the scruff of his new beard, a few days growth met his fingers and the skin beneath begged to be scratched. Erik denied it, not wanting to give the appearance of a new beard to any one curious enough to try to see within his hood, through his flimsy disguise. *You're better than this*, Victor's voice whispered, his lessons springing into Erik's mind once more.

He'd been taught to become whoever he could dream up, yet, here he was, Erik Brown, man on the run. Fugitive. He was writing his own story and it only followed the truth. Erik turned his gaze up from the concrete of the sidewalk and really started to see the world around him. He forced confidence into each step, straightened his shoulders, standing tall. He forced a devil-may-care smile to his lips. He saw a Walgreens just down the block and quickly found himself browsing the aisles.

He'd debated whether to leave his shades on but decided it'd bring more attention than it would avoid so he put them in the backpack he'd left with the clerk near the door. Last thing he needed was a bored security guard accusing him of shoplifting. He walked down the makeup aisle, looking at different foundations. Maybe if he could darken his skin, change his hair color. What if he applied subtle makeup to change his features? How many videos on the internet were there where some young woman did just that? How hard could it be?

One-hundred bucks later and two hours down the road, Erik stared at himself in the cracked mirror of a dirty gas station bathroom. He picked over his appearance, running a makeup-stained hand along a cheek caked in lumpy foundation. He clearly didn't know what color to buy as the makeup tinted his skin different shades. He'd somehow managed to make his cheeks look gaunt. The dark eyeshadow he'd applied around his eyes making them look sunken in their sockets. He wasn't sure what he'd been going for there but what he saw in the mirror surely wasn't *it*. He ran a hand through his wet hair, dyed a jet black, about the only thing he'd gotten right. He'd trimmed his beard into a full goatee and dyed it to match but the shade was at odds with that of his hair. He doubted anyone would notice though.

Erik couldn't help but laugh at himself. He'd wanted to make himself dark and handsome, but, instead, had managed to make himself look like a drug addict. As long as he didn't look like Erik Brown, he didn't much care what the end product was.

Erik changed out of the slim fit clothing that hugged his frame, his ruined slacks, his stained button-up, and donned a baggy t-shirt and baggy jeans. He added an oversized hoodie that he shrunk into. He stood in front of the mirror and scanned his new appearance and added a baseball cap. It all looked brand new, so Erik retrieved the knife from his sock and started splitting threads in the usual wear and tear places. He frayed the lining around the pockets of the jeans, doing the same at the knees. He split the cuffs of his hoodie, then tossed it onto the ground and stomped all over it. He rubbed the dirt encrusted hoodie over his jeans and splashed the mess with water to make it stain the clothing. He looked at himself in the mirror again. It wasn't great, but it'd do.

Erik walked into a coffee shop, the patrons avoiding making eye contact with him. Perfect. He bought a cold brew with the money from the stash house and took a seat in the corner. He marked his exits, came up with an escape plan while he sipped the bitter brew and then pulled out his laptop. He powered it up and hoped Kincaid had found something, that she'd emailed him back.

The loading screen took forever, doubt and worry eating at him while the bar slowly filled up. The laptop pinged softly as it finished and a notification for three new messages popped up. Erik clicked on it. Kincaid *had* responded. Erik ignored the other two emails and clicked on it.

Mark,

Bad news. Remember when we went shooting the other day? Looks like that's the place I left my ammo. Anyway, I'm in it up to my ears today.

Call me later.

Kincaid

Erik read the message, then reread it. It didn't make sense. Mark? Who the hell was Mark? And Erik had never been shooting with Kincaid. They barely knew each other not to mention… Then it clicked. Bad news. The contacts were bad news, and she wasn't talking about going shooting, she was talking about the robbery and Erik being shot at. Where had she said the unsolved murders occurred? The ones that matched the ballistics from the slug they pulled out of his fence? Liberty Row, that's the place, those are the guys, the Polish mob. Kincaid had confirmed it and she was worried.

Erik fumbled out the burner phone from his backpack with nervous fingers. He took a few deep breaths to calm himself and pulled up Kincaid's number. The phone rang and rang. It kept ringing and finally went to voice mail.

"Shit," Erik murmured, switching the contact and calling Kincaid's desk extension instead.

The phone rang a few times and then a strange voice answered.

"Hello?" It was a man's voice. It sounded tired, maybe even sad.

"Who is this," Erik said without thinking.

"What?"

"Where's Detective Kincaid?" Erik's question was followed by silence.

"Who's asking?" The voice finally said.

"A friend," Erik growled, losing his patience. "I need to talk to her. It's important."

"Yeah? Well, she can't take your call."

"This is important!" Erik growled.

"I told you, she can't take your God damn call! Take a hint!"

"Why!?" Erik was losing his patience. Who did this guy think he was?

"Because she's dead!"

Erik's stomach dropped out; he heaved a heavy breath like he'd just taken a body blow in a prize fight with Muhammad Ali. "What?" That was all he could think to say.

"She's fucking dead!" Erik could hear the man fighting back tears. "She's dead."

"How?" Erik asked, too stunned to say anything else.

"Shot. She was following up a tip…" The voice trailed off, as much in disbelief as Erik. "Who did you say you were again?" The voice followed with a renewed sense of awareness.

"No one." Erik hung up the phone and let it drop to his lap. Tears fought to see the coffee-scented air, but

Erik held them back. He clenched his fist and slammed it on the table. The patrons around him jumped in surprise, nervously avoiding his gaze as he swung it across the room.

He gave a fake laugh directed at anyone brave enough to look his way and gathered up his laptop, shoving it into his bag. He rushed out of the shop, leaving his cold brew forgotten in his wake. He rushed into the afternoon sun and rounded a corner, hiding himself in someone's back doorway. He leaned his head against the cool, rough bricks and released a strangled cry. This was on him. He'd gotten Kincaid killed. This was his fault.

Anger blossomed within him as the thought hammered home over and over again. This was his fault. They wanted him and he kept dragging other people into it. What if they found out about Kelsey? What if they went after his family? No. It was time to stop running. It was time to fight back, and now he knew where to find them. It was time Erik went on the offensive and answered their string of murders. They'd pay for what they did to Victor, to Jo.

Chapter 50

ERIK FOUND HIMSELF walking towards Liberty Row, fueled by his desire for revenge, no plan in his mind. *Be smart, be safe, be fearless*, Victor's voice interrupted. Erik hesitated in mid step, stopping in his tracks. He looked around himself and realized what he'd been about to do. He was about to commit suicide. How could he be so stupid? How could he let his emotions play him like that? He needed a plan, and quick.

He knew Jeffrey was dead, but what about the other two guys? He pictured them in his mind, but Kincaid's face kept invading his thoughts. He fought desperately to push her away, but she kept returning. "This is on you," she said, sending a shiver down Erik's back.

"I didn't mean to," Erik said to no one, eliciting some confused glances from passersby. Erik realized he was just standing in the middle of the sidewalk and gave a startled old lady a sheepish smile. "Just talking to myself," he told her, but he doubted she spoke English as she gave him a bewildered glare and kept walking.

Erik took the hint and got to moving again. He walked hunched over, hands stuffed into his oversized hoodie. He shuffled, playing up his junkie appearance, hiding his thoughts, his roving eyes behind his dark shades. His mind moved a mile a minute, shutting Kincaid out so he could think how to avenge her. Based on her tip, this was where the thugs operated. The question was, where was their headquarters? Knowing the neighborhood did him little good if he didn't know which block to stalk. He could try asking someone, but he was afraid of the heat that might bring. Then, he realized he already had the perfect cover.

With a renewed sense of direction, Erik put his tentative plan to use. He walked until he found a run-down bar, the faded Open sign flashing neon, inviting in the day drinker, deadbeat, junkie. One look at the entrance told Erik someone inside knew where to score some dope. His mind flitted back to the safe house, what had they been hiding there? Heroin, at least he was pretty sure that's what it was. He'd have to roll the dice on that one, but if memory served, Smith had mentioned the drug once or twice in connection with these guys.

Erik took a cleansing breath and walked past the trio of drug addicts nodding off along the wall around the entrance, cigarettes left smoldering and forgotten in their hands. Their eyes stared outwards but didn't even register Erik's crossing. He pushed into the bar; the door heavy against his outstretched hand. Oak, he thought. The hinges squealed his arrival and a few heads turned to regard him. Their scowls were not friendly.

Erik almost turned around and left, but instead, decided to lean into his disguise more. He looked around, scanning the small room, refusing to meet any eyes. He scratched his arm absentmindedly and made his way to the bar. The bartender waited, a pint glass forgotten in one hand, a cleaning rag in the other.

"What're you having?" He said with a thick accent.

"Beer," Erik responded, his eyes still moving about the room. "Beer and a bump," he added, not sure if his lingo was proper but going with it anyway. He really hoped *Law and Order* was up on their stuff.

The bartender grimaced, setting the glass down. "Why not forget the beer and get the fuck out of my bar?"

Erik finally locked eyes with the man, hoping he hadn't already blown his plan. "Hey, man, no trouble, no trouble." Erik held out his hands and started backing away.

The bartender shook his head, exasperated. "Wrong door, junkie fuck." He motioned towards the back door and Erik realized he was sending him to the dealer. Erik bobbed his head in understanding and beelined to the door.

Erik pushed through it and found himself in a tight coatroom. He gave the room a brief scan and realized he was supposed to go through the next door into what was most likely the alley. Erik proceeded to push the heavy door open, a blast of fetid air screaming into his nostrils. He fought an offended cough and pushed the door open the rest of the way revealing a shadowed alley. Dumpsters lined the walls and gave off the overpowering smell of garbage. Erik fought the urge to wretch and stepped out of the coatroom. He looked around the deserted alley and slumped. Had he been set up? The realization crashed home and then Erik was looking for his exit. His feet were on the verge of flight when a woman in a big black coat stepped out of another doorway.

"Money," she demanded.

"How much?" Erik responded lamely.

She shook her head in disgust, mirroring that of the bartender. "Just give me what you have, and I'll give you what it buys," she explained, her slight accent intensifying with her anger. Polish, Erik realized. Marga's accent had been faint, but the pronunciation of certain vowels told him everything he needed to know. Heroin, Polish accents, odds were good that these were the people he wanted.

"Ok, chill," Erik said in his best drugged voice. He reached into his pocket where he'd stuffed a dirty, crumpled one-hundred-dollar bill. He fought with his pocket to pull it out, making it look more difficult than it was. He finally freed it and presented it to the woman with a flourish.

She was unimpressed. She just held out a hand and accepted it, unfolding it and raising an eyebrow before looking back to Erik. "Steal a TV?"

Erik responded with nervous laughter, not having to act too much to achieve it as he wondered if he'd just blown his cover. Was one-hundred bucks too much? The woman turned away, whistled some code to an unseen companion, the shrill note echoing off the concrete walls and steel dumpsters. She didn't turn back as she retreated through her doorway,

"Wait!" Erik called after her, but she didn't respond, disappearing behind the door, the crash of a lock declaring her absolute departure. Erik didn't mind that she'd stiffed him the drugs, but he knew no junkie would let it go so he raced to the door and banged on it. "Hey! What the hell?" He called dramatically. A minute or so later, a brown bag plopped onto the ground behind him. He jumped involuntarily and stared at it for a second.

"Get the hell out of here!" Yelled an accented voice. Erik darted away from the door and looked up to a fire escape high above him. A balding man in a track jacket leaned against the rail, menace permanently etched into his scowl. Erik smiled stupidly up at him and grabbed the brown bag, trying to go back into the bar but the back door was locked. Gruff laughter rang down from the fire escape as Erik looked around the alley for an exit, really playing up his fear. Erik was calm as could be. He now had two people to watch for. Two people that might lead him to the bastards that had killed Victor.

"Run rabbit!" Called the man as Erik took off down the alley towards the street.

Erik rounded the corner and skidded to a stop. Questioning stares met him but he ignored them, stuffing the drugs into his pocket and hunching back into his junkie stumble as he made his way down the street.

When he was a few blocks away, he ditched the drugs in a public trash can, making sure to jam it in and bury it. Last thing he wanted was for some kid to fish it out and start an addiction.

It felt good to be free of it, not that a run in with the cops would be any worse for it. He was already a prime suspect in a murder, had angered the local mafia and their dirty cops, and seen one of his two allies murdered because of him. His mind ran off to Kelsey, but he quickly reined it back in. She could take care of herself. But he did need to tell her about Jeffrey, about Kincaid, he just couldn't worry about that right then. Erik needed to focus. He had a plan; it was time to fall fully into it. It was very likely it'd fail, and he'd die trying. Maybe he should call his family, say goodbye... Selene, he could call her work phone. Would they bug that? In the era of cellphones? Erik decided it was a risk worth taking.

"Hello? Selene Brown's office."

"Selene," Erik said, his voice catching on her name as a torrent of emotion tried to escape his opened mouth.

"Erik?"

"Yeah."

"Why the hell you calling my office phone? Did I miss a call or something?"

"No, just, I'm on a new phone and was pretty sure you'd ghost an unknown number," Erik lied, the words just tumbling from his subconscious.

"You are so weird!" Was Selene's expected response.

"Selene, I just needed to talk to you, hear your voice really. The last couple days have just been really tough."

"You alright, Erik? You need me to come get you?"

"I love you, Selene. You're too good for this family. I'll be in touch, later." He had to end the call or else he'd spill his guts to her, get her involved in his nightmare and he couldn't do that. He couldn't endanger her more than she already likely was.

The thought sobered him. They were being watched. If he'd had a tail, his whole family must have had one too. Best not to think about them. They knew him. They'd never believe the set up. They'd never stop loving him. Jeffrey had been a message, that's all. He was a thug, Kincaid had even said it, at least, Erik thought that's what she'd said. Self-doubt ate at him in a time when he needed all of his confidence. He needed to go back to being the man that had impressed a spook. He needed to return to the man before the murder, before Kincaid's death. And then he realized Selene was unaware of the murder in his apartment. Had she known; the conversation would've been much different. The police hadn't contacted her yet, but why not? The murder was half a day old; they should've been chasing down every lead by then and family was always a good place to start. So, what were they waiting for? Unless... unless it was a trap? It didn't matter, Erik realized. It changed nothing when it came to who he was dealing with. He had to continue down the path he'd chosen.

Chapter 51

ERIK ENTERED THE first mom-and-pop shop he came to. He browsed the clothing racks and picked out some clothes that'd help him to blend in, working class dickies with a matching work shirt, a beanie and a jacket, throwing in a pack of zip ties for good measure. He wasn't sure if he'd need them but after Jeffrey's he figured better safe than sorry. He paid for them, adding a pair of glasses, and left without a word. The clerk paid him no mind, eagerly accepting his money.

Erik walked along the street until he came to a motel. It looked like a pay by the hour kind of place, perfect for what he had in mind. He bought a room from a gaunt middle-aged man with greasy black hair and an ungroomed beard. The man's breath was sour with the stink of beer, his eyes bloodshot, his clothing stained. He barely looked at Erik.

The motel room was in a state of disrepair. It was clean, but the furniture was old, broken down. The shower was stained, the fixtures rusty. The bathroom mirror was cracked, probably an angry fist. The bed was lumpy and old, but Erik doubted he'd get much sleep on it. Plus, that wasn't why he was there. Erik disregarded the squalor he found himself in and went to work. He unloaded the backpack; the four phones, the stack of money, the makeup and the extra ammunition and magazines. His heart dropped when he realized he'd left his gun at Kelsey's.

"Shit," he groaned, burying his head in one hand while he smacked the bed with the other. "Stupid. Stupid!" He'd been so rattled by the thought of scaring her he'd been careless. Erik sighed and made peace with his situation. If things went right, he wouldn't need the gun. He'd just feel a lot better if he had it was all.

Erik repacked the bag, keeping the makeup and one burner phone out, which he stuffed into his pockets with a wad of stolen drug money. He took the bag and looked around the room for a place to stash it, finally landing on the vent beside the bed. He carefully unscrewed the grate and shoved the bag in. It wasn't perfect but it'd have to do. He carefully screwed the screws back in and dusted off the ground. He returned to the forgotten bag of clothes and took them out. He regarded the drab work shirt and the gray work pants. They looked brand new. That wouldn't do.

Erik tossed them onto the ground and walked all over them. He threw them into the shower and blasted them with water, then tossed them onto the bathroom floor, kicking them around with his foot. He picked them up, regarded them and decided they still needed work. He pulled the knife from out of his sock and went to work cutting at the fabric, not poking the knife through, but working at spots like the hems and cuffs, just as he'd done with the clothes he still wore.

He spent about an hour on the clothes, being much more thorough than the first time, drying them with the retro hair dryer he found attached to the wall next to the sink. The hair dryer gave off a metallic stink as the coils heated up within it. The thing was ancient and barely worked. It took far longer than Erik desired to dry the clothes, and when he was finally finished, he held them up in the meager overhead light. The newness was faded, hints of it still glaring through his destruction but only where someone knew to look.

They'd do.

Erik hopped into the shower and rinsed the makeup off, some of his hair dye following it. The water never got above lukewarm, but it still felt good. He dried off, eyeing himself in the mirror, his body made motley by healing bruises. Once dry, he retrieved his makeup and started applying it. This time, he tried to stay away from the junkie look. It'd been a happy accident but had drawn too many stares. This time, Erik just tried to make himself look like a tired laborer. The eyeshadow made his eyes look sunken, the foundation adding dark circles. He ignored sharpening his cheek bones as that'd made him look far too gaunt. He pulled on his battered slacks, admiring the worn fabric in the knees and along the pockets. He buttoned up his drab work shirt, fingering the fraying fabric along the cuffs of the sleeves and along the collar. Victor would've been proud.

Erik shoved his feet into a new pair of work boots, slipping his knife into one of them. It wasn't much protection, but it'd have to do until something else came along. He put on the beanie and grimaced at how new it looked but figured he could just toss it into the next patch of dirt he saw to rough it up. He'd already decided to find some mud to cut the gleam on his new boots. He shoved the zip ties into his back pocket and took one last look in the mirror and nodded his approval.

"Let's do this," he said to his reflection, a look of determination settling on his features.

Erik returned to the bar from earlier, eyeing it from across the street. He doubted he'd find one of Gerwazy's thugs there but didn't want to risk being recognized so he walked around the corner until he was facing the building the woman and the man had come out of. The man had been on the fire escape on the third floor. Erik pictured the part of the building, remembering how many windows he'd sprinted past on his mad dash out of the alley. Now, all he needed to do was figure out how many windows each apartment had, and he could narrow down his options.

He reached the front entrance and found it unlocked. He overcame his surprise and entered the building. He looked down the dirty hallway, inhaled the musty air and grimaced. Just as bad as his motel room. Low wage apartments run by a slumlord. He doubted many eyes would be watching him. He figured this was one of those places where people minded their own business. That was probably why the drug dealers operated out in the open for anyone with an alley-facing apartment to see.

Erik made his way down the hallway, passing faded doors with cracking paint. He reached the stairs and peered up them. They wrapped around from floor to floor and Erik could see all the way up to the top level. He turned around and took the hallway all the way to the other side and discovered another set of stairs. He walked back a little way and stopped in front of an apartment, knocking on a door that looked as if someone had given it a little care over the years. The paint was less faded, the cracks in it less pronounced. A dirty welcome mat was on the floor in front of it.

"Chwileczkę! Już idę!" The voice was frail, older. Erik breathed a sigh of relief and tried to remember back to the Polish Marga had taught him.

An old lady with light purple hair opened the door after fighting with the dead bolt and chain. Her eyes squinted in confusion as she looked Erik up and down. "Czy jesteś mechanikiem?"

"Mój Polski jest zły. Czy możemy mówić po Angielsku?" Erik fumbled through the words, grasping at lessons he'd learned years ago and never fully maintained.

The old woman frowned, followed by a shrug. "My English, terrible. I try."

"Thank you," Erik responded with a friendly smile.

"You repair?" Erik's smile deepened.

"Yes I am."

The old lady mirrored his smile. "Narzekałem od tygodni! W końcu wysyłają kogoś! Come in, come in."

Erik followed her inside. She led him into the living room where a TV blared in Polish, a painting of the Black Madonna hanging on the wall just next to it. Several cats skittered by as they made their way to the radiator where she stopped and turned to Erik. "Broken," she said, smacking the old metal behemoth with the heel of her palm. "Fix?"

Erik nodded, "I don't have my tools, I'll have to come back. Mind If I check the other radiators? In the bedrooms?"

The old lady gave him a suspicious look, her hands on her hips, exactly as Marga had done for all those years. "You fix?"

"Of course, I'm just looking today. I'll be back tomorrow."

"Bah!" The old woman threw up her hands at Erik and walked back to her couch. "Zawsze to samo. Nic nie zostaje zrobione." She sat down and turned up the volume on the TV, ignoring Erik as he watched in surprise.

He gathered his wits and made a show of looking at the radiator, banging on pipes, checking underneath it, behind it. He got back to his feet and walked across the room, opening the bedroom door. The room was immaculate. The bed made, nothing on the floor or draped over the rocking chair in the corner. Erik walked up to the radiator, looked at it for a second and then walked back out to talk to the old lady. She ignored him as he came to stand next to her.

"Ma'am? I think I see what the problem is. I'll bring my tools tomorrow and fix it."

"You fix?" She asked, suddenly, all her attention on him.

"Yeah. Also, do you know if all the apartments here have the same layout?"

Her face turned up in a confused frown. Erik was pretty sure she didn't understand the question, so he went to the well to try and explain in Polish.

"All apartments są takie... same? Similar?"

"Podobnie?"

"Sure."

"Yes, all podobnie... Why?"

"I have a few more I need to check, and it'll save me a lot of time if they're all the same layout," Erik tried to explain but the woman didn't understand, or at least Erik didn't think she did.

"Bah!" She said to him again, waving him off while she turned back to her TV.

Erik hesitated, but decided it was best to leave. She didn't really seem to care what he'd said, only that he was going to fix her radiator. He felt bad as he shut the door behind himself and walked back out of the building. He walked down the street, trying to forget the poor old lady. He wasn't going back, he couldn't, but he'd gotten the information he needed. Time to do some more reconnaissance.

Erik made his way outside and walked around the building until he was at the lip of the alley. He peered down it, looking up to the fire escape and counting the apartments until he reached where the man had been. Twenty windows, ten apartments, if they truly were all the same. If he approached from the street side of the building, he could count his way down, but how could he be sure it was the right one? And how could he be sure there weren't more people inside?

If he could get to the girl, maybe he could get some information from her, but if memory served, she didn't look like someone he wanted to mess with. Erik berated himself for leaving the gun at Kelsey's. He'd have to make do without it.

He walked past the alley and kept going down the street until he spotted a bum leaning against the wall of a rundown building. He had the look of an addict, unwashed, skinny. Erik slowly walked up to him. "Hey, buddy?"

The man ignored him, staring straight ahead, eyes vacant. Erik stopped just out of reach. "Buddy?"

The man finally broke his million-mile stare and looked up at Erik with a slack jawed frown.

"Hey, want to help me out?"

"What?" The man finally managed in a raspy voice.

"See that bar over there?" Erik pointed at the sleazy bar from earlier. "I need you to go in there and ask to buy some drugs."

The man perked up and looked Erik over. "What's in it for me?"

"You can keep the drugs."

"What? Then what's in it for you?"

"Do you care?" Erik hoped the idea of free drugs would be enough. He watched the wheels turn behind the bum's eyes as he weighed his options. It didn't take long before the man pushed himself up to his feet and he fixed Erik with a toothless smile.

"Drugs are mine, no catch?"

"Yep. All you need to do is go in there and…"

"Yeah, yeah. I know. Not my first time." The man held out his hand waiting for Erik to put the cash in it.

Erik pulled out two twenties and shoved them into the man's hand. His eyes brightened as he counted the bills, and his smile was ear to ear as he looked up at Erik. "You're not a cop, right? You have to tell me if you are you know."

"Do I look like a cop?" That was good enough and the man rushed away towards the bar.

Erik didn't hesitate and took off at a brisk pace to get back to the building he'd just canvassed. Erik was just behind the bum when he pushed his way into the bar and disappeared. Erik kept going past the alley and around the corner. He went through the front entrance and turned right, walking past the old lady's front door and stopping just around the corner from the stairs.

He listened with baited breath, waiting until he heard the click of feet racing down the stairs. As the sound got closer, he peered around the corner, just catching sight of the young woman as she hit the landing and turned towards the back exit. He waited until he heard the crash bar on the door sound and slipped around the corner, slowly making his way to the back door. He pulled out his knife and waited, barely breathing.

Chapter 52

THE BACK DOOR swung open and the woman stepped through it. Erik was ready. He grabbed the woman by the throat and slammed her into the wall, his blade held just level with her eye as he glared down at her. Her face drained of blood and shock painted her features. She looked like she was about to react when Erik shushed her.

"One word and I take your eye." The woman whimpered as she started to raise her hands, a scared tear leaking from one eye. "How many people are upstairs?" Erik growled.

"What?" The woman managed around her shock.

"How many people upstairs, don't act stupid. You waste my time; I cut your face."

The woman trembled against the hand around her neck. "Just one," she finally divulged.

"If you're lying to me…" Erik let the threat hang in the air and the woman trembled again. Now came the part Erik had been dreading. He made a fist around the knife, ready to punch her, ready to knock her out, but hesitated.

The woman's eyes lit up in realization and Erik watched in slow motion as her knee flew out towards his crouch. He was forced to lean into the hand around her throat as he dodged backwards. The woman gasped against the new pressure but responded with a chop of her hand on his wrist. Erik's grasp slipped just enough and the woman wasted no time in throwing a punch with her other hand, connecting with Erik's cheek.

His eye watered and he growled in pain, his hesitation gone as the woman launched into another attack. Erik deflected another knee attack and slammed his body weight against her, pinning her to the wall. All hesitation was gone as he punched her in the side of the head, connecting with a sickening thud. The woman went limp against him. It took a second for Erik to register before he backed up and released her, letting her slide down the wall into a crumpled heap on the floor.

He shook off the disgust that coated him like a second skin and picked her up, throwing her over his shoulder. He had to work quick. Last thing he needed was her waking up on him.

He climbed the two flights of stairs in leaps and bounds. He hit the landing, panting under the woman's slight weight, and counted the apartments as he passed. He was just nearing his target when the door swung open and her accomplice stepped out. Erik and the man shared a startled stare before the man's hand shot to his waist. Gun, Erik thought as he heaved the girl over his shoulder and surged towards the man.

Erik flew forward with a lunging right straight punch. He connected with the man's jaw and watched him crumble. Erik couldn't help the smile that found his lips as he realized the man was out cold with one punch. Adrenaline coursed through his veins and he looked around the hallway in slow motion, his eyes settling on the two bodies that dotted the floor around him. He jumped to work, rolling over the man. He confiscated the pistol from the man's waistband and shoved it behind his belt, letting his shirt drape over it. He dragged the man into the open doorway and doubled back for the woman. She moaned as he picked her up, a new bump on her forehead from where she'd just hit the ground. Erik grimaced upon seeing it and mouthed an apology.

He tossed her onto her bald accomplice as soon as he was through the door and shut it behind him. He took a quick look around the dirty apartment just to be sure the girl hadn't lied. Satisfied, Erik pulled out the zip ties from his pocket and went to work securing his new prisoners. The woman was coming too, but she didn't fight him as he tied her up. The man just moaned in confusion; his eyes open but not focusing as Erik bound his hands. He searched the apartment with a quick scan and settled on some dirty dish towels by the sink. He pulled out his knife and cut them into strips. He balled up one strip and approached the girl. Scared eyes met him as he grabbed her by the mouth and forced the ball of cloth past her teeth. She started to fight him but couldn't do much as Erik tied another strip across her mouth. She tried to yell around it, but it was muffled and made no sense.

"Sorry," Erik said, staring her in the eyes. "I'm not going to hurt you... no more than I already have, I mean," he finished lamely, shame bringing out the words more than anything.

"Never hit a woman," Victor had schooled him, "unless there's no other choice. If there's no other choice, you do what you have to do. Life isn't fair and the rules are never absolute. Do what needs to be done to stay alive, always."

That's exactly what Erik was doing now, he reflected as he turned away from the woman and focused his attention on the bald man. He was finally coming to, his eyes looking around in disbelief, his tongue still fat in his mouth. Erik watched him test the restraints binding his hands behind his back. He slowly started working his jaw against the stiffness setting in. His eyes finally settled on Erik.

Time to talk.

"Make any noise and I kill your friend. Got it?" Erik saw the woman's eyes bug out in the corner of his vision and his heart dropped. He wanted to turn to her and remind her he'd said he wasn't going to hurt her anymore, but that'd be giving up the game. The bald man nodded in front of him, finally coming back to himself fully. "Play your cards right and all you get out of this is a hurt jaw, OK?"

The man nodded, and Erik patted him on the knee. "Good." The man winced and Erik's heart dropped again. He hated this. This wasn't him. He didn't want to hurt them. He had nothing against them. They were a means to an end. He'd done what he had to.

"You know a man named Chudy? Works for Gerwazy Zatorski." The man just stared at Erik so he pulled Kelsey's sketch from his backpack and held it in front of his face. "Do you know a man named Chudy, yes or no? You lie to me and I kill you both."

"Yes," the bald man finally managed, a tremble of fear going up his leg.

"Can you get him here?"

"What?" Erik was getting sick of hearing that word. The frustration must have shown because the bald man didn't wait to hear the question again. "Yes. Yes! I know him. My phone." The man motioned to the coffee table beside the woman. "I call him."

"No," Erik growled from behind a triumphant smile. "No talking. Text him."

Erik retrieved the phone. "What's your code?"

"1111," the man mumbled.

Erik put it in and shook his head. He went into the man's contacts and found three different numbers saved under Chudy. He held it up for the man to see. "Which one?"

"Second one."

Erik clicked on it and brought up their past conversation. It was in Polish. Great, Erik thought. He scanned the conversation and fought the despair rising within him, and then an idea came to him. He flipped the phone into airplane mode and hit the speak and text button.

"Tell him you need to meet up with him, in Polish. You say something else; I'll kill you both."

The man nodded and Erik held up the phone. "Potrzebuję twojej pomocy. W moim mieszkaniu jest szalony skurwiel! Myślę, że próbuje cię zabić. Pośpiesz się! Send!" Erik's fist shot out and connected with the man's nose, a jet of blood shooting out his left nostril. The man groaned, his eyes tearing.

"What'd you say?"

"Just what you told me!" The man whimpered.

"Good. If you're lying…"

"I know, you kill us both."

"Right." Erik stood back up, turned the phone off airplane mode and tossed it back on the coffee table. That's when he heard the shouting coming from the alley.

"Bastards! Thieves!" It was the bum, waiting on his drugs. Erik smiled to himself and looked at the pile of heroine on the table next to a scale.

"How much does forty bucks buy you?" Erik said, motioning to the drugs.

The bald man looked at him with confused eyes. "Point two grams," he finally said.

Erik weighed out the point two grams, shoved it into a brown paper bag and tossed it out the window. The shouting immediately stopped.

"How long does it usually take for him to get over here?" Erik asked, not really caring what the answer was. He knew full well Chudy wasn't coming and that the bald man had lied to him. Skurweilu. Erik was going to have to look that word up.

Chapter 53

THE TWO CAPTIVES sat on the couch, bound and gagged. Erik sat by the front door, just to the side of it where he'd be hidden if someone breached it in a hurry. The bald man's pistol waited in Erik's grip, hammer cocked and forgotten as the minutes stretched on. Erik's mind was on Kelsey. She should be finishing class and heading to the gallery meeting. Erik couldn't keep her from his mind. He'd feel a whole lot better once she checked in, once he could tell her about Jeffrey, about Kincaid. He fought the urge to text her, but he didn't want to distract her. The art show meant too much to her.

Everyone jumped as the phone started to shimmy and shake its way across the wooden coffee table. Erik rose from his perch and walked into the living room, locking eyes with the bald man as he picked up the phone.

"Drug deal?" The man hesitated but the cant of his eyes told Erik everything he needed to know. "What's the procedure? And if you lie to me, I'll take an eye."

Erik undid the gag on the man's mouth. "Answer it and ask how much they want." It was an obvious lie and Erik didn't hesitate to send a right straight into the man's nose. The woman whimpered in fear as the man flew back against the back of the couch, his head cracking against the hard edge where the cushion ceased to be. The man groaned loudly, pain etched across his face, while the phone continued to vibrate in Erik's hand. Erik turned to the woman and undid her gag.

"Save this man from himself." Her eyes widened at Erik's implication, her gaze shooting to the groaning man, a tremor shaking her small frame as she took in the blood trickling down from his nose to mix with the dried blood of his split lip.

"Answer and say nothing, then go down to the alley and meet the junkie. Whistle up the code for the quantity, weigh it out and toss it into the alley."

"Zamknij się dziwko," The bald man murmured in a menacing voice. The woman's eyes betrayed her fear at his words and prompted Erik to send another right straight to the man's chin. The woman let out a startled cry, tears trickling from her eyes.

"Głupcze, on nas zabije!" She shot back.

Erik didn't wait for them to say anymore, answering the phone and hitting mute. Silence greeted him on the other line.

"Pomóż nam!" The bald man yelled, just as Erik had suspected he would. Erik shot him a scowl and cocked his free hand back. The man yelped and tried to curl into himself. The line clicked dead and Erik tossed it back onto the coffee table.

"I should cut out your tongue for that," Erik growled in his most menacing voice. But instead, he fixed the gags back in place and left the two captives to tremble on the couch while he met the junkie in the alley.

Erik moved through the apartment complex with speed, reaching the bottom of the stairs in no time. He opened the door and stepped out to find a young college looking kid. The young man had sunken eyes that were at odds with his meticulous appearance. His clothes were clean, his hair styled and gelled. Erik was caught off guard. The man's face brightened as he caught sight of Erik and he shuffled over.

"Fifty bucks?"

Erik felt a pang in his heart as he nodded, taking the money and turning to walk back inside, whistling some shrill nonsense he hoped sounded like a code for anyone else listening. Everything about the man said he shouldn't be buying heroin. Erik had no doubt that a painkiller addiction had brought him into that alley. Erik wanted to help him, not send him further down the rabbit hole, but he had to maintain his cover. If he could take these guys down, he'd be helping a whole lot more people than one young man.

Erik entered the apartment to find the bald man wiggling across the apartment floor, to where, Erik wasn't sure. Horror filled the man's eyes as Erik approached him and he started trying to plead with Erik around his gag. Erik ignored him, walking right by him towards the drugs and the woman. He removed her gag.

"How much does fifty buy?"

"Point twenty-five," she responded, fear dominating her face.

"Thank you," Erik said, the kindness in his voice creating a look of confusion in the woman's stare.

Erik weighed out the heroin, placed it in the brown bag and tossed it out of the window to the poor soul down below. Erik closed the window and walked up to the man still on the floor. Without warning, he delivered a swift kick to the man's side. The man screamed in agony, but the gag stopped it from being audible to anyone but Erik and the woman.

"Please stop!" She called from her seat on the couch." Stop hurting him!"

Erik spun to look at her and her jaw clicked shut as she cowered back into the couch. Her fear hurt Erik. This was the last thing he wanted to be doing. He went into medical school to help people. He'd never hurt anyone before the madness of Victor's murder came knocking on his front door and invaded every aspect of his life.

"You think I enjoy this?" He growled at the cowering woman, the truth ringing in his words. "My issue is with Chudy and his friends, though I see little to redeem the two of you. That young man is my age. He doesn't look like a junkie yet, but with your help he's going to be in a morgue in no time. You're scum. Parasites feeding on society. A part of me wants to put you both in the ground for what you're doing to these people, but you're a symptom, not the cause. I don't know you and I won't judge you. I'm sure there's a reason you're here and I'm sure it made sense to you, but so help me God, if you don't change your ways, I'll change them for you."

Erik was disappointed at the silence his little speech gathered. Two sets of frightened eyes watched him from two different places. The woman's jaw stayed clenched as Erik's scowl went from her to the man at his feet. He growled in disgust as the silence stretched for too long and he grabbed the man by his belt and dragged him back to the couch.

"I should leave you on the floor," he said as he hoisted the man back up onto the couch. "Your friends aren't coming. They don't care about you. So, how about you help me and save us all a lot of pain."

The man looked away from Erik, refusing to meet his eyes. Erik took it as confirmation that the man wouldn't talk, not to him anyway. Erik had suspected that'd be the case, so he wasn't surprised. His plan just moved to the next phase. It was never as easy as you hoped.

"I'll help you," whispered the woman in a scared voice.

Erik watched the man's eyes widen at the sudden betrayal, a slurry of unintelligible words foaming out of his gaged mouth almost instantly. Erik grabbed his face, forcing the man's eyes to his.

"Shut up," Erik commanded, his voice deep with the trappings of authority. It was the voice Victor had used when he was fed up. Erik had spent a childhood practicing it in the mirror, never using it as his solitary lifestyle kept him from becoming too close to any but

Victor, Marga and Selene. To Erik's surprise, the man closed his mouth, his eyes looking anywhere but at Erik.

Erik turned his attention back to the woman. "Why?"

"Why what?" The woman retorted. "You ask for help, I offer, now there's a problem? Maybe I don't feel like dying today like this fool, głupi drań." She spat at the bald man and he started with his unintelligible tirade once more. Erik let him, walking over to stand towering over the woman.

"Why should I trust you?"

"Up to you. It's either trust me or wait for Chudy and his friends to get here. How good of a shot are you? Because I doubt that pistolet is enough."

Erik smiled, already rearranging his plan in his mind. Sometimes it was that easy. He walked away from the woman and back to the man. He picked him up and tossed him over his shoulder.

"What are you doing?" The woman called after him in a worried voice.

"Taking out the trash," Erik responded without turning back to her. He kept walking and went into the single bedroom. He tossed the man onto the bed and pulled out the pistol.

The man's eyes widened as Erik picked up one of the pillows and stuffed the muzzle of the gun into it. Erik walked up next to the man and leaned in close to whisper in his ear.

"If you make a sound, I really will shoot you." The man's eyes widened, and he started to protest, at least Erik guessed that's what he was doing as he turned towards the wall, shoved the pillow and gun against it and fired.

Chapter 54

KELSEY LOOKED FROM the address she'd written down to the street signs hanging from the stop lights on the corner ahead of her. This was the place. She grabbed her bag, the art supplies weighing heavily against the straps. She was going to need a new bag before too long, but this one had lasted her a lot longer than the last one.

She pulled the strap over her shoulder and fought with the door handle, eventually brute forcing the battered door of her old car open. She stepped out into a sunny afternoon, a cold wind gusting down the slow city street. She fought the wind to keep her dark hair from blowing into her eyes and wished she knew where her sunglasses had gotten off to.

The sidewalk had the smell of an open sewer grate nearby and her nose wrinkled up at the offending smell that rode the wind next to her. She rounded the corner and found the red painted wooden door of the corner shop with the glass window, the name of the shop painted on it in an old-world style font. She fought the weight of the door, the push of the wind against it, and flinched at the ring of the bell heralding her entrance.

A number of eyes lurched towards her as she stumbled inside, the door slamming behind her. She gave the room an embarrassed smile and shrugged. The eyes stayed on her for a fraction of a second longer before they returned to wherever they'd been trained before her arrival.

The shop was close to empty. The smell of burnt coffee beans proclaimed it to be a coffee shop, but the lighting was unusually low for a coffee shop. That was Kelsey's first indication that something was off, the clientele of fearsome looking tough guys the second. They largely ignored her when they didn't take the opportunity to openly leer at her. She shrugged off their roving eyes as she marked their faces and decided they were not the men Erik had sent her there to find.

She hesitated but a moment before approaching the counter and ordering a Frappuccino.

"We don't serve that," the barista said with a thick accent.

"Ok, latte?"

"That neither."

"I guess I'm a little confused then, what do you serve?"

"Coffee," the man responded, little care in his voice.

"Ok, I'll take a coffee then." The man nodded and disappeared behind the massive espresso machine that sat unused on the bar. He returned quickly with a steaming cup of coffee and set it on the table.

"Cream and sugar are over there." He pointed to a small table at the far end of the room where little disposable creamer cups sat in a basket, a bowl of sugar with a spoon next to it.

Kelsey said her thanks, sipping the bitter coffee on her way towards it. She almost spit the offending liquid back into the cup but refrained. She poured three creamers into the dark coffee and stirred in several scoops of sugar before the drink became at all palatable. She retreated to a high table in the corner of the room, taking a seat on a wobbly stool before pulling out her sketch book and pencils.

As she would in any other coffee shop, she started sketching the room, oblivious to the uncomfortable stares that met her efforts. If she were going to truly give herself a chance to discover the presence of the men Erik had described to her, she had to stick around for a minute or two.

As the air in the room grew more and more stale with the quiet of discomfort, the low murmuring of men afraid to speak out loud, Kelsey became aware of the looks cast towards her corner of the room. They'd lost the lewdness of dirty men mentally undressing a young woman and had been replaced with questioning glares, as if they'd lay bare the reason for her extended presence.

Kelsey could never remember feeling less welcome, less safe and, as the discomfort continued to grow in an unimaginable way, Kelsey sought to gather her supplies strewn about the table, her offending coffee forgotten at her elbow. She cast wary smiles towards her onlookers but could see a rash boldness growing in their eyes. It was time to go, she realized, probably was fifteen minutes earlier, she amended.

She was fighting with her overburdened bag when the door slammed open, wind gusting into the room and sending her coffee toppling off the high-top table. Kelsey was oblivious to its tumble, the splash of warmth against the leg of her jeans, as she found her eyes locked with Loren, his pink scar twisting his scowl into an almost demonic glare. He paid her little mind as his eyes left hers and explored the room, his hand tucked into the folds of his leather jacket.

Behind him came Feliks, his chin tucked into the cowl of his jacket. He stumbled through the door as if pushed, his face varying shades of purple bruises and scabbed over gashes. He too locked eyes with Kelsey but was quick to avert them, his cheeks flushing.

Before Kelsey could gather her wits about her and attend to the puddle at her feet another man entered the shop. He was dressed immaculately, his hair slicked back and plastered to his skull. His bright blue eyes took an immediate interest in Kelsey, holding her within his gaze, a prisoner to the aura of power he exuded.

"My apologies my dear," he said as he walked up to her table. "This wind, what can you do?" His smile was ear to ear, confident. Kelsey just gaped at him, unsure of what to say, what to do. "Allow me to purchase you another cup of coffee?"

"Konstantyn, your father is waiting," the man with the scar said, saving Kelsey from Konstantyn's attention.

"What is that diabeł doing here?" Konstantyn said, glaring at Loren.

"He wishes to speak to you, that is all I know," Loren said with a shrug.

"But of course." Konstantyn's smile returned and he locked eyes with Kelsey once more. "See that this beautiful young woman is given another cup of coffee, on the house of course. I'll be but a moment my dear."

"Thank you," Kelsey stuttered as the man spun towards the man with the scar and followed him out of the room through a door in the back.

"Piotr, a cup please," Feliks said, breaking the trance Kelsey was trapped in. Piotr complied and Feliks delivered the cup to Kelsey. "If you stay, you only invite his advance further." Feliks warned in a low voice meant only for Kelsey before he followed the other two men out of the room.

That was all Kelsey needed to hear. She left the fresh cup of coffee in her wake and practically sprinted out of the shop. The door flew open against the wind and nearly broke off of the hinges, but Kelsey paid it no mind as she rushed away from that place, that man. She could hear the laughter of the fearsome looking tough guys in her wake. She rushed to her car and sat in the driver seat for a moment, her hands trembling too much to put the keys in the ignition. She fished her phone from her bag and texted Erik, the phone shaking in her grasp.

"They're here," was all she could write.

Gerwazy watched Kelsey rush down the street from his second story perch above the shop.

"Get on with it, father, your impromptu visit is keeping me from a particularly delicious Mexican dish downstairs."

"I think you have nothing to worry about, Konstantyn, it would appear your conquest has fled your advances."

"What?" Konstantyn said, rushing to the window. His cheeks reddened with anger as he turned towards Gerwazy. "Now who will warm me tonight?"

"Quiet, Konstantyn. We have women for just that and you know it."

"Father! What is so important that it couldn't wait for five minutes?"

"Your gamble has failed, Konstantyn. Kincaid did not lead us to Erik, she did the opposite. Instead of bringing him in she has told him to run and hide. We are no closer to this clue Peter whimpered about, and I tire of the games."

"And how is this my fault? It was you who sought merely to follow him for as long as you did. And the mess with Peter? Was he not your idea?"

"Be quiet," Gerwazy growled. "I do not wish to point fingers, only to find solutions. Sit."

Konstantyn complied, glowering at the turn of events within the last few minutes. "Those loose ends have been tied. We must move forward. We must find Erik Brown. How he has eluded us thus far is very upsetting." Konstantyn looked to say something but Gerwazy talked right over him. "Loren, pay Lars a visit, see if he's heard from his wayward brother. And you, Konstantyn, I need you to focus. You've done enough damage already with your rash decisions."

"I did nothing more than what would have been done eventually!" he protested, jumping to his feet.

"Sit down!" Gerwazy screamed at him, causing Konstantyn's legs to turn to jelly and collapse beneath him. "You had no right! You're lucky you are my blood, were you any other man you'd be dissolving in the river as we speak!" Gerwazy let the maniacal gleam in his eye wash over Konstantyn to great effect. "Find Erik Brown. He is to be your lone thought. No more worry of a woman to warm your bed. The longer Erik Brown eludes us, the shorter your leash becomes and the angrier I become. Understand?"

Chapter 55

ERIK'S EARS RANG, the pillow did little to muffle the shot. It was a lot louder than Erik had thought it'd be, but its purpose was accomplished as he looked down at the man. He stared at Erik with bulging eyes, his breath rasping out of him in frantic gusts but not making a sound otherwise. Erik could hear the woman in the next room stifling a cry. He took a deep breath and walked out of the bedroom, shutting the door behind him.

The woman stared at him in disbelief, white as snow. Her shoulders heaved up and down with barely repressed sobs, the misery of loss stamped all over her. Erik felt a pang of guilt but pushed it down as far as it'd go. He was doing what was necessary and no one had truly gotten hurt… yet.

"Consider it a favor," Erik said callously. He crossed the room, shoving the pistol behind his belt and pulling out his knife. The woman gasped, words failing her. Erik ignored it and cut her feet free. "Be smart, I don't want to have to shoot you too, OK?"

The woman nodded emphatically, and Erik pulled her to her feet, spinning her around and cutting her hands free. "Let's go," he said grabbing her by the shoulder and steering her in front of him. He pushed her forward and she stumbled a couple of steps before turning to give him a vicious scowl. Erik quickly pulled the pistol from behind his belt and shoved it into the pocket of his coat, pointing it at her. The scowl only intensified as she turned back around.

"Do anything stupid and people die. Get it? I'm not messing around." Erik saw her shoulders sag in defeat, or at least he hoped so, otherwise what was the point of his macabre masquerade? "Now, go. We need to get the hell away from here."

The woman led the way through the front door. She worked the stiffness from her wrists as she walked with Erik a few steps behind her, far enough away to be out of her range if she tried anything. Of course, if she did, Erik had no idea what he'd do, probably just let her go and go back to a new draft of the plan. Erik wasn't a killer, a thought that made him search for answers as to what he'd do when he caught up to Gerwazy Zatorski. Turn him in? The man owned the police, and had some judges, politicians, etc. in his pocket. Not like Erik could just reason with him. He didn't have what Zatorski was looking for, and he doubted Zatorski would just pick up and leave and let Erik live his best life. At this point, Erik surely knew too much. Just knowing the name Zatorski had gotten Kincaid killed. Grief surged through Erik at the thought of her, but he threw up his dam and blocked it from taking control. He had to be cold. He had to be distant, capable of anything, at least in the eyes of this poor woman. His captive. It was a role, and he had to play it to the T.

Erik's thoughts came to a halt as he caught sight of the neighbors peeking out of their apartments, closing the doors with a squeak as they saw Erik and the woman. As he'd thought, the gun shot was too loud. He hoped he'd been right about it being the kind of neighborhood where people kept to themselves as the woman lead Erik down the stairs and around the corner. The old lady Erik had met earlier was just in the process of leaving her apartment. She snarled at the woman in front of Erik.

"Szumowiny." She said, her look brightening just a bit as she saw Erik. "You repair today?"

The optimism in her eyes made Erik's heart hurt. "Yes, I'll be back later," he told her as they walked past. Once they were out of earshot Erik asked the woman what the lady had said to her, more curious than worried.

"She called me scum," the woman responded in a no-nonsense tone.

"Guess your job isn't much of a secret around here."

The woman spun around in response; eyes narrowed like a cat about to strike. Erik reacted by wiggling the gun in his pocket. She looked down at it and spun back around, the glare never leaving her brow.

"I'm no murderer, coward. I help you because what do I care if evil kills evil? In one afternoon, you've taken everything I had left. If I'm scum, you are worse." She went silent and Erik didn't blame her for her words. How could she know that her boyfriend, or whoever he was to her, was lying on their bed, his only complaint stiff muscles and a fat lip. He wasn't about to tell her. He needed her to believe he was something he was not. He needed her to believe he was ruthless and not to be trifled with. It was an act and Erik played the role as best he could.

They reached the front door and the woman hesitated. She cocked her head to regard Erik with a cold look. "Where to, morderca?"

"Take me to Chudy." The woman laughed in response, the sound sending shivers down Erik's spine. It was the laugh of someone who didn't care anymore, someone who'd given up. It was Lars' laugh when he got back from Afghanistan. Erik was well acquainted with it.

"So, suicide?"

"What aren't you telling me?" Erik queried, trying to keep his voice neutral but failing.

"What aren't you asking, morderca?"

"That your new name for me? Cute. Just start walking, left out of the door."

She snorted her disdain but followed his directions. With no other place to go, Erik had her lead the way back to his cheap motel just a handful of blocks away. The woman hesitated outside his room, the door looming in front of her, the unknown waiting behind it. Erik offered her the key, but she just stared at it.

"I'm not going to hurt you. I already told you that." Erik could hear the plea in his voice but hoped she couldn't. Her eyes didn't waver, her face frozen. "Take it," Erik commanded, trying to snap her out of her daze.

Her eyes flitted up to his and he saw cold anger behind them as she tentatively reached for the key. Erik wagged the gun in his pocket at her trying to dissuade her from doing something stupid. She answered with a scowl, snatching the key from his palm and unlocking the door. She stepped through with a deep breath, clearly bracing herself for what was to come.

Erik hated what he was doing, but he had no choice. He had to get to Gerwazy somehow and Chudy was his best bet. He was like a dog with the scent trapped in its nose. He was single-minded and hungry. He had to keep going forward, one step after tumultuous step. He forced himself to regain the confidence and composure of the part he'd played in the apartment. The walk had given him too much time to think, to care about the effect he'd have on these people long after they were free of him. They're drug dealers. Scum, he reminded himself as he reset his walls. No place for emotion here. He had to get what he needed. He had to be free of this mess, to make it up to Kelsey, his family, get back to school. For Victor.

He entered the room right behind the woman. She turned to look at him, unsure of what he wanted her to do. "Sit down," he commanded her, his internal pep talk returning the cold edge to his voice. She complied, choosing to sit on the edge of the bed.

Erik shut the door behind him and bolted it. "All the way to the back of the bed," he told her as he pulled the pistol free of his pocket and placed it on the small round table by the window. He pulled out a chair and sat in it with a heavy sigh. The woman just watched him. "All the way back," Erik repeated.

A nervous look flitted across her face but she stamped it down like a pro and complied. "You going to rape me?"

Erik was shocked by the words, letting them hang in the air between them like an accusation painted in red across someone's front door. She tried to stare Erik down but as the silence lingered her eyes started to move around the room, looking everywhere but at him.

"Absolutely not," Erik finally said, making the woman jump, bringing her eyes back to him. "As long as you help me, you have nothing to fear from me."

"I already said I would," she snapped back, venom dripping from her tongue. "And then you killed Stefan anyway." A tear leaked from her eyes and Erik wanted to tell her Stefan was fine, but he restrained himself.

"He was a liability. If I left him behind, how long before I had the Polish mob breathing down my neck?"

"I loved him!" The woman growled.

"He was trash!" Erik retorted. "I don't speak a lot of Polish, but I know some. He was calling you a slut and a bitch. He'd have sold you out in a second if he thought it'd do him any good. I did you a favor."

The woman just stared at Erik, her thoughts trapped behind her cold, blue eyes. He waited for her rebuke, but it didn't come. Instead, she just clicked her jaw shut and looked away from him, more tears streaming down her cheeks.

"What's your name?" Erik said into the ensuing silence.

"Anna." She kept her eyes on the other side of the room and Erik didn't blame her.

"Anna, I'm Erik, and I'm sorry I got you involved with this."

Anna let out a single bitter chuckle before swinging her gaze back to Erik. "You're sorry? You ruin my life and offer me a sorry?"

"No one's apologized to me yet, so I figure you're ahead of the game."

"What's that supposed to mean?" Anna demanded, the anger back in her voice, the tears forgotten once more.

"Chudy. I need to find Chudy. Can you get him here?"

"No," Anna said, her cheeks flushing.

"But you know him?"

Anna's eyes darted away from his once more, studying the plaster on the walls, her tongue still in her mouth.

"You don't know him, do you?" Erik got up from the chair, closing his eyes to fight the anger building inside. His anger evaporated with the shocking buzz of his burner phone in his pocket. Only one person had that number. Kelsey.

Erik pulled out his phone and read her text, hope swelling in his chest. "Tell me about a shop on the corner of 7th and North."

Anna looked as if she'd been slapped, her eyes widening, her mouth working up and down. "You'll find nothing but death there," she was eventually able to say. "His real name is Feliks, the man from the sketch. And if it is Feliks you want, there is another place, less guarded. A place where people like Feliks go and let loose, only open at night when the city is most quiet."

Ten minutes later, Anna was tied up on the bed, duct tape covering her mouth. "I'm sorry I have to do this, but I can't take any risks. If I'm not back by tomorrow morning, the maid will find you and you can tell the police whatever you want because I'll be dead. If I find out you lied to me, I'll be back and you'll have a lot more to worry about, understand?"

Anna nodded her head, tears streaming down her cheeks once more. Erik hated making her cry, scaring her. He hated the whole thing and hoped he'd be back in a few hours with Feliks. That'd mean everything was going according to plan and he needed that. The alternative was exactly as he'd said. Death. He'd never clear his name, avenge Victor, finish medical school or see his loved ones again. This had to work.

Chapter 56

ERIK FOUND HIMSELF at a used car dealership just down the road, a sleazy one. One of those dealerships with a rusted-out sign, a message board with just a couple letters still in place underneath. The lot was mostly beaters, cars long forgotten and little cared for, dirty windshields, black dirt still coating the wheel wells, underneath the bumpers. Erik did a quick circle around one car in particular, the phone to his ear, Kelsey on the other line.

"I'm so sorry I asked you to do that," Erik said, anger building in his chest like the flames of a dragon, white hot in their intensity, begging for a target to be released upon.

"Not your fault, Erik. I volunteered and I'm glad I did. I can take care of myself, in case you forgot, and if you were the one that walked in there…" her voice caught, the implication clear.

Erik didn't make her say it. "Yeah, I know. Just be safe, Kelsey. These guys… they're scary. This woman I'm working with…" Erik's voice caught on the lie. "The things she's told me."

"I just wish you were here."

"I know, me too. I'm sorry. I'm sorry we met at such a strange time in my life. I'm sorry I pulled you into this and I'm sorry I have to miss the art show. If everything goes according to plan though… it just has to."

"Yeah, what the hell, Erik? Couldn't have planned it a little better?" Kelsey was joking, but Erik still winced at her words. "Call, text, just check in with me. I'm not going to stop worrying about you until you do."

Erik smiled, the feeling of someone caring, and knowing what he was up against, it invaded him with a sense of confidence he had no right to. He was going to succeed. He had to.

"I will."

Erik said his goodbyes and did one last lap around the old car. It looked serviceable for what he needed. He caught sight of a man with greased back hair and a rumpled suit watching him from inside the showroom, as if the term showroom was at all appropriate for the sad cars on display inside. The man had the look of a shark, the way his eyes locked on when Erik stepped into the run-down lobby. The place screamed dirty money and Erik didn't doubt the dealership was a front, but that worked for him. That was why he was there. He needed to get an inconspicuous car with zero paper trail. He had a backpack full of cash, having taken the whole thing from the vent before he left the motel.

Anna's eyes had watched him with barely concealed interest as he'd gone to work unscrewing the vent cover. He was pretty sure he'd heard her gasp when he pulled out the bag and checked its contents, but a bag full of tightly rolled hundred-dollar bills would do that to anyone.

"Hi there, fella," the sleazy car dealer started, his pudgy hand outstretched as he walked up to Erik.

Erik ignored it and instead pointed to the car in the middle of the lot. "How much for that?"

The dealer stopped short, his cocky smile disappearing for a moment while his wheels turned. Erik could see him doing the mental arithmetic and adding in a percentage for himself.

"6300 base price but we can jazz it up a bit if you have the money." That sleazy smile curled his lips once more and Erik just wanted to be away from him and his body odor of cigarettes and ham sandwiches.

"For that piece? You're out of your damn mind," Erik responded, his voice lighthearted and full of disbelief. "I'll give you two grand for that bucket. Cash."

The dealer's eyes narrowed, and Erik couldn't help but see a resemblance to a rat. Fitting, he thought as he turned back to the car. "Paint's peeling, tires are old. I can tell that from here. What am I going to find when I pop the hood?"

"Whoa, buddy. I don't know what kind of operation you think I'm running but that is a fine automobile!" The man forced so much conviction into his statement that Erik wondered if he believed it.

"No offense but I kicked the tires a bit before I walked in. That piece of shit isn't worth six grand."

"What do you take me for? You think I keep pieces of shit on my lot?" The mock hurt in his voice brought a smile to Erik's lips and even the dealer couldn't keep a straight face. "Four grand and I'll throw in an air freshener."

"Twenty-five hundred, cash, no questions, no paperwork." Erik said the words with a confidence he didn't feel, and he watched as the ugly little man's eyes widened. He looked Erik up and down and started calculating in a new light.

"Four grand and you and that car were never here." His sneer was ear to ear as he found the upper hand. The upper hand that Erik had given him.

"Four grand?" Erik responded, watching the corners of his mouth curl even further. "Fine."

Erik stuck out his hand and the dealer shot his out to grab it, sealing the deal. Erik really wasn't sure who'd won there, but he really didn't care. He needed a car and couldn't use his real identity, not unless he wanted the swat team busting down his motel door to add kidnapping and wrongful imprisonment to his list of perceived crimes.

"You go grab the keys and I'll get the cash ready." The dealer nodded and plodded off, his heavy steps a little lighter as he celebrated his sale.

Erik quickly dug into the backpack and pulled out a roll of money. He counted out forty one-hundred-dollar bills and shoved the rest into his pocket, surprised by how much more there was in the bundle. He must have forty grand in his bag. He lamented his stupidity in not counting it all out back in the safety of the motel and searched the showroom for cameras. None. Probably because it was a front, and they didn't need the recorded proof. Erik had no doubt that his car was either stolen or full of stolen parts, but he just needed it for a bit and then he could ditch it somewhere the police would find it.

The dumpy man waddled back into the lobby and jingled some keys in one hand. "Four grand, please."

Erik pressed the wad of cash into his sweaty little palm and held his hand out for the keys. The dealer hesitated, his smile curling deeper. "Another grand and I don't tell the police some dumb fuck stole one of my cars."

Erik couldn't believe his ears and just stared at the smiling man. "Take it or leave it," he cackled, his jowls swinging back and forth in amusement.

Anger gurgled back up from the pit of Erik's stomach and filled his eyes with its white-hot hatred. The dealer's smile quivered in response as the silence unfolded between them, but the smile never fully left his lips. He was a smug bastard, far too comfortable to be anything other than a cog in a criminal enterprise.

Erik stared the man down as he shoved his hand into his pocket and pulled out the wad of cash. The dealer's eyes lit up again and his cogs started turning again.

"Make that two. You can afford it."

That did it. All of the anger and frustration that had been trapped within Erik broke free, his face turning crimson and twisting into a monster's scowl. He threw the wad of money at the man's face catching him off guard and making him retreat a step. Erik surged forward and grabbed the fat man by his shirt and lifted him up just a bit, to get him off balance, before he slammed him onto his back. He went down with a thud, his foul breath of cigarettes and coffee rushing out of his lungs, his head bouncing once on the tile floor with a terrific smack. His eyes rolled back in his head for a moment before refocusing on Erik, blurry and watery.

Erik was immediately terrified at what he was doing but forced himself to play the role. The role of a man not to be trifled with. He needed the man to fear him, fear his return. He needed him to take the money and forget all about Erik. He put his face right next to the car dealers, his eyes boring through the back of his skull.

"Keep the money, you piece of shit. If anyone comes looking for me, cops or your goon buddies, I'll be back to haunt you. Understand?"

The man just stared up at Erik, so scared he barely breathed. "Yes?" Erik growled, throwing every ounce of menace he could muster into it.

"Yeah… Yeah…" The dealer finally managed.

"Good," was all Erik responded before regaining his feet and checking the gun in the back of his belt. He turned as he did so, making sure the man saw it, and walked out of the showroom, leaving the sleazy dealer on the cold tile floor in a sea of money and his own piss.

Erik fired up the engine and drove off the lot, his adrenaline subsiding and leaving him with trembling fingers dancing along the steering wheel's hard rubber. He took a deep, calming breath and fought the bout of panic that tried to overtake him.

"Shit, shit," Erik murmured as he started to shake. He pulled over to the curb a couple blocks away and fished out his phone, calling Selene's office.

"Selene Brown's office, this is Selene."

"Selene," Erik said, her name whooshing out of him on the edge of a scared sob.

"Erik? You OK?" Selene's voice was filled with worry, her maternal instincts immediately picking up the wrongness on the other end of the line.

"Oh, Selene. Everything's so messed up. I did something, I didn't even know I was capable of it. I'm scared, Selene. Scared of what I'm becoming."

"Jesus, Erik! What'd you do? Are you OK?"

Erik ran the back of his hand over his cheeks, wiping away the tears he hadn't realized had fallen. "I... this sleazy asshole... I almost beat him up, Selene. I was so angry, I just snapped."

"You got into a fight? Are you hurt?"

"No... I mean, yeah, I got into a fight, and no, I'm not hurt, just rattled. I've never felt so angry. I've never... I just slammed the man on his back."

"Did he deserve it?" Selene always knew how to cut to the core of it. She never passed judgement, she just didn't.

"Yeah..." Erik stammered.

"And he's OK?"

"Yeah... other than probably being as scared as he's ever been, he'll be fine."

"OK then, breathe, Erik. You're under so much stress, don't be so hard on yourself! I watched you grow up, I know who you are, and one angry outburst at some asshole isn't going to change that."

"Yeah, you're right, Selene. It's just so scary, discovering what you're capable of. I just don't like who I think I'm becoming."

"Oh, Erik. You're the gentlest soul I've ever met. You're going to be OK. I promise."

"Thanks, Selene."

"You're welcome. Now go enjoy your conference and tell me all about it when you get home!"

"Yeah, see you soon," Erik said, hope swelling in his chest as he willed it to be true.

Chapter 57

ERIK DROVE THROUGH the quiet neighborhood; the sun preparing to set and release the scum that ran the night. He was able to push the whole ordeal at the dealership to the back of his mind along with everything else he refused to think about. Anna had told Erik where he could find Feliks, admitting that neither her nor her boyfriend really knew him much more than in passing as they exchanged services. Feliks would occasionally sell them a kilo of heroin, or a weapon. He dabbled in the underworld, filling many roles for the crime family Erik hunted. Anna had never heard of Gerwazy, but she was only on the periphery, allowed to exist because she got her hands dirty and kicked up the profits. Feliks was very secretive, cautious. Anna warned Erik that she'd never met him alone, that he always had an entourage of one or two thugs. He was low level, but high enough to matter. Captain of the errand boys. They liked to drink though, and she knew where.

Erik continued to drive, trying his best to be as inconspicuous as possible. He tugged the beanie down over his ears, popped the lenses out of the pair of cheap sunglasses and tried to wear them like he needed them. On close inspection it'd be obvious they were just the frames, but he didn't plan on getting that close to anyone other than Feliks. The gun Erik had taken from Anna's boyfriend sat in the cup holder just within Erik's reach. He ignored it and the implications it brought with it. His mind wandered as he drove through the darkening

282

streets, every other streetlamp popping on as he drove by as if to scream that he didn't belong.

Could he kill someone? The thought rolled around his mind, no answer forthcoming. He was no murderer, of man anyway. He'd killed his fair share of deer, rabbits and doves, but he'd always dressed them and salvaged everything he could. If forced, could he squeeze that trigger on a fellow human being? He tried to convince himself that if his life depended on it, he could. Thinking it and doing it were separate feats though and only time would truly tell.

A blinking red sign brought Erik's mind back to the driver's seat of the beater he was in. The sign said, "The Warsaw Republic" and Erik knew he'd arrived. It was one of the nicer bars he'd seen since his arrival in this poor, rundown, immigrant neighborhood. Toughs lounged outside smoking cigarettes and joking. It was a charade though, as Erik noticed their ever-vigilant eyes probing the streets around them. The bulge in a jacket signaled the presence of a gun and Erik had no doubt each man was armed and more than capable of using it. Anna had warned him of that though.

Erik coasted by and pulled over just within sight of the bar. He tucked the gun into his belt and stepped out of the car. He locked the door with the key and crossed the street. He popped the collar of his work jacket and scrunched his neck into it, letting the lapels brush his cheeks as he shoved his hands into the shallow pockets. He forced his arms back to disguise his own bulge in the back of his jacket. He walked with a purpose, keeping his eyes forward and down but cataloging everything within his peripheries. He passed an alley that drove like a dagger into a dead end between two seemingly connected buildings, a door with a red light illuminating the small cutaway. The door was like a dirty sore in the side of the building, a back door for the bar, likely for deliveries and nothing more since there was only one exit.

The red glow of a cigarette signaled a guard leaning against the opposite building and, where there was one, Erik figured there were at least two. He disregarded the alley and kept on walking. He was within spitting distance when he realized the guards at the front of the bar had gone quiet. He kept his head down and watched them from the corner of his eye. They glowered at him, cigarettes hanging from their closed mouths, hands lingered within their coats, firearms clutched and ready to rock. Erik ignored them and kept walking by. As the distance between them grew, the murmur of discussion sounded from behind him once more. Talking about me, Erik thought, a new pep in his step as he increased the distance. Jovial laughter erupted behind him and he managed to relax just a hair.

Erik continued down the street until he hit the corner and hung a right to circle the block. The buildings next to the club looked empty, the windows dark and gaping against the soft light from the streetlamps, spider web cracks spread through several glass panels. Erik briefly noted the faded paint on the doors adorning the top of each stoop. He began to wonder if the buildings just appeared empty or actually were. He fought the tug and pull of his subconscious as it tried to start a discourse on what the vacant buildings signified. He fought it with the firm thought of, does it matter? And the response nagged at the corner of his mind as he continued down the quiet street. Of course, it does.

Erik continued his sojourn around the desolate block, only the odd individual crossing his path as he went. The buildings continued their dark vigil on the empty streets below and the urge to try one of the faded doors feuded with Erik's sense of caution. So much so, that at one-point Erik found himself on the bottom step of one stoop, staring as though to bypass the thick wooden door. The roar of a distant car engine growing louder as it approached him was the only thing that broke the spell. Erik rounded the last corner, crossing the street and sneaking back to his car in the shadows. He slipped into the back seat, his eyes never leaving the guards perched outside the club. If they'd seen him, they gave no indication. Erik breathed a sigh of relief, the tension never leaving his shoulders. He draped a dark blanket over his body, the edge like a cowl over his head, his eyes just visible to anyone that cared to scrutinize the back window of the dark vehicle.

The guards continued their watch on the comings and goings of the desolate sidewalk and Erik quickly realized why his passing had been such a cause for concern. The only people that walked by the club, or on that side of the sidewalk in general, were fellow gangsters and thugs. They slapped hands in some secret handshake as they walked by, making their way through the heavy steel doors, the armored platting on the inside glinting against the streetlights as if to signal the clubs ill repute to any watching eye.

Men came and went, none of them sparking recognition in Erik's tired mind, until a black SUV, much like the one that'd followed Erik days before, crept up the street, stopping at the small open lot between the buildings. A couple of guards raced to the chain link gate and pushed it open, grunting against its heavy frame, the tiny wheels at the bottom sliding more than rolling under the weight. The car stopped and one of the guards opened the back-passenger door. A severe man stepped out, his receding hair line greased backwards against his skull, his widows peak like an arrowhead pointing towards a nose that arched gracefully to his lips, at odds with the menacing eyes that perched above it. A well-groomed goatee coated his chin, a pencil thin mustache adorning the lip above it. He moved confidently, so much swagger in each step that Erik had no doubt of his importance. The guards fawning over him, lighting his cigarette, made no difference.

Erik's heart stopped, his breath stagnant in his lungs, as Feliks stepped out of the passenger seat. Even in the meager light, Erik could see the dark bruises under each eye, the white glimmer of bandage draped across a nose that seemed off, crooked even. Feliks lit a cigarette, his lighter flourishing in his hand as he clicked it shut and jammed it back into his pocket. Anger rose up in Erik, forcing the breath from his lungs in a surprised gasp. He'd not even realized he had stopped breathing.

Feliks walked around the SUV and was met by the driver, the other man from the coffee shop, the man with the scar, his tail from just a few days ago. Erik fought the surprise that tried to disorient him, telling himself that of course he'd be there too. They work together. Erik took a few calming breaths and settled himself. No fear, be smart. They weren't expecting him. Why would they? To them, he was just a scared medical student, probably too terrified to do much more than run and hide. The thought was like a warm blanket for his nerves. He settled underneath it and regained his focus on Feliks.

Feliks stood next to the other man, puffing his cigarette dramatically. The other man patted his pockets, eventually pulling out his own pack of smokes. He opened it and then spiked it violently. Feliks laughed at him, but the laughter was short lived as the other man turned a scornful eye on him. Erik couldn't hear the words but the emotion on the man's face conveyed the message. His brow contorted, his cheeks flushing red. He shoved Feliks and pointed a menacing finger into Feliks' chest. Feliks staggered backwards under the onslaught, his eyes dropping to the asphalt. The important passenger turned around, just at the club's door, to smirk down at the beleaguered Feliks. The angry man finished his tongue lashing and the whole group burst into laughter at Feliks' expense. He cowered against it, throwing up his hands in surrender. He shuffled his way back to the driver's door of the SUV, his hand touching the handle before the important man barked down at him.

"Walk," Erik thought he said, and Feliks did just that, nodding in dejection, shoving his hands into his pockets and shuffling out of the back lot and onto the sidewalk. Erik couldn't believe his luck. He watched in disbelief as Feliks sauntered down the block, walking past Erik's car on the other side of the street without even a glance.

Erik waited for Feliks to cross the street, close enough to his car to touch it. He let Feliks round the corner and scrambled into the driver seat climbing over the center console from the back seat. He did it as subtly as he could, his heartbeat drumming in his ears, his breath coming in ragged, adrenaline-fueled gasps. He turned over the motor and used every ounce of self-control to let the vehicle glide forward instead of squealing the tires. He eyed the guards in his rearview mirror, but they were too focused on the newcomer to notice him halfway down the block.

Erik turned the corner and spotted Feliks. He was busy dragging his feet, muttering to himself as he kicked pieces of garbage into the gutter. He looked terrible as Erik cruised by him, the streetlights illuminating the damage he'd suffered to his face. His nose was broken, his cheeks bruised and scabbed. He'd been worked over, and recently.

Erik coasted up the street a little further, trusting that Feliks' path went his way. Erik had been rehearsing this moment in his mind for the last twenty-four hours. Playing the scene over and over in his head, his mind searching for any weaknesses, anything that could go wrong. He parked the car in the darkness between streetlights, scanning the area for people, witnesses, lookouts, anything.

He exited the car, his hood pulled over his head, fake glasses resting on the bridge of his nose. He continued to scan his surroundings and saw nothing. This block appeared as empty as the one the club shared. The soft glow of lights within the three-story buildings was the only proof of life, but the windows were shut, blocking out the poverty-stricken streets they oversaw.

Erik made his way to his trunk and popped it open, pretending to shuffle through something inside of it while the distance between Feliks and him narrowed. Erik continued his charade, half in the trash bag lined, empty trunk, just like he'd seen in the mob movies. Primed for murder, he thought, his heart skipping a beat. But murder was the furthest thing from his plan. His plan was fear. The shuffling steps grew louder, and Erik made as if he was trying to get something heavy out of the trunk. He looked up; his face hidden by the cowl of his jacket collar.

"Mała pomoc?" he said to the passing form that was Feliks. Feliks ignored him, or didn't hear him at all, lost in a stupor. Erik stepped onto the sidewalk, his pulse racing. "Panie!" Feliks spun around in his tracks, one hand shooting behind his back where Erik imagined a gun rested. Erik threw up his hands in surrender, trying to put Feliks at ease. "Mała pomoc?"

Feliks scowled back at Erik. "Weź się pierdol," Feliks said, venom flying from his clenched teeth. He was about to turn around when Erik shoved a hand into his pocket and pulled out a wad of cash. The move sent Feliks racing for his gun again, but he relaxed when he realized Erik was holding out a stack of cash.

"Proszę?" Erik waved the money at Feliks. Feliks straightened up and smiled.

"Kogo potrzebujesz, mojego przyjaciela?" Not for the first time, Erik regretted not learning more Polish from Marga, but his grasp was just firm enough that he caught a word here and there, enough to know he'd won Feliks' trust.

"Tutaj," Erik said, motioning to the empty trunk, but Feliks' angle didn't show him that it was empty, and he stepped around the car and peered down into the darkness, his eyes widening in realization at just the last moment as Erik clubbed him in the back of the head.

Feliks crumbled halfway into the trunk, unconscious. Erik looked around the empty street. Desolate, still. He quickly fished the pistol out of Feliks' belt, his phone from his front pocket, and pushed him the rest of the way into the trunk. Feliks moaned softly as Erik bound his hands behind his back, moving on to his feet and then shoving a gag into Feliks' slack jaw. He slammed the trunk shut and hopped into the driver seat, heart racing the whole way back to the motel where Anna awaited him.

Chapter 58

ERIK PULLED INTO the quiet motel parking lot and killed the engine. He surveyed the dark windows, the vacant customer service counter. He took a deep relaxing breath and stepped out of the car. He kept his eyes scanning as he approached the trunk. No movement, no prying eyes, but then again, that's why he'd chosen that motel. Sleazy, dive-y. Perfect for an affair, an escort, a drug deal or, in his case, an interrogation.

Erik jammed the key into the trunk's lock, and it unclasped with a loud click and popped open revealing the terrified stare of Feliks as he lay in the plastic lined coffin. Erik pulled up his shirt to reveal Feliks' gun stuffed into the front of his pants.

"You don't have to die here, OK?" Feliks just stared, his eyes growing wider. "Do what I say, and you have nothing to fear from me. Got it?" Feliks just continued to stare. "Nod your head yes or no."

Feliks snapped out of it and gave Erik a quick nod yes. "Good. I'm going to cut your feet free, OK?" Feliks nodded again, this time more quickly.

Erik cut the bindings around Feliks' ankles and pulled his legs halfway out of the trunk. He then grabbed Feliks by his coat and tugged him up into a sitting position. Feliks scanned the parking lot, his eyes flicking as quickly as possible around himself as he found his bearings, as he calculated his escape. The movement was so fast, Erik almost missed it, but Victor had trained him well in reading the body language of others.

Erik put his knife up to Feliks' neck in a flash of silver. Feliks whimpered in surprise, his breath gusting out of him as fear froze out any more oxygen from entering his lungs.

"Don't be stupid," Erik growled. Feliks let in a ragged breath as Erik moved the knife away from his throat. "Get up." Feliks hesitated but the menace in Erik's eyes prompted him to stagger to his feet, his hands still bound behind his back. "Turn around." Feliks did as he was told and Erik grabbed him by the bound wrists, the tip of his knife sticking Feliks in the small of his back. "I'm going to remove your gag. Try anything and I'll take one of your kidneys."

Feliks didn't move, so Erik took that as an understanding. He removed the gag with one hand, the knife still pressed into Feliks' back with the other. Erik tossed the gag into the trunk and slammed it shut. Feliks jumped in surprise and the knife bit into his skin. He gasped in pain but did little more, to Erik's relief.

"Walk," Erik commanded, prodding him forward with his free hand. Feliks stumbled forward but Erik kept the knife on his back, a tiny bead of blood winding down the knife's blade to rest against the handle. Erik ignored it, his eyes roving the windows, waiting for a face to appear and destroy everything he'd accomplished that night, but no such face appeared.

They arrived at Erik's room without incident. Erik opened the door with a free hand and pushed Feliks through the doorway. He stumbled into the TV stand and careened off of it to land on the floor with a grunt and a thud. Erik entered the room right behind him and quickly closed the door. He scanned the room in one quick movement and landed on Anna just sitting on the bed where he'd left her. She looked at him with surprised eyes going from him to Feliks and back again. She raised an eyebrow, as if impressed, but Erik chose not to read much into it.

Erik grabbed Feliks and pulled him upright before pushing him backwards into a chair. Feliks gave little to no resistance as he slumped into the sturdy piece of furniture. He cringed against the impact on his bound hands but said nothing. Erik pulled out Feliks' gun and pointed it at him. Feliks just looked away, not scared, just weary.

"Don't make me use this, OK?" Feliks rolled his eyes and brought them up to match Erik's.

"It took me a moment," he muttered in his soft accent, "but now I see it. Erik Brown. We were wondering where you had gotten off to." His words were strangely unconfrontational, resigned even.

"You destroyed my life," Erik responded, at a loss for anything else to say.

"Yes," Feliks conceded.

"You killed my bestefar... my grandfather."

"Not me, no, but I know who did. That is what this is about, right?"

Erik again was at a loss for words. He'd pictured this interrogation going many ways, but this wasn't one of them.

"Listen, Erik Brown. I am tired. I am tired of following you, tired of being blamed for losing you. I am tired of being smacked around, shit on, taken for granted. Just ask your questions, OK?"

"Who killed Victor."

"Konstantyn Zatorski."

"Konstantyn Zatorski?"

Feliks sighed before answering. "Yes. He was only supposed to kidnap Victor, but he lost his shit when he saw him coming up the walk and shot him instead. He is a lunatic, ask the girl. Hello, Anna. How is your father?" Feliks smiled at Anna and she cringed, her eyes darting to the opposite side of the room. "Do not worry, Anna, you will be seeing him soon. I doubt either of us are making it out of this one." He burst into tired laughter and broke his gaze from her to look back up at Erik.

"Why?"

"Why what? Why did he shoot him? I could not tell you. I know... knew nothing of your grandfather. He was just a job, an easy one. Snatch and grab. Old man at that, and then Konstantyn goes crazy and blows out the back of his head. I have seen things in this life, but that? The way he stood over him, panting, smiling, crying. He is a lunatic, I already told you."

Erik gulped down his tattered emotions, breathed in a long deep breath and centered himself. He felt his mind go empty, and he took a seat on the edge of the bed. Anna cowered just feet away from him, but he paid her little mind.

"Start at the beginning. Why were you targeting Victor?"

Feliks smirked, his eyes dropping to the floor in front of Erik. "Gerwazy told us too."

Erik shot to his feet and smacked Feliks with the back of his hand. "No games," he growled. Erik watched the anger dance within Feliks' eyes but with a little effort he squashed it and found his sad smirk instead.

"The very beginning then, OK. Well, I guess, it all started with your brother..."

"Lars?" Erik interrupted; his calm rattled once more.

"Do you have another brother? No? Ok then, yes, Lars. He borrowed money from us. They sent me and Loren to collect, break some fingers if necessary. Not my silny, but Loren, well, he is good at such things. I mostly just make sure he does not go too far. Well, this time, Konstantyn wanted to come. He was feeling especially violent and needed to get it out. Who was I to say no?"

Feliks paused, a haunted look washing over him, and Erik realized Feliks had been on the receiving end of that violence, and recently it looked like.

"Well, long story short, Konstantyn is about to go to work on Lars when he sees this picture on your brother's desk. All the rage fell out of him. Me and Loren were left just holding Lars down, even he was so surprised he stopped squirming against us. It was strange, like nothing I have seen. Konstantyn picks up the picture and just stares at it. I am too afraid to say a thing, Loren too. Finally, Konstantyn turns around and holds up the photo and asks Lars who is this man in it. Lars tells him it is Victor. Konstantyn just turns it around and looks at it some more.

"Nobody moves. What the hell is going on I remember thinking, then Konstantyn pulls up a chair and sits down in it. Do you know who this woman is? He asks Lars. Lars is not sure what to say, none of us are. That is my mother, Konstantyn tells him before punching Lars in the gut."

"What? His mother?" And then Erik remembered Smith's theory about Marga. Then Konstantyn is Gerwazy's son, Erik realized.

"Who am I to make sense of such things? All I know is that Konstantyn went to work on your brother's gut. Beat out every bit of information on Victor and Marga. He cried when Lars told him Marga was dead. He cried. I have never seen him do anything other than scream and growl. We left without the money. He took the photo, that was it. When he showed it to Gerwazy, well, I have never seen so much anger from the man. He was like a volcano. It just erupted out of him, he took a fire poker to his furniture, destroyed expensive paintings. I thought he was going to kill me just for standing in the wrong place at the wrong time. Instead, he ordered us to find Victor and bring him to him. Then he asks his bodyguard to call an art gallery, calm again, ready to replace his paintings just like that. Konstantyn insisted on going with us and the rest is, as you Americans put it, history."

"Then, what do I have to do with any of this? If it was revenge, then why me? Why not my brother, or sister, or father?"

Feliks shrugged; his disinterest evident. "I am a soldier. I do what I am told, no more. They say watch you? I watch you. They say follow you? I follow you. To me, you were a boring typical American elitist with your apartment in a nice part of town, your studies in medicine. Your mind-numbing routine. Studies, gym, sleep. Studies, gym, sleep. Bah!" Feliks looked away from Erik and let his head sag over the back of the chair. "You were annoying fly buzzing in my ear until you went to the bank that one day. What business does he have here? Loren asks me."

"So, you drugged me so you could ransack my house, Victor's house?"

"What? Drug you? What are you saying? It makes no sense. Why would we drug you? We knew your routine; we were following you. Why drug you when we already know where you are, where you will be? We lose you; we just go where we know you will be next. Simple."

The cold logic seeped into Erik's brain and sat there, an icy spike refusing to melt within the fires of his active mind. Erik watched him, scrutinized him, seeking the glimmer of a lie but Feliks gave no hint to it. It was the truth, Erik realized, his stomach bottoming out, a falling feeling working its way up his chest to sit like a bowling ball over his lungs. So, it was John Smith. He'd already admitted to as much, but there had still been a kernel of doubt in Erik's fertile mind. He fought to keep his calm, to dam the emotions trying to flood his face. He gulped against the rush and only just managed to stem the tide before it swept him under. He wasn't sure why he wanted so desperately to hide his thoughts from this man, this thug, but the need was overwhelming.

"Then who else? You said you were following me, if that's true, you should know who drugged me." Erik put a challenge into his words and Feliks perked up, his sad smile filled with contempt.

"Of course, we saw it happen. Who it was? I don't know. They rushed you on the street, put you in a van and drove off."

"And you didn't follow them?"

"Of course, we did. That does not mean we know who they are."

"And it wasn't you who ransacked my house while they had me?"

"I already said no."

"Then why did they have a gun connected to murders in this part of town? Gang murders..."

The smile slipped from Feliks lips and was replaced with a distrusting scowl. "You lie," was all he said in response.

"Nope. Detective Kincaid told me. They pulled a slug from the scene, one that was shot at me, and it matched some cold cases right here in your backyard." Erik let his words sink in for a moment. "Who killed Kincaid, was that you?"

Feliks' eyes shot to meet Erik's. "I am not a killer. I do not know who did it. Was it not you? That's what the police think." Feliks' lips curled into a menacing snarl of a smile. "Your old friend Jeffrey Grant too, if I am not mistaken."

Erik fought the urge to lunge across the room and knock the smile off Feliks' lips. His fists balled at his sides but that was as much as he allowed his anger to leak out.

"Jeffrey gets executed and you get beat up, within an inch of your life would be my guess. So, tell me, what did Loren get? He looked fine to me last I saw him, laughing with the boss, sending you to get cigarettes."

Feliks' smile once again evaporated, and his gaze fell to the floor. Erik could sense the anger boiling within him and made a mental note not to push him too far. He was a man with little to lose, inclined to make stupid decisions, and, if he was in disfavor, bringing Erik in would be a boon to his cause.

"Loren does not make mistakes, only those beneath him."

"And you're beneath him?"

Feliks snapped a glare towards Erik and nodded. "The more ruthless, the more power. I am weak in their eyes. I sell drugs to dumb fucks that get abducted by my enemies." His eyes moved to Anna. He gave her a sad smile. She whimpered against her gag and looked away from him again. "I collect protection money from beggars, and follow spoiled brats because Loren tells me to." Feliks' voice began to swell, his righteous anger finally finding an outlet, Erik. "I lure friends to their death so spoiled brats can be framed for murder! I stop to help stupid bastards in the streets so I can be abducted by stupid spoiled brats! Just kill me already! Or do what you plan to do, I am tired of the games. Tired of being yes man, stoolie, bitch."

Erik let him wind down, watching him with crossed arms, his own scowl perched on his lips. "I haven't even begun to get what I want from you, Feliks."

Defeat weighed heavily in Feliks body language as he slumped into his chair, seeming to deflate under Erik's gaze. "So be it," he replied, his tone heavy with resignation.

Chapter 59

AN HOUR LATER found Feliks bound to a chair, heavy rope wrapped around his chest, arms and legs. A gag filled his mouth as tired eyes watched Erik prepare for the next phase of his plan. Anna, just like Feliks, watched Erik with a similar, haunted look.

Erik did his best to ignore her, willing out the cold persona he'd adopted in his dealings with her and Stefan. His conscience clawed at the wall, begging him to be human for just one moment with the frightened woman watching him from her restraints on the bed. He forced his gaze to stay away from her, but his peripheral vision allowed the heart-rending sight into his mind anyway. He stuffed some supplies into his backpack, zipping it and shouldering it in a quick motion. He locked eyes with Anna and paused. Words bubbled into his brain, but his opened mouth did nothing more than breathe. The silence stretched between them, fear clouding Anna's irritated, red eyes. Erik noticed the dark circles underneath them for the first time, the mascara running in faint tracks down her cheeks and felt ashamed.

"I'm sorry," he finally said, feeling no relief in the quizzical look Anna sent back at him. "I'm sorry," he murmured again, the words hollow in his own ears as he turned and walked out the door. He plucked a long hair from his head and closed it in the heavy door so that it stuck out just below the handle. *Safety first*, Victor agreed.

Erik's beat-up car made a high-pitched squeal as he shifted gears. He knew the sound; he'd spent too much time working on the Chevelle with Victor not to. He shook his head and marveled at the audacity of that slimy car dealer. He imagined the man squirming in his seat as Erik pulled up in the shitty car and walked towards the front door. He imagined the man soiling himself in fear, begging forgiveness, promising to give up his swindling ways.

The blast of a car horn brought Erik back to himself, his eyes darting to his rearview mirror, instantly landing on the reddened face of a fat man in a sedan he hadn't noticed when he decided to change lanes. Erik lifted his hand and motioned his apology, but the man continued his inaudible cussing out of Erik and Erik was forced to push it from his mind, along with his fantasy confrontation. He yawned and realized for the first time how tired he really was. He looked at himself in the rearview mirror and noted his own dark circles showing from beneath the makeup, the redness of his own eyes.

"When was the last time you really slept?" He asked his reflection.

He drove for another fifteen minutes, passing out of the squalor of the neighborhood where he'd begun his path towards redemption. No sooner had the rundown buildings receded from his rearview than he found himself surrounded by middle class suburbia. He drove a bit further, and parked along the side of the road. He checked his disguise in the rearview, decided it'd do. He barely recognized himself.

He walked past a few storefronts, long closed for the night, hardly seeing them before he stopped in front of a pizza joint. He looked through the front window, scanning the meager occupants inside. None fit the bill of Eastern European thug, so he went in. The door chimed his entrance, and the scent of baked dough and melted cheese filled his nose. His stomach growled in response and Erik realized he'd not eaten in a while. It was as if he'd forgotten his body's basic needs. Food, sleep, water...

"Been here before?" Erik looked up into the friendly eyes of Lars Brown, older brother, tormentor, lifelong drag. Lars' smile didn't waiver. Erik forced one to his tired lips, silently celebrating his disguise. Even his own brother didn't recognize him.

"Lars," Erik started. His voice strange in his own ears, sounding as if he were being strangled. Emotions rolled over his mind, memories tugging at his attention, filling him with angst, sadness, and anger. There stood the architect of Victor's death. There stood the master of his family's pain, going all the way back to Erik's birth. Disgust must have crept into Erik's gaze because Lars stiffened, his own smile slipping into perplexity.

"Do I... I'm sorry, have we met before?" The words sounded weak, a quality he'd never seen from Lars, the brash troublemaker, the lifelong rogue.

"We need to talk," Erik responded, raising himself to full height, shaking out the weary muscles weighing down his shoulders. Lars' smile slipped completely, dread filling his eyes. *He thinks you're with Zatorski*, Victor's voice murmured in the back of his mind. *Use it*, it finished. "Privately."

Lars gave a solemn nod and motioned for Erik to follow him. They wound their way past the pizza oven, the employees that didn't even lift their gaze from the task at hand as they passed. Lars led Erik to his office, a small supply closet of a room right next to the walk-in cooler. The buzz of the refrigeration unit vibrated through the off-white wall. Lars sat heavily in his chair and looked up at Erik in resignation.

Erik said nothing, just staring down at his brother, a man he hardly knew, who didn't even recognize Erik's voice. How far they'd drifted apart. How far apart they'd started.

"What now? I already gave you everything I have. My grandfather's guns... I thought we were even?" Lars' words were tinged with hesitant rage, his fists clenched on top of the steel tabletop of his cluttered desk. A light went on in Erik's overworked mind as he realized how one of Victor's guns had turned up at Jeffrey's murder. "I'm all out of shit to give! The last thing I have is this damn restaurant and you already have a quarter of it!"

"Shut up," Erik growled, the full scope of Lars' crimes laid bare. He'd sold his soul to the devil, Erik realized. "Why?" Was all Erik could force past his own anger.

"What?" Lars looked as though Erik had slapped him. "Why? What the fuck is that supposed to mean?"

"Why'd you sell your soul to the Zatorskis, you miserable prick!"

Lars sat bolt upright, his eyes squinting in confusion, searching Erik's face, realization dawning slowly. "Erik?"

"Why'd you do it, Lars! Why? Bestefar is dead because of you! You killed him!" Hot, heavy tears sprang unexpectedly to Erik's eyes, slipping down his cheeks to drip off his chin.

The shock slowly wore off of Lars and was replaced with indignant anger. He shot out of his chair and trembled across the desk from Erik. "You spoiled piece of shit, how dare you," his rage was so intense his words whooshed out in a whisper. "How dare you! I had nothing to do with Bestefar's death!"

"Konstantyn killed him. Your god damn business partner!"

"What?"

"Konstantyn Zatorski murdered Bestefar. He shot him in the back of the fucking head, Lars. It was Konstantyn! And you lead him to Bestefar. You didn't pull the trigger, but you pointed the gun. I had to know if it was true. I had to hear it from your own worthless lips. Feliks was right. Holy shit! Feliks was right!" Tears streamed down Erik's cheeks, his voice cracking between sobs. The fatigue from the last few days overwhelmed him, and he had no defense, and all in front of his brother, his lifelong nemesis.

Lars' eyes softened, his mouth working as if to say something but only breath escaped his opened lips. His anger melted and he slumped backwards into his chair. The legs screeched against the tile floor as they begrudgingly gave under his sudden weight. "No," he whispered to himself, his eyes falling to the gleaming surface of his desk, to the spot where Erik's tears fell unabashed.

"Konstantyn. He killed Bestefar and now he's trying to frame me for a different murder, and one of Bestefar's guns was the murder weapon… and you gave it to them." Erik trembled with rage as Lars' shocked eyes found him again. "They think I know where something is, something Bestefar stole from them a long time ago."

"Jesus Christ! Are you serious?"

And so, Erik told him everything, about how Feliks and some man named Loren had been following him for weeks before he made them. Lars cringed at the mention of Loren but stayed quiet. Erik told him about Jeffrey and how he'd gotten away from him, how Jeffrey turned up dead shortly after and how Det. Kincaid was quick to follow. Lars listened in rapt silence as Erik relayed the plot of an action movie. Erik's words met with disbelief when he revealed Victor's sordid past with Zatorski, the CIA, Marga and Norway.

"Konstantyn is our half uncle, I think," Erik finished. "I'm not sure what went down but—"

"Jesus," Lars interrupted. "All this because I needed a fucking loan? Because you just had to be a doctor and tapped everyone in the family out to make it happen? Fuck, Erik! This is on you as much as me!"

Erik stood in disbelief. "Are you serious?"

"God dammit, Erik! You're so fucking selfish you can't even see it! You got everything, always have!"

"Bullshit. Don't even try that on me. I worked my ass off to go to medical school. I didn't abandon the family as soon as I was eighteen. I didn't get into trouble and make everyone's life hell! And I didn't tap the family for shit! I went to undergrad on scholarships, it didn't cost anyone a dime. Did you ever think that maybe nobody trusted you with their money because you're a lifelong screw up?"

"Fuck you," Lars said, cold fury vibrating the words.

"Did you ever think I got to where I am because I cared about someone other than myself? You're pathetic," Erik spat, done with the conversation, done with Lars, for good this time. He turned on his heel and reached for the door, not expecting Lars to throw himself over the desk and tackle him.

Erik slammed against the door with a crash and the two thudded to the ground. Erik struggled to get Lars off of his back, utilizing the jujitsu training Victor had been sure to teach him to roll Lars off his back, scrambling to get the higher ground on top of him. Erik was bigger and he was stronger, but Lars had been in the military and had trained for far longer in self-defense than Erik. He would not be thrown easily.

Erik protected his neck as he tried to spin around and get half guard on Lars, but Lars blocked him. Erik started throwing elbows behind him but found only air, that was when Lars threw his first punch, catching Erik on the corner of his cheek. Erik howled with anger, confusion and fear. His adrenaline spiked and all his fatigue was wiped away in an unbridled torrent. Strength surged through his limbs and he overpowered Lars' dogged defense to gain the upper hand.

He spun between Lars' legs and turned his piercing gaze on him. Lars met it with his own determination. Finally, the fight that'd been brewing for Erik's whole life. Erik tried to throw a punch, but Lars latched onto his wrist with one hand, the other protecting his face. Erik tried to shake it off, but Lars' grip was sure, so Erik abandoned that hand and raised the other one. He rained down a heavy fist. Trying to connect with Lars' head but Lars easily blocked it. Erik tried again, and again, and again, but each time Lars was ready. Finally, Erik grew weary of the game and bucked up, freeing a knee from the ground, he used it to ram Lars in the thigh with all his might. Lars yelped and Erik broke his grip on his right wrist. He fell forward with all his weight, ramming his elbow into Lars' chin.

Lars yowled in pain but used Erik's momentum to roll him off of him. Erik found himself in a triangle hold, the blood rushing out of his head. His vision went dark and then he was asleep.

Chapter 60

ERIK WAS PASSED out on that floor, for only Lars knew how long before he startled awake, his mind groggy, his memory hazy. He looked around the small room, slowly piecing together what had happened. He was on the floor of Lars' office, laid out on his back, a folded-up jacket under his head, a pizza apron draped across him like a blanket. A glass of water was placed next to him with a single serving Advil package and a slice of pizza.

Erik couldn't deny the ache in his head and the rumble in his stomach. He wolfed down the pizza and took the Advil, downing the whole glass of water. He laid back down on the folded-up jacket and closed his eyes. He'd only intended to reset his mind but when he opened them again the glass of water was full, and Lars was watching him from behind his desk. Erik rose to his elbows and stared at him.

"How long was I out?"

"Few hours," Lars responded, his voice still gruff, anger still flickering at the fringes. "Looks like you needed it. When was the last time you slept, or ate for that matter?"

Erik shrugged, honestly not sure. "Thanks," he said instead.

"For what?"

"For whatever this is," Erik said, motioning to the water, the makeshift pillow.

"Yeah, no problem."

Erik sat all the way up and stretched his taught muscles. He touched the raised bruise on his cheek and winced.

"Sorry about that," Lars offered.

Erik eyed the similar bruise on Lars' chin and smiled, "Ditto."

Lars reflexively brought his hand to it but stopped short, cracking a rare smile. "Yeah, kinda hard to explain to my workers. They thought someone died in here." Lars let out a gruff laugh and leaned back in his chair, his eyes going to the stark ceiling of the small office. "What're we gonna do, Erik?"

"What?"

"About Konstantyn, about Bestefar." Lars' smile evaporated and was replaced with a hungry scowl. "Their beef was with me; they never should've brought anyone else into it."

"It's not like that, Lars. Bestefar pissed them off a long, long time ago and they finally caught up to him. There's—"

"Nah. They never would've found him if they didn't crash my apartment."

"Lars. It happened. There's a lot we don't know about Bestefar. Hell, his real name wasn't even Victor! It was Per. Per Larssen."

"Why? Cuz some little piece of paper you found said so?"

"Yeah, that and the Goddamn CIA backed it up." Lars huffed out a shallow breath and turned his attention back to the ceiling. "He was a spy, Lars. Those games he used to play with us growing up? Spy games."

"The hell you talking about?" Lars' attention was back on Erik, his confusion clear. "What games?"

"The guessing games we'd play at the park, trying to figure out who people were, what they did. Creating an alias to go and see how close we were?"

Lars snorted in disbelief. "Never did that shit with me."

"Sure, he did, you just don't remember it."

"Nah, Erik. I'd remember that shit."

"Well, what about him taking us shooting, teaching us how to move and fire and find cover?"

Lars' disbelieving laugh sounded louder this time. "He didn't teach me that shit, the military did."

"Who taught you to drive then? To always sit facing an entrance, to look in reflections to see everything around you at all times? To find an alternate exit? To read people like I'm reading you right now…" Erik trailed off, noticing for the first time the sincerity in Lars' shrugs and head shakes.

"He didn't teach me shit. You don't remember, do you? Figures. We weren't close, Bestefar and me. He taught me how to be quiet when sneaking out, the feel of a palm on the back of my head when I displeased him. He taught me not to talk back. How to hate my family and how to run away. Your childhood wasn't mine, Erik. I wasn't raised by doting grandparents. I was raised by a scared as hell, slightly older sister and an absentee, deadbeat dad." Lars let his words sink in, letting his sudden flash of anger dwindle before going on. "I was old enough to not give a shit when we moved in with Bestefar and Bestemor. Although, I wish I hadn't, hearing what you're telling me. I thought the old man was just a hard ass, set in his ways. I didn't realize he was a bored, old spy looking to relive the glory days."

"That's not true," Erik said, trying to keep the pout out of his voice.

"Nah, you're right. He just wanted to train you to be a government asset without ever letting you know it, without pushing you into the family trade. Yeah, cuz all future doctors know half the crazy shit you do. What else he teach you? How to strangle someone? Bleed them out with a single strike of a knife? He teach you how to hide a body and cover your tracks?"

Erik's stomach wretched as Lars continued, his words wielded like a sword as they cut away at his happy memories. "Stop, Lars."

"He teach you how to seduce people? Turn them into assets?"

"Lars. Stop. It wasn't like that."

"He teach you to—"

"Shut the hell up! You asshole! You always do this. You pick and pick and pick. And then you wonder why everyone can't stand to breathe the same air as you... Why they refuse to give you money. You're an asshole." With that, Erik lurched to his feet, his head spinning with the sudden movement, but he refused to acknowledge it. He reached for the door handle, intent on never seeing Lars again when Lars called out behind him.

"You're right. I'm not stupid, just an asshole. Just an asshole."

Erik turned to regard Lars, picking up the defeat in his voice. Lars stared at the floor, eyes gazing through the tiles, through the foundation.

"Just tell me what to do, I'll do it."

"No way. I'm not here to recruit you. I just needed to know the truth. I needed to hear it from your mouth."

"Don't be dumb, Erik! What do you know about these guys? Cuz, I guarantee I know more. I've lived with them breathing down my neck for months! Watched as they've squeezed me dry, started to take over my business. If Bestefar hadn't died... They'd own me. Can you imagine how that feels, Erik? My freedom for Bestefar's life? I need to do this. I need to get back at them. I'm doing it with or without you."

"Fine. Set up a meeting with Konstantyn. Feliks mentioned a coffee shop and I'm pretty sure Kelsey already checked it out." Lars' eyes snapped up to Erik. Erik didn't see fear in them, just confusion. "It's the only way I'm gonna get clear of this."

"So, what, we talk to Konstantyn and this all goes away?"

"No... I... I don't know how to find Gerwazy, but I bet Konstantyn does."

"Sure. Let's just set up a meet and greet with a class A psycho and tell him to stop, to put us in touch with Daddy. I'm sure that'll work. Good plan, Erik."

"No, we abduct him, barter with his dad, strike a deal."

"Ok, and what's our leverage? Don't kill Konstantyn? Cuz, I doubt that'll do it." Condescension rang in Lars' voice and it took all of Erik's efforts to not bristle at it.

"They're looking for a ledger Bestefar stole from them way back in the day, while he was working undercover in Poland."

"And you have it?" The condescension was gone.

"No. But they don't know that."

Lars burst into mocking laughter. "And what happens when you don't deliver? They just square it up to big balls and begrudgingly let you live?"

"I can figure it out. Bestefar left clues, I just need to decipher them, but I can't do it looking over my shoulder constantly. Between the police, which Zatorski owns by the way, and Zatorski's goons, I haven't had a chance to think."

"Or eat, or sleep. Yeah, I get it."

"Listen, man. This is the way it is, I didn't choose it, so save the sarcasm, the condescension. Either you're in or you're out. I'll figure it out regardless. I have to or I'm dead or in jail. Hell of a motivator."

"Fine. I'm in. I know the coffee shop you mentioned. Konstantyn's HQ. I'm intimately familiar with it. And hey! All else fails, I'll just put a bullet in Konstantyn's head." Erik waited for Lars to laugh, to smirk a little even, but his face was determined, his fists clenching and unclenching as he imagined it. As if out of nowhere, Lars raised his hand at Erik and pretended to fire a fake gun. "BANG!"

Erik jumped, his heart racing. Lars was serious. Probably wouldn't be the first time, Erik realized. He'd done a few tours in Iraq and Afghanistan, but that was war. *And what is this?* asked Victor.

"Ok," Erik finally responded. "Put it in motion, call me at this number when you're ready." Erik grabbed a pen from a coffee cup on the corner of Lars' desk and jotted down the motel phone number on a menu mockup next to it.

"And what'll you be doing?"

"Figuring out where the ledger is." Lars gave Erik a blank look before nodding his head.

"Good luck, kid."

Chapter 61

ERIK DROVE BACK to the motel, his head swimming in the revelations about his upbring and Victor's lies. What was the purpose? Why train a child to be a spy? Had he just been using Erik? Using him to relive his glory days? Anger surged through Erik and he wanted to scream. He'd looked up to Victor, he was Erik's mentor, his best friend. Erik had trusted him, blindly. He'd sought his praise, to do right by him, and what was his reward? Danger at every turn, a life completely flipped upside down! A world built on mystery and lies? Erik finally let loose the building scream, frustrated tears leaking down his cheeks.

"I trusted you!" He screamed at the road stretching out before him. "Why did you do this to me? WHY!?"

Because I wanted you to be strong. I taught you nothing that you haven't used almost every day of your adult life. Only you can end this. Only you know what to do, because I taught you. I taught you how to survive, so, survive.

"I hate you," Erik whispered, trying to convince himself it was true, but he knew it wasn't.

Erik nearly blew past the motel he was so deep in thought, fighting to justify Victor's lies. The tires squealed as he turned into the parking lot, nearly jumping the curb onto the sidewalk before he screeched to a stop. He quickly made his way to his room, the do not disturb placard still on the handle. He checked the strand of hair in the door. Undisturbed. He breathed a sigh of relief and pushed his way into the room.

Anna watched with wide eyes from the bed, her gag still in place, hands still bound. Her mascara ran all down her cheeks and Erik realized she was sitting in a puddle of her own urine.

Feliks was still bound in his chair, utterly defeated. Erik walked right past him towards Anna.

"Sorry," he murmured as he cut the zip tie around her right wrist. "I should've let you go before I left."

Anna looked at him with terrified eyes. It hurt Erik. He undid the other wrist and pulled the gag out of her mouth. "You deserve better."

"You do this to torment me?" Anna whispered, refusing to move an inch.

"What? No."

"You murder my love, abduct me, tie me up for days and then beg my forgiveness? Will you rape me now? Then tell me how horrible you feel for taking advantage of me after?"

Erik recoiled in horror. "No! Never. I already told you. This isn't me! I'm a nice fucking guy!" Erik could hear the desperation in his own voice and decided to put some distance between himself and Anna. He leapt off the bed, back to his feet. "You helped me out and I appreciate it. Your 'love' is fine. I tied him up on your bed, told him to be quiet and shot the wall."

"What?"

"Once this is over you can reunite with him and continue to poison your neighborhood. Living the dream, right?"

"How long has he…" Her voice trailed off into worried tears.

"Less than twenty-four hours. Probably not feeling great but aside from some dehydration and soiled boxers he'll be fine. Just like you." Anna continued to stare at him in disbelief.

"This is a trick. You mock me." Fresh tears ran down her cheeks.

"I told you, from the beginning, I'm not going to hurt you. Now, if you have to go, go." Erik motioned to the bathroom, but Anna didn't move. "Or don't, just don't do anything stupid and I won't tie you back up."

"Why not just let me free?"

"So, you can go tell the police where I am, about how I abducted you? Tip off Feliks' friends that I'm coming for them?"

"I promise, I'll say nothing."

"And I don't trust you so shut the hell up and chill the hell out, please."

Anna's mouth clicked shut and her tears returned, any glimmer of hope fading from her eyes. "Oh yeah," Erik murmured taking off his backpack and unzipping it. He produced a couple to go containers and tossed one at Anna. She looked at it as if it were a grenade waiting to go off and kill them all.

"It's pizza. You hungry? Yeah? Then eat." Erik tossed a bottle of water next to her as well and sat down on the other side of the table from Feliks who looked at the container in Erik's hands. "Be good and I'll let you have my crust."

Erik opened the container and dug into it, eating it with the voracity of a famine victim. He was so focused on filling his belly he barely registered the click of the water bottles plastic lid opening. Out of the corner of his eye he watched Anna inhale the pizza and chug half the bottle of water. Good, he thought as he wolfed down a second slice.

Once he was done, Erik was true to his word. He removed Feliks' gag and fed him the crusts, gave him some water and returned the gag.

"Can I... Use the bathroom?" Anna asked just as Erik sat back down.

"Go for it." She started to wiggle free of the bed and Erik pulled the pistol from behind his belt and put it on the table, making sure Anna saw him do it. He saw her jump in the reflection of the chrome barrel and relaxed a little.

While he waited for her return, he pulled out the clues Victor had left him and started to pour over them, looking for any details that might help him. He heard the flush of the toilet and then the shower sounded. He looked up in surprise and watched the door for a minute. The sound of the water pressure changed as he was pretty sure Anna entered it. No windows, no weapons, she's just cleaning the urine off herself, he reassured himself. He went back to the message.

A few minutes later, the shower turned off followed by the click of the lock popping free. He found the bathroom door in the reflection of the gun and waited for Anna to emerge. The door slowly opened, and Erik could see Anna peeking through the opening, her wet hair plastered to her forehead.

"Erik?" She called softly from her refuge. "Do you have clothes I can use?"

Erik turned to regard her, nodding. Without a word he pulled the baggie hoodie out of his backpack along with the oversized T-shirt and pants from the other day's junkie disguise. He got up from his chair and crossed the room in a few steps, the clothes offered in his outstretched arm. As he neared the door, Anna pushed it open all the way, revealing her naked body.

"Jesus!" Erik yelped in surprise, quickly avoiding her nakedness with his eyes, looking over her head instead. Confusion washed over her features as she hesitated, covering her breasts with one arm while the other covered her groin.

"I..." She started, her confusion deepening. "I'll let you have me in exchange for my freedom."

"Anna, put on the clothes," Erik ordered, refusing to take another step towards her. His arm stretched out towards her, waving the bundle of clothes.

"I'm clean," she added, letting her arm drop from her breasts. Erik refused to look, refused to be tempted.

"Just, please, get dressed, Anna."

"I've seen the way you look at me, like you're going to take me. Now I'm offering. No guilty conscience. Just... let me go. All of this is yours." Erik could see her arms moving as she ran her hands up her slender curves, confidence building in her eyes as Erik's resolve waivered, or so she thought.

"It's pity."

"What?" she responded, unsure of whether she heard him right.

"I look at you with pity, now put on the damn clothes and get back on the bed." Erik didn't wait for her to respond, tossing the clothes in her face and returning to his chair. He watched her reaction in the reflection of a cheesy motel painting as she clutched the clothes to her chest and watched him walk away.

"Pity?" Erik watched her confusion melt away, replaced with anger. She dropped the clothes and took a couple steps towards him. He sat at the chair and put his hand on the waiting pistol and turned to regard her.

She stood just across the room, still naked and dripping. Erik locked eyes with her, still refusing to take advantage of her nakedness. Feliks, on the other hand, watched her with rapt attention, his eyes traveling up and down her body.

"You can continue to give this lowlife a show, or you can get dressed." Anna's eyes snapped to Feliks and she quickly covered herself and retreated a step. Feliks smiled at her from behind his gag, going as far as to give her a lecherous wink. That was enough. Anna bent over and retrieved the bundle of clothes and disappeared into the bathroom, the door flying shut with a bang in her wake.

Erik turned his full attention to Feliks. "Get a good look, asshole?" Feliks shrugged. "When this is all said and done, that's probably the last naked woman you'll ever see in person, so savor it," Erik growled.

Anna stayed in the bathroom for quite a while after that, soft sobs escaping from under the door, traveling into the small motel room. The gentle cries chipped away at Erik and he came to regret his words. He did pity her, her way of life, her meager, diseased existence, but he didn't blame her. Society had failed her, created what she'd become. She'd arrived there by necessity, not choice. That much was obvious, but it wasn't his place to look down on her, judge her. He considered knocking on the door and apologizing but couldn't make his feet move. Instead, he turned his focus to the clues, pouring over them with new resolve.

Hello, Erik, my barnebarn. Understand I'm sorry. Just or not, I've lied to you. How I've lied to you all. Your bestemor was the only one who knew the truth as she lived it with me in life and in death. Ultimately, if you're reading this, my death has been tragic. Let me pray it was an honest tragedy, but I suspect foul play is what has brought you here and placed my all with Marga once more.

The door creaked open and Erik's eyes shot to the bathroom's reflection in the gun. Anna peered out, looking at Erik, a mix of emotions roiling her features. She opened the door all the way and stepped out. Erik breathed a sigh of relief as she emerged in the baggy clothes. They were far too large for her and she had to hold up the pants as she crept towards the bed, her eyes darting from Erik to the bed and back again. The springs creaked as she climbed onto it and pushed the soiled bedding to the floor. She resumed her spot and stared at the back of Erik's head.

"I pity *you*," she finally said, accepting that Erik wasn't going to look her way. "I've spent a lifetime learning to survive by whatever means necessary. You just started learning. So naïve, so innocent... so arrogant, watching the rest of us from your tower. Welcome back to the ground, Erik. Welcome to the real world."

"Sounds good. Thanks," Erik responded absent mindedly, refusing to be baited, to take his focus away from probing the message he'd decoded.

Silence descended on the small room. Erik poured over the message, dissecting every piece of it, oblivious to Anna as she pouted at him, shuffling around on the bed. Oblivious to the urine streaming down Feliks' leg, another victim of Erik's inattention. He was oblivious to the world around him. *You trust Anna far too much*, Victor warned him, but each absent-minded glance towards her reflection in the gun, the plastic of the cheesy motel paintings, the corner of his vision found her where she was told to be. Only the sudden and jarring ring of the motel telephone broke him fully from his trance.

Anna gasped in surprise and even Erik couldn't help but jump a bit as the ringer shrieked its hello. Erik grabbed the phone from its cradle, not allowing it to continue its shrill song.

"Hello," he breathed into the mouthpiece, doing his best to disguise his voice.

"Erik?"

"Lars?"

"Yeah. What's with the voice? Been watching too many superhero movies?"

Erik paused, cleared his throat. "Nah, just something in my throat." Lars chuckled on the other line and Erik's cheeks reddened. "What do you want, Lars?"

"Shit's in motion, little brother. Strap on your helmet cuz we're about to get dirty. Meet me at the shop in about an hour."

"Yep." The line went dead, and Erik slowly put the phone back on its cradle.

He turned to Anna; her eyes as big as pint glasses. He got up and took a few steps towards her, she cowered away from him and then he realized he held the pistol in his hand. He couldn't really recall when he'd grabbed it, maybe when the phone had rung? It didn't matter. He shoved it behind his belt and let his shirt fall over it.

"Get up," Erik asked her as gently as he could. "You're coming with this time."

"What?" Anna gasped in horror.

"I'm not gonna hurt you, Anna. You're almost clear of this. I don't want to tie you up again, but I can't just leave you here, so, you're coming with."

Chapter 62

ANNA JUST WATCHED Erik from the passenger seat with frightened eyes. He felt terrible, what had he done to this woman? *What is necessary*, Victor reminded him. When they arrived at the pizza shop, Lars was waiting by the curb with a duffel bag.

Erik pulled over and Lars peered into the front seat, an amused look on his lips. He got into the back seat, hefting the heavy duffel onto the seat next to him.

"You Kelsey?" He asked with an outstretched hand.

"This is the other woman I mentioned."

"The one you kidnapped?" Lars responded, disbelief tinging each syllable.

"She's cool."

"Is she? How do you know?"

Erik looked over at her. She was white as snow. Her fingers trembled in her lap. Her eyes fixated on the dash in front of her.

"I just do."

Lars snorted in response but didn't push it. "She's cute," Lars finally commented, Anna went ramrod straight in response. "We can use that," Lars added, as if to clarify his lecherous statement. "Konstantyn is gonna have some guards with him. Maybe cutie pie over here can distract them while we make our move?"

Anna snapped her gaze from the dash to Erik. He could see how frightened she was in the corner of his vision as he drove. Her breath came in shallow gasps, just audible over the low drone of the radio. She looked like a caged animal about to bolt. But Lars had a good point. She could be the distraction they needed to get the jump on Konstantyn and his men. Kelsey had mentioned their… attention to her when she was there.

"Anna? What do you think? You help us out and you're free, I promise."

"No," she started, her voice bordering on hysterical. "Help you kill Konstantyn? It's a death sentence!"

"No one's getting killed," Erik tried to reassure her.

"Except me. If I help you, dead."

"If you don't? Dead," Lars said, almost in her ear.

"Lars! Back off!" Erik growled, eliciting an amused laugh from Lars.

"She's dead no matter what she does, Erik. Except, she's got a better chance if she helps us."

"Dude! We're not killing anyone, especially her!" Erik couldn't believe what he was hearing. Would Lars really kill her? Erik was so angry he hardly registered her sobs coming from the passenger seat.

"Not us, little bro. She helped us. That's the death sentence. Those thugs don't like snitches."

"I forced her!"

"Doesn't matter," Anna managed between sobs. "He's right. They will know I gave you Feliks. We're both dead. Feliks and me. Stefan too. You may not have fired the bullet, but you've killed us all the same."

The car went silent for a bit, everyone contemplating their situation. "I'll do it," Anna finally announced, surprising everyone. "Your brother is right; I stand a better chance helping you than not." She swiveled around in her seat to look at Lars. "If I am to be a distraction, I'm going to need something else to wear."

"Agreed. Erik, can we trust her with a gun?" Lars said, his grin at odds with the gravity of his question.

Lars waited in the car as Erik and Anna went into a boutique store. The clothing was all second-hand stuff, a staple in the more affluent neighborhoods. A testament to how ideologically different poverty and wealth were. The poor only had cheap, second-hand clothes to wear, whereas the wealthy sought it out and paid a hefty price for it, Erik realized as he looked at one of the price tags. Erik followed Anna as she browsed a rack of dresses, still not sure about her, even though he desperately wanted to be. Was it wise to bring her into his scheme? Erik waited for Victor's voice to tell him he wasn't being stupid, but his subconscious said nothing.

"I'm going to try these on," Anna told Erik, breaking him from his thoughts.

"Nah, I don't think so," Erik said in quick response, still battling with how much he should trust her.

"You want me to be a distraction? How much good is an oversized dress that hides all the points of interest for a man?" Erik had no response. She was right. "You can come into the dressing room if you don't trust me." Erik's cheeks flushed at the thought. "I thought not, ciacho."

"I'll be outside the door," Erik said to her back as she led the way to the dressing rooms.

It didn't take Anna long to choose a dress, which was good because, as Lars said, Konstantyn waited for no one. When she stepped out of the dressing stall, Erik's breath caught. The dress she'd chosen was a sundress with a plunging neck and a cinched waistline that accentuated her hips, the knee length hem accentuating her long legs.

"It works," Anna said with resignation.

Erik clicked his jaw shut and looked away from her, his cheeks again flushed. "Sorry," he murmured.

"Stop saying that. It means nothing at this point. Sorry for what? The list is too long. Give me the money and I'll pay for it; I saw some makeup by the counter so give me enough to cover that too." Erik handed her the money and followed her to the counter where she grabbed a tube of ruby red lipstick and mascara.

Lars whistled when they got back into the car. Anna ignored him and Erik cast daggers at him in the rearview mirror. "What?" Lars protested. "Can't compliment a lady?"

"Don't make this more awkward than it needs to be," Erik retorted, a little hot under the collar.

"It's the whole point, isn't it?" Anna said, putting on her lipstick in the mirror.

"That doesn't mean he can just ogle you, Anna," Erik said, throwing the car into drive.

"Says my kidnapper." The car went silent and stayed that way for the rest of the short drive.

When they arrived near the meeting point, Anna tensed up, her eyes looking at the old buildings with a glimmer of sadness. Erik parked the car and looked over at her, noting how her hands clutched each other in her lap.

"You good?" Was all he could think to ask. The question startled Anna out of the fugue state she'd landed in, her eyes snapping towards Erik's voice.

"I…" She hesitated. "I've not been here for years."

"What?" Lars blurted from the back seat.

Anna's eyes snapped back to the dash, her skin going ghost white again, her hand trembling as it moved thick strands of hair from her eyes. "My father once owned a shop near here. It was a corner store… It was a long time ago."

"OK, are you good though? No second thoughts?" Erik tried to keep the worry from his voice, forcing it to be warm, gentle.

"Yes," Anna replied, straightening in her seat. She turned to meet Erik's eyes. "Gun, please."

"You're sure?" Anna nodded. Erik reached under the seat and pulled out a gun, placing it gently in Anna's hand. She looked at it as if it were a foreign object, took a deep breath and shoved it into the purse she'd thought to buy on their way out of the boutique. No place to hide a gun in that dress, she'd pointed out.

"Ok, just stick to the plan and everything will be fine." Anna nodded again, and exited the car, the door slamming shut behind her as she started walking down the sidewalk, towards the meeting place. She rounded the corner and stopped, just staring. Erik and Lars both tensed in their seats.

"What's she doing?" Lars demanded from the back seat.

"Hell if I know!" Erik responded; his voice filled to the brim with worry.

Erik was about to get out of the car when she finally walked into the coffee shop.

"You don't think that's her dad's old place?" Lars said after a sigh of relief.

"Shit," Erik said, a numb feeling washing over him. What had he just done? What would be waiting for him on the other side of that door?

"Too late," he said out loud, his inner thoughts laid bare.

"What?" Lars said as he climbed into the passenger seat from the back.

"Nothing," was all Erik could think to respond.

"Having second thoughts?"

"Of course. I'm flying blind here, Lars." There was no animosity in Erik's voice, but Lars bristled anyway.

"Or you could just trust me. Jesus, Erik. I know I'm the family fuck up, but this is actually something I'm good at." Lars said his piece and turned his attention back to the coffee shop.

The silence stretched out between them, like the gulf between the moon and the tide. The energy of unsaid words pushing and pulling but never being said until Erik shattered it, another inner thought laid bare.

"Why'd you leave? Leave the military?"

Lars snorted next to him, slow to answer as his wheels turned. "I got tired of carrying people across the finish line."

That got Erik's attention. "What do you mean?"

"Listen, I love the military. Were I an officer, I'd still be in the Middle East, but I wasn't. I was a grunt. I was a 'do as your told' pawn. How many of my brothers did I bury due to bad intel or dipshit orders? Old men playing three-dimensional chess from their Barcaloungers. Me and mine just a statistic." Lars went quiet but Erik felt like he had more to say and gave him his space.

"You hit a point in life and nothing you've done makes sense. You can pick it all apart. It's all meaningless. Kill a bad guy and find ten more the next day. It's futile, all of it, that's why I decided to make pizzas. Each one replaces a memory I don't want. Each one washes a little of the stink of death off me."

They didn't talk after that. They just listened to the radio and counted the minutes until it was Erik's turn to get out of the car and makes the thirty-yard walk around the corner and into the coffee shop.

Chapter 63

ERIK'S HEART BEAT against his bones as he rounded the corner and reached out a hand to open the glass door. His eyes scanned the room just like Victor had taught him. He spotted Anna in the corner, leaned over a table while she sipped her drink, her jaw line clenched, her cleavage pushed to the max in her snug dress. No one spared Erik a second glance. She flinched as he stepped into the room, her eyes flicking towards him, her face going pale, but recovering quickly enough that the men staring at her didn't notice as their eyes quickly regarded Erik before being drawn back to Anna like moths to light.

Two brutes in leather jackets brought their heads together and said something to one another about Anna. At least, Erik was pretty sure it was about her as their eyes never left her. Erik recognized Konstantyn immediately. Same guy from the club the night before. Konstantyn didn't give Erik any attention at all, his eyes also glued to Anna's ample chest. He just sat in the corner, the two thugs between him and Erik, no windows or doors behind him, insulated from the world by threatening demeanors and dangerous minds. Erik tried not to stare, but this close, he couldn't help but see how similar the man looked to Erik's own father. How had Lars missed it?

He wasn't looking for it, Victor murmured from the depths. Erik tore his eyes from the trio of evil men and beelined for the counter. A bored man with a sleeve of tattoos and beady eyes awaited him. Erik was trying to imagine where the gun was kept behind the counter when the bell chimed behind him. Erik jumped at the sound and forced himself to calmly look behind him. Lars stood in the doorway, his body rigid with barely suppressed anger.

"Lars, good of you to join us," Konstantyn cackled. "Why so angry?" He added, following it with as much condescension as a laugh could hold.

Lars closed the distance between himself and the thugs in a couple bounding steps. They shot to their feet and their hands went to their hidden weapons, but Lars stopped on a dime and put his arms out, ready to be searched, his focus never leaving Konstantyn.

"You know exactly why, you son of a bitch," Lars growled as one of the thugs patted him down and the other one relaxed, leaning back against the wall, crossing his arms with an amused smile playing his lips.

"Truly I don't," Konstantyn replied, his face the picture of innocence. "Please, Lars, calm yourself and talk to Uncle Konstantyn." He smiled a wicked smile and patted the seat next to him.

In a flash of movement Lars brought his hands down on top of the head of the thug searching him, the click of his teeth audible to the whole room. The man dropped and Lars was able to use gravity to direct the dazed thug's downward momentum into his partner, chopping him at the knees, keeping the other man's hands from finding his gun as he tried to keep his balance. They fell into a tangled heap and Lars' gun flashed into his hand. Anna surged to her feet, her gun appearing from the purse she'd positioned on the table in front of her. Erik followed suit, spinning back to the barista. The man had a shotgun half raised when Erik's sights landed on him.

"Drop it."

Chapter 64

A STUNNED SILENCE enveloped the room, only to be broken by Konstantyn's amused cackle. "What is this then?" He pondered. "A suicide pact?"

"Shut up," Lars growled. "And surrender your weapons, slowly."

The two thugs looked up to Konstantyn from where they lay at his feet, clearly seeking guidance. They would die for this man if he asked them to, Erik realized, never letting his gaze waiver from the fake barista, just another Zatorski soldier. Had Lars not warned him, would he have realized it before it was too late?

Konstantyn nodded to his men then turned his attention back to Lars. "Do as he says, boys. Army man has a screw loose, clearly," he purred, still very much believing he was in control.

The thugs retrieved their weapons and tossed them at Lars' feet. "You too," Erik growled at the barista, trying to invoke as much of Lars in his words as he could. The barista hesitated, his eyes fighting with the idea of continuing the shotgun's deadly path. In the end, the barista put it on the bar.

"Impressive," Konstantyn smiled, his eyes boring into Erik. Erik refused to acknowledge that menacing gaze, willing it to slide off his shoulders like rain drops on a rain jacket. *Fear is weakness*, Victor whispered.

"How are you, Uncle?" Erik responded, finally training his eyes on the man.

"Uncle?" Konstantyn's grin flickered as he tried to pierce Erik's disguise, his eyes finally lighting up with recognition.

"Erik Brown! So great of you to reappear! We had wondered where you got off to." His smile deepened. "Thank you for saving us the trouble of sniffing you out."

"Of course. Anything for family." Konstantyn's Cheshire grin waivered for a moment, the lights turning on behind his menacing eyes as he pieced Erik's words together. Uncle. Family.

"Ah. So, that is where Feliks got off to." His grin returned. "Again, thanks for saving us the trouble of sniffing him out!" His laugh burst into the still air like a mental patient's wail. Not a spine resisted the shiver that shook it in response.

"I said shut up!" Lars screamed, surging forward and bringing the butt of his gun down across Konstantyn's cheek. To Lars' credit, the laugh stopped. To Lars' detriment, the action caused the closest of the two thugs to leap at Lars' legs, wrapping his bear like arms around them at the knee. Lars fought gravity for a moment before the man forced him onto the hard floor. Lars landed with a thud, his finger squeezing the trigger of his gun in response. The cacophony of the shot rang against the walls and Erik cringed into himself against it. He registered the whistle of the bullet far after the wind of its path had swept across his brow, after flecks of hot liquid sprayed across his cheek. He had barely even started to contemplate the sound when gasping gurgles drew his attention back to the barista, at whom his gun was pointed. He was greeted by a crimson geyser spraying the walls as the barista collapsed backwards, his hands clenched around a ruined throat.

Erik was vaguely aware of Anna pushing past him to get at the other thug, the one just beginning to move from his prone position on the ground at Konstantyn's feet. Shock numbed Erik's other senses, his ears only hearing a loud whine, his eyes unable to leave the frightened eyes of the dying man on the other side of the bar, and then, another shot rang out, this time, the bullet hit the bar, not next to Erik, but near enough to shake the stupor from him. He spun around, raising the gun at whatever awaited him.

"Stay down!" Anna screamed as the other thug disregarded her order and shot to his feet. Anna hesitated and that was the only thing the thug needed. He grabbed the gun in her hand, locking up the firing mechanism, making it into nothing but a piece of metal. His other hand swung a heavy fist that connected with Anna's chin. She dropped in a heap at his feet, her gun still in the thug's hand.

Erik had to act quickly, choosing to disregard the newly rearmed thug and focus on the one trying to maul Lars. Erik closed the distance in a couple strides and delivered a savage kick to the side of the thug's head. He grunted loudly in response but didn't stop fighting so Erik reared back and delivered another one. This one rattled the man's teeth and he slumped on top of Lars who did his best to climb out from under him as quickly as possible. By the time anyone could turn their attention back to the newly rearmed thug, he'd racked the gun and trained it on the brothers. He smiled victoriously as he pulled the trigger. The gun clicked lamely, and surprise blossomed on the man's face, his eyes darting to the useless hunk of metal in his hand. By the time his eyes had returned to Erik and Lars, both had their guns trained on him.

"Empty?" Lars baited him with a relieved smile. The thug dropped the gun and put his arms up, signaling the end of the fight.

Konstantyn's amused cackle filled the room again. He hadn't even moved. "Brilliant!" He crowed. "People pay for such a show!"

"Shut up!" Lars roared, about to pistol, whip him again, but Erik caught his raised arm instead.

"Chill, brother. He's baiting you!"

Lars gave Erik an angry look but lowered his arm anyway. The thug at his feet groaned loudly, rediscovering consciousness and a newly broken jaw. Lars channeled his anger at the new disturbance and landed another kick to the side of the man's head. "Stay down!" He screamed into an ear that heard nothing. "And you!" Lars continued, turning his attention to the other thug. "On your belly, hands behind your head!"

The man's eyes travelled past Lars, taking in the reddened wall behind the bar and complied, the fight gone out of him. Erik decided Lars had control of the room again and made his way to Anna. She'd only just sat up, looking around the room in a daze. Her chin was bleeding from where the man had connected. Her hand found the wound and she started working her jaw up and down, grimacing at the shooting pain that awaited the movement.

"You good?" Erik asked.

She made eye contact with him, her focus wavering for a moment before nodding yes. Erik offered her his hand and she grabbed it, letting him pull her to his feet. She stooped down to pick up her discarded weapon, and Konstantyn's mocking laughter sounded again.

"Girl, no need for that. The jig is up!" Konstantyn turned his gaze on to Lars and raised a manicured eyebrow. "Who is this girl you've brought me, Lars? Can't even trust her with a loaded weapon? I must say, I am intrigued." He swung his eyes back to Anna. She wilted under them and Erik stepped between her and Konstantyn. "Knight in shining armor, and here I thought you had eyes for Samantha."

The confusion must have shown on Erik's face for Konstantyn's smile seemed a little less sure all of a sudden.

"Who?" Erik responded.

"Perhaps not," Konstantyn conceded. "Bone I'll have to pick with your friend Feliks when next I see him."

"Only thing you're gonna see is your maker," Lars said, reinserting himself into the conversation.

"Oh, Lars, be a dear and shut up."

Lars turned bright red and Erik feared he might follow through on his threat. "Lars," Erik said, trying to draw his attention. "Take a look outside really quick, no way those gun shots went unheard. Make sure we're clear and Ann…" Erik bit off the rest of her name, his eyes shooting to Konstantyn. "Annnd me and the girl will tie these assholes up."

Konstantyn lit up, evoking a sinking feeling in Erik's chest. "Ann? Anna, perhaps? Not many options with that are there?"

Anna's face was so pale Erik could practically see the knuckle imprint in the red on her chin. "Girl," Erik barked, his mind unable to give her a fake name in that moment. *As if he'd buy it*, Victor snarled. "Tie up the unconscious one, I'll get the other guy."

Anna looked to him, a startled deer, and barely caught the zip ties he tossed at her. "Quickly," Erik said, hoping to snap her out of it. To an extent, it worked, but the color refused to return to her sharp features.

"Ann… Anna… Are you Polish, girl? I think so," mused Konstantyn as the zip ties screeched tight on the fat wrists of the two thugs. "Hmmm, your image tugs at the mind, girl. We've met before I think. Może pieprzyłem twoją matkę?"

Anna tried to hide her fear, but Erik could read her like a book after all he'd put her through. "I won't ask you to be quiet, Uncle, because you're incapable."

Erik stepped over the thug at his feet, gun raised and walked up to Konstantyn, embodying a calm he didn't truly feel. "Hands," he demanded. Konstantyn complied with a mocking smile, putting his hands out in the classic 'cuff me' gesture. Erik complied, tightening the zip ties around them. "And now," Erik said with a smile as he retrieved a ball gag out of his backpack, holding it up for Konstantyn to see.

"A little, incestual, don't you think?" Konstantyn smiled. Erik fought the urge to slap it from his lips but just gagged him instead.

"What'd you call it when you were screwing me? Uncle?" Konstantyn's smile widened and he tipped his head at Erik. One point me, Erik thought as Lars rushed back into the coffee shop.

"All clear, let's move."

Lars had moved the car in front of the shop where he left it idling at the curb. The back door was already open, a hungry mouth waiting to devour Konstantyn. Erik hustled Konstantyn out of the coffee shop and shoved him roughly through the opening, using his moment to hurl Konstantyn across the back seat. Konstantyn landed on his face and grunted. Erik paid it no mind as he shoved Konstantyn's legs in behind him. Erik continued to push the bound man until he was scrunched into the other corner, his head jammed against the other door. Fire filled his eyes as he grimaced against the indignity of what Erik had forced upon him. For Erik's part, he just smiled.

Erik slammed the door behind him as Lars and Anna filled the front seats. The passenger door had barely clicked shut behind Anna when Lars gunned it, pulling away from the curb, away from the bound thugs, the dead barista. What have we done? Erik wondered, his adrenaline finally letting off the gas and letting rational thought back into his fatigued mind. *What you had to*; Victor responded.

Chapter 65

IT TOOK KONSTANTYN the better part of the trip back to the motel to right himself in his seat, eyes boring into Erik the whole time, but Erik ignored him, his mind had reverted to the riddle of the missing ledger. It was his leverage, it was everything. Konstantyn was the bargaining chip, but the ledger... the ledger was his freedom, his old life, his path to redemption. *You hope*, Victor chimed in.

They pulled into the dirty motel parking lot, entering off a side street, the back-way in. It was an attempt to keep the clerk's eyes off Konstantyn. Erik doubted there were many that didn't recognize him in this neighborhood. Even if they didn't know his name, they knew his face and they knew who he worked for. If Gerwazy owned the police, he certainly owned the neighborhood where he hung his hat.

Lars threw the car into park and nodded to Anna. She darted out of the car and Erik had a moment to wonder if she was running before she ultimately rushed up the motel stairs, disappearing onto the walkway. She made sure the way to the room was clear before rushing back to the top of the stairs to nod at Lars.

"All clear, little brother," Lars said, his eyes trained on the windows peering down on them, silent witnesses to their crime.

Erik pulled Konstantyn out of the car and prodded him along ahead of him, the nose of his pistol in Konstantyn's ribs. Lars took up the rear, still watching the curtained windows around them.

Erik pushed Konstantyn up the steps and towards Anna. She held the door open for them, her eyes looking everywhere but at Konstantyn. *There's something there*, Victor warned Erik as they passed by her and into the room. Erik continued pushing Konstantyn into the room, forcing him face first onto the bed while the others joined them, Lars pulling the door closed behind them, using every lock available to secure it. Konstantyn landed with another grunt and quickly rolled onto his back, his smile returned. He tried to say something, but the gag blocked anything intelligible. Konstantyn seemed not to mind though for he continued his little dialogue, his dark eyes swinging over to regard Feliks who was still bound and gagged in the chair in the corner of the motel.

Konstantyn's smile deepened as Feliks' eyes widened. Feliks looked from Konstantyn to Erik and back. His fear was palpable, and he started to mutter to himself, also unintelligible behind his gag, but his mumbling quickly turned into heavy breathing and Erik realized he was having a panic attack. He sprang into action without thinking.

He rushed over to Feliks and removed the gag. Tears ran down the man's face and his breathing came in beleaguered gasps.

"I'm dead," he muttered between breathes, his voice nothing more than a wheeze. "Dead," he continued over and over.

"Easy," Erik told him in a gentle tone, holding the man like a child. "Easy," he continued until Feliks' breathing resumed some semblance of normality.

As Erik's adrenaline started to calm down, he became aware of the muffled laughter Konstantyn was trying to force through his gag. Before Erik could respond Lars strode across the room and punched

Konstantyn in the jaw. Konstantyn's head jerked back and he fell lifelessly onto the bed.

"Needs to learn to shut up," Lars told the room before making his way into the bathroom, the door slamming shut behind him, leaving Erik and Anna to exchange worried looks.

"Just kill me already, please," Feliks said from behind them. Both sets of eyes spun around to regard the defeated man. "Put me out of my misery, please. I am a dead man. Konstantyn will not allow me to live, he will not."

"Take it easy, Feliks. Konstantyn is in no position to hurt you," Erik said, trying to reassure the wretch.

"Not now, no, but will you protect me when he is free?"

"Why don't you protect yourself. Flip on them, put them all in jail. You told me yourself, you were there when he killed my bestefar. Go to the police, take them all down!"

Feliks shook his head no, refusing to meet Erik's eyes. "It is not so easy. They own the police. They own politicians, judges. I would not make it a night in a jail cell."

"Then take it higher. I have... connections."

"Just kill me. The maze has closed around me, the minotaur has found me." Feliks clammed up after that, refusing to say anything else, to make eye contact with Anna or Erik, and when Lars returned from the bathroom, he ignored him too.

Konstantyn was out for a good bit of time, the gag in his mouth probably the only reason he didn't have a broken jaw, or broken teeth at the very least. It gave Erik the chance to open his phone with Konstantyn's finger, only to reveal a set of contacts that made no sense by any linguistic standard.

"So?" Lars asked hopefully.

"Anna? This make any sense to you?" Erik held up the phone for Anna, but she just shook her head no. Erik turned his attention back to Lars. "It's in code. Guess we're waiting for him to come around."

"Shit," Lars muttered before turning the TV on and sitting down on the edge of the bed.

Erik sighed out his frustration and headed for the door.

"Where you headed?" Lars asked.

"Gonna call Kelsey, let her know I'm alright." Lars just smirked and turned back to the TV.

Erik stepped into the late afternoon light and leaned against the railing for a moment before fishing out his phone and dialing Kelsey.

"Hey! Everything OK?" Kelsey's voice held a mixture of hope and fear and Erik could only imagine the look on her face.

"Yeah, not according to the plan, but I think we've got something here. Listen, don't think about me, or this mess. I want you focused on your show. Knock em dead. And don't sell that painting of me too cheap," Erik said, forcing a joy into his voice he didn't feel.

"Maybe I should just skip the show, come to you? I don't know, I just have this feeling in the pit of my stomach..."

"No! Trust me, you're safer there than you would be here. I'm... I don't know what's going to happen, Kelsey, but meeting you? That's about the only light in my life right now, so be safe and enjoy the opening. You deserve it."

"God, I don't like it when you talk like that!"

"I'm sorry, Kelsey. I honestly don't know what to say, sometimes I wish we'd never met."

"Um, OK?"

"No! I don't mean it like that, it's just... I'm scared." The other end of the line was quiet for what felt like an eternity before Erik realized Kelsey was crying. "Kelsey?"

"Just, do what you have to do, Erik. Don't worry about me, worry about you." And then the line went dead.

"Fuck," Erik sighed, his shoulders slumping in defeat.

Chapter 66

GERWAZY STARED OUT his tented window, ignoring the beauty of the stars as they turned the hazy night sky into a kaleidoscope of shimmering light. His black town car pulled up to the curb in front of a crowded art gallery. His two bodyguards, giant men in black suits, stepped out of the car, their eyes scanning the crowd at a continuous clip. Satisfied, one stepped back and opened the back door of the luxury sedan while the other one reached a hand into the darkness of the vehicle and helped Gerwazy onto the curb. The old man was immaculately dressed in a black tuxedo. His hair thick and white, his blue eyes sharp as they too scanned the faces surrounding him. He moved with a vitality not typical of a man his age, his stride confident in each step, his back straight. The tuxedo hugged his frame, showing off the athletic physique he'd labored a lifetime to achieve.

The large men lead him down the red carpet, past the photographers who shouted questions at him, asking for a name or a quick word. He ignored them as if they spoke a foreign language. The doors to the gallery swung open before him as if he were a king in a fairy tale. The inside of the gallery was quiet by contrast to the roar of voices and the clicks of camera shutters just outside the doors. The slow lilt of stringed instruments murmured over the low chatter of the crowded gallery. A man with a clip board spotted the old man and smiled, making his way towards him.

"Mr. Z, welcome."

Gerwazy smiled, power oozing out of him, wrapping around those within his aura, beckoning their eyes to find him, their intrigue laid naked before him. He was slow to respond, holding his small audience in the pendulum of time as if the words he uttered would set the world on a new course.

"Linus, my pleasure," he responded, his voice refined, his accent almost nonexistent.

Linus thanked him again but Gerwazy simply waved him away, done with being bothered. Linus complied, melting back into the crowd of onlookers, the hum of the questions that surrounded Gerwazy enveloping him, begging him to reveal who that man was. Gerwazy paid no mind to it, instead, wasting no time in getting to the art adorning the white walls of the gallery, his keen eye searching for what exquisite pieces might replace those he'd fed to his fire. His men ushered the other patrons out of his way, gruff but respectable at the same time. They kept the others at bay while Gerwazy ran his eye over each piece he passed, alone in his man-made bubble.

He continued down the line of artwork, all done by promising young painters, all unknowing guests at Gerwazy's request, until suddenly he stopped, his attention falling on a beautiful young woman. He'd seen her before, but from where he couldn't recall. He skipped the art between him and her, pondering her familiarity until he was almost to her and his eyes found a painting of a young man standing before an open window, the sun streaming through to kiss his bare skin, and it all clicked. She was the girl from the coffee shop, Konstantyn's Mexican dish. He snapped a finger and one of his men quickly stepped up next to him.

"See that we are undisturbed." The man nodded and with the support of his companion created a small perimeter around the two.

"What a beautiful painting this is, Miss?" He offered his hand in greeting, Kelsey taking it enthusiastically.

"Martinez, Kelsey. Kelsey Martinez, and thank you, sir." Kelsey smiled at Gerwazy, unaware of his connection to Erik, his ill intent simmering below his polished exterior.

"You may call me Gerry, Kelsey. Tell me, this young man, he's so intriguing. What is his name?"

Kelsey's smile waivered, unease eating at the butterflies in her stomach. Why was that name so familiar? "Erik? He's a friend of mine."

"Quite a friend to allow you to paint him in the nude," Gerwazy smiled, his eyes completely focused on his prey. Kelsey blushed at his comment but quickly laughed it away.

"Yes, quite the friend."

"Very good," Gerwazy chuckled, his grin deepening as he read the young love dripping from her awkward little smile. "Can we step into a quieter space and perhaps I might submit an offer to buy the piece?"

Kelsey's eyes lit up, her sense of foreboding evaporating. "Absolutely!"

Gerwazy snapped his fingers at one of his men, whispered something in his ear and then turned his attention back to Kelsey. "I'm friends with the owner of the gallery, he won't mind if we step out back. It's too loud in here for talk of money."

Gerwazy smiled at Kelsey and took her hand, leading her out of the room, away from witnesses. He led her past the caterers as they prepared hors d'oeuvres at a frenzied pace. He led her through the opened garage door of the loading bay and into the alley. Kelsey's smile slowly disappeared as Gerwazy's town car pulled up next to them.

"Be a dear and get in." Gerwazy motioned her towards the door as his man opened it for her.

"Oh, that's OK, Gerry." And then Kelsey remembered why that name was so familiar and her heart stopped, her eyes frozen on Gerwazy, architect of Erik's troubles.

"Kelsey, my dear. Get in the fucking car," Gerwazy growled, the full intensity of his evil finally on display. Before she could shake free from the stupor of realization, Gerwazy's man presented a gun and aimed it at her. "In," Gerwazy snarled.

Chapter 67

KONSTANTYN TOOK A while to come around, forcing Erik to wonder if it was an act, but when he finally did, they were ready and waiting. Lars and Erik sat in the remaining chairs right in front of him, their expressions pure business. Konstantyn slowly rose from his prone position and saw them, a smile playing his lips but unable to take full form beneath the reddened evidence of Lars' fist.

"Don't speak," Lars started.

"You want to live another day, you do exactly what we say," Erik continued.

"We're gonna call Daddy Dearest and let him know we have you. We want a sit down with him. About time we get this whole thing cleared up."

Konstantyn nodded his understanding and waited for Erik to remove the gag. "Phone," he said as he tried to work his jaw loose. "Nice punch, nephew. I will be returning the favor."

Lars shot to his feet and delivered an open-handed slap across Konstantyn's cheek. "I said don't speak," he growled, fists balled, hovering dangerously close to Konstantyn.

"Phone," Erik said as he jammed the phone between the two men. Lars stepped back and crossed his arms, ready to strike if need be. "What's your father's number?"

"Just give me the phone and I'll call him."

"Nope, I'm making the call. You'll get your chance to talk to him after I confirm you gave us the right number."

"Fine." Konstantyn rattled off the number and Erik dialed, using Konstantyn's phone. A name popped up, 'Diabeł'.

"Diabeł?" Erik asked Konstantyn with a raised brow.

"It means devil," Anna said from the corner of the room. "And it fits with his father."

Konstantyn regarded her for a moment and then turned his eyes to Erik. "The man is a bastard, what can I say?"

Erik pushed send and let the line ring. It rang for a few minutes and then a refined voice answered, speaking in Polish. "Konstantyn, gdzie byłeś?"

"This isn't Konstantyn," Erik started. "This is Erik Brown. I'd like to meet."

"Erik Brown! Just the man I was hoping for." Gerwazy's quick response caught Erik off guard and the words he had rehearsed for this moment flew from his mind. "And my son, does he breathe still?" Gerwazy added, almost an afterthought.

"He does," Erik managed after a moment's breath.

"Good. As long as he does, so will Kelsey."

"What did you say?" Erik could feel the blood rushing to his face, the pit of his stomach dropping into the earth's core. His fingers gripped the phone like a vice, going white at the knuckles. Anna looked at him with renewed worry, her face going as pale as his knuckles.

"Such a strange interlacing of events. I'd set up to replenish my supply of art this evening, and instead I seem to have finally caught up with you, my boy. This goes without saying, but hurt my son, Erik Brown, and I will hurt your pretty little girlfriend."

Erik tried to control his breath as it gasped out of him in short bursts. "If you—"

"Do you understand the stakes, my boy?" Gerwazy's voice grated in his ear. *No time to fall to pieces*, Victor scolded him.

"Understood. How do I know she's OK?"

"Same way I know Konstantyn is. Trust. Trust, my boy. Come to Kelsey's apartment, 10:00 p.m. tonight. Come alone. You and Konstantyn. I say no weapons, but we both know that won't happen," Gerwazy broke into gruff laughter sending shivers down Erik's spine.

"Do you honestly expect me to believe we'll just trade hostages? No. I show up, you kill me, you kill Kelsey. I'm not stupid."

"Yes, you are, my boy. You're very stupid. If you don't show up, I kill her anyway and then hunt you down and kill you too, but all after visiting young Selene and poor depressed Michael and angry Lars... I suggest you take me at my word instead of forcing my hand. A man is no better than his word and I, Erik Brown, am a great man."

"Fine," Erik said, unable to think of any alternatives. Everything had gone to pieces. This close! Erik's mind screamed into the dark shadow of his incoming thoughts. Erik hung up the phone and looked up. Konstantyn smiled maliciously at him while Lars waited expectantly.

"He has Kelsey."

"What?" Lars inquired.

"How?" Anna demanded, drawing Erik's attention to the other side of the room.

"Luck," Erik said in disbelief.

Anna burst into a string of Polish, turning towards the bathroom and rushing into it.

"This, complicates things," Konstantyn said, his smile growing.

"Gag him," Erik said. Lars complied, forcing the ball into Konstantyn's mouth.

"How well do you really know this girl?" Lars said once he was satisfied.

"What do you mean?"

"Isn't it a bit convenient that we grab Konstantyn and then she just turns up with Gerwazy?"

Erik's blood froze and he just stared at Lars. Could she be dirty just like Jeffrey? A plant from the start? Erik refused to believe it. Refused to believe his time with her could possibly be a lie.

"No way she's in on it. No way," was all Erik could say forcing enough conviction into his words to satisfy Lars.

"You better be damn sure," Lars responded. "What's the plan then?"

"I am, damn sure," Erik lied, "and I... I don't know. He wants to meet in a few hours. Wants me to bring Konstantyn and do an exchange."

"That's suicide!"

"I know. But what choice do I have? If I don't show, Kelsey is dead and then Selene and Dad and he even threatened to kill you."

"Fuck!" Lars yelled, slamming his fist on the bed next to Konstantyn. "Konstantyn was our trump card. Everything else we could've used, Bestefar took to the fucking grave!"

"What'd you say?"

"We're screwed! That's what I said," Lars moaned, his face red, his feet wearing a track in the tiny stretch of carpet along the bedside.

"Lars. I know where the ledger is."

Lars stopped in his tracks. "What? For real? Then, let's get it!"

"Not enough time."

"What do you mean? That's our ticket!"

"Stay here, I need to make a call." Erik made it to the door before turning around. "Oh, and hands off him!"

"Geezus, Erik! He killed Bestefar!"

"And I'll never forget or forgive that, but we have time to get ours."

"Fine."

"What's going on?" Anna asked from the bathroom doorway, her eyes puffy and red. It was obvious she'd been crying.

"Give me a sec. I'll be right back."

Erik didn't wait for her response. He made his way to his car and got in. He closed the door and pulled out his phone, took a deep breath then typed in a number. The phone rang, and rang, and rang until finally-

"Persistent aren't you."

Chapter 68

ERIK WASN'T GONE long. He made sure no one was lurking around the motel before he returned to the room. Everything was as he left it. Lars sat on the bed next to Anna, watching the news with an anxious expression. Anna watched the floor in front of her, her eyes still puffy from crying.

"Took long enough," Lars grumbled. "By the way, nothing about our little operation this afternoon made the news. I figured Gerwazy would clean up the mess all quiet like. Too bad about that barista though."

Erik could see the depth of that stray shot weighting on Lars. "It was an accident, Lars. You didn't—"

"Not my first time, Erik. I'll be fine. Just one more face to a haunt my dreams. He'll have plenty of company."

"Lars, I'm sorry, I—"

"Shut up, Erik. Not looking for a cry session. Doesn't matter. Now, what's the plan? Is that takeout?"

Just like Lars. Always distant, never wanting anyone's help until they'd turned their back on him already. Erik looked down to the bag of burgers in his hand and he nodded, tossing it at Lars. "Figured we might all be hungry."

Lars tore open the bag, ripping off the paper wrapper around his burger. He inhaled it, having just enough forethought to toss the bag into Anna's lap. Anna just looked at it, as if she didn't understand what it was.

"Anna. You're free to go," Erik said.

"What?" Anna and Lars said at the same time.

Erik picked up his backpack and pulled out a couple rolls of the money he'd stolen from the stash house. He held them out to Anna. "Should be about twenty grand. You can get pretty far away from here with that. You and your boyfriend."

"Really a good idea to let her go?" Lars asked around a big bite of burger. "Didn't you force her into this, make her think you killed that aforementioned boyfriend?"

"That's exactly why I'm letting her go. This is on me. I brought her into this."

"What if she goes to Gerwazy? Huh? You ever think of that? She could give us up!"

"I don't want to go," Anna said in a quiet voice.

"What?" Erik and Lars said at the same time.

"I want to see this through."

"Why?" Erik asked in disbelief.

"Because... because I hate them. They ruined my life long before you came along."

"Do go on," Lars said, his voice steeped in sarcasm.

"They... I have history with them. You don't need to know more." Anna clammed up and turned away from the brothers, her knees coming up to her chest, her arms wrapping around them in a sad embrace.

"Fine," Erik said. "That's your story to tell. You really want this? Fine, but I can't tell you how this is going to end. My plan is risky."

"Well, get to it then so we can poke holes in it and patch it up," Lars said.

"First thing's first." Erik reached back into his bag and pulled out his headphones, walked over to Konstantyn and put them over his ears. Konstantyn didn't even try to fight him, opting to just stare his evil stare instead. "Give me your phone," he told Lars.

"What? Why?"

"Because you have shit taste in music." The lights went on in Lars' eyes and he quickly fished out his phone, unlocked it and clicked on his music folder.

"Turn it up to eleven," he cackled as he tossed the phone to Erik.

"What does he mean?" Anna asked as Erik plugged the headphones in and cranked the volume. The sound of heavy metal filled the room, muffled by the headphones around Konstantyn's ears. Konstantyn's eyes bulged and he screamed in pain around the gag, trying to shake the headphones off.

"Ok," Erik said, turning back to his accomplices.

Chapter 69

ERIK'S CAR PULLED up to the curb a few blocks down from Kelsey's. Erik exited the car, jamming the gun behind his belt, letting his shirt and jacket fall over it. He doubted he'd have it long, but as Gerwazy had said, they both knew each other would bring guns. Why should Erik be the one to disappoint?

Erik's feet were heavy, the soles of his shoes weighed down with the cement of worry as he made his way down the block. His muscles felt twitchy and weird, his breath short and wheezy. He inhaled deeply trying to dispel whatever it was that had taken ahold of him.

Calm down, boy, Victor told him, the voice so real that Erik stopped in his tracks, expecting to see the old spy step onto the sidewalk before him. *Deep breath. Push out the fear. Envision the victory. Always envision the victory.*

Erik straightened his spine, pushed his shoulders back and drew himself to his full height. He took a deep breath, then another. The cement fell off his shoes and his muscles shook off the strange feeling. Deep breath. Deep breath. The building's door loomed before him as he closed the distance, a big man in a dark suit stood just inside of it, waiting for Erik.

"Where is Konstantyn?" He asked in a thick Polish accent.

"He's safe," Erik responded.

"The boss will not be pleased." He said no more, instead, beckoning for Erik to follow him through the door and up the stairs. Erik followed him down Kelsey's hallway, to her front door with the flower around the peephole. The big man pushed it open and motioned for Erik to enter. Erik complied and the door clicked shut behind him, the big man still on the other side.

"Gun," Loren said to Erik, his own pointed at Erik's gut, his other hand outstretched and waiting. Erik complied, pulling the piece from behind his belt. "Good boy."

Loren retreated a few steps and allowed Erik fully into the studio where Gerwazy, another thug, and Kelsey waited. Kelsey looked terrified. She looked like she'd been crying but she bore no bruises or signs of mistreatment.

"Kelsey," Erik called out, her name slipping from his lips on their own.

"Erik," Gerwazy responded, stepping in front of Kelsey, dominating Erik's field of vision. "Where is my son?"

"Not far from here. You get him when I walk out of this building, no sooner."

"That was not the deal," Gerwazy said with menacing calm.

"No, but I thought maybe I could sweeten that deal, maybe not die at the end of it."

"My men tell me you are smarter than I gave you credit for. Prove them right. Let's sit," Gerwazy said, motioning towards Kelsey's breakfast table. Erik complied.

"Tell me, Erik. Tell me of this deal," Gerwazy said as he took his seat across from Erik.

"I have the ledger," Erik responded, willing confidence into his words. Gerwazy's eyes lit up but that was the only tell he gave.

"Oh?" He feigned disinterest, but Victor had taught Erik to read every bit of body language.

"That's what this is all about, right?"

"So naïve," Gerwazy said, his voice tinged with amusement. "What do you know of your grandfather? Very little I suspect."

"I know enough," Erik countered. "I know where his ledger is."

"His ledger," Gerwazy laughed. "Did you know your grandmother was once my wife? No?" Erik tried to act surprised. Sometimes there was something to gain in giving someone the higher ground. Victor had taught him that.

"I figured not," Gerwazy chuckled. "Did you know we were once all friends? Or so I thought. I can tell you don't believe me. Why on earth would Per be friends with such an evil creature as me? That's what we called him back then. Per Larssen. It's because I was powerful, and men like Per are drawn to power. You know nothing of your grandfather, my boy."

He doesn't know Victor was a spy, Erik realized with cold clarity. "Is that why you killed him? Because he stole your wife?"

"I did not kill him, Erik. I only wanted to talk to him. He was killed before I could."

"Yeah, by your psychopath son." Gerwazy's laughter surprised Erik, making him feel even more uneasy.

"Where is my son, Erik?"

"I already told you. Are you ready for my proposal or not?"

"So bold! Look at you! You certainly aren't the quiet medical student you pretend to be!"

"You forced me to change, Gerwazy."

"Did I? I forced you to drag this beautiful girl into your mess?" Gerwazy said, running his finger down Kelsey's exposed thigh. Erik bolted upright in his chair, anger turning his cheeks red, a torrent of hate ready to fly from his lips and strike Gerwazy dead. "But I must say, the relief that filled those pretty little eyes when I confirmed your story to her. It would seem she doesn't know much else about you though, Erik."

"Look at me, Kelsey." Erik commanded. They locked eyes. "I'm getting us out of this." She nodded back at him, trust flowing between them, her fear subsiding ever so slightly.

"Oh, Erik. So much confidence! I love it. Now, how is it you captured my son? I'm sure there's a story there."

"Lucky, I guess. Just like you, Gerwazy. Right place, right time."

"I see. Well, then. On with your deal."

"I give you Konstantyn, you give me Kelsey. I give you the ledger, you clear my name and leave my family alone. Your beef is with Victor, not us and you already got what you wanted from him."

"Got what I wanted from him? Loren? Hit him." Erik had no chance to defend himself the punch came so quickly. Loren connected with Erik's cheek and Erik saw stars for a second as he fell off his chair. Kelsey screamed against her gag and the room spun. Erik laid on the floor for a second trying to gather his wits. "Check him for a wire, recording device. You know the drill."

Chapter 70

ERIK'S HEAD WAS spinning. He'd never been hit like that before and the next thing he knew, Loren's fat hands were patting him down, emptying his pockets and lifting him by his shirt and depositing him back into his seat. Loren tossed Erik's phone onto the table with a clunk.

"It's recording," Loren growled.

"Nice try, Erik." Gerwazy picked up the phone and hit stop, then deleted the recording, as he nodded to Loren. "Desperate, Erik," Gerwazy said as Loren grabbed Erik's shirt collar and rabbit punched him in the mouth. Pain blossomed around the impact of his knuckles, the metallic taste of blood filling Erik's mouth as his teeth tore at the inside of his lip.

"No quick retort? College man?" Gerwazy taunted, signaling Loren back to his side.

Erik spat blood onto the floor beside him, wiping at his mouth with the back of his hand, willing the calm he desperately wanted back into his mind.

"How do you know I didn't go to the cops?" he finally managed, wiping the blood off the back of his hand on his pants.

"Because you already did, Erik, and Loren had to take care of it." Gerwazy's sick smile was ear to ear as he reveled in the glow of his own power.

"Kincaid?"

"Amongst others."

"How many cops did you kill to cover this mess up?"

"Kill? So naïve, Erik. Most we just paid off. Kincaid was the only one stupid enough not to take a bribe."

"That how you framed me for Jeffrey's murder?"

"Jeffrey?"

"Peter," Loren growled.

"Oh! Right. That fool. I'd forgotten about him. His death was merely meant to scare you into our warm embrace. Kincaid was supposed to lead us to you or get you to turn yourself in, but she was a stubborn one. Some people you can't buy, Erik. But it was worth a try. And poor Peter, put up quite a fight didn't he, Loren?" Gerwazy laughed, the humor never reaching his cold eyes.

"Broke Chudy's nose," Loren said with a twisted smile. "Clawed him up good before I put a hole in his head."

"Clear my name and I give you the ledger," Erik said, trying to ignore Loren's psychopathic grin, ignore the way he caressed the gun in his hand while he so casually spoke of murder.

"I like this kid," Gerwazy said, turning to Loren. "He does have balls, doesn't he? Why do you think this ledger has such sway?"

"You killed Victor for it." Gerwazy burst into laughter and Erik steeled himself against the fear that tried to creep up his spine.

"He died because he stole my wife." *Lying*, Victor cooed in the back of Erik's mind, but Erik could discern that all on his own.

"Then, why follow me?"

"True, I would like the ledger, but Victor's death could be enough for me," Gerwazy responded, changing gears, trying to throw Erik off.

"I thought you just wanted to talk to him?"

"I did. I wanted to talk to him and ask him how it felt walking through life with an x on his back. I wanted to talk to him about what was going through his mind when he decided to stab me in the back, steal my wife, and my fortune." Gerwazy's voice stayed calm, but his face reddened, and his eyes hardened, boring through Erik. "You see, I took Per under my arm, I gave him a taste of the good life. Power, money, women and then he stole it all from me! That watch you wear; I gave it to him and then he gave it to you. Tired of the reminder perhaps? I was a boss in Poland. I ran the factories; I was high within the party. I carved out my throne with blood. I had everything and then your grandfather came sniffing around. I should've known better, the way he asked about every little fucking thing. It was like he was writing a book about me!

"We were friends, I'm not lying. We both survived the Gestapo, the war. We were men hardened in fire. So much alike, and then one day someone came to me and said he was not who he said he was. Per told me he was a Norwegian businessman. Spoke Norwegian, had a Norwegian name and then I'm told he is an American, and then I'm shown photographs of him and Margarete... FUCKING!" Gerwazy's rage exploded out of him and filled the room with the steam of its dragon breath. "I thought, no. Margarete is my wife, devoted to me, to our three-year-old son. She would not, but there, in those photos, I see her face. I see her breasts, cupped in Per's hands. His cock inside of her. What else could I do but see him dead? I dreamt of how I'd do it, holding my son in my arms, waiting for her to come home so I could confront her, show her the error of her ways. Make her understand why Per must go. For our son, for Konstantyn. But, when I awoke, they were gone. In the middle of the night, they broke into my office and stole my fortune right out from under me."

Gerwazy's tone slowly calmed as he walked his memories, sifting through the pain, the happiness.

"No, Erik. I was not planning to simply murder Per, my old friend. I was going to give him the pain he gave me. I was going to go to work on him. I was going to use every tool the UB had entrusted me with. My son took that from me when he shot him in the back of the head. He robbed me of my justice. But perhaps I can rain down my vengeance on you?" Erik shuddered under his gaze; the breadth of his insanity fully revealed. "But then, I suppose Konstantyn would pay the same price."

"Hold that thought, Gerwazy," Erik said with a confidence he didn't feel. "I gotta get cleaned up. I'm bleeding all over the place and that's no way to conduct negotiations."

Gerwazy's face went blank, his eyes sizing Erik up, delving into his essence, his being. Erik sat up straight against it, shoulders back, head high. Gerwazy broke into a grin. "I like this kid!" Gerwazy said to Loren once more. "By all means," he said, motioning towards Kelsey's bathroom. "But be quick, I do get bored easily," he added as he ran his fingers along Kelsey's thigh again, moving closer and closer to the hem of her dress, smiling as Kelsey's eyes widened against his intrusive touch.

Erik surged forward, no plan, just anger and was met with the butt of Loren's pistol. He crumbled to the ground, vaguely aware of Gerwazy's maniacal laughter, the stream of fresh blood flowing from the new gash on his temple.

"Erik! You think you're tough? Is that it? If I wanted Kelsey, I'd take her right here over this table while Loren held you down and forced you to watch." Gerwazy returned his fingers to her thighs and a stream of anger could be heard from behind her gag. "Something to say?" Gerwazy cooed.

He motioned for Loren to remove the gag.

"Touch me again and I'll kill you," Kelsey hissed.

"Is that so?" Gerwazy laughed. Without warning, he thrust his hand under her dress.

Kelsey growled in response and sent a kick flying out towards the old man, just missing his chin by an inch. The kick was so quick Gerwazy nearly toppled off his chair to avoid it. Loren was quick to act though, grabbing Kelsey around the chest and dragging her and the chair she was bound to away from the old man.

"Get off of me asshole!" Kelsey screamed at Loren as he allowed his hands to linger on her chest. "I'll fucking kill you for that."

Loren just laughed, giving her breast a good squeeze before he put the gag back in place. Kelsey's stared at the man with a burning intensity, but he ignored her, instead, checking on Gerwazy.

"She's just a little doggy with a big bark, Loren. I am fine," Gerwazy said shooing him away.

Erik slowly picked himself up off the floor to face the devil before him. Gerwazy's eyes were cold, twin daggers pointed at Erik's heart. Erik tore his eyes from the menacing specter and looked to Kelsey. Her eyes leaked angry tears, her mascara running down her cheeks. Erik's heart sank, his fists balling at his sides, but the looming presence of Loren, his smug smile, his gun ready to give Erik a matching wound on the other temple.

"You do look a fright, Erik. Get cleaned up, and don't take long, for Kelsey's sake." Gerwazy thought about returning his hand to her naked thigh but didn't, instead opting to threaten her. "When this is all over, you'll be warming my bed. High on heroin, stuck in the reality I create for you. That is, unless Erik can be your hero." Erik fought to keep his anger in check and just stared at Gerwazy, pouring his hatred into his gaze. "Will you be her white knight, Erik?"

Erik willed his legs not to wobble as he made his way across the room, into the small bathroom. He closed the door behind him, as calmly as he could manage. As soon as it clicked shut, he rushed over to the toilet, lifting the lid just as he started to wretch. He hung his head over it and fought the urge to empty his stomach as hot blood dripped off his chin and nose into the clear water. He dry-heaved a couple of times, hot bile rising into his mouth but nothing more. Erik fell to his knees, head still over the toilet. The urge to vomit subsided and he leaned a shoulder against the cabinet under the sink. He took a deep breath then stood up.

Erik turned on the sink, letting cold water flow out of the faucet into his cupped hands. He splashed the water onto his face and looked at himself in the mirror, willing confidence to fill his skeleton like air in a balloon. He grimaced against the blood that continued to leak from his various wounds, using the hand towel to mop it up as best he could. He fell to one knee and opened up the cabinet, his hand fishing around behind the cleaning supplies, the extra toilet paper and paper towels. His heart sank, a rushing emptiness overtaking him.

The gun, the gun he'd forgotten the night he'd broken into Kelsey's apartment. It was gone.

Chapter 71

"LOOKS LIKE PLAN B then," Lars said, causing Anna to jump. "It's been too long," Lars added, turning his tired eyes on Anna.

Konstantyn laughed from the floor of the car where he lay bound, his laughter muffled by the ball gag wedged between his teeth.

"It's only been ten minutes, relax," Anna said, although the death grip she had on the folds of her dress signaled her mutual worry.

"Yeah, it's an exchange. It should take, like, two minutes. Five tops with Erik making his deal. Something's wrong."

"And what about him," Anna said, motioning towards Konstantyn in the back. "What do I do if neither of you come back?"

"Stick to the plan. This was always a possibility. Or, you could just shoot him in the head and disappear. We're the only ones that know you're involved. Either way, I don't care."

"Stupid boy," Anna responded. "Is it so easy to kill a man?"

"Sure, why not? You got something brewing between you two. Could cut the tension with a butter knife."

"It's not that simple," Anna turned away from Lars and stared out the window, her eyes moving to Erik's empty car down the street. "He took everything from me, Lars. Everything. But still, I cannot kill him. I am not him."

"The hell are you talking about?"

Konstantyn sat up in the space behind them, his eyes bright with realization, his mouth the full crescent of a smile. His laughter started slow and soft but rose into hysterics, bubbling around the gag in his mouth, his bound hands pointed at Anna.

"Finally recognize me, pieprzony gnojek?" Konstantyn nodded his head happily, his smile malicious. He pointed at Anna and then drew his bound hands across his throat, she just smirked, turning back towards Erik's car.

"He killed my father," Anna said. That got Lars' attention.

"You serious?"

"Him and his friends, his father... That shop we took him from? That was my father's. They forced him to pay them for protection, bled him dry, just took what they wanted. It was a corner store back then. They broke him, my father. He killed himself." Anna let it all out in a stream of thought, the anguish washing over her. She turned to regard Konstantyn, venom in her stare. "Death is too good for him."

An alarm sounded from Lars' phone, making them both jump. Lars turned it off, took a deep breath and patted Anna's leg. "Time to go. Give us another five minutes, we don't come back? Up to you." He handed her a knife and stepped out of the car; the door slamming shut in his wake. A gun flashed into his hand as he rushed across the street and ran down the block, disappearing around the corner. Anna watched him, waiting for him to disappear from her sight before she turned to regard Konstantyn, a smile tugging at the corners of her mouth.

"Do demons bleed?" She asked, the knife held firmly in her hand. "Perhaps we will find out."

Chapter 72

FEAR ENGULFED ERIK. Could Lars have been right? Was Kelsey really in on it? Was she a plant from the start? The way she'd just showed up that first time in the coffee shop and not recognized him the second time? But if she was a plant, why had Jeffrey freaked out when Erik lost his tail?

Erik took a deep breath and tried to clear his doubt. He'd been disoriented when he ditched the gun, was he just misremembering where he'd stashed it?

He stuck his hand back into the depths of the cabinet, dreading what he'd find, and gave it a more thorough search, pushing things out of the way until his hand brushed against something cold and metal. His veins filled with adrenaline as he pulled the gun out, relieved tears slicking his cheeks. He cocked it and jammed it behind his belt.

Erik stepped out of the bathroom to find Loren holding Kelsey, her bindings removed but Loren's arm around her neck, his gun to her head. Gerwazy stood next to him, smiling.

"No more games, Erik. I grow weary."

"It's simple, Gerwazy. Clear my name and the ledger is yours. Release Kelsey and Konstantyn is yours. What's left to debate?"

"What if I tell you that is impossible?"

"I'd call you a liar." Erik tore his eyes away from the glinting gold detail of the barrel of the gun Loren pressed against Kelsey's head and matched Gerwazy's stare, realization flooding into him. "The murder weapon is in this room, in the hands of the murderer. Is he worth more than your ledger? Your son? Because this isn't a two-part deal, it's all or nothing, Gerwazy, and where you have me, I have nothing left to lose, and the evidence is stacking up."

Gerwazy smiled back at Erik and nodded his head. "More than meets the eye, Erik. More than meets the eye. Loren, lower the gun, release the girl. Our friend will not be cowed by theatrics."

"Are you sure?" Loren said, his disappointment clear.

"Yes." Loren lowered the gun obediently. "You see, Loren, your own hubris has ruined the charade. Our friend has noticed your gun."

"Such a beautiful gun, too," Erik added. "Certainly not the kind you drop a body with and toss into the river, but here you are, ready to drop two with it. My guess is that gun is connected to a number of unsolved murders, like Jeffrey Grant, or whatever his real name was. Perhaps even the slug Detective Kincaid pulled out of my fence the night you tried to ransack my house."

"But it was Per's gun they found in the dumpster at your apartment," Gerwazy cooed.

"Yeah, and Victor always removed the firing pins prior to storing them."

Loren's face grew dark, clearly not a fan of being chastised by Erik. Clearly not happy about the whole situation. "This gun will taste your blood soon enough, pieprzony gnojek."

Erik was about to respond when everything just seemed to happen. A commotion at the door drew everyone's attention as Lars pushed his way inside, his arm wrapped around the neck of the thug from earlier, his gun pressed to the man's head.

Loren started to respond but was met with Kelsey's sharp elbow to his stomach, a heavy haymaker following as she spun around and put all her weight into the punch. She connected with Loren's chin, the crack of bone-on-bone resonating through the room. Loren, caught off balance, stumbled backwards. Kelsey didn't waste a second as she grabbed the barrel of his gun in one hand and twisted his wrist with the other. She pushed him further off balance, driving him towards the wall, using all the momentum the two had created to move the much larger man. Loren screamed in pain as Kelsey twisted the gun in his hand and ripped it out of his grasp. She jumped back as Loren roared in pain, grabbing at the fountain of blood that had been his trigger finger only moments before. Kelsey flicked the finger out of the trigger guard and racked the gun, a bullet jettisoning from the chamber, a new one clicking into place.

In the mere seconds of chaos Lars' entry had created, Erik pulled his own gun and trained the sights on Gerwazy, the last standing thug doing the same on Erik. "Your move," Erik said, cold conviction in his voice.

"My finger!" Loren roared his face red with anger. "I will kill you!" He screamed as he started to launch himself at Kelsey.

BAM! BAM! BAM! Loren staggered backwards, red flowers blossoming against the white of his button up shirt, his eyes wide in surprise as he dropped to the floor, blood gurgling from his lips in a pink foam.

Everyone stared at Kelsey as she turned towards them, the gun smoking in her hand. "I warned him," she said as she removed her gag with her other hand. She trained the weapon on Gerwazy with a trembling hand, silent fury radiating from her.

"Don't do anything stupid, Kelsey. No need for anyone else to die today," Gerwazy said in the face of her wrath. "You have your evidence, Erik. The police will be able to link that gun to a number of crimes, including those we framed you for. Now, the ledger?"

"What guarantee do I have we'll be safe?"

"My word."

"That's not good enough. Why not just shoot you now and be done with all of this?"

"I have many loyal soldiers, Erik. Many that do not share in my restraint. Many that will avenge my death by bringing their grievances to your family. Anyone that is close to you really. So, I give you my word, and that is all I can give you. I am a powerful man, Erik. My word is my reputation. Let me show you." Gerwazy slowly slid a hand into his jacket. "Just grabbing my phone, no need to be jumpy, Lars."

Lars had the gun leveled at Gerwazy, going back and forth between him and the thug in his grasp. Gerwazy fished out his phone and tossed it to Erik. "Dial 911 and throw it back to me."

"Why?" Erik responded

"Just do it."

"Fine." Erik dialed the number and hit send, waiting for it to ring before tossing it back to Gerwazy. He caught it easily and brought it up to his ear.

"Yes, police? I'd like to report a crime in progress. I think my neighbor has been shot. There was a big scary man banging on her door and then I heard gun shots. I'm worried she might be dead." Gerwazy rattled off Kelsey's address before ending the phone call and shoving his phone back into his jacket. "The ledger."

"Cemetery. Victor's headstone. There's a secret compartment."

"Good boy. Stashu, bring around the car and quickly."

Stashu lowered his gun and rushed past Lars and his captive. Gerwazy looked from Lars to Erik, his intent clear.

"Let him go, Lars. We have what we came for."

"How do you know we can trust him?"

"I don't, but we got what we needed, Lars. We've done everything we can."

"Fine," Lars said, releasing the thug.

"Good boy, Erik. Stay out of the neighborhood and you have nothing to fear." Gerwazy walked past Lars towards the door.

"What about Konstantyn?"

"I lay this mess at his feet. How many good men has he cost me? Do with him what you will," Gerwazy said, his voice emotionless as he walked out the front door.

"What the fuck just happened?" Lars asked after the door slammed shut behind Gerwazy. Erik ignored him and raced over to Kelsey instead.

"I'm so sorry," he started to say but Kelsey slammed into him, knocking the words from his lips as she wrapped him in a tight hug.

"Erik!" She said, tears welling in her eyes. "What just happened!?"

The sound of sirens interrupted their reunion and Erik turned to Lars and handed him his gun. "Get out of here. I'll handle this."

Lars nodded and disappeared back through the door. Erik turned back to Kelsey. "I'm so sorry, about all of this. I never thought you'd get involved like this. I thought I was keeping you safe, but I just pushed you right into the fire. I'm so sorry, so sorry. I never wanted any of this for—"

"Erik, just shut up and hold me please." And suddenly, the door jumped off its hinges, tumbling into the room as two cops burst through the splintered doorway with guns drawn.

"Hands up!" They screamed.

Chapter 73

A COOL BREEZE rattled the leaves above Erik's head, the icy air flowing over smooth cheeks where a few days growth had been just that morning. Dark circles still hung below Erik's eyes where they mingled with the cuts and bruises from Erik's journey. He shrugged into the warmth of his coat's wool collar, allowing the thick peacoat to absorb the majority of the chill. Erik steadied the fedora on his head with one hand while the other sought safety in his pocket. Fall was at an end, the death of winter laid out before him as tiny ice crystals fell from the sky to mingle with the headstones stretching out before him.

"So, explain something to me," Agent Smith said from just behind Erik. "How'd you hack the microphone?"

"Google it," Erik said with a laugh.

"Fair enough. Smart move, the double deception. Get him to turn off the app, toss it on the table where it could hear better and all, but how'd you know he wouldn't just smash the phone, really disable it?"

"I didn't," Erik responded.

"Ballsy move, kid."

"The thing with Lars?" Erik asked, his eyes on the headstones before him.

"Nothing to discuss. Body never turned up. My guess is Gerwazy made it disappear. Police said the coffee shop was scrubbed clean and everything."

"Why don't you ask him?" Smith just laughed in response. "Yeah, didn't think he'd be much of a talker."

"Not true!" Smith laughed. "Talking to a lot of judges and politicians. Making the FBI's job real easy. Doesn't really matter where he's concerned though. That little microphone trick you pulled has him dead to rights. Him and that Loren creep. They even got Feliks to flip after they found his skin under Peter Wacowski's fingernails. Pinned it all on Loren, said he was there when Gerwazy made the order. Even corroborated what Gerwazy said about Konstantyn... that he killed Victor. Star witness all of a sudden. Konstantyn, sure wish we knew where that bastard was. Anyway, if you hear from Anna, we sure would like to talk to her, see if she has any idea."

"Yeah, I'd sleep a whole lot better knowing that myself," Erik countered. "And the police? Kincaid?"

"Let's just say, the murder of one of your own getting covered up inspires a bit of spring cleaning," Smith said with a shrug. Erik was aware of that part though, it'd been all over the news for the last twenty-four hours, along with Gerwazy's arrest. They'd grabbed him right there in that cemetery.

"Good," Erik said as he kneeled down in front of the headstone.

"Sorry about Victor's headstone. Thought we'd have a little more time. He must've really wanted that ledger. Got Gerwazy on desecrating a grave though. Just another charge on a long list."

Erik turned to regard Victor's smashed up headstone and shrugged. "Is what it is."

Erik ran his fingers along Marga's headstone, feeling it for imperfections, clues, a trigger. He ran his hand around the back and felt a pair of dimples just off the corner. He pushed on it gently and heard a click. He stood back up, ignored Smith, and walked a circuit around the headstone before finding the slightest crack in the smooth marble. He bent over, ran a finger along it and pushed. Another click sounded and the piece slid out of the body of the stone revealing an aged black leather book. The ledger.

"Well, there she blows," Smith whistled. Erik bent over and removed it from its cubby, holding it out to Smith without another thought. "Don't even want to know what's inside? What this was all about?"

"It's over," Erik said, still holding out the ledger.

"Take a look, kid. You earned it."

Erik sighed, the book still at arm's length. Smith made no move to free his hands from their warm pockets.

"Fine."

Erik held the ledger before him, hesitating. The wind whistled in his ear as he stared at it. Finally, as if he were only waiting for his courage to build, he opened it, revealing a list of coordinates with paragraphs written in a mixture of Polish and German next to them.

"Well?" Smith interrupted.

"Coordinates," Erik responded.

"That it?"

"No," Erik said, trying to use his limited grasp on the Polish language to pick out key words. "It's… It's…" Erik couldn't believe what he was reading. "It's coordinates to paintings, gold… Nazi loot, I think," Erik finished, his eyes rising to meet Smith's. "It's a guide to stolen Nazi treasure."

Smith whistled in surprise. "Well, Gerwazy did say Victor stole his fortune." Erik couldn't help but laugh. He closed the ledger and handed it to Smith who took it this time, squirreling it away into the folds of his jacket. "Gonna make a whole lot of people happy, getting this stuff back where it belongs."

"Yeah."

"Not what you expected?" Smith said, taking in Erik's deflated demeanor.

"I just wonder why Victor sat on it for so long. Why he waited till his death to reveal it to anyone."

"Guess we'll never know," Smith said with a shrug. "Welp, been real, kid. If you change your mind, you have a number. Be a shame to let all that talent go to waste. We can always use someone like you in the company."

"That was Victor's life, and it killed him. I just want to go back to mine."

"What now then?" Smith asked.

"Promised someone I'd fix their radiator."

"Well, good luck with that," Smith laughed, clearly not believing Erik was serious.

"Thanks," Erik responded.

Erik left Smith in his wake, walking towards the cemetery entrance where Lars waited, a cigarette between his lips.

"Thought you quit after you were discharged?" Erik said, the usual venom gone from his voice.

"Yeah? Well, figured it was a good time to pick it back up. Not gonna have a whole hell of a lot else to do in prison." Lars' voice was heavy with worry.

"No body," Erik responded matter-of-factly.

"What?"

"Gerwazy got rid of the body and scrubbed the shop. No evidence a crime was ever committed. You're clear, Lars, so stomp that coffin nail out. Selene will have none of that at the next family dinner."

Relief flooded Lars' eyes; the cigarette forgotten between lips turned up in a joyous smile. "Jesus, Erik! Couldn't have led with that?"

Erik just wrapped Lars in a hug and after a moment or two, Lars responded in kind.

"Promise me you'll talk about all this with someone, just, you know, don't keep it all in. It'll eat you up—"

"Yeah, not my first rodeo, Erik. Not my first rodeo." Lars' voice trailed off as he retreated within himself.

Erik patted him on the shoulder. "Dinner tomorrow, don't be late or you'll face the Beacon."

Lars let out a soft chuckle and tossed the cigarette to his feet.

Erik was still thinking about how best to put his life back together, to get back to normal, when he pulled up in front of Kelsey's apartment. He looked over at the bouquet of roses sitting on top of his toolbox in the passenger seat and smiled. He was about to get out of the car when someone tapped on his window.

He flinched and instinctively ducked away from the noise, his foot jumping off the brake, looking for the gas, but a cooler head prevailed as Erik caught a familiar face in the corner of his vision.

"Jesus, Anna!" Erik exclaimed, rolling down the window. "Where the hell have you been? Where the hell is Konstantyn? How'd you know I'd be here!?"

Anna looked down on Erik from the dark cowl of her black hood. Her lips were painted a ruby red, her eyes darkened with eyeshadow, really bringing out the blue. She looked good; Erik realized.

"Can I get in?" Anna asked, the plea hanging on her lips.

"Yeah, sure," Erik responded, at a loss for anything else to say.

Anna rushed around the car and pulled on the door handle. "Shit," Erik murmured as he leaned across the seat to unlock it. The smell of lavender invaded his car along with her presence.

"Where have you been?" Erik asked again.

Anna looked over at him and smiled a sad smile. "I thought you were dead. You and Lars."

"Yeah, we figured that out when you and Konstantyn disappeared." Erik paused, looking over towards Kelsey's building, lost in thought for a moment. "Where'd you go? Are you OK? I mean, you look like you're doing alright."

Erik watched Anna smile in the corner of his vision. "Thank you, Erik. You saved my life."

"Nah, I did my best to ruin it."

"I was trapped," Anna started, her voice catching on the words. "I was so content with the life I'd taken, my piece of shit boyfriend, my job. I thought I deserved no better. I wanted no better, until you took it away from me. When I thought Stefan was dead, it was a relief. I couldn't go back to that life. I didn't even realize what I was feeling until you told me he was alive and then the walls closed back in on me and... I needed something to shake me, wake me up. That was you. I'm free."

"That's... that's great to hear. I'm happy for you." And he was. It was what he had needed to hear. He hadn't been aware of how heavily she'd been weighing on his heart until the burden had been lifted. "The FBI is looking for you," Erik added, almost an afterthought.

"I know," Anna said, her voice quiet.

"They wanna know what happened to Konstantyn, so they can arrest him for the murder of my grandfather, maybe get him to flip on his old man."

"He's gone."

Erik turned his full attention to her for the first time since letting her into his car. He cast a wary eyebrow at her, and she shied away from him.

"I just thought you should know."

"How?" Erik wasn't sure he wanted to know but he had to ask.

"We discovered demons can bleed. Take care, Erik." And before Erik could react, Anna had slipped out of his car and stepped into the bustle of the city.

"Jesus," Erik muttered to himself.

His phone buzzed in his pocket, an incoming call. He fished it out and his heart sprang into his throat.

Kelsey.

"Hello?" He answered, almost forgetting to breathe.

"Are you stalking me now?" Her voice was not friendly.

"What? No!"

"You don't drive a blue Honda?"

Erik smiled in realization and he peered up through his windshield towards the second floor of Kelsey's building. She stood in her window, looking down on him.

"Hey beautiful." Her frown broke into a happy smile as their eyes locked.

"Are those roses in the passenger seat?"

"Yep. For an old Polish lady," Erik joked.

"Shut up!" Kelsey laughed, putting butterflies in Erik's chest.

The End

Made in the USA
Middletown, DE
30 July 2022